Trials

of

Hatred

The War and Deceit Series
Book One

Erin O'Kane

Fires of Hatred

This is a work of fiction. Any resemblance to places, events or real people are entirely coincidental.

Copyright © 2020 Erin O'Kane, all rights reserved.

Written by Erin O'Kane.
Cover by Jodielocks Design.
Edited by Elemental Editing.
Proofread by Amber Baker.
Formatted by Kaila Duff.

Contents

Author's Note	vii
Introduction	ix
Prologue	1
Chapter 1	3
Chapter 2	13
Chapter 3	25
Chapter 4	41
Chapter 5	59
Chapter 6	72
Chapter 7	84
Chapter 8	102
Chapter 9	114
Chapter 10	142
Chapter 11	159
Chapter 12	171
Chapter 13	190
Chapter 14	210
Chapter 15	224
Chapter 16	236
Chapter 17	249
Chapter 18	271
Chapter 19	286
Chapter 20	304
About the Author	319
Also by Erin O'Kane	321

DEDICATION

Dearest Reader,

Yes, I'm talking to you, to everyone that picks up this book and gives my story a chance. Every single message, like, comment, and review means the world to me and helps to fuel this dream of mine.

When I first said I wanted to write a book, my teachers laughed at me, after all, how could an extremely dyslexic girl who could barely spell her own name ever write, let alone sell a book? Fourteen years later, I sat down and poured my heart into my first book, expecting only to sell a couple of copies to my mum. That book became a bestseller.

This story is one that I have LOVED writing, every word resonates within me, and without the support of you and my author friends, it wouldn't have come to pass.

So, this dedication goes to you, the readers and the dreamers.

Thank you. x

Author's Note

I ran a competition in my readers group for one of my readers to name a character. I selected my five favourite names and then left it up to the group to vote which name they liked the best.

The winner of that competition was Jodie-Leigh, with the name Rhydian. This character plays an important role in the story and I think this name fits him perfectly.

Introduction

<u>Hierarchy within the Kingdom of Arhaven</u>

The Great Mother
The King and Queen
The Princes
Higher Magicians High Priest

Magicians Priests
Lords and Ladies
Common folk, servants, maids
Slaves and prisoners

Prologue

The people of Arhaven haven't always lived on the Black Cliffs of Morrowmer. Originally desert nomads, they travelled, never settling in one place for too long. The Great King Magnus was the first to settle his people, creating a prosperous land for all. However, after many years of peace he became bored. He selected his best warriors and together they journeyed far and wide until they came across Morrowmer. The Great Mother, our goddess, came to Magnus in a vision and decreed he settle there, dedicating his life to her and constructing a place of peace and worship. And so, the Kingdom of Arhaven was created, passing down from king to prince for centuries.

That's when the elves came... However, there have been whispers that the elves lived peacefully nearby, until something changed. Although, talking like that would gain you a one-way trip to the executioner. We've now been at war with them for so long that no one really remembers how it started. They live in the ancient forests at the edge of our territory and have strange, unnatural magic. The Great Mother blesses people across our land to serve, worship, and protect. The strongest of these are our warriors; the magicians. They keep us safe and we thank the Mother every day for their bravery.

Who am I? I'm a nobody, a slave with no name. I'd been condemned to live out my days serving the kingdom for a crime I don't recall. But one day, I was yanked from the darkness and thrust into the light. My whole life changed after a vision from a blue-eyed magician.

I'm six hundred and twenty-five, and my whole life is about to change in ways I couldn't possibly imagine.

Chapter 1

The familiar clink of chains and the shuffle of bare feet on stone floor fills the air. Ragged breaths and coughs from chests full of infection is a sound familiar to those who live in the slave quarters. Although, calling it "quarters" makes it sound far grander than it is. The dingy, cramped space where we sleep for the few hours that are ours alone can hardly be called grand. Mold and mildew grow on the walls, and a cold draft fills the space no matter the time of the year, although the winter months claim many lives with its cruel, icy embrace.

The room itself is large, it would need to be to house the number of slaves the castle keeps. The ceilings are high, and the stone walls have arched pillars that could be considered beautiful if they had been appropriately cared for. I don't know what the original use for this building had been, but for the three years I've toiled here, it's only housed the slaves. I've been a slave since I was eight, though I was only moved to the castle when I was seventeen. It was a blessing...and a curse.

We're led out of the slave quarters, slowly making the long walk towards the castle proper. No one wants to see the slaves, so we are kept far away, guarded to ensure no one escapes. Not that anyone would dare try, unless they had a death wish. I only know of one who attempted to break free, and they didn't get far. Desperate to escape by any means necessary, they jumped off the castle wall, receiving a kinder death than what the guards would have given them.

Keeping my head down as I shuffle forward, I follow the line of my fellow slaves. Not that I *need* to follow them, I could walk this route in my sleep. Sleep... now that's something I do miss. My body and head ache from the lack of it and from the hard labour the previous day. You'd have thought I'd be used to it by now, seeing as I've been a slave for twelve years.

Today is the eve of my twentieth birthday, a day that is important within our society. It's a day when young women and men have the chance to be chosen by the Great Mother. Only a lucky few will ever be chosen, but it's something we all dream of, and I would be lying if I said I had never imagined myself in the robes of the magicians. Within our society there are three ways to be chosen—join the priesthood and serve the Great Mother, join the magicians' ranks, or be paired off with your predestined partner. For most, this will encompass attending a grand ball with a few being paired up with someone of their stature. Only a handful of people are chosen to join the priesthood each year, but most hope to be chosen by the magicians, although no one has joined their ranks in years.

A feeling of trepidation and excitement runs through me. The choosing ceremony... What will it be like? All little girls dream of attending theirs, having the chance to dress up in their finery and be paired with their prince charming. It's the law that *all* people, regardless of status, must attend the ceremony before they turn twenty, and with the next ceremony being held tomorrow, it will finally be my turn. I'm not sure how this will play out, I've never heard of a slave attending before, but *everyone* is required to be present at the ceremony. I'm sure I won't be blessed in front of all the lords and ladies, since they probably run a separate ceremony for the slaves. Right? Doubt starts to run through me. All my other rights were stripped from me, would they deny me the choosing too? That would be the signing of my death warrant.

A commotion ahead pulls me out of my musings as I come to a stop alongside the others who are gathering together. Keeping my head down, I glance out of the corner of my eye to see what the holdup is, and I'm barely able to suppress the wince that's threatening to appear on my face. A young slave girl is being pulled to the side—it's never good news when the guards single one of us out. As soon as she's been moved out of our path, we continue our trudge towards the castle. As always, guilt builds up in me as we walk past the young girl, who is now crying out for mercy. Her pleas fall on deaf ears as the three large guards start to beat her for her crime—stopping to help a fellow slave who had fallen.

The feeling of rage building up inside me is something I'm used to carrying. Rage at the guards, rage at the situation, and rage at myself for doing nothing to help her. With an inward sigh, I keep marching, but I don't avert my eyes like the other slaves, I keep my gaze on her for as long as possible. My one small rebellion.

I think I've gotten away with it until a shadow falls over me and a rough, dirty hand grabs my chin, dragging me to a stop. Instantly, I look down and try to fall to my knees, the position expected of me, but a hand on my arm stops me, roughly pulling me back up.

"Feeling sorry for your little friend?" He spits at me, his hot, acrid breath on my cheek almost making me gag. I keep my eyes firmly fixed on the ground and shake my head at his question, not daring to speak. It'll only make my punishment, and that of the young girl, even worse. I know this from experience and she won't thank me for it. A sharp pain flares across my cheek as he backhands me, a gasp escaping me at the sudden impact. Despite wanting to, I fight against the instinct to shy away and cradle my face. When he grabs my chin again and forces me to watch as the young girl is beaten, I don't fight him, I just watch, shame lining my gut that I can't do anything to help her. The only thing I can offer her is to bear witness, so she knows she's not alone. Something is screaming inside me, telling me to do *something*, threatening to overwhelm me as I push it away. I may not be able to fight or protect her, but I will acknowledge what has happened, and if she wants it, I'll be there to offer her help once we return to the slave quarters.

If we return. Many of us leave in the morning and never come back. Most of us die at the hands of our masters, their punishments harsh and cruel, or from simple infections that go untreated. For many who don't get assigned to the castle, who work in fields or mines, their hearts give up from exhaustion. Their young bodies can't cope with the manual labour, the physical work we are forced into taking its toll. The best any of us can hope for is a quick death.

Mercifully, the beating doesn't go on for much longer and the girl is dragged further out of the way and left in a slump on the ground as the cruel, cold wind whips around us. The line of slaves starts moving and the guard drops my chin, giving me a hard push. I obediently step in line once more, but a small, dark part of me seethes and burns at the way they treat us. I push it down and keep moving. After all, what could I do about it?

The rest of the morning runs as usual, and I'm assigned to clean the grand hall. The choosing ceremony will be held here tomorrow, so the castle is alive with maids and servants hurrying about getting everything ready. Other than the royal family, several lords and ladies live within the castle, the rest of them residing in the city below. A handful of priests live here as well, in addition to a few castle magicians. Then there are the paid servants and other castle staff, many of whom dwell in the city and climb up the many steps that are carved into the rock to reach the castle.

As a slave, I'm the lowest of the low and mostly ignored. This often comes in handy, so while scrubbing the floor, I get to listen to the castle gossip. It's inane, but it keeps me sane, imagining myself in the positions of others and the ridiculous situations that the noble lords and ladies of the houses get themselves into.

When I'm sure I'm not being watched, I take small, sneaking glances at the room around me. I've been here before, but I never get over its opulence. It's beautiful with large, arched ceilings and the whole back wall is taken over by three large, stained-glass windows. The scene it depicts is one that all in the kingdom know well —the story of King Titus, who led us to victory against the elves in the battle over the Black Cliffs of Morrowmer, the cliffs we now call home.

The room is currently decked out with vases upon vases of flowers. I'm lucky to have been assigned this room today, as all of this will be gone the day after tomorrow. It's quiet except for the sound of my scrubbing brush, and a brief sense of peace runs through me. It's easy to forget we're at war when I'm in this room.

The sound of footsteps and chattering voices startles me back into action. I jerk my head down and pick up my pace, scrubbing at a spot on the floor with a renewed vigour. I cannot afford to get punished again. I was lucky this morning that the guards didn't check my marks, as I would have been bound to get a harsher punishment.

When slaves become the property of the royals, they're branded with an identification number. If we step out of line, we are branded with an X. Four Xs and you lose your usefulness, and then you're sent to the camps where you are worked to death digging graves for those who die fighting in the war. My life here may be tough, but it's nothing compared to the misery of the camps—working for twenty hours a day, shovelling mud and hauling around the dead until you collapse. Slaves don't last long there.

I have three of these marks branding my arm, meaning I'm one away from this fate. Although my misdemeanour this morning wasn't enough to earn another brand, my punishments tend to be harsher, longer, as I'm considered a troublemaker.

"Did you hear that Prince Jacob will be attending the ceremony tomorrow?" The excited voice of the servant jolts me out of my reflections, my interest piqued. I always listen for information on the royals, it's best to know as much as I can about my captors. Prince Jacob is the youngest of the three royal sons. From what I've heard, he's quieter than the others, spending more time in his library than mingling with the court ladies like his older brother Michael. I thought he was around my age, and I must have been right if he'll be attending the ceremony. I wasn't aware the royals attended the choosing ceremony. Although it's a part of our religion, I had assumed the royals would be above it all, seeing how they're blessed by the Great Mother.

The maids continue to chatter as they arrange more flowers—beautiful lilies, dahlias, and other, more exotic flowers I've never seen before—into the large, amphora style vases. The colours are bright and the scents so vibrant that even the dreariest of souls would struggle not to find a little bit of peace in this room.

"Do you think he'll be paired up?" the second servant asks, hanging a garland of bright red and white flowers.

"Oh, I doubt it," the first servant replies with a scornful look on her face. "The royals don't have to follow the same rules as the rest of us mere mortals. They pretend they do, but we all know the truth. He'll probably only be there to play along with the little farce they have going on," she continues on blithely, oblivious to the shocked look on her companion's face.

"Mary!" The outraged tone of the servant has me glancing out of the corner of my eye as I continue my task. This part of the floor is surely clean by now, but I'm caught up in the gossip. "You can't say things like that, someone will hear you. It's treason!" Her words are hushed as her eyes dart around the room, aware of the ever-present guard standing outside the hall.

"It's true and you know it! He'll probably only be attending for a chance to be chosen to join the magicians. Not that anyone has been chosen for years." Mary is trying to defend herself, but her voice is quieter, as if she knows she has stepped out of line.

The two maids are quiet for a while, continuing to

arrange the flowers in the awkward silence caused by Mary's rash words. Shuffling forward, I feel my heart sink as I see the footsteps the servants have trodden onto my clean floor. My knees ache underneath the thin shift that covers my body, and my hands cramp from gripping the brush for so long, my fingers wrinkled and bleeding from the labour. I struggle as I stand, my whole body screaming in pain and my muscles cramping from being hunched over for hours. But I ignore it, reaching for the bucket of dirty water. Head down, I shuffle to the small room attached to the back of the hall, the clink of the chains around my ankles the only sound, echoing around the arched ceilings. Mercifully, they have running water in this part of the castle, so I don't have to walk to the well in the courtyard like I know many of the slaves in the older parts of the castle have to. Emptying the bucket, I fill it with fresh water and begin my slow walk back to where I had been working. Whispers follow me as I trudge forward, the heavy bucket and hours of labour making me slower than usual.

"Is that the slave they were talking about?" one whispers to the other, causing my heart to stutter. I'm used to being ignored, and attention is never a good thing for a slave.

"I think so, she's older than the others. And that long dark hair and pale skin...she's different from the others. It must be her."

I'm used to sticking out due to my appearance. The people of Arhaven are blessed with tanned, bronze skin and golden hair thanks to the strength of the sun that beats down on the land. My black hair, green eyes, and pale skin would have made me stick out whether I was a slave or not. No matter how long I work under the sun, I never tan. I don't remember my past, so I have no idea where I originally came from, but I've heard whispers from the other slaves about the people from the mountains who share my characteristics.

"I hear she'll be terminated tomorrow."

I nearly stumble at her words, shock coursing through my body. I hurry as fast as I can to my corner and drop to my knees, straining my ears to hear what they have to say. Perhaps they have the wrong slave...

"Why, what has she done?"

"She turns twenty tomorrow. They cull the slaves at that age."

"Why do they cull them?"

"You know that all citizens are required to attend the ceremony in order to be blessed, but slaves aren't allowed. Without a blessing from the Great Mother, your soul is lost. Those with lost souls are killed before they can become a danger to society," Mary explains, but I tune out the rest of the conversation, my blood turning cold in my veins.

I knew I was one of the older slaves, but I didn't realise I was the eldest. It's true that many don't make it past childhood, and I've never seen an elderly slave... Dread lines my stomach and nausea rolls through me. Closing my eyes, I take a deep breath and try to calm my racing heart.

Keep calm, it's probably just a rumour.

"I've never heard of slaves being killed when they turn twenty!" the quieter servant exclaims to Mary. At this point, though, I'm not really paying attention, since Mary's previous words are ringing in my ears.

"That's because they hardly ever live until that age." I can feel the weight of their stares on my back. "Shame, she's a pretty little thing. I wonder what she did to get sold into slavery," Mary comments, before I hear two sets of footsteps walking away from me.

It's only at this point that I let the scrubbing brush fall from my abused hands and I wrap my arms around my torso.

I'm to be executed tomorrow.

Chapter 2

The rest of the day drags, my brain reeling from what I've learned. I barely see the hall I'm cleaning, my thoughts spinning and tumbling in my head. They can't be right, I haven't done anything wrong, why would they kill me? Sure, they kill slaves on a daily basis for the smallest of offenses, revelling in handing out punishments. So why am I so surprised? Did I truly believe, deep down, that they would let me take part in the ceremony? And if what they said is true, that slaves can't receive the blessing at the ceremony, then the only other option would be death.

As part of our religion, we worship the Great Mother and are taught through readings. Everyone has to attend these readings, even the slaves get a short reading once a week. These readings teach us about the Mother and the blessings she bestows upon us. Priest Rodrick is the one to deliver our readings. He's a harsh, weaselly man who obviously feels only disdain towards the slaves. Our readings are always about repenting, about how lucky we are the Great Mother chooses to give us another purpose. They say we can hope to redeem ourselves in her eyes by serving our royal family. But occasionally, he will give a reading on the choosing ceremony. Everyone knows what happens to those who aren't blessed. Without the Great Mother in our lives, we have no soul, it's ripped from our bodies, so even if I were to escape, what kind of life could I lead without my soul?

The clocktower chimes, informing me it's the seventh hour past noon and time for me to head back to the slave quarters. Although, to be honest, the grumbling of my stomach is more regular than any clock. Fighting against the nausea that's swimming through me, I push to my feet and collect my brush and bucket, shuffling over to the storage room, my weary limbs making me sluggish. I step into the room and set down the equipment with a tired sigh. Knowing I'm alone in the chamber, I take a moment to stand up straight, stretching out my exhausted limbs. A flash of movement catches my attention, and before I can stop myself, I look up. I don't know what makes me do it, I've been a slave long enough to know to keep out of the way and be invisible, but something inside me fights against my instincts.

A woman is staring at me, looking shocked at seeing me here, her dark eyes wide. She doesn't say anything as we stare at each other, and I can't help but open my mouth. To say what? I don't know, but I instantly stop as she opens her mouth to speak, fear flooding through my veins. Fear that quickly turns to stupidity as I realise what I'm seeing. A mirror.

Slaves are forbidden to use mirrors. We're taught that using them is vain and vanity is of no use to us. So seeing myself now is a surprise and I flinch away from what I perceive. Of course I've seen my reflection in the water troughs, but it's not the same, and only for a second, so I don't catch the attention of the guards.

I have no idea where the mirror came from, it's never been here before. Perhaps one of the servants moved it into this room to get it out of the way for the ceremony? Glancing around to see if anyone is watching, I bite down on my lip with indecision. My first instinct is to bow my head and walk away, pretend I never saw it and be thankful to the Mother that no one was here to witness me finding it. If I'm caught looking in the mirror I'll get punished, and I might even earn a fourth brand for it. Is looking at my reflection really something I'm willing to risk being sent to the camps for?

Something twists within me.

If the maids were right, you're going to be killed anyway. Look at the mirror, take back your identity, a dark voice encourages, and I realise it's right. Hands shaking, I take a step forward, the jingle of my chains a constant reminder of what I am. But as I raise my chin to look in the mirror, I see I'm more than that.

I have pale skin, partially from years of being kept in the dark, and my cheek is red and swollen from where the guard hit me, but otherwise it's unblemished. The rest of my body hasn't been so lucky, I'm covered in scars. My long, black hair falls against my face, and I raise my hand to push it back behind my ear. My pale pink lips quirk up into a semblance of a smile. How did I ever mistake myself as anything other than a slave? My skin is marked with dirt and my filthy shift hangs from my body. Looking back up at myself, I see the tension around my eyes, but something that also looks like determination.

Disturbed, I turn away from the mirror and start the walk back through the castle. Eyes downcast, I try to be invisible, but the chains announce our presence and our status, so everybody knows what we are. Nothing, criminals of the kingdom. The other slaves don't talk about their lives before, so I don't know what they did to deserve this. Perhaps they're like me and don't know what their crime was.

As I reach the courtyard, I'm shocked to see that it's full. My hair falls from behind my ear and covers my face as I instinctively bow my head, giving me a veil to hide my frown as I try to gauge what's happening. Guards line the walls of the courtyard and, as one, they step across to block the entrances, leaving me with no way out. Looking around, I see mostly servants and slaves, but the odd visiting lord and lady dot the space, one of the only times all of us would be together.

"Citizens of Arhaven," a booming voice calls, instantly catching our attention as the courtyard falls silent. His rich red clothing and the symbol of the Mother embellished in gold thread on his coat instantly identifies him as a priest. "We have a traitor in our midst."

A sick feeling washes over me and before I can stop it, my body instinctively takes a step back. A couple of people eye me suspiciously before turning to the speaker. Thinking back over what the maids had been whispering about, my mind starts to play tricks on me. Maybe this is how they would do it?

But I haven't done anything to be branded a traitor, I try to assure myself, but my thoughts keep twisting, trying to convince me that this is how I'll die. Paranoia makes me shake, my limbs trembling.

This can't be happening. I'm not sure I totally believed the maids, but I hadn't ever thought they would kill me publicly.

The anger that burns within me, the feeling I work so hard to push aside, to bury deep, starts to boil up. The desire to live, to fight, rises to the surface. I'm not ready to die. Gazing around, I search for something I could use as a weapon. I've never fought before, but I'm strong from years of manual labour. I wouldn't last a minute against the guards, but if I can take them by surprise, perhaps I could get away. Scanning the ground, I see only the smooth, paved ground and I curse my luck.

"Bring her in." My head jerks up at the priest's words as muttering fills the courtyard. Relief turns to horror as I see who's being dragged in, her hands bound behind her back and her ankles cuffed with the same chains that bind mine.

Mary, the maid who had been talking about the royals in the hall I'd been cleaning earlier. Someone must have reported her for her slander, and now she has to pay for it. The gag doesn't stop her muffled cries for help as she looks at the crowd—seeking aid or sympathy, I'm not sure.

"This…*woman*, has committed a great crime and betrayed our blessed royal family," the priest sneers with disdain, the crowd making the appropriate sounds of disgust, their voices raising as they shout insults at Mary. "She is therefore branded as a traitor." The whole time the priest speaks, I keep my gaze locked on the bound woman. Her eyes are wide with fear as she realises that her people have turned on her. All because she said something they didn't believe.

"The usual punishment would be execution. However, the Great Mother has chosen to be merciful." The priest smiles benevolently, and I hear several praises to the Mother, but I can't help the sinking feeling that runs through me. Arhaven is not a merciful nation and I suspect this act of mercy may make Mary wish for death. The priest clears his throat, bringing everyone's attention back to him as he turns to Mary, his face devoid of all emotion save for a sick gleam in his eye. "You shall be stripped of your name and identity and henceforth be known as Slave 1023. You shall work for the royals and try to redeem yourself to the Great Mother." Mary's cry of despair can be heard despite the gag in her mouth as the guards strip her of her servant's uniform, the observing crowd muttering under their breath. Left in only her modest underwear, she shivers under the bitterly cold wind and the watchful eyes of her people.

The sizzle of hot metal can be heard as the branding prop is brought into view, causing a scream from Mary as she struggles uselessly against the guards. People shuffle around uncomfortably, realising what they are about to witness, but I stand frozen. I've been in her place and remember how scared I was, but I wasn't old enough to realise what I was missing out on. Mary must be seventeen or eighteen and knows exactly what this is going to mean for her. The guards unbind her hands and hold out her arm, and no matter how much she struggles she can't get away, her wide eyes watching in horror as the brand is lowered and pressed to her skin. Her piercing screech fills the courtyard and one of the watching ladies faints, as many servants look away, unable to watch. I can't help but notice that all of the slaves in the area are standing stock-still like me, watching the branding of a new slave who's about to join our ranks.

Mary sags back in the guards' grip, sobbing now. The guards' begin to drag her away to the slave quarters when a voice calls out.

"Wait." The guards pause, confused frowns lining their faces, and I get the feeling this show isn't over yet. The priest has a message to put across and he isn't done. "Slave 1023 has a traitorous tongue. If we send her away without further punishment she will speak lies and slander to our other slaves." Ice floods my veins as I understand what's about to happen, and my fellow slaves obviously realise the same thing as they bow their heads, not wanting to witness the following punishment. Watching the branding, sure, we've all been through that, so we watched, showing our solidarity or even curiosity at having a new slave join our ranks. But if I'm right about what I suspect is coming, well, no one deserves that. Even the guards look disturbed, but they dutifully obey orders and bring Mary back, pushing her onto her knees before one of the justice pillars.

The three pillars come up to about hip height and have verses from the Scared Slates, our religious texts, that demand justice for sins committed. I've only ever seen them used once, and the memory is imprinted into my brain. I don't even remember his crime, but I remember his punishment. The man was burnt alive... He often visits my dreams.

Mary is bound to the pillar, her sobs loud as they remove her gag and rest her chin on the flat surface. "Remove her traitorous tongue," the priest orders. Many members of the audience cry out or turn away, unable to watch, but I notice that not a single one of them protests or tries to stick up for Mary. Fists clenched, I take a small step forward, to do what, I don't know, but a hand grips my arm and I freeze in my tracks. Quickly looking down at my arm, I see a small slave at my side. She avoids my eyes but shakes her head slightly, and I know what she's saying.

Don't do it.

I don't know what I was about to do, or where the urge came from—the need to do *something*, anything—but it would only get me killed or earn me a fate the same as Mary's. The sting of tears pricks at my eyes, but

I won't let them fall and I stand tall as Mary's tongue is held out and sliced off with one smooth movement. Her screams make me wince, but I refuse to turn away or bow my head like the others.

The priest is practically glowing, looking gleeful as his eyes skim across the horrified audience who were unable to watch. That is until he sees me and his smile quickly turns into a frown. Thankfully, the guards step aside from the exits and, as one, the slaves quickly slip away before the priest decides to start making an example of us. I escape among the mass of moving people.

THAT EVENING, I'm curled under the scrap of fabric I use as a blanket, staring into the small fire the others have managed to start. I have no idea what they managed to find to burn, but I like watching the flickering of the flames. Images of Mary keep playing through my mind and my anger seems to move and grow with the dancing blaze. I remain separate from everyone, I always have. There's no point in making friends when you're a slave. Plus, there's a hierarchy system, even amongst us, and I want nothing to do with it.

A soft mumble of voices as some of the younger slaves talk catches my attention, their words too quiet for me to make out, but as I glance over, I see their faces are serious and tense. I wonder what they are talking about. They're young, they must be about eleven or twelve. A ghost of a smile flickers up at the corner of the younger one's lips before she nods and lies down by the fire, the conversation over. The small action, nearly insignificant, brings up a memory.

I was once walking through the courtyard when two

children of visiting nobles ran in, their laughter filling the space as they chased each other. The sound nearly caused me to stumble, so joyful and happy, it was foreign, and I wondered what it would be like to be like that. To be so carefree.

As I look at the two young slaves curled up by the fire, something burns inside me. They should be playing and laughing, they shouldn't be down here working until they drop from exhaustion. Frowning, I push up into a sitting position and glance around me, that dark little voice slithering back into my thoughts.

None of them should be here. They're children. What could children possibly do to deserve this fate? The thoughts take my breath away and I shake my head firmly as if I can throw them from my head.

You were a child too. What crime could you have committed?

Those words are dangerous. Priest Rodrick is always telling us that our servitude is a blessing, that we should be grateful the royals chose to keep us alive and give us that opportunity. I should be happy that the Great Mother wanted to give me a chance to redeem myself. I must have done something terrible to earn this fate, the royals wouldn't enslave children otherwise, surely?

The sound of heavily booted feet echo around the room, bouncing off the stone walls and sending a wave of fear through us all. No good ever comes of the guards visiting the slave quarters at night. Knowing that someone is coming, we do what we do best—shrink into the shadows and blend into the background. As the footsteps come closer, I realise that they are dragging someone behind them, their body being pulled along the dirty floor. When they drop the body unceremoniously to the ground, I think for a moment the person is dead. But then a wordless moan escapes the motionless form as the guard kicks them in the ribs. The other guard looks around in disgust, his eyes briefly landing on me before he pulls a scroll from his belt. Heart pounding, I feel like every eye in the room is on me. Is this it? The decree announcing my death?

"809, come with us, you've been chosen by the Great Mother to serve in other ways." Silence follows the guard's words and I can't help my relieved sigh. I immediately feel bad as a pretty young slave pushes to her feet, her eyes wide. Quiet praises to the Great Mother fill the room as she steps around the body that's still unmoving. As she reaches the guards, their eyes gleam with mirth as they wrap their meaty hands around her skinny upper arms. It's a blessing, to be chosen to serve the Great Mother in the way I suspect she will be. Serving the Mother in any capacity we possibly can is drilled into us every week by Priest Rodrick. But then why does it feel like she is walking to a fate worse than death?

As a female slave, we can be chosen to serve the Great Mother in ways the males can not—to bear the children of the barren wives of noblemen. It's said that only those who have truly repented can be chosen to serve the Mother in this way. I've seen some of them walking the halls, their bellies round with child, their eyes dull and lifeless, and their bodies covered in bruises. Once they have birthed the babe, they are sent to the king's brothel to work. No longer a slave. I wonder, is it truly freedom though? They're still forced to work in the brothel.

The guards leave with the trembling girl and the steady moaning from the person left behind turns into a wail. People around me share nervous glances with each other, worrying that the noise will call down the guards, but no one makes a move. Usually I would keep to myself, after all, no one helped me when I was thrown in here as a small child. I had to learn to fend for myself and witnessed firsthand what happened to those who didn't adapt. So that's what I did, I learned how to survive. I don't know if it's the prospect of my impending death that makes me bold, but I push up onto aching feet and walk over as quietly as my chains will let me.

Crouching by the body, I place my hand on their shoulder, and as they shy away I recognise them. Mary. After we didn't see her for hours, I thought she had died from her wounds like many do when they first come here.

"Mary." My voice is rough as I reach for her, and it makes me wonder when I last spoke. Long enough ago that I have to think about it. Hisses fill the room and Slave 879 sneers at me.

"625, do you have a death wish?" she whispers, her tone full of venom as her eyes drop to the girl crying on the floor. "She's 1023 now. Nothing else." Turning away, she shuffles back to the group of slaves that look to her for guidance.

Guess we aren't getting any help from her then. Not that I expected it. 879 has always disliked me. Originally, she tried to recruit me to her group, but I refused. Since then she seemed to have a personal vendetta against me, trying to trip me as we walk to our assignments or make me spill a bucket of water, anything that would get me punished.

Returning my attention to Mary, or 1023, I realise she was right about something. If the guards caught me calling her by her real name, then having my tongue removed would seem like a blessing in comparison to the punishment I would receive. Turning Mary over, I see her face is covered in bruises as she flinches away from me. I reach out again to help her, but she yelps, attempting to scramble away from me.

She makes a series of inarticulate noises, trying to speak before wailing as she realises she can't. Turning, she crawls towards a corner as far away as she can get from us.

Standing in the middle of the room, I frown as I watch her, my body swirling with emotions I can't put a name to. The others around me settle down for the night, accepting their fates. Returning to my corner, I numbly sit down, glancing at the brands on my arm.

Is this how I will die? As a nameless slave? Curling up, I try to fall asleep, Mary's crying a desolate lullaby. For the first time in my life, I pray.

Chapter 3

That night I dream. I'm surprised I even managed to sleep after what I learned yesterday, but my body was so exhausted from a day of hard labour that it demanded rest. In my dream I was chosen, chosen to join the magicians. Magic rarely graces humans, but the Great Mother blesses a chosen few to become magicians —our greatest protectors. Fewer and fewer have been picked over the years, but the war against the elves is still rife. Some say the Great Mother is punishing us for our sins, which is why less people are being chosen to wield her magic. I'm not sure what I believe, but the thought of having magic is intoxicating.

I must have been in a deep sleep, because I'm jolted awake by a sharp kick in my side. Bolting upright, I glance around and see guards have arrived. Not hearing them coming, something I'm always listening for, shows how exhausted I am. No one tries to warn me.

"625! On your feet!" The words are shouted at me, demanding that I comply with their orders. I shake my head to clear my clouded thoughts before a creeping sense of dread and fear rolls through me. My body aches from sleeping on the cold stone floor, but I try to shake off the discomfort, not daring to stretch out my abused limbs. Standing before the guards, I feel small, my shoulders hunched forward and head dropped so my face is hidden behind a shield of dark hair as if it would protect me from what's to come. I fight to keep myself from shuddering as fear rolls through me like a wave. They don't deserve to see my fear, but I can't help the tremble in my fingers. No good has ever come from being called by our number.

Their rough hands grip my upper arms tightly, and I'm reminded of the girl who was taken last night. Is that to be my fate? Without another word they begin to march me away. Peering through my hair, I glance around, trying to meet someone's eyes to see if anyone will do anything to try to stop them. No one says anything, the room is silent. Not one person meets my panicked gaze, but I see expressions of sympathy as some of the slaves I knew better turn their heads, unable to watch. I don't know why I'm surprised, why would they risk themselves for me when I wouldn't have done the same?

A movement catches my eyes and hope flutters in my heart until I see who it is—879 wearing a smug expression, her gaze meeting mine as I'm taken away. Anger boils in my veins again, but instead of pushing it aside I welcome it. It's not going to save me, but I refuse to willingly accept my death. For now, though, I keep silent, seething, as I'm half dragged into the castle.

"Let's hope he gets this over with quickly. I want to be back in time for the ceremony," one of the guards grumbles, his companion grunting in agreement.

As we enter the courtyard, my anger stutters for a moment as I think I'm going to be bound to one of the pillars, but they keep walking, taking me deeper into the castle, through the winding corridors until we reach the chapel. I've never been here, and if not for the circumstances I would be admiring the intricately carved marble pillars and arches. Priest Rodrick is waiting at the altar at the front as I'm dragged through the sanctuary and shoved to my knees when we reach him. Head bowed, my chest heaves as my breathing speeds up, the hammering of my heart so loud in my ears that I'm sure they're bound to hear it.

Rodrick steps closer, his familiar scent of incense clouding my nose until I can see his shoes. One of the guards grips my hair and wrenches my head back, and I can't hold back the gasp that escapes my lips. The priest runs his eyes over me, a small smile playing at the corner of his lips. I get the feeling he's enjoying every moment of this.

"As a slave, you forfeited the right to the choosing ceremony," he begins. His words are aimed at me, but his usual booming voice fills the space like he's giving a reading to a large crowd. "The Sacred Scrolls say that those who do not attend a choosing ceremony before their twentieth birthday will lose their soul and become an abomination. We *cannot* allow that." His voice is grave, making it sound like my death sentence is a sorrowful moment. That anger turns in my stomach again. I know the truth. The priest *hates* the slaves, he is enjoying every moment of this.

Footsteps echo and I see more guards enter the room, the flash of black and gold making my blood run cold. The black priest uniform is saved for only one man—the executioner. The man who carries out the will of the Mother herself. I guess I should be flattered that they think I'm dangerous enough to warrant so many guards, their beady eyes watching me wearily as if I'm going to turn into a monster at any moment.

"Today we send 625 back to the Great Mother." Rodrick looks up and presses his fingers to his forehead in the gesture of the Mother. He turns his attention back to me and frowns, disgust in his eyes as he looks at my dirty clothes. "Pray that you have repented enough for her to grant you a place in her eternal embrace." The sound of swords being removed from scabbards makes my heart race as the guards take weary steps closer, as if I'm going to lose my soul immediately and turn on them.

However, it's the executioner I keep my eyes on. His face is blank of expression, but I get the feeling he doesn't want to be here, the weight of his blessed role taking a heavy toll on him. Something flips within me then and a sense of peace fills me, peace and determination.

"No." It's the second word I've spoken in twenty-four hours, but my voice is clear and steady.

"No?" Rodrick crows, his scolding tone heavy as I flick my eyes over and sneer at him. "You think to deny the Mother?" I may not be able to move, but I can make my feelings clear.

"I—"

"Silence! I refuse to hear another word from your tainted lips!" Rodrick shouts, spittle flying from his lips as he works himself up into a rage, the large sleeves of his gown rippling as he gestures sharply.

"Wait. I want to hear what she has to say." The Executioner's voice is low and rough, like he rarely gets the opportunity to speak. My eyes flick around the room, from person to person, gauging their reactions. They seem uncomfortable. This isn't going how they'd expected, and Rodrick has turned a shade of red that makes me worry. Not for his health, but men who get that angry tend to lash out, to make what should have been a quick punishment tortuous. Dragging my eyes away, I meet those of the executioner. I've always been scared of him, everyone is, not just the slaves, but all the people of Arhaven. We've all heard the stories of the executioner, but at this moment, I'm not scared.

The room is silent as he waits to hear what I was going to say, and I realise that these will be my last words. I best make them count. There are so many things I could say. I could beg, bargain, or swear. But as I look inside, I realise what I must tell them. Clearing my throat, I start to speak.

"The slaves...they're children. You're killing *children*. What could they possibly have done—"

"It's as the Mother wills it. We don't question her." Rodrick's sharp voice cuts me off, swiftly followed by a slap to my face that has me reeling. Had the guards not been holding me in place, I'm sure I would have fallen back. Storming forward, he grabs me by the front of my shift, bringing his face close to mine as he hisses at me. "You've had your say—"

"Stop." The voice is unlike any I've heard before, power seemingly embedded into the words as Rodrick stumbles back. Lazy, strolling footsteps fill the room as the stranger walks up behind me as if he has all the time in the world. Perhaps he does.

"Mage Grayson." The priest's tone relays his shock and fear as he greets the high magician. My blood runs cold as he comes closer, my skin tingling as his magic fills the room, crawling over my body the nearer he gets.

I had known the magicians would send a representative to the castle for the ceremony, but I hadn't realised it would be *him*. Mage Grayson is one of the eight High Magicians of Arhaven, the strongest of all the magicians. The trials they have to go through are enough to cause nightmares, and Grayson is one of the youngest and strongest to gain that position. I've only ever seen him once. He doesn't come to the capital often since he's usually out on the battle front or at the magicians' keep, many miles from here.

His energy feels suffocating as it envelops me fully and he finally steps into view. His magic seems to stutter as he takes me in, his eyes scanning my slight frame. As my head is still being wrenched back, I don't have any other choice but to look at him, so I make the most of it. He's tall and tanned, like most of the people in Arhaven, but his hair is darker, not black like mine, but different enough that he would stand out in a crowd. He's good-looking, but in a way that powerful men are, not classically beautiful. His sharp jaw and piercing dark eyes make him seem like he's constantly contemplating something.

"Release her," he commands, waving his hand at the guards who immediately let go of me, taking a hasty step back. I slump to the floor, the toll of the day leaving me drained. I'm not sure how much longer I can take the constant threat of death. The magic I felt earlier changes to a gentle caress, my body suddenly feeling renewed, and my aches are taken away as my heart settles. Gasping as the tingling sensation leaves my body, I push myself up, back straight as I wait for whatever is going to come next. I keep my eyes down out of habit, but I can see the priest spluttering and red as he looks between me and the mage.

"But—"

Grayson glances over at the priest with his brows raised, his lips quirking up at Rodrick's barely restrained frustration. "I think I can take care of her." He wiggles his fingers and I gasp as a band of magic suddenly snaps around my waist, making me arch my back at the sudden tight feeling. The magician's eyes return to me with a frown. "This is the slave you've been so worried about?" He sounds amused and I see the guards' discomfort as Rodrick turns a deeper shade of crimson, insulted by the magician's words but unable to retaliate. No one would dare go against the word of a high magician.

"She's about to be returned to the Mother," the executioner answers, his first words since Grayson entered the chapel. A look passes between the two of them that makes me think they know each other.

"What's her crime?"

"She turns twenty today," Rodrick supplies, his voice calmer now that he is back in his element. Grayson frowns as he turns back to me, his gaze reassessing as a wave of his magic travels up my body and lifts my chin, like a phantom hand. My whole body stiffens, my instincts screaming to keep my eyes dropped, to not meet his eyes with my own.

"Hmm, that makes things more complicated," he murmurs, still looking at me intensely as if he's trying to figure me out and what he sees is lacking.

No. I won't die a coward. Feeling determined, I flick my eyes up, looking directly into his. Shock covers his face before he quickly schools it into a smirk and turns to face the priest. "But I didn't mean that. Why is she a slave, what did she do?" There's a pause and I listen eagerly. Perhaps I'll discover the reason behind my slavery.

"Does it matter? It is as the Mother wills it," the priest responds quickly, dismissing the matter with a gesture of his hand.

"You're right, it doesn't matter." My heart stutters at the magician's words before he starts to speak again, addressing the guards still lingering in the room. "Change of plans, gentlemen, the slave comes with me."

"What?" Outraged, Priest Rodrick stalks towards Grayson, throwing a disgusted look at me before turning back to the magician. He appears scornful, and I know he's not used to people denying him. "Why would I possibly allow that?"

"Because the Mother wills it," Grayson replies, repeating the priest's earlier words back to him, the corner of his mouth fighting a smile. "Because I received a vision. This girl is crucial to the war, she will play an important role. I'm not sure what yet, but I can tell you this—if you kill her today, we will lose the war."

Silence meets his declaration, and for a moment I think I'm dreaming, I have to be. I'm a slave, I'm nothing, how could I have anything to do with the outcome of the war? The war that has been going on for centuries? The magician stares at me like he's thinking the same thing and I quickly lower my gaze again out of habit. I may have a way out of this and I don't want to ruin that by pissing him off.

"Well, you're too late. She's twenty, she'll become a monster, and you can't stop that." Rodrick's voice raises, his pitch higher than it had been previously, his face beginning to redden again at the prospect of the magician taking me away. Grayson turns sharply to face Rodrick, and from my position I can just about see the look he gives the priest.

"Do you think it was purely luck that brought me here just before you killed her?" His words are sharp and I decide right then I don't ever want to piss off this man. I see the priest stiffen as his hands are suddenly bound to his side by a glowing band of magic, reminding everyone in the room just what he's capable of. "Don't fight me on this, Priest Rodrick."

Released of his magical restraints, the priest falls to the ground, gasping as he sketches out the symbol of the Mother on his forehead. "Of course not, I would never think to question the plans of the Great Mother or the magicians that serve her," Rodrick wheedles, his voice honeyed as he bows his head. He says all the right words, his voice nothing but compliant, but I know he's angry. As he pushes to his feet, he glares at me, proving I'm right. But he's not just angry, he's furious. I've seen expressions like this before. People who are humiliated tend to become more vicious and cruel. I make a vow that if I survive this, I will try to never be alone in a room with this man.

"Stand up." The command is spoken quietly, but the magic rolling against my skin is a reminder of how powerful he is. Standing on shaking feet, I bow my head as I wait for them to tell me this was all a sick, cruel joke. "Thank you for your time, Priest Rodrick," Grayson addresses him formally, but I can hear his condescending tone and know his thanks isn't sincere. Turning his back to the priest, he walks to my side, glancing down at me with a stern expression. "Follow me. I wouldn't try to run." An echo of the magic he'd used to bind me earlier flickers against my waist and I know running would be pointless.

Without another word, the magician strides out of the room, his dark cloak with golden lining snapping behind him. Ignoring the stares of Rodrick and the guards in the room, I hurry to follow Grayson but my chains make me slow. Throwing a look over his shoulder, he makes a noise of frustration when he sees how far behind him I am, and his eyes zero in on my bound ankles.

"Can't you go any faster?" he demands, but I see something flicker in his eyes as I quickly drop my gaze and hurry to try and catch up before I anger him. The chains are cumbersome, and I've never tried to run in them before. My foot catches on one of the paving stones, and before I realise what's happening, I'm falling forward only to be jerked to a sudden halt. Glancing down, I see a glowing pillow of light has caught me, stopping me from slamming into the hard ground. With wide eyes I look up at the magician watching me with a frown. When he sees me looking at him, his expression quickly turns to one of impatience. My heart in my throat, I push up to my feet and bow my head as he walks over and inspects me for damage, lifting my arms and spinning me around. He grabs my chin and grunts when he sees the bruises on my cheeks and those peeking out of the top of my clothing.

"Come," he instructs, as he turns abruptly and begins to walk again. However, this time he's slower, taking smaller strides as he waits for me to catch up. Shuffling just behind him, I feel my body start to tremble again, and I wrap my arm around my torso in comfort. Glancing over his shoulder, he sighs and drops back so we are walking side by side. I could be punished just for being this close to him, but who knows the consequences if I upset him by moving away? We walk this way in silence until I feel his eyes on me again.

"What did you do to deserve being made a slave?" I don't answer, seeing how I don't have an answer for him. He snorts and I catch a glimpse of him shaking his head as if he thinks I'm being difficult.

"You didn't try to plead for your life." His voice is

quiet, and had I not been standing next to him, I might have not heard him. It's not a question, but he seems to want an answer. How do I answer that? "Most people I know would beg for their life. I've even seen battle hardened soldiers pleading to the Mother." I feel his eyes on me again and this time I don't shy away, instead, I keep my gaze straight ahead. "But not you," he ponders, as if I'm some puzzle for him to figure out. He continues to lead me through the castle, taking me into the deeper parts I've never been before. Slaves don't usually come this far, we're kept away from the royals.

"I know you can speak, I heard you before." Frustration is clear to hear in his voice now and that bubbling anger wraps its claws around me. Before I can stop it, I'm opening my mouth.

"I only speak when I have something worthy to say." My voice is weak and scratchy from lack of use, and I quickly throw my hand over my mouth as I realise what I've said. He stops and I know I'm in serious trouble. People don't speak to the magicians like that, especially not the high magicians, and slaves shouldn't speak *at all*. By implying that he was not worthy of a response from me, I was gravely insulting him.

Having my tongue removed would seem a tame punishment compared to what the magicians could do to me. Images of my skin being slowly peeled from my body rolls through my head as I fall to the ground, prostrating myself before him. My forehead presses into the hard floor, although this part of the castle is carpeted, so there are some small mercies. My breath pants out of me while I wait for him to speak or move or *anything*. When he does, it's not what I expected. A shocked laugh chokes out of him and he pauses as if surprised that he laughed.

"You've got backbone. Good, you're going to need

it." Still pressed against the floor, I frown into the carpet, wondering what he's talking about. I don't know what the magician wants from me, and his actions confuse me, so I stay on the floor awaiting his instructions. "Although, this throwing yourself on the floor is going to be an issue." His voice suddenly gets closer and I feel a hand on my arm before he pulls at it to help me up. Lifting my head, my eyes lock with his, and it takes me a second to realise what he's doing. He's kneeling before me, offering me a hand. A high mage, one of our premier people in society, is kneeling before a slave.

Shuffling back in alarm, I pull my arm away from him. He's breaking the rules, but it won't be him that gets punished. Seeing my terror, he frowns and slowly stands. "I won't hurt you. Not unless you try to run," he tells me, waiting for my curt nod before gesturing for me to get up. Hurrying to my feet, I start to follow him again, our tense silence making the walk awkward. I can't help but think over his words, about why I didn't beg for my life. I didn't want to die, but at that moment I knew I had a chance to say something, to speak up for those who couldn't. Begging wasn't going to spare my life.

"Why plead for my life when there are hundreds of children being killed every day?" I whisper, my words barely loud enough to be heard, but I know he's heard me because from my peripheral I can see him staring at me intently.

After a moment of silence, he huffs out a breath and turns his attention to the corridor ahead of us. "You are not what I expected."

I want to reply, to ask him what exactly he expected, but I have already pushed enough boundaries today, so I duck my head and keep moving forward.

You're not what I expected either, I can't help but think, trying to watch him out my peripheral. His uniform is similar to the one soldiers wear—a double-breasted jacket covered in gold buttons. But where the soldiers wear dark green, the magician's wear dark blue and have a cape. High magicians have gold lined capes, but their power is what really gives them away. I'd expected a high magician to be powerful, but I'd grossly underestimated exactly *how* powerful he would be. That kind of power comes with responsibilities, and I had expected him to be cruel and distant towards me, like the priests, but so far he's surprised me.

I still have no idea where he's taking me, and I've lost track of where we are in the castle thanks to the twisted route we've taken. Perhaps he's done that on purpose so I can't run?

Reaching a wide, opulent corridor, we stop outside a set of double doors, the wood carved with swirls painted in gold.

"We're here," he tells me, and my brow creases in confusion. Where is *here?* He pauses, glancing down at me as if waiting for a response, but what he forgets is that I've been mostly silent for the past twelve years. I'm used to my questions going unanswered, so after a time you stop asking. Reaching out, Grayson touches the golden door handle, simply laying his hand on top of it. *What is he waiting for?* Confused, I stand at his side. When I feel a flash of magic and the sound of the lock turning, my question is answered. Pushing the doors open, he strides in and my eyes widen at the sight before me.

A huge living chamber greets me, every item in the room gleaming as if it had just been polished. The walls are painted a cream colour with lush, deep red carpeting. The furniture is made of walnut and upholstered with fabric the same shade of red as the flooring. Mage Grayson has already walked into the room, removing his cloak with a sigh before hanging it up on the set of hooks screwed into the wall. Rolling his neck and stretching out his arms, he gazes around the room.

"I haven't been here in years, yet it always looks just how I left it," he mutters, running a finger along the wooden dresser as he walks over to the plush, upholstered couch. Settling against the large cushions, he frowns as he notices me still standing in the open doorway, eyes wide.

"Are you coming in?" His smile is teasing and something flips inside my stomach. I try to swallow back the sick feeling that seems to have taken residence inside me. I shouldn't be here, I will get a fourth brand for sure if one of the guards catches me.

They were going to kill you anyway, what's the harm in taking a look? the rebellious part of me insists, and I realise it's right. Lifting my foot, I slowly step over the threshold, holding my breath as I walk fully into the room. The doors shut behind me suddenly, making me spin to see who's behind me, only to see…no one. Hearing a chuckle, I turn again to see Grayson wiggling his fingers at me. Magic.

Feeling stupid, I look away and try to take in as much detail as I can without making it obvious.

"You're free to explore the room as much as you like."

Busted. I ignore his smug smile as I stare up at the glistening chandelier hanging above us, wondering how long it took the crafter to create such beauty. "There are shields around the door and windows, so don't get any ideas about trying to escape." His voice turns harsh, his eyes glowing with his power as he calls it to him, and I can't help but flinch away from him. The power subsides and he frowns, shaking his head at whatever thought he was having. "You're safe in my chambers, no one will hurt you here," he continues, oblivious to the horror that his words have caused.

His chambers. He's brought me back to his chambers. An image of the slave that was taken away last night flashes through my mind and I take a step away from him, shaking my head as my hands form into fists. I won't be saved from death only to end up having to service a magician.

"No." My denial is firm and clear.

"No?" He pushes up from the couch and takes a step towards me, but stops as I bare my teeth at him, a feral hiss escaping from behind my clenched teeth. Frowning, he gestures towards me. I've adopted a fighting stance, ready to run or fight should I need to. "I don't under—" I interrupt him with a shake of my head.

"I won't lie with you."

My words finally register and he looks like he's just been punched in the gut before anger crosses his face. "Mother above! Is that what you thought I brought you here for?" Frustration and disgust line his face and the room starts to shake with his magic. It begins with a small, fine tremble, and then builds until even the walls seem to quake. Inside, I'm terrified, but I stand my ground. He must be trying to trick me. I should have learned by now that no help is offered for free. Keeping my chin up but my eyes cast away, I gesture around me.

"Why else would you save me from the executioner just to bring me to your room? I know what happens to the slaves they take away." The room instantly stops shaking and Grayson seems to sag with the weight of what I've said.

"Fuck. No, I—" A knock at the door has him pausing. Sighing, he gestures to a door on my left. "Go in there, you will find a bathroom. Clean yourself up. I'll send someone in to help you in a bit. Once you're done, come join me out here," he instructs. Looking at the door, I feel a sense of foreboding, but I give him a short nod before slowly heading towards the door he waved at.

I step into the room, pausing in the doorway and hearing only silence behind me, except for the subtle rattling of my chains. Looking around, I notice a large, four-poster bed, and when I spot the bathroom I hurry over, shutting the door firmly. Pressing my head against the white painted wood, I whisper prayers to the Mother. As I try to catch my breath, I hear Grayson talking animatedly to someone, someone who does *not* sound happy.

Mother help me.

Chapter 4

The bathroom is like nothing I've ever seen. The room is so white and clean I'm afraid just touching something will make it dirty, which will be sure to earn me a punishment. A large, sunken tub takes up the whole right side of the room and is big enough for at least three people to sit in comfortably. Cabinets line the wall to my left, a huge mirror covering half the wall. I step to the side, not wanting to face what I might see in the reflection. I turn my attention to the various bottles of lotions that line the top of the marble countertop. I have no idea why one person would need so many. Then I realise with a blush that no man would have this much, and I must be looking at something that belongs to his partner. I know he's not married, thanks to the gossip from the servants who always forget that the slaves are listening to their whispers. However, I didn't know that he had a partner, or any…lovers. How would she feel knowing a slave was locked away in her partner's bathroom, using her lotions? Looking away with a shudder, I step towards the tub.

The sound of footsteps outside the door has me spinning and lunging for the little silver lock, sliding the bolt across. Taking a step back, I wrap my arms around myself. I know that against a magician a tiny lock wouldn't keep him away, but this small piece of metal has me feeling more secure anyway. Suddenly, despite the brief moment of security I'd felt, everything that's happened in the last few hours hits me. I start to tremble, my stomach rolls, and I only just make it to the toilet before I'm vomiting into the basin. Retching, I empty the meagre contents of my stomach as if I'm purging my body of the events of the day. Replaying the magician's words in my head, I press my forehead against my braced arms and try to calm my breathing.

Safe. You're safe. He said so, no one will hurt you, I repeat over and over until the shaking stops and I can sit back on my heels. I shouldn't trust him. Why would he offer me safety? He knows I'm twenty, so why is he delaying the inevitable?

I don't know why, but I believe him and decide to enjoy my reprieve. After a moment I'm feeling stronger, so I push up and walk back to the bathtub, reaching toward the two silver knobs. Turning one to the right, my mouth twitches up in some semblance of a smile as hot water starts streaming from the tap and into the tub.

I don't remember ever having a bath, it's not a luxury slaves get to enjoy. So when I overheard women discussing the pleasure of enjoying a relaxing bath, I never understood. The rough washing downs from the guards certainly don't count. Every month they gather a group of slaves, strip them naked, and pump freezing water through a hose, dousing us to remove the dirt and grime that covers us like a second skin. It's a humiliating and painful occasion. Washing is a necessity to stop us from getting sick, not something to bring pleasure.

However, as I run the bath, I can't help the small flicker of excitement that fills me at the prospect of getting truly clean.

The sound of flowing water echoes around the room and, cautiously, I flick my gaze up to see that the large mirror has steamed up. Releasing a breath I hadn't realised I was holding, I take a step towards the counter and stare with wide eyes at the rows upon rows of bottles. I only ever learned basic letters and words before I became a slave, so as I stare at the bottles the letters on the labels start to swim in my vision. Blindly, I reach forward and grab one, not knowing or caring if it's right. Pulling the cork from the top, a sweet, floral smell greets my nose before I dump half the contents of the bottle into the bath. Bubbles soon start to form and I reach to remove my shift, but something stops me. Voices.

Frowning, I shuffle over to the door, trying to be as quiet as my chains will allow. I know that the Mother frowns upon spying, but I've been rescued from death only to be told that I've been seen in one of the great magician's visions. It's been one hell of a day. Besides, I doubt I'm in her good books anyway, so what's one more misdemeanour?

Pressing my ear against the bathroom door, I hear the sound of footsteps, like they're pacing the room. I could have sworn I heard voices, but right now I can only hear what I assume is Grayson pacing the length of the chamber. What's caused him to be so tense? Does he think I'm going to try to escape? Or is he regretting his decision to save me from the executioner? I'm about to pull away from the door when the voices start up again.

"Are you sure it was her?" That's not Grayson. The voice is male, and older than the magician who brought me here. He sounds...disapproving. I can't say I blame him. When Grayson had an image of a girl who would be influential in the war, I'm betting they were hoping for one of the noble ladies. Not a slave girl who has reached the end of her usefulness.

"Yes," Grayson answers, his voice firm. Whatever vision he saw, he fully believes in it. "As soon as I saw her, it was like a bolt of electricity shot down my spine. I don't know why, but she's important."

"She's a slave. A nobody." The disgust in the older man's voice is nothing I'm not used to, but today it twists something inside me.

"She has a part to play in the war. We can't kill her." Grayson's smooth response is quick, but it strikes me like a physical blow.

"Then what do we do with her? She might be dangerous," the older man counters, but I barely hear him.

We can't kill her.

Pulling away from the door, I stare at it in shock, not really seeing it. They truly aren't going to kill me. I hadn't let myself believe it when the magician turned up and whisked me away. Death is only a slip of the foot away when you're a slave, the slightest transgression or error can lead to your execution, your body just one more to add to the mass graves outside of the city. I've always known I would live a short life, but then I was shown a glimpse of something else.

Hope.

Shaking my head, I take a step back. Thoughts like that are dangerous. The only way I've gotten through the last twelve years is by living a day at a time, and that's what I need to do right now. Focus on surviving today. Taking a deep breath, I frown as I see a dark, dirty smear on the door where I was pressed against it. Mother above. If they see that they will know I was listening to their conversation. Something wet touches my foot and I smother the shriek that tries to escape. Spinning around, my eyes widen in horror when I see the bathtub is overflowing with bubbles. I'll get a flogging for this for sure. A pounding on the door has me jumping into action, leaping forward to turn off the taps and desperately trying to scoop the bubbles back into the bathtub, but they continue to flow over the top.

"What's going on in there?" Grayson's voice is muffled through the wooden door, but I can hear the command in his tone. "Open the door," he demands, as my eyes dart around the room, desperately looking for a way out of this. Only there isn't one. Sinking to the floor, I feel my chest tighten as I try to stop the flow of water and bubbles towards the door. The water is hot, almost scalding, but I ignore that as I grab handfuls of bubbles, desperately trying to throw them back into the tub. He doesn't wait for me to comply with his orders, and I feel the tingle of magic run over me as the little lock on the door undoes itself.

The door swings open and I lower my head as I wait for his response. He says nothing, the only sound is the gentle splashing of the water overflowing onto the floor. Belatedly, I shift my position so I'm prostrate before him, my forehead pressing against the wet floor, soapy water stinging my eyes as it continues to make its path towards the magician's boots.

"What in the…" Grayson exclaims but he trails off, and I can almost feel his eyes burning into me. He's silent for a moment and I keep myself as still as I can until I hear a noise of disgust. Fighting the urge to look up, I focus on my breathing, trying not to choke on the bubbles that are starting to surround me.

"I told you she'd be trouble," the older man chides, before he walks away with clipped steps, leaving me alone with the magician. This is the biggest bathroom I've ever been in, but suddenly the room feels small, constricting.

"Get up," he demands quietly, and as I push up from my position, tilting my head, I see him looking around the room with a frown before he drops his gaze back to me. Bowing my head to avoid eye contact, I hear his sigh before his knees appear in my field of vision. "I thought I told you to stop throwing yourself onto the floor." His voice has a teasing edge to it, but I daren't risk that he's not joking and remain in my position on the floor. I hear his sigh as he takes another step closer to me, but he doesn't bother kneeling, not this time. Is that because of my reaction last time, or because a slave isn't worth getting his smart uniform wet for?

"You're not in trouble, get up." There is definite frustration in his tone now and, deciding not to push him any further, I scramble to my feet. Daring to look up, I watch the high magician as he surveys the damage to the room. A wry smile pulls at his lips when he reaches for the bottle I'd chosen.

"I applaud your good taste in scents, but did you need to use so much? This is expensive stuff."

I can't help it, I stare at him. This is a high magician, one of the men who protects our kingdom, but here he is, talking to a slave about his favourite perfume. Are all of them like this? Somehow, I don't think they are. The magicians have a scary reputation for killing first and asking questions later, their training brutal and their Goddess-given powers lethal.

Wide-eyed, I continue to stare at him, drawing a blank at his expectant expression. His eyebrow raises when I don't respond. I *think* he's joking. He hasn't reprimanded me, which he would have done had he been truly angry at the mess. He sighs again at my lack of response and waves his hands in a complicated gesture that has the water and bubbles starting to clear.

"I'm sorry, I've never used it before," I whisper, as I watch him working his magic, the tell-tale tingling sensation running over me stronger than I've ever felt it before. Questions simmer up inside me, but I push them away. I've always been inquisitive and it's landed me in trouble more times than I can count, but I'd have a death wish if I questioned a high magician.

"Mother above!" The high pitch exclamation has me spinning around to see a stern-looking woman gaping at the mess. "Mother above! What is going on in here?" Her gaze lands on me for a moment, and I brace myself for a beating, but her eyes soon narrow on the magician.

"Jayne, I was trying to help our guest. I was distracted and I didn't notice that the water overran," Grayson lies smoothly, and with a flick of his hand the floor is spotless. The woman, Jayne, stares at him, unblinking, and for a moment I think she is going to call him out on his lie. Letting out a huff of air, she shakes her head, the corner of her mouth pulling up into a smile.

"Well, at least you cleaned up after yourself." She tuts, trying but failing to hide her smile as she bustles into the room.

"It's good to see you again, Jayne." His voice is warm, and for a moment I don't see the imposing high magician, I see a young man who's been away from home for a long time.

"You as well, dear. You don't visit me often enough," she chides gently, before shooing him away. "Now, leave us alone, it's not proper that you're in here alone with a young lady."

I look down at the shackles around my ankles and barely manage to hide my snort when she calls me a lady. Shifting on my feet, the metal rattles and I frown. Those are going to make bathing difficult. Skin tingling, I glance up to see Grayson staring at my legs intently as his fingers dance in intricate movements. A quiet click sounds from the cuffs, but it may as well have been a gunshot. It reverberates through me as they fall to the floor with a clatter. Mumbled voices fill the room around me, but they fade away as I stare at my now bare ankles.

For twelve years those have been bound to me, the only constant in my life. I hadn't thought I would ever see them removed. Even in death slaves are buried with their shackles. My skin stings where the air hits the raw wounds from the too tight metal bands, but I pay no heed to it. The pain is nothing compared to what I'm used to receiving. I lift a grimy foot and place it back down softly, marvelling at how quiet my steps sound without the chains rattling with my movements. Jayne says something to Grayson, her voice sharp, and I raise my head quickly and see her whipping him with a towel.

Stomach twisting, I stumble back, waiting for the retribution he will bestow upon her. To touch a magician without their permission is a crime. What Jayne just did would be considered a capital offence. But that's not what happens. The two of them ignore me as Grayson laughs and holds his hands up in surrender.

"Okay, I'm going!" Throwing the older woman a fond smile, he strides to the door before turning to look at me. He seems to pick up on my distress, noticing I've shrunk back into the corner of the room. For a second I think he's going to say something or take a step towards me, but his expression changes into a frown. His gaze drops to my ankles and then the cuffs. When he meets my eyes again, he looks every inch the magician, his hard eyes boring into me as if he can see all my secrets. I'm instantly reminded that although he may have saved me from the executioner, he could easily kill me if I was to upset him. I must never forget what he is capable of. After another couple of agonising seconds, he dips his head slightly and leaves the room, pulling the door firmly shut behind him.

As soon as he leaves, I feel like I can breathe again, and I blow out a breath I hadn't realised I'd been holding. Jayne turns to survey me, and I use the opportunity to do the same. She's shorter than me and of the typical Arhaven build, with slender shoulders and narrow hips. Her hair, which I'm sure was once fair and golden, is now peppered with grey and pulled back neatly. She's wearing the dark blue uniform of a magician's servant, the same colour worn by their masters. She must have been working in the castle for a long time to have been granted this position, plus she seemed to know Grayson well.

Her blue eyes scan over my thin frame, my lank, dark hair that's falling into my face, and down to my raw ankles. Unable to hold her shrewd gaze, I drop mine to the floor. I'm waiting for her to belittle me or force me to my knees once she works out I'm a slave. But the blow never comes. Hesitantly, I lift my head, and for a second I think I see sympathy in her eyes before she quickly schools her expression. Sighing, she gestures towards the bath.

"Go on then, get in," she instructs, as she places her

hands on her hips, watching my every move. Taking small, careful steps, I tiptoe towards the huge tub. As I reach it, I grab the bottom of my shift, but stop to glance over at Jayne, who just raises her eyebrows at me. "Come on, no need to be shy. We have the same equipment." Biting my lip, I nod. She's right, after all. Plus, after what I've been through today, removing my clothing in front of another woman is nothing. This is no worse than when we're chosen by the guards for monthly inspections.

To make sure that the slaves aren't hiding contraband, the king holds regular inspections, and should anything be found or guards have suspicions about a slave, then a personal inspection of that slave can be authorised. If you're chosen, you're taken to the courtyard, stripped of your clothing, and forced to stand naked until the captain is assured that you aren't carrying contraband. Of course, none of us ever are. I never got chosen when I was young, it wasn't until I became older that the guards started to notice me more. Now I'm lucky if I make it a month without being picked.

The memory of the guards disgusting gazes makes me shudder as I pull my shift off over my head, dropping it unceremoniously to the floor. Turning my back to Jayne and reaching out to grasp the side of the bath, I freeze as her shocked gasp echoes around the room.

"Mother above," she swears, before the sounds of her shuffling alert me to her coming closer. "They branded you? What did you do?" Her voice is horrified.

I know what she's asking—what did I do to deserve being punished in this way? Anger boils up inside me, and I don't know if it's because of today's events or if it's because I feel safer around her, but I can't stop the bitterness that coats my words.

"All slaves are branded this way the moment we become slaves, to remind us that we belong to the king." The brand at the bottom of my spine, although long healed, always looks red and angry. It throbs under Jayne's stare, as if talking about it makes the pain fresh. The king's symbol, branded on me forever, marks me as his property. If she was upset by that, then she would hate the mess of scars on my stomach.

"I knew about the numbers. But not this…" She trails off and I flinch as I feel her fingers brush over the mark. I learned from an early age that the only time someone touches you is to inflict pain, so I brace myself against the bath as I await the blow.

"Will you stop acting like I'm going to beat you?" Jayne commands, some of her fire coming back into her voice as she seems to shake away the shock of seeing my brand. Spurred into action, I lift a foot and place it into the water, hissing quietly as the water stings the raw skin of my ankles. Jayne doesn't say anything as she guides me into the water, but I can see her frown from the corner of my eye. Easing down into a sitting position, I wait expectantly as Jayne bustles around.

"You soak some of that dirt off and enjoy the hot water. I'll be back shortly," she directs, before she walks out of the room, shutting the door firmly behind her.

Dumbstruck, I look around the room. My whole life has been guided by the instructions of others. *Clean here. Move this there.* I've never had time to myself to "enjoy" anything. What do I do? My mind is spinning, thoughts flashing through my head before I have a chance to fully comprehend them, but I soon find my eyelids drooping as the hot water soothes my muscles. Hesitantly, I lean against the sloping side of the bath and rest my head back, after all, no one's here to see me.

Watching the steam rise from the hot water surrounding me, I reach out to touch it, smiling slightly as it eddies around my fingers, swirling in the air. My smile drops as I think about what will be awaiting me once I leave the bath and face the magician who saved me. He took the blame for me. And lied. *Why?* Frowning, I shake my head, trying to rid it of thoughts of Grayson, and tell myself to just be thankful that he did. Sinking lower into the water, I close my eyes and let myself pretend, just for a moment, that I'm someone else.

The sound of somebody tapping on the door has me opening my eyes and I realise I must have fallen asleep. Sitting up, I frown at the still closed door. Why aren't they coming in? The knock comes again and I realise with shock that they're waiting for me to respond.

"Yes?" I croak, but Jayne must hear me because she walks in, shutting the door behind her before moving over to me, a ghost of a smile playing on her lips.

"It's relaxing, right?"

"Yes," I reply, my voice a little stronger this time. She seems different now, but I can't put my finger on why. Handing me a sponge, she gestures for me to face the wall. Turning in the tub so my back is to her, I hear her puff out a breath as she sinks to her knees behind me. There's a pause, and I get the impression she's trying to work out what to say.

"I'm going to wash your hair," she explains as she gently reaches out and gathers my dirty locks. I don't really want her to touch me, but I get the feeling she's not going to hurt me.

"Okay," I murmur, trying to relax as I begin to rub the sponge against my arms. I grimace when the sponge soon turns black. A soft tug encourages me to tilt my head back, and Jayne pours warm water over my hair. I worry about the water going onto the floor again, but I can hear it splash into some sort of bowl. A sweet smell fills the air before her hands are on my scalp, massaging something into my hair. I fight against my instincts to shy away, and after a moment I start to enjoy the pleasant feeling.

Rinse and repeat, rinse and repeat. It seems to take a while and Jayne mutters under her breath about the amount of dirt coming from my hair. Once she's done and I've scrubbed my skin clean, the water left in the bath is grey with muck. Gesturing for me to stand, Jayne tries to help me out, but I quickly and ungracefully climb out myself, ignoring the slight look of hurt that crosses her face. When I stand, I see the expression has disappeared and she passes me a large towel, wrapping it around me. Without waiting for an answer, she pulls out a chair from beneath the counter and gestures towards it.

Suddenly, it goes dark as something is placed over my head. Heart pounding, I thrash around, trying to knock off the covering.

This is it, they're trying to kill me. They're going to take me away. The thoughts are nearly consuming as my chest heaves, my eyes stinging as I fight tears. I was stupid to trust them, and I'm going to die for that mistake. The cover is removed and I squint against the light. I see a shocked looking Jayne standing in front of me, her hands outstretched as if to comfort me. But she doesn't, instead she hovers there, unsure. Panting, I meet her eyes for a second before looking away, wrapping my arms around my middle.

"I'm sorry, I forgot…" She trails off and I can hear her regret. She slowly reaches for my chin, guiding my face up until my eyes meet hers. "Whatever life you had before today, it's in the past. It's going to be a learning curve, for you and for me. I'll try to be more careful, if you can work on trusting me?" She's asking the impossible. I don't trust anyone, that's a luxury I can't afford to have.

"He told you about me." A statement, not a question. She knows I'm a slave, yet she doesn't treat me like one. I examine her face as I wait for her response. She seems wary, concerned. She treats me differently than others do. Most people don't see *me*. I'm usually perceived as a nuisance, like something unpleasant they just stepped in. Jayne is treating me like, like...a normal person.

"He told me you're important, and I trust him," she responds. I hold her gaze long enough to ascertain that she's telling the truth before dropping my head again. Sighing, she guides me towards the chair. Pulling my towels closer, I perch on the edge of the seat, ready to jump up if I need to. I don't think Jayne's going to hurt me, but I'm in an unfamiliar place and old habits are hard to break.

Jayne moves slowly and positions herself so that I can see what she's doing. I'm not sure if she's doing it on purpose, but I'm grateful for it. Raising the towel, she proceeds to dry and comb out my hair. We're silent as she works, but it's not a cold, strained silence, and I find myself enjoying being in her company. Once done, she comes to stand behind me and guides my head up to look in the mirror. I go to glance away out of instinct, but I find I can't move my eyes from the image I see.

It was only a handful of hours ago that I looked in the grimy mirror in the forgotten closet, but the difference between those hours is shocking. I don't recognise the young woman sitting in front of me. Her dark hair falls around her face in shiny waves, thick and full. Her face, while pale, looks soft and clean compared to the gaunt, haunted looking reflection from before. But it's my eyes that hold the biggest difference. I've always thought my almond-shaped eyes were too big, eternally seeing things people want hidden, and sure, I still look too thin but there is something in my eyes that's altered. I look like someone determined. But determined for what?

"You're very pretty. I didn't notice before under all that dirt." The comment is said lightly, but I can hear the undercurrent of disapproval in her voice. Disapproval at me, or disapproval at how we're treated to make us that dirty in the first place? Hastily, I look away and push off from the stool. Those thoughts are dangerous.

Seeing that she's made me uncomfortable, her face pinches before she nods, patting a pile of folded fabric I hadn't noticed before. "Get changed into this, call me once they're on and I'll button you in," she explains, before quietly leaving the room.

Letting out a soft breath, I slowly turn to the bundle of fabric. It's the dark, rich blue of the magicians. My heart thuds painfully in my chest. Surely she brought the wrong one? To dress me in this colour is making a statement, the magicians are claiming me. But for what? What could an ex-slave offer a high magician? Reaching out, I frown as I notice my hand shaking and force myself to slow my breathing. This is ridiculous. Scowling at the offending piece of clothing, I grab it and fight my way into it, ignoring the softness of the fabric and the flurry of excitement and nerves that I refuse to let surface. The fabric flutters down to just below my knees, the snug sleeves cutting off just above my elbows. I refuse to look in the mirror as I call out to Jayne to let her know I'm dressed. It's silent for a while and I wonder if I haven't spoken loudly enough, but I turn away as the door opens, baring my back for her to button up the dress.

"Can you button me up please?" I request quietly, boldly. I still don't know what's happening, but I like Jayne.

Silence follows my question. Did I say something wrong? I can feel her eyes on my brand again, my skin tingling under the weight of her stare. Shuffling my weight, I pull at the fabric, unused to such tight clothing, feeling awkward in the silence. I open my mouth, to say what I don't know, when I feel her hand brush the skin on my back. My skin erupts into goose pimples, a soft gasp escaping my lips as she touches my brand. It's only for a second, but I swear something within me pulses at the contact, except before I can work out what *that* was, she starts to button up the dress. We stay silent as she gently tugs at the fabric, fastening the fiddly buttons. She doesn't brush my skin again, and the strange pulsing sensation stays buried.

"This colour suits you," a deep male voice comments. Grayson's voice. Spinning as if the room's on fire, I back away from the male.

"I thought you were Jayne." Breathless, I startle as my back hits the wall behind me, stopping my retreat.

"I gathered that." A sly smile graces his lips.

This is all a huge joke to him, my fear is an amusement. Anger twists inside of me and I take a step forward, fists clenched at my sides.

"So, you took advantage of that and continued to let me believe you were a woman?" I can't stop the indignant words, but as soon as I've said them, I clasp my hands to my mouth as if I can pull them back. Dead, I should be so very dead. Instead, he grimaces and puts a hand to the back of his neck.

"Well I…wait…" He trails off as he sees my expression, his eyes narrowing as he takes in my sudden change in demeanour. "You can speak your mind when we're alone. I will never punish you for that."

We shall see, the small angry part of me whispers, but I brush that aside and slowly drop my hands to my sides. My brain takes a couple of moments to realise what he's said. *When we're alone.* Taking in the man before me, I assess him in a new light. He isn't going to hurt me, and he genuinely seems concerned that he said something to upset me. A high magician concerned about offending a slave is enough to make me laugh. Pushing away from the wall and with a bravado I don't feel, I meet his gaze.

"Do you plan to be alone with me a lot then?" I hadn't meant to make it sound sexual, but in the enclosed space of the bathroom, even I have to admit it sounds like I'm coming on to him. "I mean, I don't… I…" Trailing off, I cringe as his concerned expression starts to grow into an amused smile. "You confuse me," I admit, my face burning. His smile drops a little at my words, but he forces it back in place quickly enough that most people wouldn't notice. But I'm a slave, we notice the smallest changes, it's what keeps us alive.

"When you're ready, come into the reception room and we'll explain what's going to happen." Taking a step back, Grayson grabs the door handle and pulls it open. One foot out of the door, he turns back to look at me. "I truly am sorry for making you believe I was Jayne. I stepped out of line."

Nodding in response, I watch him leave the room, shutting the door quietly behind him. Frowning at the space the magician had just been standing in, I raise my hand to my temple where a headache is beginning to form. That man confuses me.

He's dangerous and I need to be careful around him, I conclude. And not just because of his magic. It's too easy to forget what he is, but more importantly, it's too easy to forget who *I* am.

Chapter 5

I'm not sure what I was expecting to see, but Grayson reclining in an armchair with a book in his hands was not it. Standing in the doorway, I wait for him to notice me, but when he doesn't, I use the opportunity to look around. A wall of bookshelves takes up one side of the room, and two arched windows fill the far wall. A large fireplace dominates the wall opposite, with four armchairs situated in front of it. Although the room is full of books and furniture, it feels…empty. There are no pictures or decorations on the walls, no personal touches of any kind. The magicians don't spend much time here, they are busy fighting on the front line or at the academy, but still… this is his home. Doesn't he have a family or loved ones?

My eyes are once again drawn to the books on the far wall, their colourful spines calling to me. I must make a sound as Grayson glances up and follows my gaze to the bookshelf. With a ghost of a smile, he closes his own tome and pushes up from the chair, gesturing for me to come into the room.

"Do you like reading?" he inquires, watching me carefully as I step over the threshold. As I walk towards the shelves, I marvel at being able to move freely now that I'm without my chains. I shake my head as an answer to his question before returning my attention back to the books, running my finger along the leather spines. I've never had access to books as a slave, but I feel drawn to them. I have vague memories of someone reading to me as a child. I don't remember who it was, or even what the stories were about, but I remember her voice. On the tough nights, the ones where my back was screaming from the lashes I'd received that day, or my feet were bleeding from walking barefoot several miles to the stone quarry, those were the nights I'd hear her voice and I'd dream about knights, damsels, and winged horses.

The room is silent and I get the feeling he's waiting for a response. "I can't read," I answer with a shrug, pulling a thick book from the shelf and running my fingers over the embossed title.

"What?" His voice is shocked, and when I shoot a look over my shoulder he's shaking his head, a thoughtful look on his face.

"I learned my letters, but I was eight when I became a slave, so…" Shrugging, I turn and place the book back on the shelf. I don't need to explain why I never learned to read, educating the slaves isn't exactly something the king worried about.

"You were eight? You were just a child." I'm not sure how to respond to his soft, shocked words. Surely this isn't news to him? He's one of the king's high magicians. Slaves are enemies to the kingdom, criminals who have been granted leniency from a death sentence because of our age.

Thankfully, I'm saved from answering when Jayne walks into the room with a tray full of steaming mugs. "All the slaves are children," she tells him, not meeting my eyes as she unloads the cups onto the small table between the chairs. She's right, the slaves are children. I'm the eldest slave, and although we don't swap ages, I'm pretty sure that none of them are older than seventeen. Most of us don't last longer than a year.

Jayne's voice is carefully neutral, but I get the distinct feeling she disapproves, not that she'd admit to it. Those kinds of opinions are dangerous and you never know who's listening. I feel the weight of Grayson's stare, but keep my focus on the books, the conversation making me uncomfortable.

"I'll teach you." Turning, I gape at him open-mouthed and realise that Jayne is doing the same thing. "Everyone should be able to read," he defends with a shrug as he walks up to the bookshelf, placing the leather bound book back onto one of the rows. Turning, he heads back to the chairs and I watch him as he takes a seat then looks up at me expectantly. Opening my mouth to ask a question, I freeze as my eyes are drawn to the small table next to him. It's not so much the table, but what's on it that causes ice to run through my veins and my hopes to come crashing down around me.

Chains.

I'd been stupid to think that life would be different. He promised not to kill me, he didn't say anything about a better life. My ankles throb painfully at the thought of them being reattached. I stare at him for a moment before flickering my gaze to Jayne, who's watching me with a pitying expression. Pushing away the sick feeling in my stomach, I drop my head and slowly walk towards him, stopping before his chair.

"What are you doing?" He sounds amused, but I stay silent, holding my position. I don't think he'd hit me for moving, but one of the first lessons you learn as a slave is to be silent and still, and old habits are hard to break. I can hear him sitting up and leaning forward in his chair. "Opal, what's going on…" He starts, his fingers brushing lightly against my arm, but he trails off as I flinch away from his touch.

Opal? Is he talking to me? The thoughts fly through my head in a confused rush, my hands trembling slightly at the uncertainty. Part of me is insisting I look up and refuse to ever wear those chains again. I would rather be put to death than shuffle around like a ghost. But I can't say that. I *want* to live. Jayne puts down her tray and strides over to us, standing by my side. Through the veil my curtain of hair offers, I can see her cross her arms over her ample bosom. My breathing quickens, my eyes locked on the chains.

"Come on, Grayson, you're a smart boy, use that brain the Mother gave you," she scolds. She's reprimanding a *high magician* like he's a child, the same magician who could kill her with a snap of his fingers. She's asking for death by speaking to him that way. However, she doesn't seem to care. "She thinks you're going to put those blasted chains on her." To my amazement, Grayson cringes at her rebuke, glancing at the chains that lie on the table just to the side of him.

I can hear her talking and Grayson mumbling a response, but I'm not understanding what they're saying. My breaths are still coming too fast as my hands and body continue to tremble. I want to be strong, I don't want them to know how much this is affecting me, but I can't hide it. My vision starts to blur and my head feels light, and I have to fight away the nausea that threatens to overtake me. Suddenly, my hair is brushed from my face and Grayson is kneeling on the floor in front of me. "Listen to me. You're safe," he says earnestly, but how can I believe him? "I'm sorry, I should've got rid of those bloody chains," he apologises, but I'm not fully paying attention, my thoughts circling.

Jayne mutters something, but I can't hear what she says, my panic all-consuming as I focus on the magician's wide eyes.

"I blew up a goat," he blurts out, and silence follows. I blink at his admission, the absurdity of what he's saying sinking through my panic and causing the trembling in my arms to lessen.

"You did what?" Jayne asks, her voice holding as much shock as I'm feeling. He turns to glance at her for a moment, smiling bashfully before looking back at me. His face settles into an expression of determination.

"When I was in training, I was much stronger than the others, and they bullied me because of it. One day we were practicing shooting targets with our magic, and they wouldn't let up, they kept taunting me. I was so mad, I could feel the anger and rage building up inside me, but I knew I couldn't afford to lose control. So, I channelled it into the target. The more they taunted, the stronger I threw my magic," he explains, his features twisting. I know there's more behind this story, but he carries on, so I keep my observations to myself. "This was exactly what they wanted, and they turned the target into a goat just as I shot a blast of magic towards it." Blinking again, I try to concentrate on what he's saying.

A goat. The fearsome magicians are messing around turning targets into goats? I think to myself, trying to imagine a young Grayson surrounded by other young magicians.

"It exploded?" Jayne questions, her voice disapproving, but I can see a smile tugging at her lips.

"No." He grimaces. "I tried to change the intent of the magic, which is very hard to do after the magic has left the body." He stops, rubbing the nape of his neck with his hand before continuing, "I wasn't strong enough to stop the magic, but I was able to change it."

"What happened?" My voice is small, but I see Jayne smile slightly and nod her head in approval out of the corner of my eye. My breathing has calmed and my heart is starting to settle as I focus on Grayson.

"It blew up the goat."

"You said it didn't explode," Jayne points out, and he sighs before conceding with a nod.

"No, it didn't. It blew it up, literally. It grew." Silence follows his words again before the room is filled with Jayne's bellowing laugh. A hint of a blush colours his cheeks, but he smiles ruefully as he watches the older woman collapse into a chair with laughter.

"You made a giant goat?" I query, trying to push away my own amusement but the corners of my lips twitch up.

"Yes. Bloody thing ran off into the forest, never saw it again," the magician mutters as he reclines in his seat, a smile toying at the edge of his lips.

A strange feeling bubbles up inside until a barking laugh overtakes me. Throwing my hands over my mouth, I look at the magician in shock. There haven't been many opportunities to laugh in my life, and I don't remember much before I was a slave. Grayson chuckles at my shocked expression, and before I know it, I'm laughing again. Not the loud, braying laugh of Jayne, but a shocked, joyful giggle.

After a moment, Jayne pushes up from her chair and walks over to me, gently steering me to the seat she just vacated, still chuckling and muttering something about a goat under her breath. Sitting on the edge of the seat, I shuffle around awkwardly, unused to sitting on cushions. An unsettling feeling runs through my veins.

"Feeling better?" Grayson asks, and I know he's not inquiring about the seat. Stilling in the chair, I look up at him appraisingly as I decide how to answer him. Just looking at him like this should lead to a punishment, but he simply leans back in his chair, his eyes steady on me. Perhaps it's the stress and trauma of the day, but I decide to ask him a question.

"Why did you tell me that story?"

He hides his surprised look quickly, but I can tell he didn't expect me to answer him, and certainly not with a question of my own. "I scared you. I shouldn't have left the chains out. You needed something else to focus on."

"Why the goat story?" He's right, I was panicking, all thought and reason had fled my mind. He could have told me anything, but he deliberately chose something that would cause him embarrassment.

"I wanted to see you smile." I ignore the uncomfortable emotion that his words stir in me and change the subject.

"Why am I here? What's going to happen to me?"

Jayne makes a noise of exclamation as she bustles back into the room with a tray of drinks, placing them down on the table before me. "Grayson, have you not explained anything to the poor girl yet?"

"I'm getting there!" he exclaims, and I can't help but wonder what the relationship between them is. She's a maid, so she can't be his mother, but she acts so familiar around him it's like they're family. "Do you know anything about magician's visions?" he questions, pulling my attention back to him.

I've heard mentions of them, the whispers of slaves, but it's only ever been hearsay. Shaking my head, he nods once in acknowledgement before continuing, "The visions are sent to us by the Great Mother. Most of us will go our whole lives without receiving a vision. These visions always hold truth and come to be, but they are not always clear in their message. We have magicians who have dedicated their lives to trying to understand and interpret these visions." He pauses to check that I'm keeping up with him so far and I nod, accepting the glass of water Jayne shoves into my hand. "I have been lucky enough to receive three visions." Leaning forward, he receives a glass of steaming dark liquid from the maid before adding cream and sugar to it. A bittersweet smell greets me, and I find my mouth watering as I watch him stir it. "I don't suppose you've had coffee before?"

Busted. Flicking my eyes from the cup to Grayson, I see that he caught me looking, but he doesn't sound angry, in fact, he sounds curious. When I shake my head, he gestures for Jayne to pour another cup.

"I didn't think you'd like it. Horrible, bitter stuff," she comments, but does as instructed, filling a cup with the dark liquid and gesturing to the cream and sugar. Shuffling forward, I copy what Grayson did, adding a splash of cream and sugar before sitting back in the chair, looking up at the magician expectantly.

"Can you tell me more about the visions?" I inquire, holding the warm cup close. This simple beverage, a luxury I've never been given before, fills me with a strength I didn't know I had.

"They are sacred and illegal. Those who ignore visions don't tend to live very long thereafter." I think over his words, tentatively bringing the cup to my lips. My mouth bursts with flavour as I sip the liquid and force myself not to pull a face. Jayne was right, it is bitter, but the cream and sugar soon follow through and I find myself taking another sip. Grayson watches me with a blank expression as I drink, and I slowly lower my cup, meeting his gaze.

"I was in one of these visions?" He's already said as much, but I need to hear it again. Why would I, a slave girl who has nothing, not even her name, be in a sacred vision?

"Yes." He's shut down again, the embarrassed young man telling me a story about blowing up a goat replaced by a shrewd magician. But I've seen that part of him now, and I know he doesn't mean me harm. I'm purely a puzzle he can't work out.

"What does that mean?"

"It means I couldn't let you die today." I flinch at the simplicity of his words. He didn't save me because it was the right thing to do, he saved me because his *sacred vision* told him to. I must never forget that he doesn't care about my welfare, no matter how well he pretends to. Seeing my reaction, he sighs and uses his free hand to scrub at his face, his whole body softening. "There's something bigger than us at play here. You're important to the outcome of the war, I just don't know how or what that outcome will be."

"Are you saying that I could be the reason we lose?" Sitting forward, I frown as I wait for his response. How could I have anything to do with the outcome of the war?

"I'm saying that we don't know. But you *are* important to the Mother, you have her symbol on your body, after all. I get the feeling she's been looking over you for a very long time." His voice softens again, and I feel his gaze on my body as if he can see straight through my clothing to the mark he claims is on my skin.

"Wait. Her symbol?" That's not possible. I would

have noticed if I carried the Mother's symbol. Wouldn't I?

Nodding, he gestures over my shoulder and I frown as he responds, "Yes, just below your brand."

"My birthmark?" At the small of my back I have a very dark mark that I've had all my life. It's in the shape of a smudged crescent moon with two dark moles on either side of it. I guess if you squinted then it could look a little like the Mother's symbol. Her full symbol is covered with elaborate swirls, the crescent moon bordered by two stars.

"That's not a birthmark." I'm about to argue, but something about the way he says it stops me. A tingling sensation runs over my skin as I look about in confusion. It's a bit like when Grayson is using his magic around me, but lighter, not as…sticky. It always feels like I'm walking through treacle when someone uses magic, but this is different. Looking at Grayson, I notice he has a bright, blissful expression on his face, and I know he's feeling it too. Seeing that I'm watching him, he tilts his head and his eyes light up in a way I don't understand as he takes in my flushed cheeks.

"You can feel it too." It's not a question, but I nod anyway. Grayson goes silent as he leans back in his chair, his expression thoughtful. Shuffling in my seat, I glance across at Jayne who's watching us with a brilliant smile. As if coming to a decision, Grayson nods to himself and shifts forward. "If you can feel that, then the Mother has blessed you. This changes things," he explains, but his voice is distant, as if he's saying it more to himself than to me.

"What was that?" My voice is quieter than I had intended, awe filling my tone as I watch the magician.

"Her touch. Only those she's blessed can feel her touch."

"How could I be blessed? I haven't even been through the choosing ceremony." My gut churns with worry as I mention the ceremony, still unsure how they are going to get around that stumbling block. Without the ceremony I will lose my soul. I'm sure Grayson's well aware of this, but he doesn't seem to be in a hurry or at all concerned that I'm about to become a soulless being.

"That's what I need to talk to you about." Pushing up from his chair, he starts to pace the length of the room. Watching him warily, I look across at Jayne and see she doesn't appear worried. In fact, she's poured herself a cup of coffee. Taking a sip of my coffee, I wait for the magician to finish his musings. "I knew you were important, but now I know the Goddess has blessed you..." He stops pacing and nods to himself again, sounding more sure.

"What do you mean?" I ask from behind my coffee cup, not sure I want to hear his response. This day has been a whirlwind and I feel like I'm in a dream. In the stretch of a couple of hours everything has changed, and I have yet to decide if it's for the better.

"You're going to attend the choosing ceremony."

Choking on my drink, I splutter and put my cup down with a cough. "What—but I'm a slave!" I look over at Jayne for support, but she just shrugs in a way that says "don't ask me."

"Not anymore," he declares, striding towards me with a determined look on his face. Shying away from the sudden movement, I cringe as he kneels down in front of me. "I need to keep you around. The Mother has made that clear. I thought we were going to need a secret ceremony, but things are different now," he insists, and I know I don't fully understand the implications of being blessed, but it's helped him come to a decision. That's when the thought hits me.

A secret ceremony. This would have worked. The blessing has to be performed by a priest, but the rest of the ceremony is pomp and circumstance. The only part required to link the soul to the body is the blessing.

They truly mean to bless me. I'm going to go to the ceremony after all. Pushing away the flicker of excitement that threatens to overwhelm me, I focus on the issues surrounding me. This is absurd and has to be a joke of some kind. However, a little part of me, the part that always guides me, tells me this is all happening as it should. Could this be the Mother advising me? Another thought strikes me.

"If I'm already blessed, why do I need to attend the choosing ceremony?"

Grayson seems surprised at the question, but he nods in acknowledgement. "Some people, usually those who are of great importance, or who are destined to be powerful magicians, are blessed by the Mother before they attend the ceremony. When they arrive for the formal blessing at the ceremony, it's clear who these powerful individuals are. They're marked in a way that lets us know they're someone we need to focus on." Pushing up from his crouch, he walks away from me, but I hear his final words loud and clear. "Everyone has to have a choosing ceremony, it's the law."

Everyone except for the slaves, I think bitterly to myself, wondering how many of these blessed people have been amongst us and were missed. I'm no different than them…so why am I sitting in the warmth, clean and dry as I sip coffee, while they're outside working?

"There's a choosing ceremony taking place tonight,

you will be part of it," Grayson declares, his words pulling me out of my thoughts. Frowning, I open my mouth to protest but Jayne beats me to it.

"Grayson! You think I can get her ready in time for that?" the maid splutters, putting her cup down on the tray with a loud clack as she pushes up out of her chair, rounding on the magician. Her expression is frightening, and even Grayson looks uncomfortable.

"I have faith in you." He flashes her a charming smile and she starts to thaw. His expression turns serious as he continues, "Besides, we have little time. She turned twenty today."

Arms crossed, she faces off with the magician for what feels like minutes, but must only be seconds, before she lets out a huge sigh and nods. She turns to me and I fight the urge to hide behind the chair as her appraising eyes run over my form.

"Well, we best get to work then."

Chapter 6

Pain racks my skull and I try not to wince. Who knew that getting dressed up would be so painful? Another tug at my dark strands and I grimace. Jayne mutters under her breath again, making me smile. Apparently, it's a moment of pride when a maid's charge attends the ceremony, and she seems to have adopted me. Thus, being given so little time to get me ready is something she begrudges. I've learned in the short time I've been with her that Jayne is very proud of the work she does for Grayson. I'm not quite sure how I feel about this, but a small part of me is starting to care for the loud, bossy maid who doesn't give a damn that her master is a high magician.

Sitting in front of the large mirror in the bathroom, I obediently remain still as Jayne continues to yank on my hair. In this position, with my head bowed, I keep looking at my now painted nails. Jayne had muttered a curse when she saw them chipped and dirty, but had them clipped, filed, and buffed until they looked neat in no time. She then applied a liquid that stained them a rich dark blue that matches the dress I'm currently wearing. The magicians' colour. Grayson's colour.

"How did you meet Grayson?" I inquire, but bite my

lip as soon as I say it, convinced I'm asking too much. To my surprise she makes an approving noise.

"Huh. I was there when he was born," she replies, and I can hear the smile in her voice. "Tiny little thing, but as I held him in my arms that day, I knew he would do great things."

"His parents?"

"Died in the war. Magicians too, but much weaker, barely enough magic between them to light a fire. Grayson was Goddess blessed." Again, her pride shines through in her voice, her fingers still flying across my scalp as she styles my hair.

"You raised him?" I press, nodding as she makes a noise of confirmation. This makes much more sense—how she can get away with scolding him and talking to him like she's his parent—because she *is* like a mother to him. If his parents were both magicians, they would have been on the front line where they were desperately needed. Children are only a hindrance on the war front, so they stay behind in the family home until their fates are decided at the choosing ceremony.

"Are you from Arhaven originally?" I question. I've noticed her accent is slightly different than the other maids and servants who work here. Grayson has the smooth, cultured accent the magicians and priests seem to gain through their training.

"Oh no." She spins me on the chair so my back faces the mirror and guides my head up to look at me. Her eyes assess her work before she nods and reaches for a brush and tray covered with various tools.

"I'm from a small village far in the north, close to the mountains," she explains, as she searches for the tools she's looking for. "That's where I started working for Grayson's family many, many years ago." Raising a tiny brush, she reaches for my face. As I start to pull away, she gives me a warning look which is enough to make me sit still as she reaches for my face again. Brushing the tool across my eyelashes, she continues her story and I let her distract me. "My family are millers, and that's what I was destined for, but I've always been fascinated with magic. After my choosing ceremony, I went up to Grayson's family estate and demanded they give me a job." Laughing, she reaches for a second, smaller brush that she dips into a black liquid. Gesturing for me to close my eyes, she continues her story. "I should've been flogged, but the master of the household took pity on me."

Raising a bronze disk up against my face, she mutters, "You're so pale, I don't have a powder pale enough." She frowns and puts it down with a shake of her head. "Hmm, your skin is remarkably unblemished for a slave, I think you can get away without it."

"The slave masters always made sure my punishments didn't damage my face." I'm sure I was destined for the whore house, and every time the guards visited the slave quarters at night, I would dread that they were coming for me.

"Mighty considerate of them." Her tone is careful, and I'm reminded of what happened to Mary when she spoke against the royal family. I get the feeling she disapproves of how the slaves are treated, even though she hasn't said as much, and I know there's a story there, but she doesn't know me well enough to share it.

We sit in silence as Jayne continues to apply the makeup to my face. It's quite a nice feeling to have someone else attending to you and I find myself getting sleepy. My eyelids are heavy and I have to force them to stay open.

"All done," she announces, and I turn to look in the

mirror but she jumps in front of it, blocking my view. "No, wait until you have your dress on."

Tilting my head in confusion, I look down at my new, freshly pressed outfit that she helped me into less than two hours ago. "But I'm already dressed." Making a rude noise, she gestures for me to leave the room and follows behind me, guiding me through Grayson's quarters and towards a dressing room.

"You can't go to the ceremony dressed like that." Her flippant tone makes me freeze, but she doesn't seem to notice as she walks into the room and straight up to a huge rail of clothing bags. Pulling one of them to her, she unzips it, peeks into the bag, shakes her head, and pushes it back, reaching for the next one.

"This is the finest thing I've ever worn." My voice is cold and she glances over her shoulder as she hears my tone, her face softening as she explains.

"You're going to the ceremony as a family friend of Grayson's, who has come to Arhaven to serve him and learn more about court, you need to wear something of that stature."

Frustrated, I gesture to the dress I'm wearing. It's smart and well made, and I don't understand why this isn't good enough. I've never had anything this nice and it seems like such a waste that I'm having to change out of it. "If I'm posing as a servant, shouldn't this be appropriate?"

"No, girl. Most servants save up for years to earn enough to pay for their ceremony dress. If you wore this, you would stand out, and that's exactly what you don't want to do."

I understand what she's saying, and if that's the role I'm going to be playing then what she says makes sense. But I can't help feeling uncomfortable. Here I am, being pampered and dressed up like a doll, when my fellow slaves have nothing.

"Found it!" Jayne calls out, dragging me from my thoughts as she carries a mass of dark fabric over to the centre of the room. I don't look at the dress as she hangs it up, I simply turn my back to Jayne so she can undo my zip. Silently, I climb out of my clothing and stand still as she lifts the dark blue fabric over my head, pulling it down over my hips and guiding my arms through the sleeves. I stay still as she fusses around me, fixing the dress and pulling it into place. Eventually she guides me to a large mirror that takes up nearly the whole wall.

Lifting my head, I gasp at what I see before me. I don't recognise my own reflection. My hair hangs in dark waves with a braid circling the top of my head like a crown. My cheeks have been brushed with a slight blush, which makes them look chiselled rather than gaunt from lack of food. My eyelashes are long and my almond-shaped eyes are rimmed with a dark kohl. Light pink gloss colours my lips, which part in shock as I see the garment I've been dressed in.

The gown is dark blue like my previous outfit, but it's so dark that in some lights it looks black. Sleeves made of lace cover my arms, the dark flowered pattern concealing the scars that litter the skin there, and the neckline dips low enough to hint at the lack of cleavage malnutrition has robbed me of. The bodice is tight around my waist, cinching in before flowing out at my hips, the large, expansive skirts surrounding me with the same lace flowers decorating the hem. Jayne appears at my side and looks at me with such pride in her eyes that it turns my stomach.

"Wear these, they will cover those awful marks on your arms." Pressing two large metal cuffs into my hand, she takes a step back. Looking down at the jewellery, I carefully slide them onto my wrists, realising that they cover my slave marks completely.

It's the most beautiful dress I've ever seen, which makes me wearing it all the more outrageous. "I can't wear this." My breath hitches, part of me screaming in protest for saying these words. I should keep quiet, enjoy wearing it until they realise their mistake.

"Don't be silly. It fits like it was made for you," Jayne says as she circles me, gently pulling and repositioning the fabric. Reaching out a hand, I grab her softly as she walks around me, pulling her to face me.

"Jayne, they will stone me alive if they realise I'm a slave." Fear makes my voice tight, but something else is awakening within me, something I fear far more than them realising I'm a slave.

"Was." Frowning, I stare at the maid questioningly. "You *were* a slave, not anymore," she corrects tenderly, patting my hand in reassurance. This is by far the most frightening thing she has said to me yet.

"I don't know how to be anything but a slave," I whisper back.

"I know. It will be a hard adjustment, but we will help you. Plus, I think the Mother has great plans for you," the maid coos with a knowing smile.

"Jayne, why does Grayson have dresses in his room?" This dress was obviously made for someone, and the thought that I'm wearing his mistress's dress makes me uncomfortable.

"It was his sister's. She died before she could ever wear it." Grief lines her voice, and I know now is not the right time to ask about the woman this dress was made for. "I never understood why he kept it, but I think I know why now," she replies cryptically. I examine the maid, and under my stare she seems to shake her thoughts off before casting a critical eye over me, circling around me, straightening the fabric of the dress, and picking off an invisible piece of lint. "Right, you're ready. Let's go."

Shooing me out the door, she shushes me as I try to stall, leaving unasked questions on the tip of my tongue. I'm not ready for this. I'm a slave, not someone to be dressed up and paraded in front of the whole kingdom. Wringing my hands, I fiddle with the cuff covering my slave marks. They are going to know. They will see past the pretty dress and recognise me for the imposter I am.

As if she can read my mind, a hand slips into mine and I look up sharply at the maid by my side. Her usual careful expression has softened, and she offers me a gentle smile. "Stop. Trust in Grayson. Trust in the Mother."

There are a hundred things I could say to her, like the fact I had believed the Mother had abandoned me long ago, or cynical questions like why would Grayson risk his neck for me? But someone makes a noise of surprise which distracts me from my queries. In my haze of confusion, I hadn't realised that Jayne had led me back into the reception room where I'd seen Grayson with the book in his hands earlier. Scanning the room, I see it was Grayson who made the noise. His eyes are locked on me, his intense gaze making me shift uncomfortably, but I can't seem to look away from him. He's imposing and impressive in his ceremonial uniform. The tailored, double-breasted jacket emphasises his impressive physique, the golden buttons with the king's symbol gleaming for all to see. A half cloak is over his left shoulder, the leather strap coming around under his right arm to keep his sword arm free. It's all symbolic, this uniform is never meant to be worn in battle, but it looks extraordinary all the same. Rich, golden embroidery of the king's symbol, a swirling sun, runs along the bottom of the cloak, a constant reminder of who he works for. The dark blue fabric is striking against his tanned skin and blond hair, which has been combed into place.

I prefer him with his hair messy. The thought flits through my head and I quickly push it away as a blush stains my cheeks. I shouldn't be having those kinds of thoughts about the protector of our realm! Almost as if he can read my mind, the corner of his lip twitches up and horror runs through me. *Can* he read my mind? Before I have a complete meltdown, he takes a step forward, breaking our locked stare.

"You look —" He stops abruptly when he realises Jayne is also in the room, coughing awkwardly before straightening his back and nodding at the dress. "Good work, Jayne."

"Smooth," she mutters quietly under her breath, but not quiet enough for him not to hear it, which is clear from his raised eyebrow. "Grayson, I taught you better than this, compliment the lady!" she chides, and I don't miss the slight flush of his cheeks before he nods and walks straight up to me.

"You look so much better now," he murmurs, his blue eyes sparkling as he stops a step away from me. I try to bury the amusement that comes from his awful compliment, but when Jayne snorts I can't hide it anymore, and a startled laugh escapes me.

"Oh, Mother. I give up," the maid grouses with a huff, throwing her hands up in exasperation, but there's affection in her tone.

"Sorry." He winces, and his apology leaves me

dumbfounded, the absurdity of the situation shocking me yet again.

"I shouldn't be doing this." Pulling at the metal cuffs on my wrists, I twist them off, the scars and tattoos marking me for what I am on full display. A hand reaches out and captures my wrist, and I turn my head away, not wanting to see the magician's expression.

"I thought we'd spoken about this. You're not doing anything wrong," he assures me, and again it's like he can read my thoughts. This entire situation feels wrong. It's like I'm in a dream being pampered while the other slaves continue to suffer. My traitorous heart so desperately wants this to be real, but my brain has learned not to believe things that are too good to be true. "The Goddess has blessed you. She stopped your death by sending me the vision of you." Grayson lets go of my wrist and reaches for my chin, gently guiding my face towards him, not stopping when I flinch from the contact. "You need to believe this. Your old life is gone, you're no longer Slave 625."

"Then who am I?" The words sound weak and lost. I wish I sounded more confident, but that's exactly how I feel—lost.

"She's right, Grayson, she needs a name," Jayne speaks up, and I don't miss the concerned frown she tries to hide as I meet her gaze.

"Do you remember your old name?" Voice soft, Grayson brings my attention back to him. I shake my head and he looks thoughtful, pacing the silent room as he thinks. He'd called me Opal earlier, will this be what he calls me now?

Suddenly coming to a stop, he spins and runs his eyes over me before nodding to himself. "You are Clarissa, a family friend who I've known for years. You've come to the capital to learn more about court and the kingdom. You will be staying here and attending events with me, and during the day you'll be working with the maids." He frowns at this part and sighs with resignation. "I need to keep you close, and the only way the priest will allow this is if you're still working."

He can't be serious. "Won't people think it's strange that a lady is working as a maid during the day?" There is no way they will buy this whole act if I'm seen mopping floors, and I'm not surprised the priest wants to keep me working. This will go against everything he preaches, that the only mercy for a slave, an enemy of the kingdom, is death.

"They won't notice. The upper class rarely pays attention to anyone but themselves or those they're trying to impress." That I can believe, but I'm not so sure the other maids and servants will be the same. I've seen how quick they are to gossip and speculate.

"The maids will notice," Jayne comments, and as I glance over, I know she's thinking the same thing I am.

"Hmm, you might be right. Besides, that hair is pretty different…" As he trails off, I self-consciously raise my hand to my dark hair. It's always made me stand out. One year, when the beatings had become too much, I tried to hack it off with a broken piece of glass, desperate to be rid of it. It hadn't worked, I was stopped before I could do much more than the first few cuts, but when I saw my reflection in a pool of water, I sobbed. It had felt like I was losing a part of myself, my heritage that I knew nothing about. I haven't touched it again since, so it hangs halfway down my back.

The thick, syrupy feeling of magic fills the air again and pulls me out of my deep thoughts. Glancing up, I look straight to the source of the magic, seeing a smug expression on Grayson's face as he finishes a complex gesture with his hands. Opening my mouth to ask what he just did, I stop at Jayne's shocked gasp, and I whirl around to see what caused her reaction when golden curls fly into my vision.

Wait. Reaching up and grabbing a handful of my hair, I see it's no longer the dark and wavy locks I'm used to, but bright, golden ringlets. It's my turn to gasp as I look over at Grayson, trying to hide the shock and outrage that's running through my bloodstream. I don't know why I'm so angry that he's changed my hair, but it feels *wrong* on a soul deep level.

"What?" he asks, throwing his hands up as if to defend himself, but he's not looking at me, he's looking at Jayne who's giving him a death glare.

"Will you stop throwing that stuff around? It's a Goddess given gift and you use it like it's going out of fashion. Besides, you should ask a lady before you change her hair, it's rude. I've taught you better than that," she admonishes, and I can't help the small smile that pulls up my lips despite my outrage.

"She's Goddess blessed! That's why we're having this whole conversation!" he argues, frustrated, and I realise that although they may not be related by blood, Jayne is a mother to Grayson is every way that's important. "Besides, it's not permanent. It will only be blonde for events where you're acting as a lady, when you're a maid it will be back to normal."

Frowning, I reach up to touch the unfamiliar curls. They even *feel* different, the sticky, heavy presence of magic coating my hair. "You think this will be enough?"

"I have to admit, I wouldn't recognise you. Take a look yourself," Jayne professes, and guides me towards a wall mirror by the doorway. A shocked gasp escapes me as I see the elegant woman before me. I'm taken aback by the dress again as it frames my body, accentuating what shape I have and hiding what years of living on scraps has done to my body. Although it's my hair that shocks me the most. I hadn't been prepared for what I saw before me. Light blonde curls, similar to Grayson's, frame my face in a way that makes me look so different.

I look like a lady. I must say this out loud, since Jayne snorts at the same time Grayson steps up behind me, a half a smile pulling at his lips.

"Well, that was the point," he says, before offering me his arm. "Right, Lady Clarissa, we have a ceremony to attend and we're running late."

Chapter 7

The walk to the chapel is short, but every step closer feels like lead. Without the chains around my ankles my steps should be light, but I'm so used to walking with them that my whole gait feels wrong...off. Never thought I would miss my chains. It's almost like I've had them for so long that without them I'm missing a part of me.

The weight of all the eyes on me feels like it's going to drag me down. Blending in and going unseen is what has kept me alive for this long, but now I'm receiving all this attention and my whole body screaming at me to *run*, to *hide*. They're going to see through the magic and the pretty dress to the dirty slave beneath. Mercifully, Jayne selected a pair of flat shoes for me to wear, but when you're used to walking barefoot, shoes just feel restrictive. The skin on my ankles is raw from my chains and were carefully dressed by Jayne before soft stockings were rolled up my legs. Wringing my hands, I can't help but fiddle with the metal cuffs circling my wrists and hiding my marks, making sure they're still firmly in place.

"Stop fretting. I can practically feel you rejecting the magic, it's making my skin itch," Grayson reproaches gently, as he links his arm with mine, pulling me closer to him.

Startled, I stop playing with the cuff and glance up at him in shock before looking down at our linked arms. Physical touch is something I learned to hate and fear. The guards' faces would always twist into disgust if they ever had to touch us, but Grayson's expression is impassive as he rubs small, soothing circles into my palm. I don't know whether to be pleased or disturbed by his touch, but I do find something about him soothing. Since we left his rooms, something about him changed. He stands straighter and his face has fallen into a careful mask, devoid of any emotion. We continue to walk in silence, but I play over his last words, something about them bugging me.

"Is it possible to reject your magic?" I've never heard of anyone doing it before, but my education is sorely lacking, especially where magic is concerned.

"It shouldn't be, unless you had your own magic." His voice is low to avoid anyone overhearing us and his eyes dart to me, taking in my stunned expression. "You don't," he quickly says. "I would've sensed it by now. Although, as I've told you, there is something different about you. Perhaps it's just because the Goddess has blessed you. She has plans for you, after all." Even though it's not the first time I'm hearing it, it's difficult to keep my expression neutral as he tells me I've been blessed…that I'm "different."

It's never been something I'd considered. Magic was only granted to those who the Great Mother deemed worthy, but with Grayson continually telling me I'm blessed, that I'm something *special*, a little part of me can't help but start wondering, *hoping*. After all, that's what all little girls dream about, right? Being told you're special and then swept away to learn magic? It's a romantic notion, even if our magicians are used as our best soldiers in the war. Even in the slave quarters that's something I hear whispered between the younger slaves before they get the hope beaten out of them. Some of the older slaves would get angry with the youngsters, hissing at them to quit their foolish dreaming, but I didn't mind. Anything was better than seeing the blank, zombie-like look that the broken slaves wear.

"I'm glad I kept the dress," Grayson starts, pulling me out of my thoughts. From the corner of my eye I can see him running his gaze down my body before quickly looking ahead, a small frown pulling at his brow. "After my sister died..." The pain in his voice is raw as he trails off. Looking up at him, I'm about to tell him he doesn't have to continue, that he doesn't need to explain, but as he meets my gaze, I see something harden in him. "I was going to get rid of it, but something told me to keep it. It suits you." His words are curt, and for a moment I wonder what I've done wrong to make him start acting this way with me. That's when I realise.

Shit.

I once overheard someone explaining illusion magic. They said it had to be based on something, you couldn't just will it into being. Therefore, for Grayson to change my hair like this, he would have had to base it off something—or *someone*—he's seen before. Standing there before him in his sister's dress, it's no great surprise where he got the inspiration from.

"How did she die?" The words are out of my mouth before I can stop them, and I see his steps falter for a second, but he quickly recovers. I regret asking as his face darkens. I feel him pulling away from me, but just as I'm about to tell him not to answer, he clears his throat.

"She was my shadow." I almost don't hear him, his voice low. A lord dressed up in a smart suit strolls down the corridor towards us and Grayson pauses, dipping his head in acknowledgement as the lord bows in respect. We continue walking through the castle in silence as the man passes, our steps slow because of my unsteady gait in these unfamiliar shoes. "As soon as I was accepted into the Magician's Academy, that was what she wanted to do too," he continues quietly, surprising me. "She was just about to attend her choosing ceremony and I'd managed to get leave approved so I could come back to see it. I was just a regular magician at the time." Hiding a smirk, I nod my head. Something makes me think that Grayson was never just a *regular* magician. "She travelled to the border to meet me, I told her not to, that it was too dangerous, but she did it anyway." My heart sinks, knowing what is coming next as I hear the pain in his voice. "There was an attack. The elves had been waiting for me. I don't know how they found out I was coming back, but they were there to intercept me. When Opal came through, they ambushed her carriage. I was rounding the corner and saw them attacking, but I was too late. She didn't stand a chance."

"What did you do?" I'm almost scared to know, but according to Grayson, I'm somehow a crucial piece to this war, so I need to know what I'm up against.

"I killed the first one with a bolt of power so strong it threw me back ten meters. As soon as they saw the smoking remains of their comrade, the others fled." A smile twists his lips, but there is no happiness there, only anger and pain. "I tracked the others down and killed them." He stops walking, pulling me to a stop next to him. "I wish I had taken my time, made them hurt. Instead, I ripped their hearts from their chests like they did to me when they killed Opal." His voice is dark as he tightens his grip on my arm, almost to the point of pain. "Do I scare you? Does it bother you that I killed those elves with my bare hands?"

This is a completely different Grayson to the one who had knelt down in front of me in his rooms, who told me an embarrassing story to make me feel better, and who rescued me from the executioner. This Grayson is one of the high magicians, who gained his position with magic, strength, and blood. I should be shaking, fearing for my life, bowing and grovelling for him to spare me, but I don't. I see beneath his mask because that's exactly what it is—a shield to protect him from what he's seen and had to do in the name of his king. I don't answer him, but whatever he sees on my face makes him frown before blowing out a large breath and brushing his hand through his hair.

"Let's go, or you'll miss your ceremony." He sounds resigned but straightens his shoulders and offers me his arm again. We walk the last few steps to a large door that leads out into one of the grand courtyards, the Queen's Courtyard. I've been here many times as a slave to collect fresh water to clean with, and have always admired the fountains with their bright, ceramic tiles and the exquisitely manicured flowers. However, seeing it now and being able to openly admire it is something different altogether.

The courtyard is made up of three castle walls and a fourth wall with a large, open archway that leads to the main courtyard at the front of the chapel. The main courtyard is a harsher place, made of cold, grey stone arches—a place of judgement—whereas this courtyard was created for peace and beauty. They say that the king crafted this courtyard for his love, so she would have a place to go to mourn the passing of a loved one. Although, if you believe the rumours, this loved one was more than *just* a friend. Not that anyone would dare say that, other than in the hushed whispers of the palace gossips.

The side door to the chapel stands open and I can hear the murmuring of nervous voices as the acceptees prepare for the ceremony. Fear lances through my core and I pull Grayson to a stop as I shake my head. He can't seriously make me do this. Why can't I have a private ceremony? He's one of the high magicians, for Mother's sake, can't he pull some strings?

"Stop." His firm voice cuts through my panic before he reaches for my shoulder and spins me around to face him. "Stop panicking. You've faced far worse than this." I can't look at him, my eyes frantically darting around in case anyone's watching. The courtyard is empty now, and the noise coming from the open door of the chapel is rising. The ceremony is about to start.

"They'll know, they'll see through me." My voice is quiet, but even I can hear the fear there.

Afraid they'll work out who you are, or that Grayson's wrong and you're not special after all? the dark little voice whispers, and my fear transforms into anger. But that soon falters. What if Grayson *is* wrong?

"They won't," he replies, shaking me gently until I finally meet his gaze. The mask is gone, and in its place is the young man I'm beginning to know. "Trust in the Mother. Trust in me." Staring into his eyes, I come to a shocking realisation. I don't trust him, not fully, not yet, which is no surprise, but I realise that I *want* to trust him.

That's a dangerous thought, but I don't have time to worry about that right now. Taking a deep, shaking breath, I nod sharply, cataloguing the slight look of shock that crosses his face before his mask slides back into place. Linking our arms, he strides towards the chapel, my skirts billowing out behind me as we hurry inside.

The inside of the chapel is beautiful, but in a cold, gothic way with tall stone arches and twisting columns. There are rows of chairs filled with finely dressed nobles and parents facing towards the altar where the high priest is watching us all with a stern expression. Behind him, a huge, stained-glass window depicting the Great Mother shines down on us, the only colour built into this otherwise dark and oppressive space. The sun has already begun to set, but a beam of light shines through and lands on us, bathing my pale skin in colours. Closing my eyes, I take a deep breath and imagine that I can feel the sun's warm rays on my flesh, taking strength from the heat.

"Clarissa." Grayson's irritated tone calls me out of my bubble of calm, and from his frustrated expression, and the amused looks from the people around me, I get the feeling it's not the first time he's called my name.

"Sorry...Grayson." I stumble over his name, aware of the eager expressions and listening ears around us. Jayne explained to me that while I was Clarissa, I would be expected to call him by his given name. A close friend wouldn't call him a high mage in public unless in a formal setting, but the words feel hot on my tongue, like I'll be struck down for uttering them.

"Relax. Look, the princes have arrived," he comments, and I welcome the distraction, following his nod toward the thrones that sit just to the left of the altar. There are five of them in total—the king's in the centre is the grandest, with the queen's throne to the left, and the three thrones to his right belonging to his heirs. All of the seats are empty save for the last two, and I see that Grayson's right, as the two youngest princes, Jacob and Michael, take their seats. The ladies that were standing closest to me must have heard Grayson's words as they eagerly look over at the thrones before turning to giggle and gossip with their neighbours. Fighting the urge to roll my eyes, I study the princes.

I've seen them around the castle, but never had the opportunity to actually *look* at them. The youngest, Jacob, is the tallest, and looks completely out of place in his smart, double-breasted uniform as he pulls at the neckline of his jacket. His hair is just slightly too long, and he keeps having to shake his head to keep it from hanging in his eyes. If rumours are true, Jacob prefers the company of books over people and has caused the queen many sleepless nights as he rejects all of the potential marital prospects she presents him with.

Michael, on the other hand, is the complete opposite —all charming smiles and dimples, not a hair out of place on his head. His ceremonial uniform fits him comfortably and he sits on the throne like it's his favourite place to be, not a hard, cold, marble pedestal.

A hush falls over the gathering people and heads turn toward the back of the chapel. Frowning, Grayson does the same, only for surprise to light up his face.

"The queen has chosen to attend," he tells me quietly, and I glance over my shoulder to see he's right. Her black dress flows out behind her as she strides towards her throne, her face tight with an emotion I'm struggling to place, her guards following closely behind her. "That's a bold choice of clothing to wear." At my confused expression, Grayson lets out a small sigh before explaining, "The queen has been in mourning since her…friend died. She always wears something black, usually a band on her sleeve, but for her to dress completely in black to the ceremony…" My eyes widen in understanding. Whatever reason the queen has for attending today, it's not for the ceremony.

I continue to watch the queen. She subtly nods to the lords and ladies who bow their heads to her, but she doesn't stop until she reaches her sons. Her blank expression cracks slightly as she bestows a smile on them both before taking her throne.

From what Grayson said, I get the impression the queen rarely attends the ceremony, so why would she choose to come today, and why in full mourning? Questions start to rise inside me, but before I can even think to voice them, haunting music fills the chapel, a single woman's voice joining in, her beautiful singing calling out melodious words that are not our own. Whatever language she's singing in just adds to the melancholy beauty of the song.

Grayson starts to move away and panic laces through me and, without thinking, I grab his sleeve, stopping him in his tracks. Frowning, he looks down at my hands on his uniform before raising his eyes to my horrified ones. I just grabbed a high magician, my life should be forfeit. However, he surprises me once again as he leans forward, his face pulled into a look of concern.

"What's wrong? Why are you looking at me like that?" His voice is low as he steps toward me. When he flicks his gaze over my shoulder, I'm reminded that we're not alone.

"Where are you going? What do I do?" Even though I try to keep my voice equally as quiet, I can't help but wince when my voice comes out high and panicked. I get some looks from the people closest to us, their hushed whispers making me blush. Grayson frowns at them and they instantly fall silent, the thought of having a high magician's displeasure far outweighing their need to gossip.

"I keep forgetting you're…" he trails off as his face pulls into a frown again, stopping on the word.

"A slave," I reply bluntly. I have no idea where my audacity has come from. For twelve years I've followed the rules, stayed silent, completed their manual labour, but something has been awakened within me and it's not content to remain quiet anymore. Some emotion twists Grayson's features and he grabs my shoulder before pulling me towards the little side door we entered, moving me farther away from listening ears. I'm sure he's going to tell me off for speaking to him like that, especially when we are around other people, but he runs his eyes over me and something softens in his face.

"Not anymore," he assures me, his voice certain before he glances over his shoulder, frowning at whatever he sees there. "We don't have much time, but I'll try to explain the ceremony as best I can. I'm going to go stand with the other offerers, you'll stand with the acceptees. There will be a brief service and then the priest will call one person at a time. They'll ask who is offering you to the Mother, I'll step forward and say the ritual words. They will then ask you if you accept the Mother's blessing, which you respond with 'yes.' You will then be blessed and will join me on the other side of the altar," he explains, his eyes tracking my face. "It's simple, just copy the other acceptees." A faint smile covers his lips as he tries to reassure me. "You'll be fine, trust in the Mother."

I open my mouth to speak, having no idea what I'm going to say, but we're interrupted by someone clearing their throat.

"Mage Grayson?"

As if he's been struck, Grayson's back straightens and his mask falls firmly back into place, every inch the high magician. "I'm coming," he barks, and I see one of the priests hurrying away to avoid any further rebuttal from the magician. Eyes still on me, Grayson seems to be waiting for something, so I give him a ghost of a smile and nod my head.

Walk up to the altar, say yes, then go stand with Grayson, sounds easy enough, I think to myself as I watch the magician tidy his uniform and walk into the chapel.

Now alone in the courtyard, I take a couple of moments for myself, closing my eyes and enjoying the peace of the fresh air against my skin and the soft sounds of trickling water from the fountains. If someone had told me this morning that I would be attending the ceremony in a beautiful dress as a lady, no longer a slave, I would have called them crazy. Even in my wildest dreams I had never seen this future.

Opening my eyes, I take a deep breath and walk back towards the chapel door, the words being sung calling to me, even in a language I can't understand. There is something magical about it. The music ends as I step through the door and the acceptees closest to me watch me with narrowed eyes, all except one who shuffles closer to me. One of the younger priests steps up onto the altar and bows low to the high priest, who nods his head and moves to the side where he proceeds to cast his gaze over us.

"Your Royal Highnesses," the young priest begins, pride lining every word as he addresses the queen and her sons before turning to the rest of the audience. "Lords, ladies, and esteemed guests, welcome. Today is a very special day for our acceptees, the day they will be blessed, and a very special few shall be chosen for a better calling." There is a pause as excited whispers break out from the acceptees standing with me. "These young people are about to turn twenty and as such will become part of our society."

I look around at the individuals standing with me with a new understanding. A part of me had thought that they shared a birthday with me, which was why the ceremony was today, but in reality that wouldn't be practical—there are too many young people here to share the same day of birth. Thinking back on what I know of the ceremonies, which isn't much, I know they take place four times a year, so they must invite the acceptees to the ceremony closest to their birthday. Glancing around at the people near me, I see a sea of taffeta dresses and smart suits, everyone's dressed in their finest clothing. A frown pulls at my brow, I'd thought the servants were included in the ceremony, but I seriously doubt any of them are standing with me now. I've overheard servants discussing the ceremony and how they have to save for years to afford a suitable outfit.

I catch movement out of the corner of my eye. At the back of the chapel, the grand doors open to reveal a line of nervous, well dressed people the same age as me, along with what must be their parents still in their serving uniforms.

"I can't believe they still let them in." Spinning around, I see a stunning woman in a bright fuchsia gown glaring at the new group with disgust.

"Excuse me?" My voice is quiet, confused. She can't mean what I think she's implying. I'm not even sure if she's talking to me. Glancing around us, I see no one else is paying attention and she directs her icy blue eyes onto me.

"The commoners." Her disgust is clear in both her voice and her expression, and I feel that ball of anger light up inside me again, but thankfully someone else speaks up before I can get myself into more trouble.

"Are you saying they shouldn't be blessed?" a short, busty redhead with skin almost as pale as mine whispers, stepping closer to the two of us. "You know what would happen to them if they didn't receive it, right?" Disgust also lines her voice, but I get the impression she is revolted by the other lady's attitude, not the commoners. I can't help but wonder what she would think if she knew she was standing with a slave.

"No, that's not what I'm saying, Aileen," the lady in fuchsia responds with ice in her voice. I get the impression that there is no love lost between the two of them. "We'd never have anyone to serve us if we didn't allow it, after all. I'm just saying that they should have their own ceremony and let this one be *private*. They let any old riff-raff into this one," she says, looking Aileen up and down with a sneer on her face before turning to look at me again, her eyes taking in the grandness of my dress. "I don't know who you are, but you would be wise to take heed of who you are associating with."

Fighting to keep my face straight, I simply incline my head an inch, forcing myself to be polite and hoping she doesn't sense the anger that's burning within me. I don't want to be making an enemy on my first day of freedom. "Thank you for the advice."

Aileen snorts and the woman in fuchsia mutters something under her breath before turning and pushing her way to the front of the other acceptees. I guess I wasn't convincing enough.

"She's a piece of work," Aileen mumbles under her breath as she turns back to watch the ceremony, the high priest still droning on. I should probably be paying attention, but instead I focus on the redhead in front of me. Her dress is a mixture of greens and blues in crisscrossing patterns, and it's easy to see who her offerer is—a man with the same shade of ginger hair and a kilt in a similar crisscrossing fabric.

Opening my mouth, I go to reply, but the high priest calls the first acceptee forward. It's a woman, and although she looks nervous, an excited gleam in her eye tells me otherwise. Striding up onto the dais, she drops into a curtsy before the royals and then turns a bright smile to the high priest. He starts the ceremony, calling forth her offerer who speaks the ritual words, the woman eagerly accepting the blessing. I'm not sure what I was expecting to happen, but a tingle of electricity running down my spine was not it. Eyes wide, I look around the room to see if anyone else noticed it. A few others appear confused, startled, but as I glance over at Grayson, he watches me knowingly and gives me a reassuring nod.

What's that supposed to mean? Biting down on my lip, I turn my attention back to the woman on the platform, who's obviously trying her best to hide her disappointment before she is guided off the stage and the next acceptee is called up—this time, a young man. His footing is strong as he steps onto the dais, repeating the process of bowing to the royals and the high priest. The ceremony carries on much the same. One of the ladies is blessed and chosen to join the priesthood, a little cheer rising up from the audience as she's led away. A couple of the acceptees are partnered up in a blessed union, but no one has been chosen to join the magicians as of yet.

"Lady Clarissa of Lake Haven." There is a low murmur as people begin to whisper, and as the time stretches on and no one steps up, the high priest frowns before calling the name again. "Lady Clarissa."

"I'm assuming that's you, seeing as I grew up with all these idiots and none of them are Lady Clarissa or from Lake Haven," Aileen mutters, giving me a tiny push in the small of my back.

Mother above! I curse internally, before taking a deep breath and stepping forward. Totally unused to the name I had just been given, I'm shaken, and I pray to the Mother that no one notices, or if they do they just put it down to nerves.

Taking slow, steady steps, I accept the hand of one of the guards who helps me up onto the dais. Dropping into an awkward and wobbly curtsy before the royals, I hold it for a second too long before hauling myself up again, my eyes catching on the princes as I start to move away. In doing so, I'm not looking where I'm going and my feet, so unused to wearing shoes, tangle up in my skirts and I begin to fall. Hands clutch my shoulders and my already flushed cheeks deepen to a shade of red as I realise Prince Jacob is kneeling in front of me and stopped me from sprawling on the dais before them. With a frown, I recognise he shouldn't have been able to reach me in time, and I notice a hint of sticky, sweet magic rolling over me.

Eyes wide, I scrabble back from the prince, my words breathy. "My apologies, Your Highness."

So much for staying under the radar, I chastise myself as I stand, brushing down my skirts and ignoring the fluttering feeling in my chest as the prince chuckles.

"I'm not used to ladies throwing themselves at me, that's more my brother's forte," Prince Jacob teases quietly with a small smile. I smile back tightly in return and take a step away from the charming royal. I'm sure

Jacob has his fair share of female attention, despite his studious nature. "Are you okay, Lady…"

"Clarissa, Lady Clarissa of Lake Haven." I stumble over my name, but he simply smiles and nods his head.

"I look forward to seeing more of you in the future. Perhaps I can show you around the Great Library?" the prince suggests, and I open my mouth to respond but someone appears at his shoulder. I quickly lower my gaze as I realise it's his more intimidating older brother. I've heard rumours about Michael, the middle son. Other than his popularity with women, it's said that he has barely any patience and beats his servants. I want as little to do with him as possible.

"Brother, stop bothering the lady, no one wants to see those dusty books except for you." I feel his interested gaze on me and it twists something inside me. Jerking my head up, I look into Jacob's eyes and give him a small, but genuine smile.

"No, I would love to, Your Highness." The look of surprise on both their faces is almost worth it, but Michael's soon turns into something else—the thrill of a challenge.

"Your Highnesses, is there a problem? We must continue with the ceremony." I never thought I would be grateful to be interrupted by the high priest, but it's the excuse I need.

"Yes, you're right, thank you, High Priest. Please continue," Jacob says with a nod of his head, heading back towards his throne, his brother following behind. But as I take my final steps towards the altar, I can feel their eyes on me. The high priest who was conducting the ceremony waits a moment for everyone to settle, giving a few stern looks until the whispers drop away.

Clearing his throat, he adopts the serene look of a benevolent priest.

"Who here is offering Lady Clarissa to the Great Mother?"

"I am." I almost sag in relief when I hear Grayson's voice, someone familiar. Knowing there is someone here on my side makes me stand taller as he reaches my side. "I, High Mage Grayson of Lake Haven, offer Lady Clarissa to the Great Mother. May Clarissa be blessed and chosen in a way that serves Her will." The room is silent with bated breath as the high priest turns to look at me with an expectant expression.

"Lady Clarissa, do you accept the blessing from the Great Mother and accept the path She has chosen for you?" His words hit me like a physical blow as I realise this is more than just accepting a blessing. I'm saying an oath that not only will I be blessed, but I am also *accepting* a goddess given fate. Until today, I hadn't thought that was possible, I wasn't even sure I fully believed in the Great Mother. What if the fate She has chosen for me is not one I would have chosen for myself?

You were a slave, anything is better than that, my inner voice comments, and I realise it's right. This truly is my chance to be something different, *someone* different.

"Trust in the Mother," Grayson whispers, his voice only loud enough for me to catch. Nodding, I look up at the frowning high priest and say the words that will seal my fate.

"I accept."

For a moment, nothing happens, and I begin to think I was overthinking the oath I just took.

After all, they're just words, right?

Electricity jolts down my spine, but it's different than how it felt when I was watching the others. With the previous attendees, it was like little shocks, varying in strength, but this is something different altogether, like I've been hit with a bolt of lightning. It doesn't hurt, but it's like my whole body is alive, every nerve ending alight with feeling, almost to the point where it's too much. My back arches as the sensation intensifies and I crumple to the ground, blackness engulfing me. The last thing I hear is Grayson calling my name.

Chapter 8

I lie there in the darkness, relishing the feel of *nothingness* after the onslaught of electricity, until I slowly start to get the feeling I'm not alone. I'm not scared, this isn't the darkness of nightmares, but more the darkness of a safe place with a loved one. The presence grows stronger, but I get the feeling they won't approach until I'm ready. I don't know how I know this, but they exude love and patience, making me feel comfortable in their space, because wherever this is, I've been brought here. There's no doubt in my mind that I'm no longer in the chapel in Morrowmer. My body may be, but my mind is nowhere in Arhaven.

"I can feel you," I say out into the darkness, feeling foolish, but I know they will hear me.

"As I can feel you, beloved."

Beloved? Confusion rolls through me and a feeling of gentle amusement emits from the unseen presence. I can't hear the voice, but I can *feel* it deep in my soul. I get the impression that she's female and in her embrace I do feel loved, even though it's something I'm struggling to wrap my head around.

"Is it so hard to believe that you are beloved to me?"

Letting out a humourless laugh, I look around the

darkness, my voice bitter. "But I am nothing. A slave, a criminal."

"These are all the names that man has given you. They have taken much from you, your identity included." A wave of emotions rolls over me, none of them my own—anger, frustration, and an overwhelming sense of sadness. "I know you by a different name…however, you are not ready to hear it just yet, so for now, you will be known as my beloved."

"Who are you?" There is only one being this could be, but She would never appear to someone like me.

"I think you know that already, child." Her words hit me like a physical blow, and if I wasn't already sitting down, I would have been knocked back.

The Great Mother.

When I can finally think, I ask the question that's plaguing my thoughts. "Why am I here? Why me?"

There's a pause before the Mother replies and the darkness around us seems to ripple and change. "That is more complicated to explain, and I have little time, we're about to be interrupted."

"Interrupted? By who?" How can the Great Mother be interrupted? She's all powerful and the thought that there's someone strong enough to break through this connection is terrifying. No one should have that kind of power. The darkness ripples again and I swear I can see shapes moving in the distance, twisted, grotesque shapes made from nightmares.

"Our time is up." Her words are rushed and urgent. "Know this, stay close to him, he will protect you."

Confused, I push up onto shaking legs and spin around in the darkness, looking for the Mother, questions rolling through my mind. "Him... Do you mean Grayson?"

"I must go. Be strong, beloved. Don't trust the priest." Her words are distant as I feel her presence start to fade. The space around me constricts and I feel like I'm held in a tight grasp as the world seems to shake. The Mother's loving embrace disappears completely and an inky, evil feeling starts to surround me. I know it's no longer the Goddess holding me, but something different, something hungry. Fear takes over my body, but I can't move, not even to tremble as my breath stutters in my chest.

"No! She does not belong to the likes of you!" The Mother's booming voice turns feral as a blinding light fills the space, so bright it breaks through my closed eyelids. A scream unlike anything I've ever heard before fills the area, tearing at my mind, and I feel something warm and wet trickle from my ears as I fade into the darkness.

"BACK OFF! GIVE HER SOME SPACE!" The voice is loud and close to my head, making me wince. The sound of shuffling feet and shocked voices bounces around the room, aggravating my already pounding head. Why is everything so loud? Something brushes my hair and I screw my eyes shut as I try to sort through my jumbled thoughts. "Clarissa, can you hear me?" A low voice cuts through my confusion, and I open my eyes to see the concerned face of a high magician leaning over me.

"Grayson?" Trying to sit up, I realise that my upper body is resting on his knee, my head cradled in his arms. I think I hear him utter a prayer of thanks to the Mother, but as I painfully turn my head to look at him, his expression is blank. "What happened?" I inquire as I sit upright, pulling away from Grayson's warmth, fighting the shiver racking my body that I tell myself is from the cold and not from the lack of a certain man's arms.

"I was hoping you could tell us that," the high priest spits as he steps closer, his whole presence giving me the heebie-jeebies. The words the Mother whispered to me ring in my ears—*don't trust the priest.* Did She mean the high priest? Priest Rodrick who lurks behind the high priest with a sickening smirk on his face? Or all priests?

"Give her some space," Grayson orders, and I'm surprised when the high priest does so, although not without his upper lip curling in disgust. The magician ignores him and turns back to look at me. He's still sitting on the floor next to me, letting me take my time, not rushing to make me stand or worrying about getting his clothing dirty like many of the nobles would. "After you accepted the blessing, your body arched back and your skin began to glow before you collapsed. I managed to catch you before you hit the floor. Just before you woke up, your skin started to glow again and symbols appeared on your wrists. Then you woke up."

There's something he's not saying, and I get the impression he doesn't want to say it in front of our current audience. Frowning, I lift a hand to my throbbing head only to touch something wet, and when I remove it, I see that it's blood. Before I can even open my mouth, Grayson is handing me a handkerchief and I lift it to my ear, dabbing at the small trail of blood before switching to the other side. In the…vision, I had felt my ears bleed when that *creature* had screeched before the Mother saved me from him.

It was real. Whatever had happened in the darkness, it wasn't a dream or a delusion, it had been real. The Mother blessed me.

"What are you?" The words are vicious, and I look up to see Priest Rodrick has snuck past the high priest and is leering down at me with hatred in his eyes. And I know that despite the disguise, he knows who I am.

"What do you mean? You know who I am."

A humourless laugh leaves his twisted lips as he takes another step closer, the promise of violence in his every move. "I do, you're a disgusting traitor." His words are loud, and I look around to see if anyone overheard, but they are all too busy involved in their own gossip to pay attention.

"Shut your mouth, priest." Grayson spits the word like it's a curse, his voice venomous as he pushes up to stand, taking a few threatening steps towards Rodrick.

"You can't talk to me like that!" The priest's face turns red with anger, so used to being respected and feared that his hands shake with his rage, aching to punish the magician for his insult. However, he would never lay a hand on a magician, let alone a high magician, and Grayson knows that. Rodrick, to his credit, stands his ground as Grayson takes another threatening step towards him so they're almost chest to chest, the magician lowering his voice.

"You know I can, or need I remind you and the rest of this chapel?" He stares down the priest, waiting to see if his words hit their mark. I don't doubt that he would do exactly as he threatens.

Gulping, Rodrick turns pale but just shakes his head, gesturing towards me to make his point. "She doesn't deserve the blessing. She should be executed." His voice is strong despite his obvious fear.

"You don't get it, do you?" Grayson whispers to the man before stepping back and making his voice louder so all gathered around can hear. "You think the Mother would bless her, especially in such a dramatic way, if She didn't want the girl to survive for Her purpose?" Gazing around the room, I can see people nodding and leaning together to whisper as they look over at me, still in a puddle of lace on the floor as I watch the exchange.

"It's not right. There's nothing in the scrolls about a blessing like that. She's *different*. How can we trust her?" Rodrick turns to the high priest, waiting for his agreement. However, the high priest just shakes his head grimly before gesturing at me.

"You saw the marks on her arm. The Goddess has claimed her."

"Claimed me?" I cry out. If I knew what was good for me, I'd keep quiet, but I'm unable to hold back the exclamation and all heads turn back to me. I fight the urge to drop my head and hide behind my hair under all the attention, and my skin tingles as their eyes run over my body, my face, as if trying to figure out my secrets. Grayson must see my discomfort, as he steps away from the priest and moves to my side.

"I'll explain later," Grayson murmurs as he crouches next to me, his hand reaching out to cup my chin. His expression is sympathetic, as if he knows exactly what's going through my head. Offering me his hand, I shift my legs beneath me, and with his help I stand, reaching out and gripping onto his cloak as a wave of dizziness runs over me. "Steady, blessings can make you feel a bit lightheaded, the bigger the blessing the stronger the after effects."

Now he tells me, the voice inside me whispers, and I find myself smiling slightly at the snarky comment. Taking a deep breath, I steady myself and let go of his cloak once my head clears, the tingling still running over my skin, albeit it's far less intense since I "woke up" from the blessing. It's a strange feeling, not painful, but like I have an electrical current flowing along my body. I feel powerful.

Raising my arm up, I study my skin. I can't see anything different apart from the new mark that appeared when I woke from the blessing. "How long will this feeling last for?" My voice is quiet, my question mostly to myself, but Grayson gestures for me to follow him as we leave the chapel. The sound of the high priest's echoing voice follows us as he continues with the blessing now that I've left. "And shouldn't we stay for the rest of the blessing?" My question is half-hearted, an oppressive feeling that I hadn't noticed before lifting from my chest the farther we walk away from the chapel. Peering over his shoulder, Grayson gives a small shrug, the corner of his lips pulling up.

"No, there are some benefits of being friends with a high mage," he jokes, before he continues, "What feeling is that? Freedom?" His interested expression tells me that he truly wants to know, but I'm still caught on what he said previously.

There are some benefits of being friends with a high mage. Friends. Is that what this is? What we are? I've never had a friend before and I've never felt the need for one, so this feeling is foreign to me. Sure, there have been times when I've been lonely. Even when you are surrounded by others you can still feel alone, but nothing is ever going to change that, so there is no point mourning something that isn't going to happen. Grayson slows his pace so he's walking by my side and raises his eyebrows in expectation.

"No, that's not what I..." Trailing off, I look around as we stroll through the Queen's Courtyard, soaking up as much of the calming, fresh air as I can before we walk back into the castle. Grayson remains silent as he waits for me to finish my explanation. Raising my hand, I wiggle my fingers in his direction. "I meant this tingling sensation."

"What do you mean?" Something about the tone of his voice makes me turn to look at him as he speaks. His brow is furrowed as his eyes lock onto my raised hand.

"My skin feels…alive." Trying to explain the feeling that is so alien to me is difficult, and I struggle for the words. "I feel strong, stronger than I have in years." My body feels better than it has in a long time, the exhaustion, aches, and pains of hard, physical labour and sleeping on a cold stone floor has vanished, replaced with this strange, exhilarating feeling.

I'm so focused on my body and trying to find the words to explain that I don't realise he's stopped moving until I hear his hushed voice behind me. "It's not possible."

Concern runs through me when I see his expression, and I take a step towards him. "Grayson—" I don't know what I was going to do, what I was going to say, but something in his face hardens. Rushing forward, he grabs my arm, his eyes wide and urgent.

"Show me," he demands, his voice different than the Grayson I was beginning to know, and it reminds me that I don't *actually* know this guy. The barriers I usually keep so tightly around me had begun to slip. Frowning, I pull my arm away from his tight hold, wrapping it around myself.

As if that would protect you, my inner voice says snidely. I don't want Grayson touching me with that look on his face. "Show you what? What's going on?" I demand as I shift into a defensive position, my voice tightening, but Grayson doesn't seem to be paying attention as he starts pacing the corridor we just entered, our voices echoing along its length.

"It can't be, she didn't show any of the signs…a different type of blessing altogether…" I don't catch everything he says as he mutters to himself, pacing the short width of the corridor. Muttering strange words under his breath, the fingers on his left hand start moving in complex patterns, and the familiar feeling of magic falls over me, wrapping around me and making all my movements more difficult. It doesn't stop me from moving, but whatever he's doing is making me edgy.

"Grayson! Whatever magic you're using on me, stop it!" My voice is sharp like a whip and his head shoots up, his dark eyes meeting mine.

"You can feel my magic?" he asks quietly, and I feel like my answer is important to what happens next.

"Yes, it feels like I'm walking through treacle." Shifting uncomfortably under his gaze, I reach for an explanation. "Should I not be able to?"

"Only other magic users can feel magic being used, and that sensation you're feeling is the blessing of the Mother settling on you, literally every pore will absorb it. You shouldn't be able to feel that either, not without magic," he explains as he stalks towards me, every muscled inch of him rippling with tension. Stopping just out of reach, he waits for my response.

It takes a moment for what he's saying to sink in before my mouth drops open and a startled laugh escapes me. It sounds strange, more like a bark than the happy, carefree laughter I've heard from some of the castle children. "Are you saying I have magic?"

A confused frown pulls at his brow again and he shakes his head as if to deny what I'm saying, but he simply holds out his hand. "Show me your mark again."

With a frown of my own, I take a small step to close the gap between us, his words more an order than a request. Holding out my arms, I remove the cuffs and flip my wrists so he can examine the skin there. I haven't had the chance to properly look, but when I do, I gasp at what I see. A delicate pink mark in a language I don't recognise sits just above three black X's and the slave number branded into my skin. The mark actually sits right above where the cuff was covering my slave marks, answering my unasked question of how he knew it was there. Reaching towards me, Grayson touches the mark, tracing it with a large finger. The mark glows as his power rolls over me.

"You can read it?" I inquire, my words breathy as a warmth fills me, the loving caress I'm beginning to associate with the Mother making a small smile appear on my lips. Grayson's eyes jump up from the mark and whatever he sees makes his eyes widen, something within him softening before he gives me his own smile.

"Yes, it's the Mother's sacred language, the language of our magic. These words hold power." His tone is quiet, revered, as if we are in the chapel paying our respects, not in some abandoned castle corridor.

"What does it say?" I have to know. The unknown is dangerous, even though I'm sure this mark is a blessing and a gift from the Mother.

Grayson's thumb continues to rub over the sensitive skin of my wrist, his eyes never leaving my own. "My beloved." Something flutters within me and a blush colours my cheeks as he whispers the translation to me. I know he's just telling me what the mark says, but hearing those words awakes something within me.

It's been a day full of awakenings. Don't forget who he is, I remind myself, and I realise with a jolt how close we're standing. Clearing my throat, I take a hasty step back, pulling my wrist from his gentle grasp, subconsciously rubbing at the tingling skin as I mourn the loss of his touch.

Pull yourself together, I berate myself as I take a deep breath and glance around to check no one has seen us. I may not have grown up as a lady, but I've been around enough to pick up on etiquette, and I know standing that close to a man will only spread rumours, rumours which I would rather avoid. My main goal is to get through all of this and remain unseen. Which is very difficult to do while wearing a dress made of starlight and receiving a blessing that makes my skin glow. Sighing, I see Grayson is still watching me with undisguised interest.

"What happens now?"

My question seems to shake him out of his daze and his eyes run over me shrewdly, as if assessing I'm dressed appropriately. "You need to go to the ball."

Groaning, I look at him in horror. I'd hoped I could skip this part, after all, only the lords and ladies are invited to the ball. "Do I have to?"

"Yes." Laughing, he grins at my expression, straightening his uniform before he begins walking down the corridor once again. He glances at me questioningly as he passes me. Following behind him, I stare at his back, my thoughts spinning as I try to conjure a way to avoid going as he continues to talk. "I'll join you after I've taken care of something."

When I finally process what he said, I freeze, staring at his back as he carries on walking, unaware of the terror running through me. He's sending me into the viper's nest with only a pretty dress and magicked hair to protect me. "Wait, you're making me go in by myself? I don't know what I'm doing!"

"I'll escort you back to my rooms. You'll wait there until your escort arrives to take you to the ball. Once I'm free, I'll join you." Realising I'm no longer trailing after him, he pauses and looks over his shoulder at me. "We don't have to stay there long, just long enough to show our faces, then we'll leave. You will be safe," he assures me as he lowers his voice, seeing how much I *don't* want to be doing this. I have a decision to make here—make a fuss and refuse to go or trust him. The words of the Mother float through my thoughts again.

Trust in him. Trust in *Grayson.*

"Promise?" I hate the tremble in my voice, but if Grayson hears it he doesn't react. Instead, his smile widens and he holds his hand out to me again.

"I promise."

Chapter 9

The reflection that stares at me isn't one I recognise, but the beautiful, confident woman continues just to look back at me. The curled golden hair, makeup, and dress isn't just what makes my reflection unrecognisable, although that's part of the reason. It's nothing that I can see, at least nothing I can place my finger on, more like it's an aura around me. Instinctively, my right hand moves over to touch the mark on my left arm, tingles rippling from the mark the moment my fingers graze it. A gasp escapes my lips, my body feeling alive with the power of the Goddess. Gripping the edge of the sink, I brace myself against it until the feeling subsides. I shake my head with wry amusement as I raise my arm to examine the mark. Now that I'm alone, I have time to inspect the pink symbol.

At first, I'd thought it was just a symbol in the sacred language, but it's more than that. An intricate, swirling pattern surrounds it, creating the image of a crest. My skin is smooth and undamaged, unlike the flesh around the brands below my Goddess mark, where even after many years the skin is scarred and puckered.

"Clarissa, are you okay in there? Your escort is here." Jayne's voice is muffled through the door, but I can hear the note of concern in her tone. Jerking away from the mirror like it might bite, I close my eyes and take a steadying breath. I've been jumping at every noise that reaches me through the locked door of Grayson's bathroom. I feel safe in here, and I know that a little lock is nothing compared to even the weakest of magicians, but I've never had the ability to lock myself away before and I find it comforting.

"I'm coming," I reply, and I hear her walk away from the door. I wonder about the lack of security around Grayson's rooms. Is he not worried that I'll run away? Until this morning, I was a criminal, and now I have free rein of his rooms. There's nothing stopping me from leaving. Is that what Jayne is worried about? That I will leave?

Making a rude noise, I shake my head. Where would I go? Why would I want to leave when Grayson has offered me everything and a chance at a new life? I was surprised at the lack of guards as we walked back to his rooms, but then again, if the magicians, our protectors, are unable to protect themselves, then we're all in deep trouble.

Stop putting it off.

Opening my eyes, I take a step toward the locked door, reaching out for the handle, but then I realise I'm not wearing the cuffs to cover my slave marks. Shaking my head at my near miss, I turn and grab them, placing the metal bands over my wrists, so only my Goddess mark shows through the gauzy material of my sleeves. With one last look in the mirror, I turn my back and open the bathroom door, following the sound of soft voices into the sitting room.

As I enter, I see Jayne handing a steaming cup of tea to a young-looking magician sitting in one of the chairs.

As soon as they see me enter, the magician abruptly stops talking and jumps to his feet, knocking the cup out of Jayne's startled hands.

"Lady Clarissa!" he exclaims, wincing at the sound of the cup smashing on the floor, tea soaking into an intricately woven rug. "Oh crap, I'm so sorry," he blurts, turning to look at the mess he's created, then glancing back at me, his head turning comically between the two. A blush spreads across his cheeks and I decide to take pity on him, a small smile turning up the corner of my lips.

"It's okay." At my simple words he seems to relax, a cheeky smile thrown my way before turning back to the amused maid and the smashed cup. Closing his eyes, he mutters under his breath and the feeling of magic starts to caress my body. His magic feels different than Grayson's, weaker, and it comes in waves rather than the constant force I'm used to from the older magician. Eyes widening in awe, I watch as the fragments of the cup rise from the floor and fuse themselves back together, the stain on the floor disappearing completely. Plucking the now fixed cup from the air, he hands it back to Jayne with an apologetic smile.

"Sorry, ma'am, I can be a little clumsy," he admits. The maid takes the cup and places it down on the little side table with a smile and slight shake of her head, muttering something about clumsy magicians before turning to face me.

"Ah, you're ready. You look lovely, dear," she praises, as she walks over to greet me, her hands tugging at the skirts of my dress and smoothing out the fabric. "Mage Wilson is here to escort you to the ball. He will stay with you until High Mage Grayson can join you." Her explanation has me glancing over her shoulder at the magician in question, who's now pretending not to listen as he examines the teapot.

Lowering my voice, I meet Jayne's eyes. "Can I trust him?"

"Grayson trusts him," she declares, as if this is enough of a reassurance for me. Is it enough? Jayne must see my reluctance as she pats my arm in comfort. "I know his mother, she's a good woman. He's young—" There's a crash behind her and she winces at the loss of more porcelain as a shouted apology reaches us. "And clumsy, but trustworthy." She holds my gaze as I watch her shrewdly. I learned pretty quickly how to identify when someone's lying, the tone of their voice changes or their ticks give them away, everyone has them. But looking at Jayne, I'm pretty sure she's telling the truth. Nodding, I drop my eyes and take a step back, waiting for her to introduce us.

"Don't drop your eyes, a lady would never do that." Quickly lifting my eyes to her, I feel my stomach clench in nervous anticipation. "You command the room, eyes up, back straight." Following her instruction, I roll my shoulders back and attempt to straighten my spine. It's difficult. Years of hunching over, scrubbing floors, and bowing have altered how I stand, but tonight I am to pretend I'm a lady. Shaking my head at how my life has changed in such a short space of time, I await her next instruction. "Walk slowly so your steps are even, you don't want to fall in front of everyone. This ball is just as dangerous as the ceremony, words can be just as sharp as swords." Her warning rings in my ears... she's right. I can't afford to fall in front of everyone. "Just act like you own everything and everyone and you'll be fine."

"How much does he know?" I ask with a nod towards Mage Wilson.

"He knows you are new to court and don't know its ways, that you are Goddess blessed and important to Grayson." I shouldn't be so pleased at those words, *important to Grayson*, but I can't help but preen a little.

You're important to the outcome of the war, not him personally. He's just making sure that you don't mess it up, my snide inner voice chirps, but I push it aside, I need to be confident tonight.

"Okay, I'm ready," I announce, and Jayne steps back with a smile so I can walk towards the magician. "Mage Wilson, was it?" I call out, bringing his attention to me once again.

I take in the man before me and force a smile onto my face. He looks young, but he can't be any younger than twenty-three as there hasn't been a magician chosen at the choosing ceremony in years. His eyes are bright and he has the typical Arhaven tanned skin and light hair, although his eyes are a deeper, darker blue than most. He's tall, and has a slim build, and his smart blue uniform looks stiff and new. It's similar to Grayson's, but this uniform is a basic, solid blue with buttons lining the front of the double-breasted jacket. The high magicians have gold buttons, epaulettes, and a cape with a golden lining.

"It's a pleasure to meet you, Lady Clarissa. Please, call me Wilson," he gushes, his smile wide as he hurries forward to meet me. His excitement is infectious, and I find my smile widening as I watch him. When he offers me his arm, I eye it up, waiting for Jayne's nod of encouragement before linking my arm with his.

As he guides me towards the large doors, I feel his flickering magic just before they open wide, seemingly by themselves. Glancing across at my companion, I can see the concentration it's taking for him to use his magic this way as he obviously tries to impress me. For some reason I feel the need to praise him, to give him the response that he's looking for. I don't know why, I've only just met this man and he is using Goddess blessed magic to please a woman, but the smile that appears on his face when he sees me watching makes my heart warm.

"Thank you. I don't see magic used very often," I offer with a smile, as we step through the doors and start walking down the corridor towards the grand hall. It's a fair walk and I follow Jayne's advice, taking each step slowly and carefully.

"Well, I've never met anyone with a Goddess mark before," he responds cheerily, his eyes going to my wrist quickly before flitting back up to my face.

Tilting my head to one side, I consider the mage. I hadn't wanted to spend this walk in conversation, but his words make me curious. Glancing around, I see that we're alone, I wouldn't want anyone else overhearing and working out that I know so little about our culture. "Are they not common then?"

"No, my lady."

Pursing my lips, I consider what he's just told me, questions swirling in my mind. I'm so used to not asking, to keeping my thoughts to myself, but I find it difficult to stop now that I've started. "Are magicians not marked by the Goddess?" After all, magicians are granted magic by the Mother, so surely they would be marked in some way.

"Our mark is our magic," he explains, lifting his hand and demonstrating by making a small ball of light appear in his palm. My eyes widen in surprise. "Our choosing ceremonies are a little less dramatic than yours though," he jokes, and I can't help the small snort that slips from my lips. Delighted, he joins me in laughter, coaxing a giggle from me. It's short, but genuine, and I take a second to bask in this moment before we reach the ballroom where everything will change. The chatter of people reaches us as we continue our stroll, and I clear my throat, wanting to ask another question before it becomes too loud to talk.

"How do you know that you've been chosen to be a magician?"

"Our magic will show itself in some way, that's usually an indication as to what our specialty is. For me, I started hovering above the podium," he says nonchalantly, but my eyes widen and I pull him to a stop and turn to face him.

"You can fly?" My words are breathy and I probably look like a fool, but I can't help it, I have to know what it's like. I've always dreamed of being able to fly, of escaping the world below and going wherever I want with no walls to hold me back.

"No, I can lift myself for a few seconds, but I'm still learning to control my telekinesis." I frown at the unfamiliar word and he quirks a smile as he begins walking again. "I forget you don't know much about us. I can move things with my mind."

Nodding at his explanation, I follow him silently, lost in my thoughts as the noise grows louder and we round a corner to see the elaborate entrance to the grand hall. String instruments play, their beautiful music filling every space in the large room. I pull Wilson to a stop and stare into the hall that's decked out with candles and grand chandeliers, with tables to the side filled with more food than I've ever seen before. In the centre of the hall is a dance floor where many lords and ladies twirl in unison in a swirl of chiffon and lace. My heart thuds painfully inside my chest, anxiety gripping me tightly.

They're going to see through me.

Wilson reaches out and gently pulls me around so I'm facing him, not a smile to be seen for the first time since I met him, his expression sincere. It's something I'm not used to seeing. "I won't let anything happen to you." He speaks slowly, emphasising the words, and I just stare at him in shock.

"Why?" I don't mean to ask the question, but I'm so shocked that this man would put himself on the line to protect me that it comes out before I can stop it.

"Because Grayson says you're important, and because it's the right thing to do."

Because it's the right thing to do. His words ring through my ears and bring a sad smile to my lips. He may be young and naive, but his heart is pure. I can see why the Mother chose him to wield her magic. He would never kill or harm unless it's necessary, and I know he would die to protect me. I don't know how I know this, but something inside guides me and tells me this man is a good person, my mark tingling as if the Mother herself had organised us to meet. Who knows, perhaps she did.

"I think, in another life, it would be easy to love you." I don't know where these words come from, I've never loved anyone, nor do I know what love feels like, but it feels like the right thing to say. I can also see the two of us, aged and holding hands as our children charge around us, a home full of happiness and laughter, but I know that's never going to be a life allowed to me. The Mother has other plans for me.

Wilson's face shutters for a moment before he blinks and smiles widely at me. "Well, how about we settle on friends then?" He says it with such enthusiasm that I laugh, his smile is contagious.

"I'd like that."

"Now that we have that sorted, are you ready for your ball, Lady Clarissa?" The way he says this makes it sound like the ball is in my honour and it makes me smile again as I nod. Nodding in return, he straightens out his uniform and leads me to the entrance. There's a small group of people outside the door, and as we reach them, I see they are waiting to be admitted into the ballroom, each couple being gestured forward before they are formally announced and enter the grand hall.

One of the stewards sees us and suddenly pales, hurrying forward and bowing low. "My apologies, I didn't see you there. Please, come forward," he insists, his nerves obvious from his shaky words. "Excuse me, please move," he orders the waiting lords and ladies as he pushes through them. I give Wilson a confused look, but he just shrugs and leads me forward despite the grumbles and protests of those waiting.

"Mage Wilson, escorting Lady Clarissa of Lake Haven." The booming voice of the steward is almost lost to the music and loud voices, but those near the door hear and I see the whispers start. Before I know it, it feels like the whole hall is watching us as Wilson walks me in.

"Are all your entrances like this?" I whisper to Wilson, seeing his tight smile as he guides me over to one of the food laden tables. He looks just as uncomfortable as I am. I can feel eyes on my back and it's making my scars burn, like they can strip away my clothing and see me for what I am. I don't know how Wilson and Grayson do this. If people whisper everywhere they go, under constant scrutiny… it'd be maddening.

"They're not looking at me," he whispers back, handing me a glass of sparkling liquid from a passing waiter before grabbing his own. It takes me a moment before I understand.

"Why are they looking at me like that?" I hiss, gazing around and seeing that everyone is still watching us.

"Because you're a beautiful woman who received a Goddess mark. They're jealous," he answers with a smile. I know he's right, at least about the mark, but I can tell there's more he's not telling me. That also doesn't explain why the steward looked so scared when he saw us. "They'll get bored soon enough, just ignore them."

Deciding to take his advice I nod and straighten my back, turning to face out into the ballroom, and I can't help but admire the dancers and all their beautiful outfits. The place is glittering with jewels, with some of the ladies wearing so much jewellery that I'm surprised they can stand up straight. Wilson keeps me company, pointing out certain people of importance, telling me their ranks and the rumours surrounding them. For a magician, he knows a lot about the gossip of the aristocrats, then I realise he probably grew up with these people before he was chosen.

Raising the glass to my lips, I sip the sparkling liquid, pulling a face at the tart flavour and slight burn as it travels down my throat. Frowning at the glass, I raise it to my face, eyeing the liquid suspiciously.

"You're acting like you've never had sparkling wine before," Wilson comments with a chuckle, taking a large gulp of his own drink. If Wilson's drinking it, then it must be safe to consume.

"I haven't," I confirm, eyeing the glass again as I sniff the contents. It smells both sharp and sweet at the same time, the whole thing making gentle popping sounds as it fizzes. "What is it? It burns."

"It's alcohol, made from grapes." I give him a look. I've tasted the fruit before when I worked in a lord's grape field, and this tastes nothing like them. They are crisp and sweet, this "wine" is bitter and tart. He laughs at my expression, as if he truly hadn't believed me when I said I'd never had wine. "What kind of place did you come from where they didn't have wine?" he exclaims like this is the most tragic thing he's ever heard of, but I can only give him an awkward shrug, his question hitting a little too close to home. I don't know how to act like a lady, and if I'm not careful, I'm going to expose myself. "Have a few more sips, you'll get used to the taste, it'll help you relax too."

"Is it that obvious how uncomfortable I am?" I question with a bitter laugh before taking another sip of the wine, trying to school my expression as I scan the crowd around us.

"No, I'm just good at reading people," he responds with a shrug, before gesturing towards a group of ladies who are gathered at the other end of the hall, their heads close together as they talk.

A loud trumpet fanfare fills the room as the music suddenly cuts out, the lords and ladies looking around with wide eyes, their whispers the only sound in the sudden quiet. Wilson stiffens next to me, and when I glance over his face is tight, an expression of dislike so unlike the happy magician that I've seen so far that I do a double take. Seeing my shock, he schools his expression into a carefully blank mask. I wonder who he learned that one from...

"I didn't think they would come." Opening my mouth to ask who he's talking about, I'm stopped by the steward as he makes his announcement.

"Presenting, His Royal Highness Michael Arhaven, and His Royal Highness Jacob Arhaven."

As if by some unspoken signal, everyone drops into a

low bow, all except for me. My eyes are locked onto the person who is staring straight at me, his eyes boring into mine as if they know all my secrets. That person is Jacob, the youngest prince of Arhaven.

"You have to bow," Wilson hisses beside me. Ripping my eyes from the prince, I realise that no one has risen from their bows or curtsies yet, waiting for some sort of signal. Everyone in the room seems to be waiting with bated breath and a blush rushes to my cheeks as I drop to the floor in my haste to curtsy, my head dipped low. Sound returns to the room again and a pair of legs appear in front of me.

"We need to work on your curtsies." The voice is amused, and as I glance up, I'm relieved that it's Wilson and not someone else, like a crowned prince for example. He offers me his hand, which I accept gratefully, and he helps me up to my feet. Seeing my glass now lying on the floor, the contents leaking across the marble, I let out a sigh. I brush down my skirts to check for stains, but I'm relieved to see that they weren't marked from my little trip to the floor. Wilson, seeing what's happened, flags down one of the servants and passes me another glass with a smile.

Accepting it with a small smile of my own, I place my hand on his arm. "Sorry."

"What for?" His voice sounds genuinely confused, his expression open as if I've surprised him with my apology. Laughing bitterly, I gesture around me, not just at the mess a servant is cleaning up, but my mannerisms and the fact I could have been dragged away for treason for not curtsying to the royals.

"I don't make a very good lady." As soon as I've said the words I regret them, a real lady wouldn't say something like that. I make it sound like I'm a child *playing* at being a lady rather than Lady Clarissa of Lake Haven. Thankfully, Wilson doesn't seem to look too deeply into my words and takes my hand.

"I think you make the perfect lady." Turning my head to look at him, I can't help but laugh at his smile and roll my eyes. What a sweet talker.

We go back to small talk as we watch the antics of the nobility around us, although I can't help but keep shooting looks over at the thrones at the front of the hall. Two of the five are taken as the two youngest princes watch us mingle, neither of which have left the dais. However, Michael has his fair share of ladies keeping him company, many of whom are practically sitting in his lap, their fake laughter heard from the other side of the hall. I can feel his eyes on me though, but it's not him who's making my skin feel like it's alive.

Jacob, the youngest prince, has been staring at me since he entered the room, as he is now, only looking away for a second when a server brings him a new glass of wine. I've been trying to avoid looking over there, not wanting to meet his gaze, but I use this reprieve to examine him. I wasn't this drawn to him before the ceremony, it's only since my blessing that I can't seem to look away. He's handsome in a geeky kind of way and I can tell from the way he's sitting awkwardly in his chair that he's not comfortable here, unlike his brother who's revelling in the attention. Receiving his glass, he scans the crowd again before his gaze lands on me, his eyes locking onto mine, and try as I might, I can't pull my gaze away.

"Clarissa, come and see this important thing over here," Wilson declares, effectively breaking my stare with the prince as he steps in front of me. Smiling with relief, I take his offered hand as he links his arm with mine.

"Thank you," I whisper, as we weave through the

crowd, but I swear I can still feel the prince's eyes on my back. "Where are we going?" I ask, as I realise he's just taking me to the windows on the other side of the hall. There's nothing here. Each large, arched window has a little alcove, a few of which are occupied by couples who wanted to get a little alone time. People watch us as we cross the hall, but no one makes a move to talk to us, and I realise that Grayson picked well when he chose a magician to escort me. The eager looks turn wary when they see the blue uniform.

"You looked like you needed rescuing," he explains with a chuckle, and I realise he's right, he *is* good at reading people. I expect him to make a comment about the prince and my apparent inability to stop staring at him, but he doesn't say anything. Reaching an alcove, I lean against the stone arch, relieving some of the pressure on my feet. I'm used to being on my feet all day, my soles thick from walking barefoot, but shoes are still new to me and they are rubbing in places I'm not used to. Thanks to my skirts no one can see me take them off. I stand on the cold stone floor with a quiet sigh of relief and from Wilson's smile, I'm sure he's guessed what I'm doing.

Looking at him I give him one of my own smiles, small and fragile, but honest. "You were right. Thank you—"

"Lady Clarissa." A sharp voice cuts through the space between us, the tone instantly putting me on my guard as I turn to look at the person addressing me. It's a group of ladies headed up by a beautiful woman at the front. I don't recognise any of them and she appears a little older than the others, perhaps twenty-five or so. She's wearing a beautiful, flowing green dress the exact same colour as the soldiers' uniforms, and I realise that

Wilson pointed her out to me earlier. She's the daughter of the general of our human army.

"So you're the one everyone's been talking about." I've been trying to remember her name, but as she looks me up and down with a sneer, I decide I don't care. A lady steps up to the rude woman and whispers something to her, and I suddenly realise that I recognise her, not by her face, but by her bright fuchsia dress. She had been the lady at the ceremony who warned me away from Aileen and wanted a private ceremony for the higher classes. Whatever she says to the woman who's leading the pack of ladies makes her eyes widen as she roams her gaze over my body. "*She* received a Goddess mark?" Her eyes jump back up to meet mine and I see her mind calculating and working away before she smiles, thinly disguised venom still present as she takes a step closer to me. "Can I see it?"

Raising my eyebrows at her audacity, I just give her a look that I would give to the slaves that would get bold and try to steal my hard-earned meal. A look that promised violence and would usually be enough to scare them away, but not this woman. "And you are?"

"I'm afraid it's in a place that would be considered rude to reveal in polite company, Lady Theresa," Wilson jumps in, answering my question for me and being far more polite than I would have been. Turning her attention to the magician, her gaze turns predatory, the ladies behind her watching with interest.

"Mage Wilson, what a surprise to see you here. I haven't seen you at one of our balls since our choosing ceremony." Her sickly sweet voice makes me want to roll my eyes. I've seen enough behaviour from the nobility that fills the castles halls to recognise her fake attempt at being friendly. She is only out for her own gain.

Suddenly under the scrutiny of five eager women, he shuffles from foot to foot uncomfortably, but clears his throat and returns her smile. "I'm usually too busy to attend, but High Mage Grayson asked me to escort the beautiful Lady Clarissa here and I was too happy to oblige." A little part of me wants to preen at his words, but the other part of me just wants to get out of this situation as quickly as possible. These words seem to be a trigger for Lady Theresa, and she pulls her attention from Wilson back onto me. Eyeing my outfit up and down once more, she purses her lips, a sly smile pulling up the corner of her mouth.

"Hmm. I don't remember ever seeing you when I visited Grayson in Lake Haven, Lady Clarissa." She says it innocently, but I know what she's implying—that she knows Grayson *intimately*. I know she's trying to get a rise out of me, that she's jealous of my connection with the high mage, but what she doesn't know is that there is nothing between us. Not that I'm going to let her know that.

"Oh really? Funny, he's never mentioned you before." I have no idea where the words come from, but even Wilson lets out a shocked laugh before covering it with a cough.

I can't believe I just said that. She's going to kill me. Mother above, where's Grayson when I need him? I fight a flinch as her expression drops into one of anger, I can't afford to let her know she scares me. However, just as quickly as it appeared, it leaves and is replaced by a raised eyebrow. Whatever she's going to say will be aimed to hurt, but just at that moment someone clears their throat behind the group of ladies, effectively interrupting her.

"Excuse me, Lady Theresa, I was hoping to speak with Lady Clarissa for a moment?" The words are spoken like a question, but there is enough authority in the voice that choosing not to comply is not an option. Like a bolt of lightning has struck her, Lady Theresa's back straightens as she whips around to face the person who just addressed her.

"Why, Your Highness, what a lovely surprise to see you here tonight." Horror runs through me and I feel like I'm frozen to the spot, and even Wilson seems unable to move beside me. "How is your mother?" Theresa continues, not noticing or caring for my discomfort, her reply simpering and voice soft and gentle, nothing like the sharp words she was slinging at me just moments earlier. I have no idea which prince has decided he needs to talk to me. The excited gaggle of ladies in front of me has formed a barrier between us and I've never been more grateful. Shooting a look across at Wilson, I gesture towards the exit, pleading with my eyes that we make our escape, slip away while the prince is occupied. Although, I can hear from his short, clipped answers that the prince is losing patience.

"I would give almost anything to avoid this, but it's inevitable," Wilson whispers back to me, his face tight and completely unlike the happy magician I'm beginning to know. "He's been staring at you all night, it was only a matter of time." Bitterness seeps into his voice, and I get the impression that he and the prince have a history.

"That's fascinating, Lady Theresa, but I must have some time alone with Lady Clarissa," the prince finally says, cutting off whatever she'd been babbling on about. I don't see Theresa's face, but the expressions on the other ladies' faces tell me enough—she's been blown off, and she's not happy about it.

"Of course, Your Highness," she answers demurely, and takes a step back. The look she gives me as she does is enough to strike fear in any sane person, but I'm not paying attention to her, my focus on the now-visible prince Jacob.

Stepping past the ladies, he moves in closer, stopping just in front of me. If I reached out my fingers would brush against his formal wear. Green, the royal colour, but like the higher magicians' uniform, his double-breasted jacket has golden buttons and is lined with gold. His cape is made from golden thread and, of course, a golden crown sits upon his head.

Wilson nods his head in a semblance of a bow and I quickly sketch out an awkward curtsy. The prince watches me with knowing eyes, the corner of his mouth twitching up into a smile before he turns his gaze to the magician at my side, his expression morphing into a frown.

"Mage Wilson," the prince acknowledges dryly.

"Your Highness." Wilson sounds like he's being forced at gunpoint to utter the words, his voice tight like just speaking the honorific is painful. Silence stretches and I glance between the two of them awkwardly as they stare at each other. There is definitely some history between them, in fact they look around the same age so they may have grown up together. I'll have to ask Wilson later. Reaching over, I place my hand on the magician's upper arm, snapping him out of his staring match as he turns to look at me, an apologetic smile in place. My attention is brought back to the prince, whose gaze is trained on my hand on Wilson's arm, an emotion I can't identify swirling in his eyes.

"I'll go and get us some food, Lady Clarissa," Wilson tells me with a small smile, but I can tell he doesn't want to leave me alone. Honestly, I don't want him to leave either, but the unrelenting stare from the prince shows he's not going to back down. Wilson looks at the prince again and levels a hard stare at him. "I won't be far away if you need me." The words are aimed at me, but I feel like he's talking to the prince too, a warning hidden within his words.

He takes a step away from me and I watch him leave, my heart aching with the loss of my safety blanket. *Safety blanket.* Eyes widening, I realise he's one of the only people I've ever felt safe around and that's something I never thought I'd experience, especially not with someone I've literally just met. A cough brings my attention back to the prince who's wearing that half smile again. It's the kind of expression that someone who knows a secret about you would wear. He makes me nervous.

"Lady Clarissa, I wanted to properly introduce myself. I am Prince Jacob Timothy Arhaven." His words are tinged with a hint of pride and I can tell how proud he is of his kingdom. "I thought you looked like you needed rescuing." His words are said with that half smile and are very similar to what Wilson had said to me not that long ago.

"Thank you, Your Highness," I reply quietly, keeping my eyes low as I clasp my hands together in front of me, playing with the metal cuffs that hide my slave marks. He wouldn't be so eager to meet me if he knew who I truly was. The prince remains quiet for a moment and I can feel his eyes exploring my face, waiting for me to... well, I'm not sure what he's waiting for me to do, so I simply wait. I can't afford to make a mistake here, anything I do wrong could end up with a one-way trip to see the executioner.

"What do you think of the city of Arhaven?" he asks suddenly, and I raise my eyes to his mouth, occasionally flicking my gaze up to his eyes, only to drop eye contact after a second. His gaze is so intense I can't hold it for long. My mind plays over his question. Why is he asking what I think of the city?

Of course, he thinks I've just arrived, to learn about the court. I've lived in the castle for many years now, but honestly, I've never seen the city and some parts of the castle I've seen today were new to me. In a way, I have just arrived, it's funny but since the threat of my death has been removed, I'm seeing everything in a whole new light.

"I haven't had the chance to see much of it yet, Your Highness. But what I've seen of it, I like very much," I reply truthfully. Lying to the prince didn't sit right with me, although I don't know why, after all, his father is responsible for enslaving hundreds of children. I shouldn't want to be anywhere near him, but I find I feel the opposite. "I particularly like the Queen's Courtyard, it's very peaceful there."

"Please, call me Jacob. May I call you Clarissa?" I don't know much about court etiquette other than what I've witnessed, but I'm pretty sure this is unusual and I should be flattered. I'm still struggling to remember my full title, so I simply nod. "In that case, Clarissa…" My name sounds like a caress on his lips and something within me heats, and I have to pinch my arm to stay focused on what he's saying. "I would love to escort you to my favourite place in the city, if you would like?"

My eyes meet his, curiosity making me bolder. "Where is that?"

"It's a surprise." A full smile graces his face and for a second I'm blown away. He looks like a completely different person when he smiles like that and I decide that's the person I want to get to know.

"I'd like that," I reply tentatively, a small, fragile

smile on my lips, and I'm surprised at how true my statement is. The prince's whole face lights up and it transforms him, making me want to do anything he asks.

Why do I feel safe around these men? I've spent my whole life distrusting people, especially men, and suddenly I'm not only talking to them, but *trusting* them with my safety.

You're a fool, my inner voice chimes in, and doubt starts to creep into my mind. Can I trust the son of my captor? "I'd have to check with Grayson first though."

"Yes. The high mage." Jacob's face shuts down at the mention of Grayson, and I wonder what the prince's problem with the magicians is. At first, I had thought he just disliked Wilson, but the distaste in his voice as he mentions the high magician is obvious. Those two are the closest thing I have to friends, can I trust a man who doesn't like them? Questions and doubts swirl through my mind and I take a small step backwards to put some space between the prince and I.

I can feel his eyes on me, calculating and boring into my soul. Opening my mouth to excuse myself, he beats me to it, holding his hand out for me to accept.

"Will you dance with me?" My eyes jump up from his hand to his face, holding his intense gaze for a second before I look back down at his hand. Anxiety swirls through me and I feel my fingers start to tremble.

All noble ladies know how to dance. He'll know you're a fraud, my inner voice taunts as I stare at the offered hand.

"Clarissa?" The prince's voice softens, concern lining his words. "You're shaking, have I offended you?" He takes a step closer, stopping when I hold up my hand. I need a moment to compose myself and I can't think when he's close to me.

Breathe, stay calm. Not knowing how to dance is not a crime, just be truthful, I say to myself, using it as a mantra. Taking a deep breath, I clench my hands into fists, stopping the tremble, and meet the prince's gaze.

"I don't know how to dance."

He's silent for a moment, surprise lining his features. Tilting his head to one side, he considers me before nodding, that half smile twitching on his lips. "I'll teach you," he offers, holding his hand out to me once more. "I won't let you fall, I promise."

Hesitating, I go through my options. I could say no, I don't think he would do anything, but he'd be offended and I don't want a pissed off royal on top of my other problems. Also, part of me *wants* to say yes. The part of me that loves being in this beautiful dress and having men look at me like I'm worthy of something. The little girl inside of me that never gave up on the fantasy of someone rescuing her. Decision made, I nod my head and place my hand in his.

As he leads me out onto the dance floor a hush falls over the crowd, like the whole room is holding its breath. I can feel the gaze of everyone's eyes on my back, but I push it out of my mind and focus on the prince—on Jacob. Extending his arm, he leads me around in a circle before pulling me into his embrace, guiding one of my hands to his shoulder, and the other he clasps in his own hand. Pausing, he waits for the music to swell before leading me into a simple set of steps. Biting my lip, I look down at the floor as I mouth his whispered instructions, wishing I could see my still bare feet. Instead, I just have to trust that he's leading me into the right steps, and in reality, I'm surprised at how simple it is.

"See," he comments, pulling my gaze from the floor. "You're dancing. If you have a proficient dance partner, then you don't need to know the steps."

My footing feels clumsy, but after a while I relax and find I don't need to keep staring down. Raising my head, I see that the prince's intense gaze is locked on me, and after a moment I have to glance away, choosing to stare just over his left shoulder. We spend the next few songs just dancing in silence, the beautiful music and simple, swirling steps lulling me into a sense of comfort in the prince's arms. At this moment, I don't feel like 625, I feel like Lady Clarissa, a young noblewoman who's being treated like a princess. I know it's not real, but for this moment, I'm going to enjoy it.

"You don't talk much," Jacob comments, as we move into the next dance. I've noticed that people around us have been changing partners after each song ends, but Jacob simply keeps dancing with no signs that he'll stop anytime soon.

"I'm sorry, Your High—I mean, Jacob." I stumble over his name and his lips twitch in amusement, letting out a short laugh at my apology.

"Don't apologise for that, it's refreshing." Lifting his arm, he guides me under it, pulling slightly at my waist so I'm spinning under his arm. The move makes my dress spin and glitter under the lighting and a small surprised laugh escapes me before he pulls me back into his arms. "Tell me what you're thinking."

Exhilarated from the spin, my mouth pulls up into a small smile as I watch him watching me. "I'm thinking you're not what I expected."

"No? What were you expecting?" Lips twitching once again, he fights a laugh at my comment, intrigue glimmering in his eyes. I fall silent as I consider his question. I'm obviously not going to tell him my initial impressions, but he has surprised me. He's very guarded, unlike his brother who is lounging on his throne and throwing away smiles and compliments to any pretty woman who comes close. With Jacob, I feel like I have to earn his smiles, and when he does, it ignites something within him. There's something different about him, something I want to explore, but I get the feeling he doesn't let anyone in.

"I'm not sure, I can't get much of a read on you," I muse out loud. He pauses at my comment, his eyes shuttering. Frowning, I open my mouth to say something when a look of determination enters his eyes and he pulls me closer, staring down at me as the other dancers move around us.

He lowers his head, and whispers in my ear, "Well, we will have to rectify that, won't we?"

"Good evening, Your Highness." Grayson's deep voice comes from behind me, startling me so much I jump back from the prince guiltily. I glance between the two of them. Thankfully, Jacob doesn't seem to mind as he squares off with the high magician. The dancers around us stop and back away, retreating to the alcoves and, as I glance around, I can see everyone is huddled into little groups, watching us and whispering to each other. Wilson suddenly appears at my side, startling me as he puts a gentle hand on my arm and leads me away a few steps. The atmosphere between the two men is tense as they stare at each other, and I'm suddenly really aware of how powerful both of these men are. Grayson has his magic, but Jacob has something about him that screams *dangerous*.

"Grayson, I'm surprised to see you here, shouldn't you be on the front lines, protecting us as is your Goddess given duty?" Jacob challenges, his voice low and threatening. Grayson merely smiles at him, but it's not a nice smile, it's the kind that promises violence.

"The Mother has given me the role of guarding and assisting Lady Clarissa. I wasn't sure why, but since she received the mark at the blessing, I see the reasoning now." I stiffen as he mentions me, but he doesn't turn from his staring match.

"Yes, she is special, isn't she?" Jacob counters, his face twisting into a smile of his own before he turns to face me. "Lady Clarissa, it was a pleasure being your first dance partner." His eyes flicker to Grayson, and I know this was said as a jab at him. Stepping towards me, Jacob takes my hand and kisses the back of it, his eyes locked on mine. "I look forward to spending more time getting to know you." Without another word or look at Grayson, Jacob spins and strides away to the dais where his brother is sitting.

"What were you talking about?" Grayson's demand has me frowning, and I turn to face him with a raised eyebrow.

"Hello, Grayson, nice to see you too." I'm still not sure where this attitude has come from, but he just nods, rubbing his face with his hands as if he can scrub away the stress that is lining his face.

"Sorry, he just—You need to be careful around the royals." I don't bother to say anything to this, merely nodding in agreement. He's right, the royals are dangerous. If they ever found out who I really am, they wouldn't be so eager to get to know me, the king particularly. Our king is not a kind one, I've witnessed that firsthand.

"Now that that's over, Clarissa, will you honour me with a dance?" Wilson cuts through the awkward tension between Grayson and me, dramatically bowing and offering his hand up to me. I can't stop the smile at seeing him act this way as I place my hand in his.

"How could I say no?" I say lightly with a small grin, as he leads me farther onto the dance floor, a stunned Grayson watching us with an emotion I can't name. But, as I glance back at him, I can't help feeling that he's disappointed. Pushing those thoughts to the back of my mind, I turn my attention to Wilson. "Although I'll warn you, I'm still new at this whole dancing thing."

THE REST of the evening passes in a blur. It feels like I'm in a dream and that I'll wake up and find none of it is real, so I make the most of it. Wilson really is a terrible dancer and was nearly escorted from the hall when he fell onto Prince Michael's lap after a particularly vigorous reel. Grayson joined me for one dance, but he was quiet and lost in thought.

We leave around eleven, but the party's still going strong, more wine and liquor being poured as people start to pair off and disappear into dark corners. Wilson walks back with us, only leaving once we arrive at Grayson's rooms. With a quick goodbye, he winks once at me before he disappears around the corner.

Holding open the door, Grayson gestures for me to head inside, which I do, only to find the room empty. I'd expected to see Jayne waiting for us, but realise belatedly that she's probably sleeping. Magic rolls over my skin and as I turn, I see Grayson waving his hand over the door before looking at me. His eyes are dark and I can't read his expression, but he starts walking without saying anything, simply gesturing for me to follow him. Biting my bottom lip, I trail after him, wondering what caused his bad mood as I play with the cuffs at my wrists, nerves running through me. Taking a different door than the one we used before, he leads me down a corridor that has several doorways.

"That's the bathroom, down there at the end is my room, in case you need me," he explains, pointing first to a door on our right, then gesturing to a door set into the end of the corridor. Taking a few more steps, he reaches a door on the left, opening it with a twist of the handle. He doesn't step inside, simply opens the door and nods his head towards the room.

"This is your room, you will be safe in there. I've spelled it so no one can enter unless you give them permission." His voice is curt, his face lined with fatigue, but I'm too distracted to question why. Eyes wide, I take a few small steps into the room, almost afraid he's joking.

"You did that for m-me?" My voice breaks. I've never had my own room, and not just that, but the fact no one can enter, not even Grayson... I don't think he realises quite how much this gift means to me, to someone who sleeps with one eye open and hasn't felt truly safe for most of her life.

His eyes snap up to meet mine, and whatever he sees there makes his harsh expression soften. "It's nothing, a simple spell." He tries to wave it off, but I won't let him, not something like this. Reaching out, I grab his arm before he can turn away from me, no doubt leaving to head to his own room.

"Thank you, Grayson," I whisper.

Dipping his head in acknowledgement, his lips tug up into a small smile. "You're welcome, Clarissa. Sleep well."

And with that, he turns and walks down the corridor, opening and entering his room without turning back. The sound of his door closing and a lock sliding into place makes me wince. It's as if he couldn't get away from me fast enough. I'd dwell on that later, but for now, I have a bedroom to explore. Stepping inside, I look around with wide eyes, a small smile appearing on my face as it clicks shut behind me.

I'm safe.

Chapter 10

That night, I dream.

I dream of a slave who discovers she's a princess and is whisked away to live out her days in a castle. Except everything turns out not to be as perfect as it seemed. Waking up in a tangle of limbs, I feel like I'm still in my dream being swallowed by a large cloud. Thrashing around, I escape from the sheets that are twisted around me and look around the unfamiliar room. I realise that the cloud that's swallowing me is actually the large, soft bed that takes centre place in the room Grayson had led me to the night before. My room, at least for now.

It doesn't help that I'm still wearing my dress from the night before. I hadn't been able to undo the fiddly buttons that fastened the garment together, and there was no way I was going to ask Grayson to do it. Not after the mood he was in last night. Biting down on my lip, I climb out of the huge bed and pull my tangled skirt with me. I'll need to sneak out and see if Jayne is available to help, but for now, I want to snoop. Last night I'd been so tired I had quickly checked the room for escape routes and places to hide before climbing into bed. The combination of the stress from the day, the amount of walking and dancing, coupled with the fact that I felt truly safe in this room helped me have an undisturbed night. Well, until the nightmare anyway.

A knock on the door distracts me from my thoughts and I freeze at the unfamiliar sound.

"Clarissa? Are you awake? May I come in?" Jayne's voice reaches me through the door, and I let out a sigh of relief and nod my agreement.

Idiot, she can't see you, my inner voice sneers, and I let out a small laugh before calling out, "Yes." The doorknob rattles but no one comes in. Walking over to it, I frown, hearing Jayne's frustrated sigh at the other side of the door.

"I think you have to say that I can come in. Grayson did say that the spell requires specific words to open it."

"Oh. Yes, you may come in." As soon as I speak the words a jolt of magic tingles over my skin and the door opens seemingly by itself to reveal Jayne with her arms full of dresses. I step to the side as the maid bustles into the room, placing her burden on the end of the bed before sorting through the clothing, walking up to the wardrobe, and hanging up the garments. Tilting my head to one side I watch in fascination as she works, admiring the colours and rich fabrics as she "umms" and "ahhs," setting aside a few dresses and placing the other ones neatly away. Finally done with her task, she turns to look at me, her welcoming smile changing into a look of disapproval.

"You slept in your gown?" Stepping over to me, she gestures for me to spin around so she can help me undress.

"I couldn't undo the buttons." Shrugging, I look over the outfits she's laid out for me.

"You should have called for me, I would've come to

help you." There's a pause as she starts working on the many fiddly buttons and I breathe a happy sigh as the fabric eases. I get the feeling that Jayne wants to say something else, but she holds her tongue, simply continuing to help me undress. "When I didn't receive a call, I thought perhaps Grayson had helped you out of your dress." I frown, not understanding the tone of voice she uses as she mentions Grayson helping me out of my dress. She wiggles her eyebrows as she—*Oh*. My face flushes red with her implication and I quickly shake my head. I'm not a virgin by any means, a quick fumble with one of the stable slaves at the house I used to work in took care of that, but it had been raw and needy, taking our own pleasure from each other's bodies. I never saw him again after that, but I hadn't been upset, there was no love, or even feelings towards each other, just another slave disappearing like so many before him.

"Oh, don't look so scandalised," Jayne says with a wicked laugh, her cackle making me want to smile despite the embarrassment that I feel at her question. Finally free of the dress, I stand before her in only my undergarments. Turning, I find her frowning at my back with a look of such sorrow that I want to reach out and comfort her.

"It's okay, they don't hurt anymore." She's seen my scars before, and to be honest, the ones around my ankles and my stomach are far worse than the many on my back, but they seem to upset her anyway. I make sure my back is facing away from her, I don't wish to upset her further, but her frown deepens and she reaches out and turns me around.

"No, don't turn away. I want to see what our kingdom is capable of." I have to bite my lip as she speaks, trying to hold still as she gazes at what years of slavery has given me. "How old were you when you got these?" Her hand touches the skin on my back and I jump under her touch, flinching away with a hiss of air between my teeth. I know she's not going to hurt me, but I've learned to associate any touch on my back as a punishment.

"It wasn't just one occasion," I answer with a shrug, brushing off the matter as if it's a menial, everyday occurrence, and truthfully, I don't remember how old I was when I received my first lashing, but I remember the pain. Jayne suddenly appears in my field of vision, shaking her head at me as she reaches out and lifts my chin and adjusts my shoulders, making me stand taller.

"Right, enough of that. You're safe now." I hadn't even realised I was hunching forward, pulling my limbs in close as if to protect myself. Standing tall, I let Jayne faff around me as her words ring in my ears. A sense of guilt has fallen over me since I woke that I can't seem to shake. I may be safe now, but the other slaves aren't, they still have to suffer like I did, if not worse. Not that there is anything I can do about it, what use would one former slave be?

You're just too scared to even try.

I don't acknowledge my inner voice, instead following Jayne's instructions, slipping away to wash before returning to her knowledgeable hand to help me dress for the day. She's picked a loose summer dress, and although the fabric is plain and the cut is modest, it's still the second nicest thing I've ever worn. The sleeves come to my wrists, neat little cuffs covering them. It'll make doing tasks difficult, but I still don't know what is going to happen today. The upper part of the dress is loose with a scooped neckline, the waist cinching in before flaring out to above my knees. Simple blue strappy sandals complete the look. I was surprised at the colour of the dress, a rich dark blue like Grayson's uniform, but the colour looks nice against my pale skin so I don't mind. I suppose seeing as I am his "guest" here, it makes sense that I wear his colours.

Stepping out of my room, I follow the directions Jayne gave me back to the sitting room where I find Grayson reading a paper while holding a steaming cup of liquid. He raises his head from his reading as he notices me enter, pausing for a second before gesturing for me to sit down. He'd been so quiet last night I worried that I'd done something wrong. Perhaps it's because I was speaking with the prince, or it's leftover emotion from whatever issue he had been dealing with after the ceremony. Biting my lip, I step towards the table and take the seat opposite him. There's an empty plate waiting for me and the table is brimming with so many different foods, it can't possibly all be for us.

"Your hair has changed back. I prefer it like this." I can feel him staring at me as I settle into my chair, but I try not to look at him, focusing instead on the impressive spread of food on the table. I had noticed this morning that my straight black hair had replaced the curling golden locks from last night, which just confirms that today is going to be different. I was glad to see my own hair back, I don't recognise myself with blonde hair, but I have to admit it was nice to fit in. My dark hair is just another reason I stand out. A bitter smell fills the room, and I try to discreetly sniff the air as I realise that it's coming from Grayson's cup.

"It's coffee," he says with a chuckle, catching me, his gaze intense as I give him a small half smile. "Would you like some?"

Shaking my head, I pull my hands into my lap,

fiddling with the cuffs of my dress, nerves plaguing me as I look at the food laid out on the table.

"Help yourself," he instructs, taking a pastry from a tiered serving stand. I can feel his eyes on me as I try to decide what to have. I have no idea what any of it is, and I don't want to ask, not after how he was last night. But he seems different this morning. Seeing some slices of bread, I reach forward and take a piece, putting it on my plate and breaking it up into small pieces, eating one segment at a time. Seeing a glass of water at my side I reach for it and peer into the crystal clear liquid. I've never seen it so clear before. Lifting the glass to my lips, I take a sip and pull away in amazement. I don't know what they've put in the water, but it tastes crisp and fresh, sweet even. The water that we drink is the same water that the horses drink and it's always flecked with dirt. I suspect many deaths were caused by that unsanitary water.

"You're quiet this morning."

Dropping the piece of bread I was fiddling with, I look up at the magician, biting my lip as I try to figure out what to say. That I'm worried he's mad at me? That I don't know what anything on that table is and my stomach is cramping at seeing so much food? That I'm worried about the priests? I haven't forgotten that I have to work with them, and the change of my hair only confirms that this will start today.

"What happened last night? You said you needed to check something." I don't know if my fear made me bold, but something in my gut tells me that I need to know the answer, that this is important.

Sighing, Grayson puts down his cup of coffee and rubs at his face with his hands. "I had to talk with the other High Magicians." Leaving my half-finished breakfast on the plate, I finally look up and meet his gaze. "About you."

My throat constricts painfully, and I have to reach forward and take a gulp of water before I can ask the burning question. "What did they say?"

"We've never had anyone react to a blessing like you did. You can feel magic, so you should *have* magic, yet you don't." Leaning back in his chair, he runs his eyes over me like I'm a puzzle he can't figure out. "However, those who are blessed sometimes gain gifts. We think this might be your gift from the Mother." Blinking, I look down at the place on my arm where my Goddess mark is hidden by my sleeve, my whole body tingling as if just talking about it makes it react. I've never heard of people gaining gifts at blessings before, other than magic of course, but I've never attended or spoken to anyone who's been through one, so there is probably much I don't know. His explanation doesn't quite add up, as I've always been able to feel magic, it's just more pronounced since the blessing, but I keep that to myself. Thinking over what I know so far, and what Grayson's just told me, I tilt my head to one side as a thought comes to me.

"So, I'm like a magic detector?"

A bark of laughter has me looking up in time to see Grayson smiling at me, something I haven't seen since the blessing yesterday. "Something like that."

Ignoring the fact that Grayson's smile makes my insides feel all tingly, I reach for another piece of my bread, not really hungry but just wanting something to play with. "You appeared mad when you got back."

His sigh seems to fill the room and he scrubs at his face again, wincing as if what he's about to say is causing him pain. "I tried to get you out of the deal with the priests." Dropping my mangled breakfast, I look up quickly but dread builds as I see his frustrated expression. "Don't look at me like that, I haven't even told you what I'm going to say yet," he snaps, and I'm quickly reminded who I'm talking to as his magic seems to flare around him. Dropping my head, I stare at my plate, feeling his magic recede and seemingly get reabsorbed as he sighs again. "Clarissa, I'm sorry. I'm just frustrated. I rescued you from slavery, but the priests just won't let you go," he explains, and I can hear the regret in his voice, knowing that he's sorry for snapping at me. Tentatively, I glance back up at him.

"They refused and demanded that you start today. I don't know what they will have you doing, but if they harm you in any way..." His whole face darkens and my fear spikes as his magic rolls out of him once again, but it feels different than the last times I've felt it. It feels dark, malevolent. The force of it seems to grow, getting stronger as it comes closer to me, and I realise in a panic that it's going to engulf me.

I squeeze my eyes shut as I wait for it to hit, but after a few seconds, I open my eyes in confusion. I can feel the magic, it's hovering just inches from me, but it feels different. Slowly lifting my hand, I reach out into the magic. Grayson watches me with interest, and I know I'd probably look odd to a non-magic user, reaching out into nothing. It's not something I can see, but I can feel it, like a shield around me. My fingers touch it, and it seems to change yet again, twisting around my hand and enveloping me in a cocoon of warmth. The magic doesn't feel malevolent anymore, but there is an undercurrent, like it could switch at any moment.

"I've never seen my magic react that way around someone." Confusion laces his words, but his face is blank. Embarrassed, I pull my hand back as silence fills the space between us. I have no response for him, I don't understand magic and have no idea why it's different around me.

"Is that all you're going to eat?" Grayson raises an eyebrow at me, disapproval coating his words.

"I've already eaten more this morning than I would eat in a day." I don't bother to explain that my stomach is already cramping. The sweet pastries are calling to me, but I know that eating too much rich food will just make me sick. Jayne comes into the room as I speak and starts clearing away our plates, shaking her head in disgust.

"We need to start increasing your diet, you're all skin and bones. I should have thought of that already." She rolls her eyes at herself as she continues to stack up our plates. "But we'll do it slowly, no rich foods. We'll start with soups, bread, fruits, and then go from there." Arms laden with plates and trays, she smiles at me as she leaves the chamber. The urge to jump up and help fills me, and I push back my chair to do just that, but Grayson clears his throat and I return my attention to him.

"When I arrived at the ball, you were dancing with Prince Jacob." His tone is light, like he doesn't care about the answer either way, but I can tell from the small tightening around his eyes that he does. It isn't really a question, but I nod anyway. "You should be careful around him. Around all the royals."

I know this already, they were the ones that sentenced me, after all, not to mention that they're the rulers of this kingdom who deserve a certain amount of respect if you wish to keep your life. However, I suspect there is a different reason that Grayson wants me to stay away from them. "Why?"

Shaking his head, Grayson pushes up from the table

and straightens out his uniform and changes the subject. "We need to go. The priests are expecting you."

Swallowing down my fear, I push away from the table and follow Grayson out of his rooms and towards the chapel.

I CAN FEEL myself shrinking the closer we get to the sanctuary. I try to stand tall like Grayson, but the weight of uncertainty makes it impossible, my head dropping as I take slow, careful steps. Last night, when I had my blonde hair and I was dressed like a lady, I almost felt like one. It was my armour, protecting me, and without it I feel like the broken slave girl that I am.

Realising I'm trailing behind, Grayson turns, a question on his lips before he takes in my appearance, and a frown mars his blank mask he wears outside of his rooms. Striding over to me, he backs me against the wall, his broad body and cloak hiding me from anyone that happens to be walking through this part of the castle.

"I won't let him harm you, he won't lay a hand on you." I flinch away at his harsh tone, even though it's not aimed at me. "He won't make it pleasant, but he can't physically hurt you." His magic flares around me as if in confirmation. Reaching out, he gently touches my chin, bringing my head up so I meet his eyes. "Stop this, don't let that bastard strip away everything you're starting to become."

He's right. Taking a deep, shaking breath, I nod in agreement. This improved me, Clarissa, might be new, but I already feel different. I never would have dreamed of walking amongst royalty, or meeting Wilson, the sweet magician who kept me safe at the ball. Not to mention the new, blooming friendship with a high magician.

Pushing away from the wall, I blush as I realise how close I am to Grayson, but thankfully he takes a step back, allowing me to brush down my clothes anxiously. He stays silent as I sort through my thoughts before I nod once more. "I'm ready."

He assesses me with a blank expression then returns my nod and gestures for me to start walking alongside him. With a small curl of my lips I begin moving again, back straight as I take slow, steady steps. The dread and fear is still there, but I control it, trusting in what Grayson said. The priests can't hurt me.

WHEN WE ARRIVE at the chapel, Priest Rodrick is waiting for us with a sick smile on his face, but it's his gaze that makes me pause. I've seen that look before, it appears in his eyes when he's about to punish one of the slaves, a sick gleam that says he enjoys inflicting pain on others. How he got accepted into the priesthood, I have no idea.

I refuse to look down as we stand before the priest, and something else flickers in his eyes. Grayson must see it too, as he growls low, pulling Rodrick's attention to him.

"You know the rules."

Priest Rodrick simply smiles, but it's without any warmth as he turns his gaze back to me. "I won't lay a finger on her." The way he says it makes me shudder. There are ways of making someone suffer without touching them, and I know this priest is an expert at that.

"I'll know if you do," Grayson growls before turning to me, his hand brushing my shoulder, pulling my gaze from the priest. "I'll come and collect you later." I can tell he doesn't want to leave me here, but he doesn't have a choice. Nodding, I give him a twitch of my lips. It's a pathetic attempt at a smile, but he accepts it anyway. Turning away with a swish of his cloak, he immediately leaves the chapel. I don't want to think about how pain lanced through me when he didn't look back.

"So, 625, you've returned to me." The voice is close, so close I can feel his breath against my skin, and I flinch and spin around so I'm facing the priest. Never turn your back on the priests, a lesson all slaves learn quickly, and one I already seem to have forgotten. The urge to shy away is strong, ingrained in me, but I keep my back stiff as I face him down, remembering what Grayson said.

"I'm not a slave anymore. My name is Clarissa." It's shaky and quiet, but I see the shock on the priest's face the moment I say it. There is something freeing in it, and I feel the muscles that have frozen me in place start to loosen, allowing me to stand tall. Except Rodrick's face twists into one of cruel amusement, a grating laugh echoing around the sanctuary. I can't help but compare him to a spider as he creeps around me, his beady eyes locked onto me as if I'm his next meal.

"That *magician* may have taken you from us, but you will always be 625. Under all those pretty dresses and smiles, you are still a worthless, filthy slave, and I get to be the one to remind you of how lucky you are." He spits the word "magician" as if it's filthy, continuing to walk towards me as he talks. I feel myself freeze again as he tilts his head to one side, examining me. "The Great Mother has seen some…purpose for you." Shaking his head as if he couldn't understand why I would have been chosen, he reaches out as if to touch my chin, stopping an inch away from me. I can feel whatever magic Grayson wrapped around me start to react, little sparks of white light jumping and fluttering around me.

Rodrick's face tightens as if he's in pain, but he keeps his hand there, as if proving a point. "We don't know what that purpose is yet. However, we don't trust the magician, so we are keeping an eye on you too. Just remember that, *Clarissa.*" My new name on his tongue makes me feel sick and I jerk away from him, not wanting him anywhere near me. His warning was clear enough. No matter what I do, they will always be there, watching me.

Straightening, the priest continues to observe me for a moment before turning and beginning to walk out of the chapel. "Follow me," he demands, not bothering to turn to see if I obey his command. He *knows* I will do as he says, and I'm sure if I didn't he would find a way to hurt both Grayson and me. And, for some reason, the thought of Grayson being harmed makes my chest hurt.

We walk in silence through the main courtyard, past the justice pillars, before entering the castle and turning left. We could have easily left the side door and gone through the queen's courtyard, but I suspect he wants to remind me of my place. The cold, rough stone pillars, which instil fear in even the lords and ladies, have been stained red from the blood that's been spilled over the years. One of the punishments for the slaves is to scrub the blood from the pillars, but we could never remove the stains, so inevitably the slave would be punished for not completing their task.

Walking farther into the castle proper, we don't come across many people, and I suppose I have the ball to thank for that. It's still early, and while these corridors would usually be busy, thanks to all the alcohol that was flowing last night, I imagine they won't be up for some time. We are deep in the castle now, in a place I've never been, which makes me nervous. A large tapestry hangs on the wall, depicting one of our past kings in battle against the elves. It's similar to all the other tapestries, but Rodrick stops in front of this one, lifting it and revealing a wooden door. My eyes widen in shock as he removes a ring of keys from his robes and opens the door that leads to a stone staircase. My fear doubles.

There were rumours spread by the servants and slaves about a monster that lives in the castle, deep in the bowels where the king keeps it locked up. When one of the castle slaves would disappear, it was said that the beast had taken them, but I had always put it down to a story. Slaves disappeared all the time, and it wasn't because of a mysterious beast. But now, staring at the staircase and the orange glow that greets me, I'm suddenly unsure.

Rodrick turns to me and gestures for me to start walking down the stairs, his expression promising violence if I don't. My breathing speeds up and my hands tremble, but I step forward and begin to descend down into the underbelly of the castle. I'm plunged into darkness as the door shuts behind us, the air turning thick and stale as we go deeper, the priest close behind me. As my eyes adjust to the darkness, I realise that the orange glow is coming from the lanterns hanging on the walls. I don't know how long we descend, but we must be well below the castle by now.

"We have a special job for you." Rodrick finally breaks the silence, his voice bouncing off the stone and distorting it, making it echo around me. Spiralling down and down, I start to feel dizzy and wonder if we will ever reach the bottom just as a brighter glow appears against the walls. Reaching the last step, I see a large room lit with more lamps, and guards with crossbows sitting on benches that line the room. There are eight of them down here, all armed to the teeth, and a large metal door in the centre of the far wall.

"What you will see behind that door is something you can't speak a word of. If you do, you will be killed, Goddess mark or not. Do you understand me?" The malice in the priest's voice is clear and he makes me jump as he stands just behind me, so close I can feel the heat from his body, but I don't move as I continue to stare at the metal door. It's one of those reinforced ones that requires several keys to enter, and I know, without a doubt, that whatever is behind that door will change my life forever, the mark on my arm tingling in agreement. Why would they need such a large, heavy-duty door?

"Answer me!" Rodrick barks, making my ears ring. I jerk my head into a shaky nod of agreement.

"Yes."

Rodrick circles me, coming around to face me, a twisted smile on his face as he runs his eyes up and down my body. "Then go in there and clean until the room is spotless." He pauses. He's always enjoyed being dramatic and he doesn't disappoint this time. "If it's not, one of the guards will have to punish you."

"But you can't hurt me," I remind him, and whatever magic Grayson put over me tingles against my skin as if to prove the point. The grin Rodrick gives me makes me nervous.

"Oh, I can't, 625, but the guards can."

So that's how he's going to get around it. Looking around the room, I notice that all but one of the guards is watching me with a hunger in their eyes. Whether that's a hunger for my flesh or a hunger for my pain, I'm not quite sure, but I know they won't hesitate to administer my punishment.

A push against my back has me stumbling forward,

my steps shaky as I walk towards the huge door. My heart is pounding so loudly I can hear it in my ears, but I don't miss the low chuckles of the guards as they watch.

"He's killed all his other minders. Five people have died this week," the guard closest to me states loudly, and I know this is for my benefit. His comment hits me like a blow to the stomach, but I straighten my back as I reach the door.

"How long do you think she'll last?"

"An hour, tops."

The guards continue to joke and bet about my life as if it's just a game as I stand in front of the door, waiting for someone to let me in. I refuse to cry or let them see how scared I am. Grayson is right, they don't deserve to see my fear.

"When you see him, don't stare, and don't look him in the eyes, it sets him off." The quiet voice makes me jump and I jerk away from the person who's just appeared at my side. Eyes wide, I realise it's the one guard who hadn't been watching me, the quiet one who didn't join in the other guards' taunting. "The cleaning stuff is just on the other side of the door."

Why is he being nice to me? The other guards are getting great sport out of trying to scare me, but this one is helping me. Why? Is this all part of their game? My trust isn't easily earned, but I get the feeling he is truly trying to help me.

"Thank you," I mutter, as I look up and meet his eyes, so I don't miss the slight widening or shock before he quickly hides it.

"Try not to get killed, 625," he says loudly, so the other guards can hear as he fishes in his pocket for a chunky metal key before twisting it in the lock. The clunk of the latch is loud, like the pounding of my heart, and I watch with bated breath as one of the other guards produces a second key, handing it to the first guard.

Once the door has been unlocked and the keys returned to the safety of the guards' pockets, several of them step forward and grip onto the edges of the door. The other guards raise their crossbows and aim. As if by some unspoken signal, the guards pull, their muscles bunching under their uniforms as they haul open the heavy door.

"May the Mother be with you, 625," the quiet guard whispers in my ear, before another shoves me in. The guards' laughter follows me as I enter the darkness.

Chapter 11

The door shuts behind me, the locks clunking into place and sealing me in with...whoever "he" is that the guards kept talking about. It's dark in here, but I can see a glow coming from around a corner just ahead of me. My mind starts to play tricks on me, the stories told amongst the slaves prominent in my thoughts. Dragons, beasts, and monsters so terrifying that they cause you to die of fear just by looking in their eyes. Is that what the guard was warning me about?

Don't look him in the eyes.

No, dragons haven't been seen in centuries, there's no way that the king has managed to capture one and keep it a secret below the castle. That doesn't mean there isn't a monster in here though, and I've learned the hard way that monsters don't have to look scary or hideous to be evil.

My eyes start to adjust, and I realise I'm in a short corridor that looks like it opens up into a room. To my right, I see an alcove full of mops, buckets, and other cleaning supplies just as the guard had told me. Reaching out, I grab a broom and clutch it to my chest like a lifeline. It's not going to do much to protect me against a dragon or another horrible beast, but it makes me feel better. Taking a few steps forward, I pause as I reach the end of the corridor and assess what I know so far. I'm deep beneath the castle, locked away with something dangerous. They wouldn't have this much protection against it if they didn't fear whatever was here.

What is it, and why have they kept it a secret?

It's hot down here, so much so I can feel sweat start to bead on my forehead and the small of my back. Now that I'm farther away from the door, I can hear a deep roaring sound, not what I'd imagine a dragon to sound like, but like the noise a large fire would make. I can also hear a banging. I hadn't heard it before over the roaring noise, but now I realise it sounds like metal against metal.

Frowning, I step out from the corridor to see if my guess is right, my fear forgotten for a moment as my curiosity gets the better of me.

I was right, it's a forge.

The room is large with high, arching ceilings. We must be really deep below the castle if they managed to create this. Along the whole back wall is a large forge, the flames licking at the coal inside. Anvils and other paraphernalia that I've never seen before lie out on work tables. I haven't gone far into the room, the wall to the corridor acting like a shield in case I need it against whoever, or whatever, is locked away in here. I'm confused, if this is a prison for a monster, why is there a forge in here?

Movement catches my eye and I jump back behind the wall, peeking out after a second to see what it was. Confusion floods me, and I tentatively push away from the wall and walk out into plain sight, not that he can see me. He has his back to me, and an emotion I've never experienced before rolls through me, I can't quite put a name to it. It's like I'm being drawn to him, like a physical pull that I have to resist with every fibre of my being. Unaware that I'm standing at the back of the room, the man picks up a sword, striding over to the forge and thrusting the metal into the flames. I don't know how he can stand to be so close to the fire, the heat even from here is scorching. As he stands there with his back to me, I decide to examine him, tilting my head to one side as I take him in. He just looks like a normal man, so why is he locked away down here?

He wears dark leggings that hug his muscular legs, but what really catches my attention are the muscles on his shirtless back that move and ripple as he stokes the fire. His skin is pale like mine and his back is covered in scars. This man has experienced pain, you can tell from the scars that weave a story on his flesh and the way he stands. He's tall, and although muscular, he's also slim in build through years of hard labour. I can't see his face, his long blond hair casting a curtain to hide it, the rest of the hair falling to just below his shoulder blades.

I bet he's pretty. I'm not sure where that thought came from, it's certainly inappropriate seeing as this guy may be the death of me. *People don't get locked up for no reason*, I tell myself, but something niggles in the back of my mind, something that has been deeply buried but wants to be heard.

"Come to torment me some more?"

I almost drop the broom that's clutched to my chest as he speaks, his accented voice reaching me from the other side of the room. I can't work out where his accent is from, but then again, I haven't visited much of our kingdom, so that's not surprising.

"I can hear you breathing, don't think to trick me again." His words are like a whip, lashing out and making me gasp. How can he hear me breathing from there? No human can hear that far. The man whirls around with unnatural speed as he hears my gasp, his face contorting as he sees me. "A girl?" he growls, spitting into the forge with disgust, the fire sizzling in response. Pulling the blade from the fire, he walks to the anvil, his eyes flicking over to me every few seconds as if he's trying but just *can't* look away. Despite the guard's warning, I can't take my eyes off him. That feeling that I should be here, that something important is happening, guides my actions. Everything I've learned and seen here is starting to pull together in my mind, and a sense of dread starts to rise within me.

Reaching out, the man grabs a hammer and starts to pound the sword. His whole body ripples with his strength, and it's as if I'm watching in slow motion as his hair shifts, revealing the sharp points of his ears.

"Elf." The word tastes like acid on my tongue, ringing around the room like an alarm, time suddenly returning to normal speed as I stumble back. I'm going to die, that's why the priest sent me here, he doesn't have to kill me, the enemy will. That way he gets his wish and manages to escape punishment from Grayson, and if I somehow survive this encounter, it's not as if I can tell anyone about it. They would kill me if they ever found out I'd told someone, and other than Grayson, no one would believe me.

"Those scum are now sending in a girl to do their dirty work?" His richly accented words reach me, and I find my anger and hatred growing. This is the enemy, even as slaves we had that ingrained into us—elves are evil and untrustworthy. Why would they have an elf, a sworn enemy to Arhaven, working below the castle?

The pounding of the hammer on the anvil rings in my ears and I watch, transfixed by his movements. I should be scared, but I'm filled with a mixture of awe and hate. It's a strange combination, that feeling tugging at my chest again, but I can't pull my gaze away from him. His face is distinctly feline, his almond-shaped eyes tilting up at the ends, the dazzling green of his irises obvious even from this distance. I was right, he is pretty. His long hair that I first thought was blond in the light of the forge is actually white, with his distinctive pointed ears poking through as he works. Placing his hammer down, he picks up the sword, pointing it at me before throwing it in a bucket of water on the floor next to the forge, the hot metal hissing.

"They think I won't kill you?" he sneers, stepping towards me threateningly. My heart seems to stop in my chest, but I stand my ground as he eats up the space between us with his long legs, stopping suddenly as if he's jerked backward. A familiar clinking of metal makes me frown. His expression is feral, and I pull my gaze away and look down at his feet, my eyes widening at the chains that encircle his ankles. I shouldn't be surprised, he's not here willingly, of course he's going to be shackled.

He's like me, my inner voice whispers, but I force that thought away. We're nothing alike, he's an elf, he's the enemy. Years of sermons from the priests flash through my head, reaffirming the same message. Elves are evil. Yet here, locked away underground and chained next to a burning forge, I can't help but compare us.

As a slave, you were also an enemy to the kingdom. Shaking my head, I look back up at the elf, his eyes narrowing and his lips lifting in a snarl as I meet his gaze.

"No, that's exactly what they hope you'll do," I reply honestly, standing my ground even though my body betrays me, my hands shaking as I ball them into fists.

He's inches from me, if he reaches out he could grab my arm, but instead he watches me with narrowed eyes as if I'm something completely alien to him.

"What unholy magic is this?" Again, he spits the words out, like every second he is forced to talk to me pains him.

Perhaps it does, I know I'd rather be anywhere else than here right now. Again, some part of me whispers that I'm lying, that I'm exactly where I need to be. A noise of frustration escapes me before I can stop it, pushing those traitorous, confusing thoughts deep down.

"What do you mean?" I shouldn't be talking to him, encouraging conversation, but I can't seem to stop myself.

He seems to struggle for his next words, gesturing to his chest and letting out a noise of frustration when I look at him in confusion. "You don't have the word in your language." His tone implies it's my fault that he can't find the word he needs, as if I was the one to create the language, and I find myself narrowing my eyes. "The pull," he finally grits out, as if the words pain him, stopping my angry retort before I could voice it. Fear surges through me. *He can feel it too?*

"I don't know what you mean."

Liar. It's the first thing I noticed about him, even before I realised he was an elf.

"Liar," he growls, echoing my inner voice, his face twisting into a scowl. "I know lying is second nature to the male scum, and it seems like it's passed on to the females too." Taking a menacing step towards me, I can hear the groaning of his chains, the metal screaming under the pressure as he battles against it. "Shame."

He's so close I can feel his breath against my skin, causing the little hairs there to stand up as tingles run across my whole body. He watches my reaction with interest before stepping back, and I realise he was just showing me that if he wanted to, he could break out of the chains restraining him. Frowning at his retreating back, I realise that there has to be something else keeping him here. If what the guards say is true and he's killed five of his "minders" and he's strong enough to break out of his chains, not to mention that he's surrounded by weapons, why has he not escaped? A glint catches my eye and I realise he's wearing metal cuffs around his wrists too, and another sense of familiarity strikes me. However, his cuffs have some sort of symbol etched into them, but I'm too far away to make it out. He reaches the flames and returns to making his swords.

Realising the conversation is over and I've survived, I back away into the small corridor to retrieve the cleaning equipment. I may have made it out of that interaction alive, but I've still got the guards to deal with, and I don't doubt that they'll follow through on Rodrick's threat. I can't hold it together anymore, and as I reach the alcove, I fall to my knees as my body shakes, adrenaline coursing through me, my breaths coming in fast, erratic pants as I try to control myself. Curling in on myself, I squeeze my eyes shut as I try to steady my breaths, inhaling deeply and holding it for five seconds before blowing it back out again. Over and over I repeat this until I feel more in control. I don't cry, I don't allow myself to shed any tears, but this has always been my way of coping when I get overwhelmed. It doesn't tend to happen much anymore. I've seen too much as a slave and have become desensitised to things that *should* make me feel overwhelmed. I don't know whether that's something to be thankful for or not.

Once I've regained my composure, I pick myself up

off the floor and grab a bucket. I spot a tap at the back of the alcove, so I make my way over to it. There's no sink, simply a faucet and a drain in the ground. It makes me wonder where it leads to. Are there more rooms like this under the castle? It seems strange to put in a drainage system this deep down if it's just for one room, especially seeing that the room contains a prisoner. However, I push these thoughts aside, considering they aren't going to help me now. I need to focus on the job at hand. Filling the bucket, I reach for the mop, suppressing a sigh when I see that there's no cleaning fluid or soap, which is going to make this task almost impossible. Turning off the tap, I lift the bucket and carry it back out to the room, looking around to find the best place to start. Hammering noises call my attention, and as I glance over my shoulder, I see the elf watching me behind hooded eyes. Shying away from his expression, I decide to start in the far corner, as far away as I can get from him. Carrying the bucket over to my chosen corner, I raise the mop and dunk it into the water and start scrubbing the floor. I groan when I lift the mop a few moments later, seeing the thick layer of brown sludge covering it. Glancing back down to the floor, I realise it's just as dirty as it was when I started, if not worse. I've just managed to turn the dirt into mud. Rinsing the mop, I carry on, fighting against my growing despair as I only seem to be making more of a mess.

"What are you doing?" The clinking of the hammer against the anvil stops as he asks the question. He sounds frustrated, like he didn't want to ask but he couldn't help himself. Keeping my head down, I continue to mop the floor, hoping he will just accept my answer and go back to whatever he's doing.

"I'm cleaning."

A snort reaches my ears and this time I can't stop myself from looking up at him. Our eyes meet for a second and I hold his gaze. I swear his eyes widen before he's frowning again and staring at the floor I'm mopping. "No, you're making a mess."

As if I don't already know that. Pulling my gaze from the elf, I return to the task at hand. After refilling my bucket of water several times and stubbornly scrubbing at the floor, I start to see the fruits of my labour. I realise that the floor is actually marble, beautiful white marble with veins of red coursing through the stone, but it was covered in so much dirt and dust that you couldn't tell. What kind of prison has marble floors? The elf doesn't talk to me again, but I feel his eyes on my back as I work, much like how I keep stealing glances of him as I walk to replace my water.

The squealing of rusty metal fills the room and I turn, realising they're opening the door. I have no idea how long I've been down here, without any windows it's difficult to tell the passing of time. Two guards enter, holding up their crossbows as they walk in, their eyes scanning the room until they land on the elf. They position themselves on either side of me, their bows aimed at the elf who ignores them. A more senior-looking guard comes in, followed by two smiling goons behind him, and I realise that even had I managed to get the floor spotless, it was never going to be good enough. Looking down at the floor, he laughs and shakes his head.

"You call this clean? You've made it worse!" Shaking his head again, he turns and nods at the two guards who followed him in before leaving the room. The guards grin at each other before stalking towards me, violence lacing their features. Dropping the mop, I raise my hands to protect myself, realising too late that I could have used the mop as a weapon. The punch to my gut has me gasping in pain, dropping to my knees as a sharp pain rips through me. Once I'm on the floor, they go to town, their booted feet kicking at me until I'm gasping for air.

"Enough," one of the guards holding a crossbow barks out, and I glance up at him as my attackers pause, seeing that he's the guard who warned me before I came in. "The priest said only to mark her where no one would see. That's enough or she won't be able to walk." So that was Rodrick's plan, mark me where Grayson wouldn't see. He obviously hasn't banked on me having my own maid who would report everything to the high magician. My attackers smirk at me before striding out, leaving me in a crumpled heap on the floor.

"Get up," the kind guard orders, his crossbow still trained on the elf, who I've noticed has stopped working, his eyes boring into me.

With shaking limbs, I push up from the floor, not able to hold back the groan of pain as something in my chest shifts. I've broken ribs before, and I remember how painful it'd been, and I'm sure I've broken them again. The guards tense and I look up to see that the elf has taken a step forward, his eyes locking onto mine. We stay like that, our eyes fastened on each other, and it's not until the other guard barks at me to move that I finally break eye contact, pushing up onto weak legs as a hiss of pain escapes my lips, then I start the painful walk back into the guard room.

Rodrick's waiting for me, a gleeful smile on his face as he sees me limping toward him. He'd be handsome if it wasn't for the sick gleam that's always in his eyes. He doesn't say anything, he simply gestures for me to start walking up the spiralling staircase. This nearly has me groaning out loud, exhaustion making my limbs heavy, my body screaming in pain. Each breath I take is excruciating, but I don't want to be down here any longer than I have to be.

My world narrows down into forcing myself up the stairs, one foot at a time, each step agony, but I won't let them win. I've lived through worse beatings than this before, and it's not so much the physical pain, it's the psychological aspect. The guards are very good at conducting a punishment in the most agonising way possible. They didn't have to beat me in front of the elf, they could have easily taken me out into the underground room and done it there. It would have been safer for them, less time around the elf, but instead they did it as a message. To me, to him. The humiliation of being beaten in front of your sworn enemy, them demonstrating that you are *nothing*.

Finally, after what feels like a lifetime, we reach the top of the staircase, the priest pushing past me to open the door. If I'd had the energy, I would have pressed myself against the wall, avoiding as much physical contact with him as possible, but I feel drained, both physically and mentally. I barely remember the walk back to the chapel, moving on auto pilot until a flash of blue and gold catches my attention. Relief fills me and I collapse to the ground, exhaustion taking its toll.

"What in the underworld did you do to her?" Grayson demands, his voice furious, his magic pulsing out from him in response to his anger. Striding over, he kneels in front of me, touching my chin gently to bring my eyes up to him. Whatever he sees there seems to reassure him before he turns the full force of his fury on the priest.

"*I* didn't do anything," Rodrick responds, as he faces off against the magician. His smile is easy, but his back is ramrod straight and there's a tightness around his eyes that tells me he's scared of the magician. Turning to face me, his smile turns sickeningly sweet. "I look forward to seeing you tomorrow, *Clarissa*." Grayson growls at the way he emphasised my name, like it's a curse word, but Rodrick is already leaving. Grayson continues to watch the priest walking away, but he glances over at me, his mask cracking a bit at whatever he sees.

"Are you okay?"

Am I? I hurt, I'm exhausted, but Rodrick hasn't broken me, he hasn't won. Nodding once, I try to shrug but can't hide the wince that the movement causes. "Can we just go please?"

Frowning, Grayson nods and leads me back to his rooms in silence.

Chapter 12

"Holy Mother!" The cursing has me glancing up, seeing Jayne in the reflection of the mirror staring at my back in horror.

As soon as we returned to Grayson's rooms, I retired to the bathroom to clean up, the dress I'd been wearing was filthy from scrubbing floors all day. I'd been staring at myself in the mirror, trying to work out why I felt so different. I didn't look any different than how I looked this morning, but *something* had changed. I seem to be doing that a lot lately, staring into mirrors and not recognising the reflection. Sighing, I'd just shook my head and attempted to undo my dress. Thankfully, Jayne had joined me shortly after and helped unbutton the back of the dress.

Dropping the fabric to the floor, I stand in only my underwear and examine the damage, which seems to be mainly focused on the right side of my stomach, although if Jayne's reaction is anything to go by, I'm assuming my back is bruised too.

"Jayne, I'm fine, I've had worse beatings than this." My voice is quiet but practical, no use wasting energy on being upset over something that's already happened. I notice her eyes being drawn to the mass of old scars on my stomach as I speak, curiosity and sadness clear in her expression. She hasn't asked me about them, and I'm not ready to tell her, not yet. Images flash through my mind —light glinting off a knife, pain, blood, maniacal laughter. Screwing my eyes shut, I push the memories away, focusing on my breathing again. I'm safe. *Safe*.

"I'm telling Grayson, this is disgusting. They can't treat you like this," Jayne blusters, throwing her hand in the air as she paces behind me, gesturing towards my bruised body. I don't respond, just turning so I can see my side profile in the mirror and wince when I see the black and purple bruises marring my skin, wrapping around my side and up my back. I'm lucky they didn't break any of my other bones. Grayson would have found out one way or another. "What did they have you doing?" she asks quietly, and I quickly meet her eyes in the mirror before pulling my gaze away just as swiftly.

"Just cleaning." I keep my voice light, but I know I haven't convinced her by the snorting noise she makes, and out the corner of my eye I can see her shaking her head as she watches me.

"I've left some clothing for you on the side, you should be able to dress yourself." There's a pause and I know she wants to say something. I turn to face her, watching her expression, but eventually she just shakes her head and smiles sadly. "I'll be just outside if you need me."

Finally alone, I let out the low groan I've been holding in, gripping onto the porcelain sink to help steady myself against the waves of pain that rack my body. I can hear voices outside the bathroom, they're quiet, so I can't tell what they're saying, but I recognise Grayson's deep tone. His voice raises in an exclamation and I have just a few seconds of warning before heavy footsteps stride to the bathroom and the door slams open.

Through the reflection in the mirror, I can see Grayson's face—a mixture of embarrassment, shock, and anger as he takes me in. We stand in shocked silence for a couple of seconds, my heart beating fast as I wait for his reaction. I could try to hide, to cower away or scramble for something to cover myself, but I don't, he's seen me now and I'm not ashamed of my body. Sure, I hadn't exactly planned on him seeing me in my underwear, but I won't let him or anyone else make me feel ashamed of my scars or wounds. Each one tells a story, shows that I survived.

"You said you were okay." Voice quiet, he takes a step into the room, softly shutting the door behind him as he walks to my side, examining the bruises that colour my skin. He's silent and looks calm, but the stillness in his limbs and the dark anger in his eyes tell a different story. I was scared of Grayson when I first met him, his show of power frightening, but this change in him worries me more.

"I am okay," I say again, turning to face him, but he is too busy looking at the mess of scars on my stomach. "Grayson," I call softly, placing my hand on his arm to get his attention. When he finally looks up at me, I flinch away from the cold fury in his eyes. I know I need to change the subject, to get him to stop looking at me like that, and I remember when he told me that ridiculous story about the goat.

"I'm pretty sure it's rude for magicians to burst in on ladies getting changed." My sudden change of subject seems to work as he blinks and takes a step back, a frown marring his face.

"Sorry," he murmurs, meeting my gaze for a second

before dropping his back to my bruises. "I want to heal you." His deceleration is so abrupt that it takes me a couple of moments to process what he said.

"You can do that?" The words escape me before I can stop them and I bite down on my lip, worried that I might offend him. After all, he is one of the high magicians, their magic seemingly limitless, but I'm still learning what magicians can and can't do. Every magical act, even things they think of as trivial, is a wonder in my eyes.

Thankfully, Grayson doesn't seem to be offended, his eyes still glued to my skin. Shifting uneasily, I clear my throat and he finally looks up, his intense expression making me take a sharp intake of breath. Thoughtfulness, that underlying anger, and something that looks like…concern. Why would he be concerned? Does healing magic require a greater toll than other magics?

"Yes, but it involves me touching you, I have to have skin-to-skin contact for it to work."

Oh. He's worried about how I would feel about him touching me? A small frown pulls at my brow. Would I mind the magician touching me? I've generally avoided any touch for the last twelve years of my life, and since Grayson saved me, I've had more physical contact than I have during my whole time as a slave.

Or he's worried about touching a slave, worried he might catch a disease from your disgusting skin. The nagging voice of doubt plays at the back of my head, but I push it away. This isn't just any magician, it's Grayson. For whatever reason, he wants to help me. Studying his rich blue eyes, I realise I'm staring at him and quickly look away, nodding my head in agreement.

Taking a step closer, he kneels on the floor and reaches out slowly, his eyes on me the whole time, and I know if I told him to stop, he would. Gently touching my side, his hand slides over my skin and I have to bite my lip to stop a throaty moan from escaping, his touch is like a balm. Skimming around my side, his magic rolls over me before his fingers land lightly on the Goddess mark on my spine, the mark I had always thought was a birthmark. It looks very different than the mark on my wrist that I received at my blessing. With his magic rolling over me, a shockwave rocks my body as he presses against it, a gasp escaping me as energy fills my body. I feel powerful, like I could crush a human skull in my hand, and I peer down at my arms, expecting them to look different, but they don't. Twisting my hands so I can see my wrists, I note that my brands look the same, the black Xs standing out against my pale skin, but my Goddess mark from the blessing is glowing. A sharp flash of pain in my side has me wincing, but the feeling is nothing compared to the rush of healing magic surging through my body.

Grayson removes his hand and the feeling starts to fade, but my body still buzzes with the sensation of that power running through me. A rare smile blooms on my face as I turn my head to look at the magician. Except he's staring at his hand like he's afraid it might bite him.

"Grayson?" I hate how unsure my voice sounds, how needy I've become since I met him. I'm shown a little bit of kindness, and all of a sudden, I'm clinging to it, constantly needing reassurance.

At my voice his eyes flick from his hand to me, and then back again. Reaching out, he gently grabs my wrist and examines my mark, which is still glowing softly. "Mother above," he mutters so quietly I almost don't catch it.

Pulling my hand away, I wrap both arms around my middle, suddenly feeling exposed in front of him. The look of confused wonderment in his eyes is almost too much. When he looks at me like that, I feel naked, vulnerable. "What's going on?" My voice is sharp with demand, needing him to snap out of whatever trance he seems to be in.

"You're healed."

Barking out a humourless laugh, I drop my arms and turn to face the mirror again, examining my unblemished skin and pressing gently against my ribs. I shake my head with amazement when I feel no pain.

"Wasn't that the point?" Twisting my body from side to side to test the healing, I feel light and strong, better than I've felt in years. Grayson's silence meets my question and I stop twisting to turn to him, anxiety churning in my stomach. "Grayson, you're making me worry."

Pushing up to his feet, he frowns down at me, touching my shoulder gently as he spins me around, as if searching my body for an answer. "I don't know what just happened."

Is he being purposely dense? Perhaps he's joking with me. I have little experience with jokes, but I suppose this could be one. "You healed me?" I retort, my statement sounding more like a question, the corner of my mouth twitching up into an uncertain smile. Realising he's scaring me, he lets out a breath of air and scrubs his face, leaving his hair in an adorable mess.

Wait, did I just think that he's adorable? He's a high magician. No. I can't afford to think that way, not now, and certainly not about him. He's my saviour and the only thing keeping me away from the gallows.

"Yes, but I've never seen a healing like that before, and I've healed hundreds of people," he explains, and I have to bite back a sigh. Another way that I'm different and unknown, which is never a good thing. In uncertain times like these, the king doesn't want anything or anyone that he's not one hundred percent sure he can control. "It was like your body sped up the healing process." My ears prick with interest at his comment. So I may be different, but my body is healing quicker? Is that from the blessing, another gift from the Great Mother, or something about me that reacts to Grayson's magic? "For damage as extensive as yours, it should have taken about an hour of chanting, not seconds." His eyes are drawn again to the glowing mark on my wrist. It's starting to fade now, but it's still eerily noticeable.

"What are you saying?" Realising I'm still standing in just my underwear, I turn and grab the pile of soft clothing that Jayne had left for me, glancing over my shoulder at Grayson. "I have my own magic?"

"No, I'm sure you're not a magician." He doesn't sound certain, like he's trying to convince himself, and I can't deny that a part of me is disappointed. To have my own magic, to be able to protect myself and help others is a pretty thought, and one I hadn't realised how strongly I felt about until Grayson said it wasn't possible.

Turning back to face the bundle of clothing, I unfold what I thought was a dress but turns out to be a soft, pretty tunic with long, flowing trousers, all in shades of dark blue. Where did he get all these clothes from, and so quickly? Did they belong to someone else before me? That thought makes me cringe, so I push it away and slide the loose tunic over my head, marvelling at the soft fabric. I can feel Grayson's eyes on my brand and my birthmark-turned-Goddess mark, but I ignore him, bending to step into the trousers. I realise they are high waisted, with a pretty jewelled belt that ties around the tunic, synching it in. I haven't seen many of the ladies wearing clothing like this, but I have to admit it's pretty and comfortable. I'd pick it over the tight dresses any day. Soft matching silk slippers are on the floor by the sink, which I slide on before reaching for the metal bangle-like cuffs that cover my marks on my wrists. I shake my head at the irony. I've traded one set of cuffs for another, except these help me stay free. If anyone was to see my slave marks…Shaking my head, I turn to face Grayson who is still watching me with an odd look on his face.

"My magic acts differently around you."

I have no idea how to answer his statement and he seems to be saying it more to himself than to me. Now dressed appropriately, I walk past him and go to open the door as he calls my name. I stop, but don't turn, I'm tired of being looked at by him like I'm a puzzle he can't figure out, something to be fixed with secrets to be discovered. But I will hear him out, I owe him that much.

"Mage Wilson is joining us for dinner, does that suit you?"

A genuine smile crosses my lips at his question. It's small and fragile, but it's real. I haven't seen Wilson since the ball yesterday, and I'd like to see him again. Frustration forgotten, I look over my shoulder at the magician, my smile bright, and something in him changes, his whole body relaxing as he returns my smile with his own.

"Yes, I'd like that."

He opens his mouth to reply, but I hear a familiar voice on the other side of the walls and, smile still in place, I open the door, stepping out into the hallway.

"Good, because he's already here." Grayson's voice follows me, humour in his tone as I follow the corridor around until we reach the main sitting room. Wilson's sitting on the arm of one of the sofas while he blatantly flirts with a blushing Jayne. "Flirting with my maid, Wilson?"

As if the sofa had suddenly set on fire, he jumps up with the look of a startled deer, his eyes widening even more comically as he sees me with the high mage.

"Clarissa, Mage Grayson, I—we were just…" Something I've learned about Wilson is that he gestures when he talks, and he's so flustered by our appearance that he forgets he's holding a cup of tea in his hand. We watch, as if in slow motion, as the cup flies from his hand and the contents end up on the floor, splashing a large part of Jayne's skirt in the process. Making a startled noise, Jayne jumps back, her horrified eyes on her skirt and the mess now all over the floor. Wilson produces a handkerchief and hurries over to her, trying to dab at the fabric, but she bats him away.

"What is it with people spilling tea on this carpet?" Grayson's muttering has my face pinched tight as I try to hold back my laughter, but Wilson's guilty, wide-eyed expression that has him looking like a sad puppy is enough to push me over the edge as a giggle escapes me. The light, joy-filled noise makes everyone stop and look up at me, the rest of the room quiet, and I quickly stop, self-consciously lifting a hand to my hair, which I realise with shock is black.

Wilson only knows me with magicked blonde curly hair, not my straight, naturally dark locks. He only knows Lady Clarissa, and in the space of seconds I've ruined that whole charade. Panic thrums through me as I turn to Grayson, gesturing to my hair. Seeing my worry, something about Grayson changes. His body seems to grow as he takes a step closer to me and looks around for whatever threat has me panicking. I can feel his magic as he calls it to him.

"Grayson." When he doesn't react to me saying his name, I frown, realising he's not hearing me. Something else has taken over him, some protective instinct I can't get through.

"Grayson," I say again softly, placing my hand on his chest. I'm painfully aware that we're being watched by both Jayne and Wilson. My voice must break through as he looks down at his chest, seeing my hand and following it back to me. His eyes are feral, he doesn't look like the Grayson I know.

"He's gone into *euisa*," Wilson whispers, his voice awed as he watches his mentor with wide eyes. "You need to talk to him, calm him down."

"He's what?" My words are shrill and Grayson growls at the panic in my voice, grabbing me with a large hand and pulling me behind him, putting himself between Wilson and me. I have no idea what this *euisa* is, but he seems to get more powerful by the second, his energy growing evermore.

"*Euisa*," Wilson repeats, as if I should know what it means, wearily eyeing up the magician. "I forget that you don't know anything about us," he mutters quietly, before turning his attention to me. "It's the killing zone. It's a state that all magicians can go into, like a trance. It usually happens on the battlefields, all other feelings disappear, and only the urge to kill and protect remains." His explanation only makes me more anxious, which in turn makes Grayson growl again, taking a menacing step towards Wilson. I'm stuck behind a magician who's gone into some kind of killing trance, of course I'm going to be nervous, but the worse I get, the angrier *he* seems to get. "Something about you has set him off, you need to talk to him! Calm him down!"

Me calm him down? I barely know that man. Why

would my panic about Wilson seeing my natural hair set off this "killing trance?" He was pretty wound up about my injuries from the guards, perhaps he was close to the edge anyway and all he needed was my panic to set him off.

"Any time, Clarissa!" Wilson calls out, and I realise Grayson has taken another threatening step towards the young magician.

"Grayson, stop," I shout, biting my lip as he turns with supernatural speed, like a predator hunting down his prey. His eyes lock onto me, assessing each of my movements. *Mother above, help me, guide me,* I pray, sending my pleas up to the Mother for her assistance. I feel my wrist tingle as he takes small, predatory steps towards me.

"He's stopped drawing power, but the amount that he's holding at the moment is enough to blow the whole wing off the castle," Wilson warns me in hushed tones, which only aggravates Grayson, the magician spinning to growl at the young mage. A tingling sensation rolls over my body and I suddenly know what to do, the presence of the Mother filling me like a reassuring hug.

"Grayson." He spins again, dropping into a crouch, his teeth drawn as his feral gaze locks onto me again. Taking small, gentle steps toward him, I drop into a crouch so I'm on the same level as him and I reach out, placing my hand on his cheek, ignoring the narrowing of his eyes. "Come back, I need you." His body seems to shudder as I speak, his eyes closing as he leans into my hand. "I'm safe, come back, I need you," I repeat, my voice soft as I try to coax him back.

Opening his eyes suddenly, I let out a sigh of relief when I see they're back to normal, and I go to take my hand away from his cheek, but his arm comes up in a flash and holds my hand there. "Just—wait. Just for a second. Please." His voice is ragged, and it pains something inside me as he closes his eyes again and sags forward into my body, resting his head against my shoulder as he keeps my hand pressed to his cheek. It's an awkward position, but I don't mind. I'm sure when I look back on this I'll analyse and question what happened, but right now, this feels right.

After what feels like an hour, but must only be minutes, Grayson sighs and releases my hand, sitting back on his heels as he runs his gaze over me.

"You're okay?" When I nod, his expression changes from one of relief to a deep frown, making his face look stern. "I could've really hurt you, what were you thinking?" Standing, he stares down at me as he fights to keep his voice even, to stop the anger I can see simmering in his eyes. I push up onto shaky legs and twist the cuffs around my wrists.

"I was worried about you. I didn't want you to kill us because of some misplaced sense of guilt." His expression makes me stop, anything I was planning to say further lost.

"What?"

Shrugging, I try to think of a way to phrase the words. "You were feeling guilty that the guards beat me even after you said I wouldn't be harmed, and it set off this…trance?" My words trail off towards the end at his incredulous expression. I obviously didn't pick the right words.

"Is that what you think? That I felt guilty?" A bitter laugh escapes him as he runs a hand through his hair. "Yes, I was furious that the guards harmed you, and I *will* be taking it up with the priest, but that is not what 'set me off.'" My confusion must be evident on my face since he shakes his head, the anger draining out of him. "Is it that hard to believe that I might actually worry about you? Not just because of the vision, but because of *you*?"

"Oh," is all I can think to say, his words freezing me into place. How could someone like him care for someone like me? I understood that the Mother had given him a task to look out for me, and I'd believed he was angry because he thought he was failing that.

A cough has me blinking and looking past Grayson's shoulder to see that we still have an audience. "Well, that was entertaining," Wilson remarks with a grin, winking at me as Grayson groans and turns to face his guest. Jayne watches us with a knowing look.

"Sorry, it's been a difficult day," he says to the other magician, who opens his mouth, no doubt to respond with a cheeky comment, but Jayne interrupts them with a clearing of her throat.

"Excuse me, but dinner is ready." She may be a maid, a servant to one of the high magicians at that, but her tone leaves no room for argument as she turns and leaves the room.

"Thank you, Jayne," Grayson calls after her, before gesturing for me to follow. "Let's go sit down, I'm sure you have questions." That's an understatement, but I simply nod and follow Jayne through into a room I haven't been in before. It's bright with several arching windows built into one wall, a large varnished wooden table in the centre and five carved, wooden chairs along either side with one at each end. I've seen tables like this before, when I was a serving slave in one of the houses, but I've never sat at one.

"Clarissa," Wilson calls as he gestures to a chair he's just pulled out. At first I think he's showing me how to do it, and I'm about to tell him I know how to move a chair, until I realise that he's pulled the chair out for me. To sit at. Like a lady. Like the lady I'm supposed to be playing. I can't quite muster a smile, but I nod my thanks to him as I walk over and take the seat, glancing up at him as he pushes it in behind me. He goes to sit in the chair opposite me, with Grayson on my left at the head of the table. I can feel their eyes on me, but I stare down at the table, lost in thought as Jayne starts to bring in plates of food.

Glancing up as a dish is placed in front of me, I give Jayne a thankful nod and half a smile before looking at what she brought me. I have a bowl of what appears to be broth and a small plate with some meat and a tiny amount of gravy. I'm thankful that she's given me something different, as the full plates the others have would be way too much for my little stomach. The men have meat, potatoes, and gravy with some rich-looking side dishes, and if Wilson is surprised at my meagre meal, then he doesn't comment. Reaching for my spoon, I hold it awkwardly in my hands as I watch Grayson hold his fork, trying to copy the position with my fingers. Scooping up some of the broth with the spoon, I try to pour the soup into my mouth, but just end up spilling it. Feeling eyes on me, I glance up and see they are both watching me with undisguised amusement. Wilson makes a gesture with both his hands and I frown at him for a moment until I realise what he's doing. Putting the spoon down, I lift the bowl to my lips and sip the broth, my eyes closing in pleasure at the flavours. Bread and broth are the foods they feed the slaves, but I've never tasted anything like this before, the flavours, while subtle, make me want more. Taking several deep swallows, I place the bowl down and breathe deeply, my stomach turning at the sudden onslaught. I remember what Jayne said yesterday

—I need to take it easy, not rush or overeat, otherwise my stomach will just protest and make me sick. Glancing up, I see the two of them watching me as they eat their meals, the silence between us stretching.

"I'm sure you've got some questions." Grayson finally breaks the silence, repeating what he'd said earlier. Flicking my gaze between the two of them, I lean back in my chair as I try to put my thoughts into order.

"Why isn't Wilson surprised at the change of my hair colour?"

Barely looking up from his meal, Grayson reaches for a glass of what I assume is wine on the table before him. "He knows." I nearly choke on the water I'm sipping and slam my glass back down on the table.

"*Everything?*"

"Most of it." I just stare at him in silence until he sighs and finally looks up at me. "After the ball last night, I realised we needed someone else on our side who knows about you."

On our side. He's said something like this before, and I don't miss the slight emphasis on those words. He only decided to tell Wilson the full story after I'd been dancing with the prince, is that what changed his mind?

"And none of this bothers you?" Incredulous, I gesture to my hair and remove the metal cuff on my left arm so he can see the ugly Xs that mark me. Wilson just shrugs, smiling at me with that carefree attitude I'm learning is normal for him.

"Personally, Clarissa, I prefer your hair like this." He gestures towards my mane, and I self-consciously reach up and twist a strand around my finger. Silence fills the space between us again, but it's comfortable and companionable rather than awkward. I sip at my broth a bit more and pick at the meat on the plate in front of me.

"I know you have more questions."

"What happened in there? Wilson said it was...*ei-eui-essi*—" I struggle over the unfamiliar word, it feels awkward in my mouth.

"*Euisa*." The way he says it makes me shiver, the little hairs on my arm standing up at the slight accent that coats the word. Funny, that didn't happen when Wilson said it earlier. "It's a state that all magician's, with training, can reach. It allows us to access our raw power without having to chant or use gestures to cast the spell." I can't help but stare at him as he speaks. His voice is different, the gravity of his words starting to sink in. "In that state, we are not ourselves, our personalities are gone. It allows us to focus, to ignore all other distractions." Nodding, I try to swallow, but my throat is dry, so I reach for my glass, sipping at the cool water. "Somehow, seeing you so panicked made me protective and set off *euisa*." He sounds just as confused as I am, and although I want to shout and demand explanations, I know it won't help.

"Does that happen often?"

"I've never seen it off the battlefield," Wilson chimes in, still going through his meal like it's the first food he's seen in weeks. "It was pretty intense, I thought you were going to blow us up." He chuckles, but it's not the carefree laugh I'm used to hearing from him, it's an awkward, nervous laugh. It's then I realise how much danger we had been in.

"He truly could have killed us?" My words are quiet, light, but I'm suddenly acutely aware of how close I am to him. Is that anger and power still there? Am I sitting next to a timebomb? Grayson turns to me, an unreadable expression on his face as he thinks over my question.

"Could you sense how much power I was drawing to me?"

Nodding, I shudder as I remember how it felt being so close to that much power, what it felt like when he touched my Goddess mark earlier whilst using his magic. "Yes. I've never felt anything like it."

"If I'd released that amount of magic..." He trails off, and I see the guilt in his eyes as he shakes his head, poking at his half-eaten meal. The magnitude of his words is staggering, and I can tell he is waiting for me to freak out about what almost happened, but I don't see it that way. If I had looked at every what-if in my life, I never would have survived. Uncertainty is the constant companion of a slave, never sure if you will live to see the next day, so what-ifs are useless to me. Putting down my cutlery, I push my plate away, suddenly losing my appetite.

"It was my fault, wasn't it?"

"Why would it be your fault?" Glancing up from my plate, I frown at his question. Of course it was my fault.

"You said so yourself—your magic is different around me. Like when you healed me, it's...*more*," I reply, and Wilson actually stops eating and glances between the two of us.

"Wait, back up. I heard you mention the guards hurting you earlier, but they beat you so badly Grayson had to heal you?" Disgust lines his voice and I can see the shared look between the two magicians.

Grayson turns to Wilson, his frown deepening as he consults with him. "Yes, but she was healed in seconds."

"That's not possible," Wilson mutters under his breath as he stares at his plate, contemplating what his mentor just said before glancing back up at the older magician. "I mean, I know your magic is powerful, but

I've never heard of someone healing that quickly. Not even the healers can manage that."

As the magicians discuss my recovery, I can't help but think of the healers who reside in the castle. Some of the magicians are chosen by the Mother to train to become healers, although it's rare and most of them are needed on the front lines to help heal our troops against the onslaught of the elves' attacks. All magicians can heal, but it takes a lot of discipline and hard work, so the healers are coveted.

"Clarissa, can we try something?" Grayson's voice snaps me out of my thoughts, and I realise he's waiting for a response. Looking at him wearily, I wait for him to explain before blindly agreeing. He seems to realise this and gestures towards the other magician. "I want to see if you can amplify Wilson's magic too, or if it's just me." Biting my lip, I glance between the two of them. I am learning to trust them, but I need reassurances, and all of this is completely new to me. They want to use me in their experiment, but magic still makes me nervous. What if it goes wrong, or someone gets hurt?

Wilson nods in agreement, his ever-present smile still in place as he looks over at Grayson. "What do you need me to do?"

"Create a globe light," Grayson instructs, nodding as Wilson cups his hands together and whispers in a different language. I can't quite hear the words he uses, but I can feel the magic in them rolling along my skin as a small ball of white light hovers above his hands. "Good, now, Clarissa, can you come here?" Pulling my gaze from the ball of light, I slip out of my chair and walk slowly around the table. "Wilson, place your hand on her, directly on her skin."

I do as he says, offering Wilson my hand and placing

it in his as his face twists in concentration, staring at his light. As soon as he touches my skin, I gasp as a tingle of magic rolls through me, the light in front of us glowing so bright it's almost blinding.

"Whoa," Wilson murmurs, as he slowly starts to pull his hand away. The light fizzles into a hundred smaller lights before they disappear as soon as he loses contact with my skin.

"You amplify magic." The hushed, awe-filled words have me turning to Grayson, frowning at the change in him. Although he's looking at me, he isn't really *seeing* me. "You don't just detect, you amplify."

"Mother above," Wilson whispers as he takes in Grayson's words, his eyes widening when he realises the implications. I don't understand, my frown deepening as I look between them.

"What does this mean?" I demand, losing patience as they stare at me with wide eyes. Grayson seems to realise that he's scaring me and tones down some of the awe, his face spreading into a wide grin.

"This is the reason the Great Mother sent you to me." Leaning forward, he reaches out a hand and cups my cheek, a look resembling pride shining in his eyes. "You could help us win the war."

Chapter 13

Sleep escapes me once again as I wake up in a cold sweat for the tenth time tonight. Dreams of booted feet kicking my body, all to the beat of a hammer and anvil, and the lilted laugh of an elf tormenting me as I beg for a mercy that never came.

Pushing the light sheet off my body, I swing my legs around as I sit on the edge of the mattress. When I'd gotten ready for bed, I'd noticed the heavy blankets, but knew I couldn't sleep with all that extra weight, too used to sleeping only under a scrap of fabric despite the cold winter chill that seemed to plague us in the slave quarters. So, to make me feel more comfortable, Jayne had found a lighter sheet I could use. Despite that, the fact the mattress was so soft and felt as if it was swallowing me, I found myself tossing and turning all night.

I can see light creeping through the window at the far end of the room, so it can't be long until Jayne will come in to wake me. However, it's still too early for me to be up, and, as I glance at the twisted bedding adorning my plush mattress, I shudder. I'm still exhausted from yesterday's labour, even after Grayson healed my injuries, but I can't find rest here.

Standing up, I turn and grab the sheets and one of

the many pillows that adorn the bed. I carry my load over to the rug in front of the unlit fireplace in my room and kneel to construct a makeshift bed. After folding one sheet on the ground and placing the pillow on one end, I lie down and pull the final sheet over myself. Instantly I feel better, more settled, like some part of me felt as if it didn't belong in the huge, luxurious bed, especially while hundreds of children are enslaved and sleeping on rough stone floors.

I'm not sure how long I'm down there for, but I must have fallen asleep because when I next open my eyes, I see Jayne frowning down at me. And there's light streaming in through the now open curtains.

"Why are you on the floor?" She sounds more confused than frustrated, but I can tell she's angry, so I push myself into a sitting position, my cheeks going pink as I glance over to the bed. I was hoping to put the bed back together again before she came into the room, I didn't want her thinking I'm ungrateful, but she caught me before I had the chance. "Is there something wrong with the bed?"

"No, it's just...too soft, I feel like I'm sinking into it," I hurriedly explain, waiting for her to snap, to discipline me for wasting a perfectly good bed, or making the sheets dirty for putting them on the floor. She crosses her arms as she watches me squirm, not saying a word as I quickly work at gathering up the sheets, wincing when I see smudges of dirt.

"Why do you look like you're waiting for me to hit you?"

Avoiding her gaze, I place the pillow on the bed, brushing off any filth and dust that I find. "I made the sheets dirty..."

"I don't care about the sheets." Glancing over my

shoulder, I see her watching me intently. I try to look for any signs of deception, to see if she's lying, but why would she lie about sheets? She's never hurt me or given me a reason not to trust her before.

"But you looked angry when you saw me on the floor."

"I'm angry because you looked so at home sleeping on the floor. No child should be comfortable sleeping on the floor..." She looks like she wants to say more, but she bites her lip, looking away for a second before turning back to me. "I'm angry at the situation, not the sheets, I promise."

Watching the older woman carefully, I hand over the sheets clutched to my chest as she holds out her arms for them. She's said similar things before, hints that she doesn't agree with having slaves, and I'm sure that Mary's public punishment is still bright in her mind. Perhaps there are more people out there that share her feelings, if they stood together and... No, the king would never allow it, they would be silenced before they could even utter a word. Jayne is quiet under my watchful gaze, simply depositing the old, dirty sheets, and pulling out a new set from a chest of drawers in the corner of the room. Eventually, she looks up, seeing me standing there awkwardly with nothing to do. She takes pity on me, her stern expression softening into a gentle smile as she gestures towards the bathroom.

"Go wash up, I'll help you dress when you're ready. Grayson is waiting in the dining room for you." Nodding gratefully, I hurry into the bathroom and run the bath, my mind thinking over the dream that was still plaguing my thoughts.

. . .

NOW BATHED and clothed in a rich blue day dress, I head towards the dining room, pausing outside the door to clear my mind. Brushing my hand down the front of the dress, I marvel again at the softness of the fabric. The floor-length dress is another variation of the deep blue the magicians wear, with a front panel that runs from waist to floor, which is embroidered with the Great Mother's symbol in golden thread. The top of the dress is fashioned to imply I have a cleavage, whilst still managing to cover most of it. A lace panel that extends from the neckline and forms a high collar hides the fact that my collarbone sticks out. The matching lace sleeves with wide cuffs must be custom made, as they effectively hide my slave marks while still showing off my Goddess mark.

Taking a deep breath, I push open the doors and walk into the dining room, my eyes cast down until I remember the role I'm supposed to be playing. Raising my head and meeting Grayson's gaze is harder than it should be, but he simply smiles and nods in approval.

"Good morning, Clarissa." His voice is deeper than usual this morning, almost husky, like I'm the first person he's spoken to today, and for some reason that makes me feel warm inside. "You're looking lovely today." My cheeks glow with a blush, my whole body feeling even warmer now as I'm tinged with embarrassment and pride at his compliment. He gestures for me to sit, so I walk up to the large dining table, taking the seat opposite him. The table is full of food, more than we could possibly eat, but I notice there is far less than the day before, which pleases me. When people are starving it seems grotesque to have that much food go to waste. Reaching toward a large metal pot, I scoop a ladle of porridge into my bowl—one of the only things I recognise and feel familiar with. A glass jar with a golden liquid catches my eye, the sweet smell making my mouth water.

"Try it." Caught out, I look up at the mage, who's watching me with a half smile, sipping at his cup of bitter coffee that he seems to like so much. Reaching out, I pick up the glass, noting the way the liquid moves. It's thick, more like a syrup than a juice like I thought it was. Lifting it to my nose, I inhale the sweet, slightly woodsy smell.

"What is it?"

"Honey. It's nice, sweet." At his assurance I reach for a spoon and scoop a small amount into my porridge, stirring it in. I'm acutely aware of his stare as I lift the spoon to my lips and let out a small surprised noise. He's right, it *is* nice. Reaching forward, I grab the jar again, pouring a large portion into my breakfast. Ignoring the chuckling magician, I eagerly mix the honey into the porridge, almost closing my eyes in bliss as the flavours burst on my tongue. It's rich, and after a few spoonfuls, I have to slow down, my stomach protesting after years of gruel and stale bread. As I reach for my glass of water, I feel a sticky wave of magic wash over me, and when I glance up, I see out of the corner of my eye that my hair is blonde again.

"I'm not working for the priests today?" When Jayne had dressed me in a gown this fine, I'd assumed that was the case, but I hadn't dare hope.

"No." His face darkens, and I have to fight the urge to look away, to cast my eyes downward, but this is Grayson, I need to get used to keeping eye contact if I'm to masquerade as a lady. Grayson puts down his coffee cup and leans back in his chair as he contemplates me. "I spoke with Priest Rodrick and we have come to an agreement. You get today off and will return tomorrow."

A mixture of relief and dread war within me. The thought of having a day's reprieve from the priests is one that makes me want to fall to my knees and thank the Mother. Returning tomorrow, whilst not surprising, makes my stomach twist with nerves. Grayson suddenly leans forward, reaching his hand across the table as if he was going to hold mine, to comfort me. "I have reiterated that you are no longer a slave and shouldn't be treated as such." He knows as well as I do that the priests, especially Rodrick, don't give a damn. To them I will always be Slave 625. Burying those thoughts, I idly stir my porridge.

"What am I required to do today?"

Smiling at my question, Grayson shrugs his shoulders. "You aren't required to do anything. I have to attend some meetings, so you have free time to do as you wish."

"Oh." Blinking, I lean back in my chair. Free time...to do whatever I wish...a concept I've never thought of before.

We finish up our breakfast, with Grayson making an awkward attempt at small talk with me which just makes us both cringe, before he heads out to his meetings. Standing up, I slowly walk through Grayson's rooms, contemplating what I could do with my free time when a shaft of sunlight lands on me from one of the arched windows. Lifting my hand, I examine it under the sunshine, enjoying the gentle heat that warms it. It still looks the same, faint pale scars marring the skin, but yet I feel like I'm seeing it in a whole new light. Turning to face the window, I gaze out and enjoy the view.

Grayson's rooms are blessed with an outside wall, so

it looks out over the Black Cliffs of Morrowmer. It's beautiful, especially in the sunlight, which is trying to break through the clouds. There isn't much in Morrowmer except the city of Arhaven where our ancestors decided to settle and build the capital. There are stories of this land once being owned by the elves, saying we fought for the land. Although, many think the long-dead kings settled here because it is easily defendable against our enemies. The whole back of the castle is poised on the end of the cliff, the city sprawling before it, with large walls circling it, protecting it from the outside.

Deciding to make the most of the pleasant weather, I say my goodbyes to Jayne and head out into the corridor. I wish I had paid more attention when Grayson first brought me here, as these corridors all look the same and seem to be a maze. Eventually, I see sunlight illuminating the end of the hall and I hurry towards it, seeing that I've made it to the Queen's Courtyard. This is not where I was planning on coming, although, if I'm honest with myself, I didn't have a particular place in mind. But it's quiet and peaceful here, even if it is close to the chapel.

Shuddering at the thoughts of the priests, I shake my head and walk out into the courtyard, taking a seat near one of the tiled fountains, a small wooden bench built up against it for that very reason. Turning to look at the fountain closest to me, I admire the different colours and patterns on the tiles, the water crystal clear as it falls into the coloured basin. Each fountain is surrounded by beautiful flowers, their scents filling the air. Closing my eyes, I enjoy the tranquillity of being alone in this place, the gentle sound of the trickling water lulling me into a state of calm. I'm not sure how long I stay in the courtyard exploring each fountain, admiring the flowers, and just enjoying having the time to myself. No one comes through while I'm there until the sun reaches its apex in the sky, the bells of the clock tower tolling the midday meal, and then I hear the footsteps of others as they make their way towards the food hall.

The thought of entering the hall by myself, with everyone staring at me, is enough to make me feel sick. My stomach is still full from breakfast, so I decide that it's not worth the stress. *Perhaps I'll just explore the castle some more?* Nodding at my new plan, I push up from the bench and walk down the corridor that's parallel to the one I'd entered the courtyard from. I don't think I've ever been down here before, it's quieter than the main corridors with little arched alcoves along the wall. There are no windows, but it's lit with lamps and it feels warm, welcoming. I let my mind wander as I walk, my hand brushing over the stone wall, thinking over everything that has happened in the last couple of days, how my life has changed completely. I feel blessed that the Mother has chosen me for some purpose, but I can't help but feel guilty. Not that I'm doubting the Mother, I know she has picked me for a reason, but I feel guilty that *I* was picked when the other slaves, *children*, are left to work until they die. I'd never thought about it much before, the injustice of it all, when I was one of them. What crime could I possibly have committed at the age of eight that deserved enslavement?

I'm so lost in thought that I don't notice the foot sticking out of one of the alcoves. I trip over it, stumbling to my knees with a surprised cry.

"Mother above!" a male voice cries out, and I feel my cheeks blazing red with a blush. I recognise the voice, but I can't quite place it. A hand reaches out and rests on my arm and I look up, my eyes widening in dismay. "I'm sorry, are you okay?" Prince Jacob asks, a smile spreading across his face as he realises who I am, his eyebrow raising, giving him a charming, if not cheeky appearance. "Lady Clarissa of Lake Haven, why do I always find you at my feet?"

"Your Highness." I pull away fast, as if his touch burns, realising I just tripped over a *royal*. If this had been Rhydian, his older brother and the heir to the throne, then this could have ended really badly. I don't know much about the eldest prince, but I've heard stories that make me shudder. "I'm so sorry, I didn't see you there, I was lost in my thoughts..." I ramble as I try to stand, my feet getting tangled in the skirts of my dress, and it's only when he reaches out to steady me, his hand landing lightly on my waist, that I realise something. "You remembered my name." It's more of a statement than a question, but he answers me anyway.

"Of course I remembered your name, you intrigued me."

So much for keeping a low profile. If anything, more people seemed to notice me now—the pale stranger who arrived at the ball on the arm of one of the magicians, and left with another. I have no answer for the prince's statement, and I flounder, trying to come up with something to say. My conversation skills are severely lacking after twelve years of being mostly silent. Thankfully, the prince saves me by asking me a question.

"Where were you heading? Not many dare to venture down to the royal family's private quarters." His smile turns into a grin and I feel myself paling as he speaks.

I was entering their private quarters? Shouldn't there be guards stopping people from coming down here? Something seems to occur to him and his smile dims, a hint of a frown pulling at his brow. "Were you here to see my brother?" He tries to keep his voice neutral, non-judgemental, but I can tell that my answer is important.

"No!" Realising what he's implying, my eyes widen even further. I don't know why, but I *need* him to know I wasn't going to see his brother. "I had no idea, I am so sorry, I was just exploring, I—" My words come out in a rush and I can feel my hands start to shake again, his keen eyes picking up on my movements.

"It's okay, I believe you." His touch leaves my waist and he captures my hand, which was quivering slightly. "You were exploring?" His face softens, and I notice he starts to rub his thumb over the back of my hand in a way I'm sure he thinks is comforting, but instead awakens something inside me. "Why don't I live up to my promise and show you the library?" I hadn't really been paying attention to what he was saying, my focus on the movements of his thumb, but at the word library my ears perk and I finally meet his eyes.

"I would like that."

His smile is so bright that he almost blinds me with it, and guilt rises within me. I'm not who he thinks I am. He lets go of my hand and turns, reaching back into the alcove he'd been sitting in. Peering around him, I realise that a sitting area had been built into it, a closed book resting on one of the cushions. Picking up the tome, he tucks it under one arm and offers his free one to me. "In that case, allow me to escort you, Lady Clarissa."

Linking my arm with his lightly, I duck my head, waiting for him to say he was joking or that he made a mistake. "Thank you, Your Highness." He reaches out and touches my chin, making me flinch away from him at the sudden gesture. He pauses, his hand hanging in the space between us, his eyes narrowing for a second before he slowly lowers his hand, placing it on my shoulder instead.

"Please, when it's just the two of us, call me Jacob." I open my mouth to protest—I couldn't possibly call one of the princes by his first name—but at his raised eyebrow I simply shrug. He starts to walk, and as I'm tucked against his side, I simply follow. Thankfully, he treads slowly, my feet still unused to these shoes that Jayne insists I wear. We stroll in silence for a few seconds, and I'm not quite sure what comes over me when I turn my head to look at him, our eyes meeting.

"Then you must call me Clarissa."

I seem to take him by surprise, but he simply smiles again and nods in agreement. "Very well, Clarissa."

We walk again in silence for a couple of minutes, but it's a comfortable silence, and I'm grateful for it. I would never know what to say to one of the princes. We don't see many people as we walk, but those we do see quickly bow, and I don't miss the stares and the whispers.

Who is she? Why is the prince with her? Where is she from?

The whispers seem to follow us, like they're being carried on a phantom wind, my insecurities shadowing us.

"So how does High Mage Grayson know you?" Jacob inquires casually, but I get the impression he's looking for a certain answer. I'm not sure how much Grayson has told them, and I bite my lip as I consider my reply.

Keep it simple, tell him only the basics.

"We grew up together in… Lake Haven." If he notices my stumble over the name of a town I supposedly grew up in, then he doesn't point it out, simply nodding. He is very good at making his voice even when he speaks about Grayson, but I can't help but pick up on the tightening of the muscles around his eyes every time the mage is mentioned. "You don't like him?"

Jacob looks at me quickly, surprise coating his words. "You're very observant." It's not a question, so I simply nod in agreement. When seventy percent of someone's communication is in their body language, and you're one second away from receiving a beating, it pays to be able to read what they're *not* saying out loud. "It's not that I don't like him, I have nothing against the mage personally," he explains, shooting glances at me, probably worried I'm going to run back and tell Grayson every word he says. "It's magic I have a problem with." This surprises me, and I'm sure he can tell as he nods at my unspoken reaction. "It's brought us many technological advances, and the magicians fight our war—we would be far worse off without them. I just...it seems like an abuse of the Mother's power." I stay silent for a moment after he finishes clarifying, thinking over his words. He has a point, the magicians don't always carry out the Great Mother's will, and there is nothing making them use the power for good.

"But if she grants them the power, surely she is happy for them to use it as they need?" I muse. A look of surprised delight enters his eyes as I challenge him, like a part of him is waking up.

"That's the difference, Clarissa. She's given them this power, and it's their job to use it in a way that suits her purpose." He echoes my earlier thoughts, cutting off as a couple of courtiers walk past us, bowing to the prince before disappearing around the corner. "I guess what I'm trying to say is that I don't like how powerful they are, their seemingly limitless power—it makes me nervous. What's to stop them from trying to take over the kingdom?" He's right, and in a way, I agree with him, but there are some, like Grayson, that would never allow that.

"They never have before, why would they begin now?" My question seems to change something about him, his face darkening, and for a second I think I've offended him. He pulls me to a stop, lowering his voice as he pulls me closer to him so only I can hear.

"Things are changing, Clariss—" His voice low, urgent, until a cough has him pulling away.

"Prince Jacob." Turning to face the person who spoke, I instantly decide I need to avoid this individual. He stands with his hands behind his back, his chest puffed out as he stares down his nose at us, and a fake smile is pasted across his face. I don't know what it is about this person that I dislike, but every fibre of my being is screaming that this man is bad news.

The change in the prince is immediate. His friendly smile disappears and a careful mask slips into place, much like Grayson when we leave his rooms. Jacob is standing so straight at the arrival of the newcomer that I realise for the first time how tall he is. The stranger takes a step closer, his eyes running over me and landing on my chest. Without realising I've taken a step closer to the prince, I feel Jacob tighten his grip on my arm instinctively.

"Advisor Merritt," the prince reluctantly greets the man, to which the man gives him a spindly smile. He reminds me of a spider, waiting in a twisted web to reach out and grab his next victim.

"It's nice to see you without your nose in a book." *That's a backhanded compliment,* I think. But the prince just snorts a laugh. I'm surprised this man is able to blatantly insult one of the royal princes. *Who is he?*

"Ah, well, you will be disappointed to know that I am

just escorting Lady Clarissa to the library. Plenty of books for us to get lost in there, I'm sure." Jacob's tone of voice is anything but friendly, and I get the impression that there is no love lost between these two.

"So, this is Lady Clarissa." Advisor Merritt turns his head to look at me, his beady eyes boring into me. His tongue pokes out between thin lips as he licks them slightly, the movement making me shudder. I try to pass it off as a shiver in the drafty corridor, but I know I don't manage to pull it off. "I've heard much about you and your…unusual choosing ceremony. I expect great things from you." I've been in some situations that still give me nightmares, so I know, deep down, that this man promises pain—his whole aura radiates violence.

"We must be leaving, Advisor. The books aren't very patient." Jacob is already leading me away as he speaks, and the advisor makes a noise of disgust but simply nods. However, I keep watching him as we walk away and I don't miss the look of pure hatred he shoots at the prince before his eyes shift and lock with mine. Like a bolt of electricity shoots down my spine, I gasp, my body arching. If it weren't for the prince holding me up, I would have fallen to the ground.

"Clarissa! Are you okay?" Jacob sounds panicked, like he actually cares for my safety, which seems ludicrous given the fact he only met me the other day.

"*He's dangerous. Leave the library early tonight, don't go back after the evening meal.*" Staring up at the ceiling, back bowed, I have no idea where these words are coming from, except that I have this surety that if the prince doesn't heed my words, he will be in great danger.

"What are you saying?" I can hear the frown in his voice, laced with a tinge of fear. "How do you know I go to the library in the evenings?"

As quickly as it came, the feeling leaves my body, all except for a tingling in the small of my back and by my Goddess mark on my wrist. Absentmindedly, I rub at my wrist until the prince pulls my hand away, exposing the glowing mark. "I don't know what just happened, but I have a really bad feeling about that man. Who is he?" Jacob simply stares at the mark before raising his wide eyes to my own.

"Merritt is one of my father's advisors. A fowl man, but I never would've thought he'd pose a risk to me." He frowns as he helps me stand, taking a step back from me, appearing lost in thought. A flash of fear runs through me, but I realise after a second it's not my terror, more like an *echo* of fear, of a feeling that will come to pass. I suddenly know with a surety I can't explain that I'm feeling Jacob's future fear. Reaching out, I grab his wrist, pulling him to a stop. The prince frowns at my arm. I'm sure I'm gripping him tight enough to hurt, but as he looks up at me his expression softens as he takes me in.

"Don't underestimate him." My voice shakes with the echo of fear that's seeping through me, my body trembling slightly. Whether it's my words, the surety in my eyes, or some little voice that whispers to him like the one that guides me, he nods.

"Okay, I won't. I promise." Taking a step closer to me, he places his other hand on my shoulder, lowering his voice so only I can hear him. "I'll return straight to my rooms tonight. I promise, Clarissa."

Suddenly aware of many sets of eyes watching us, I take a step back from the prince, putting space between us. I'm not sure where or when the advisor disappeared, but since then the corridor seems to have filled with people, all of whom are pretending not to watch us.

"Would you still like to visit the library? Or would

you like to retire to your rooms?" I can tell that he's expecting me to answer with the latter, and perhaps that's what a real lady would do, but I have no intention of doing so.

"Of course I'd still like to see the library!" I exclaim. Does he not want to take me there anymore after my little outburst? A sense of disappointment that I'm not prepared to examine rolls through me, but I shake it away. "Why, do you need to be elsewhere?"

"No!" he replies hurriedly, before smiling ruefully at me. "You're not what I expected." Offering me his arm again, I look at it critically like it might bite me before nodding and linking my arm with his. He snorts with laughter and starts to lead me towards the library.

"Is that a bad thing?" I query after a couple of seconds. I had debated not saying anything, I'm supposed to be blending in, after all, but everything I do just seems to make me stand out all the more. Besides, I want to know his answer.

"No! You're the first lady I have found that I can actually have a debate with, without you simpering and answering only to please me," he explains, as we walk through the castle, dipping his head in acknowledgment to the lords and courtiers who pass us. I follow his lead, not sure on the protocol for greeting others whilst I'm with the prince. After a pause, I realise he's waiting for me to reply, and I scramble for something to say.

"Ah, I was raised differently." Not a lie, he has *no* idea how differently I was raised. If he realises that he's arm in arm with one of the slaves that serve in his castle…I don't even want to think of the consequences.

"I think I should visit Lake Haven," he says with a little laugh, and I respond with one of my own, deciding his comment doesn't need an answer. It's better to keep my mouth shut so I don't dig myself into any more holes.

The prince continues to lead me through the corridors. The library is on the opposite side of the chapel, built onto the back of the castle. I've never been, but I've seen it from outside. The walls are rounded, covered with gleaming windows. It looks beautiful at night, with lights shining out, the large glass dome on top making it appear as if it's glimmering. I'm filled with excitement at the prospect of going inside, not that I'd be able to read anything, but the prince doesn't need to know that. Reaching the large double doors, I look up with awe at the beautiful carvings etched deep into the wood, with golden accents painted to highlight the beauty of the work. The doors are open, but I have to wonder how they managed to move them, given as they are four times the height of a man and thicker than my torso. As soon as the prince guides me through into the library, the whole atmosphere seems to change. My jaw drops as I take in the opulent room—it's easily as big as the ballroom, if not bigger. It's six floors tall with the domed ceiling making it even higher. The ceiling is painted with beautiful depictions of flowers and plants around the glass dome. There's a large open space with desks for studying in the middle, the natural light from the large windows making it a perfect place to read. Rows upon rows of large bookshelves fill up the rest of the space, with wooden ladders strategically placed around the room available to reach the higher shelves. The large, curved windows along the back wall have a carpeted area before it, complete with comfortable looking leather seats. Two spiral staircases parallel to each other lead up to the next floor, golden handrails gleaming.

"Your Highness," a gentle voice greets, pulling me

out of my dazed stare. A middle-aged lady is pushing up from her desk to the right of the large doors, which I'd missed as when we'd walked in, my attention was fully caught on the room. She has a kind face, but I get the impression she could be a force to be reckoned with if you were on her bad side.

"Annalise, this is Lady Clarissa of Lake Haven, she is new here and wanted to see the library." I smile slightly at the woman, clasping my hands in front of me as her gaze takes me in. For some reason, I want this woman to like me. "Clarissa, this is Annalise, the head librarian. She's in charge of the library and there is nothing that she doesn't know," Jacob states with a large grin, laughing as Annalise rolls her eyes, her lips pulling into an amused smile.

"That's very kind of you to say, Your Highness," she replies with a fondness that gives me the impression she's used to him saying things like this. It's Jacob's turn to roll his eyes dramatically.

"Oh, come now, don't start that 'Your Highness' nonsense again, I've only just trained you out of it."

Laughing again she inclines her head toward me. "You have company." Jacob raises his eyebrow and turns his head to look down at me.

"Clarissa doesn't mind, do you?" Eyes widening, I take a small step backward, or at least I attempt to, but Jacob is still holding onto my arm so he simply pulls me back to him.

"Don't put her on the spot, that's cruel. Wicked boy," Annalise chides, but it's with a long-suffering smile that piques my interest. These two interact in a way that is far more familiar than librarian and prince type relationships. Studying the two of them, I can't help but wonder what relationship they share. I'm pretty sure they're not romantically involved, it's more like that of mother and son. Feeling my stare, Annalise turns and offers me a smile, but I get the impression she's examining me as much as I am her. "What do you think of my library, Clarissa?"

Caught unaware, I blink but glance at the library around us, answering honestly as a small smile graces my face again. "I've never seen anything as magical. It's beautiful."

"I like this one. She's much better than the simpering fools that usually follow you around." Jacob makes a startled sound at her backhanded compliment, which I'm sure is her way of testing me out.

"Annalise!" Jacob barks, his voice sharp, but I stop him with a gentle hand on his chest.

"I like this one," I tell him, repeating Annalise's words, tilting my head to the side as if examining her closely. "She tells the truth unlike the other simpering fools who have tried to get your attention today." Annalise chuckles as she winks at me, reaching forward and capturing my hand in hers.

"You and I are going to get on well."

AFTER MEETING ANNALISE, Jacob takes me on a tour of the library. I can feel his gaze on me as I walk slowly beside him, my eyes wide with awe, fingers trailing over the spines of some of the books. I love it here. The hushed, comfortable quiet, only able to hear the whisper of turning pages, the scribble of pen on paper, and the muted voice of Annalise at the front desk. Even the smell of the books is comforting, like it's triggering an old memory at the corner of my mind, but not quite enough for it to come fully.

We spend the rest of the afternoon in the library, just exploring the hidden coves and treasures, before the sunset bell tolls to indicate the evening meal. Jacob walks me back to Grayson's rooms, and as we reach the door we both pause awkwardly. I don't know how these things usually go, should I curtsy, or—

"Thank you for making my dull afternoon all the more interesting, Clarissa."

"I enjoyed myself, thank you for showing me the library. I loved it."

"Good." He smiles and I can tell he wants to say more, but for whatever reason he holds his tongue and starts to walk away.

"Wait!" I call out, the echo of urgency from earlier still ringing through my mind. He turns, a hopeful expression on his face. "Remember what I told you earlier."

His face darkens at the memory, but he nods, taking my hand in his and raising it up to his lips, pressing a gentle kiss against the skin there.

"Good night, Clarissa."

Chapter 14

I wake the next morning with a feeling of dread. I'm to work for the priests again today. Yesterday had been one of the best days of my life, a day where I didn't just exist, but actually *lived*. I'm still not sure what to make of Jacob. He's not at all what I expected. In public he always seems so removed from everything that's going on around him, or he's lost in a book. However, when he was showing me around the library, I saw someone who was playful and kind. As soon as we had left and were in public, he returned to the more distant prince I've heard whispers about.

Grayson had retired to his rooms late, so late he missed the evening meal, but Jayne kept me company. He was in a dark mood when he did finally return and had simply bid me good night before retreating to his bedroom. I went to bed myself after that, but I hadn't slept well, the combination of the soft mattress and dreams of Priest Rodrick laughing as his guards beat me and the elf watching with dark, furious eyes.

Getting out of bed, I pick out a book at random off the small bookshelf that is built into the wall of my room and curl up on the bay window seat. I flick through the pages, tracing some of the words with my fingers. I can't read, but I make up my own stories, and I am completely lost in a world of my own making when Jayne comes to help me dress for the day. Garbed in the same simple, but well-made dress I had worn the day before last, I sit in front of the mirror as Jayne brushes through my dark, straight hair.

Ready for the day, I walk into the dining room, finding Grayson already sitting at the table, reading a stack of papers with a serious expression.

"Good morning," I say softly, not waiting for him to look up before taking my seat opposite him at the table, helping myself to porridge with a spoonful of honey. Looking up from whatever he's reading, his face seems to darken even more as he sees me in my maid dress. It's nicer than anything the maids wear, but it's what I've come to call the simple, well-made outfit, as everything else he has me dressed in exudes wealth.

"Morning. How are you feeling today?" he asks, keeping his voice carefully neutral, but I get the impression he's wearing one of his masks again, as his eyes spark with anger.

"Fine," I mutter, as I stir my porridge absentmindedly. "I'm working for the priests again today?" I already know the answer, but I have to check, trying not to look as disappointed as I feel as I see him nod out of the corner of my eye. We fall into silence as he sips his coffee, watching me as I take a small spoonful of my breakfast. I'm not really hungry, my stomach churning with nerves, and Grayson's foul mood only makes it all the more unappetising.

"If you would tell me what they have you doing, I might be able to do something to help," he probes, his voice dangerously calm, but I simply shake my head, not meeting his eyes.

"I can't." He makes a noise of displeasure before turning back to his papers. We sit in awkward silence as I play with my food and he pretends not to watch me as he drinks his coffee.

"I heard that you spent the day with Prince Jacob yesterday." This time my gaze does shoot up, and I see his eyes narrow as he notices my reaction. Tilting his head, I can't help but compare his expression to that of a predator stalking their next meal, except *I'm* the meal.

"Yes?" The word is light, innocent, but why don't I feel that way? I've done nothing wrong, simply been shown parts of the castle by one of the princes, yet Grayson is making me feel like I'm guilty of something.

"You should be careful, the princes are not to be trusted." His comment is interesting. As one of the high magicians, he serves the king and princes, so to state they can't be trusted is a bold and dangerous thing to say. Taking a sip of water from my glass, I avoid his intense gaze again, shrugging my shoulders slightly.

"I'm still learning who I should and shouldn't trust."

Grayson makes a pained noise and I look up to see an expression I can't quite work out. It looks like anger and betrayal mixed into one before he quickly wipes it away into that mask of cool anger.

"I hope that wasn't aimed at me." When I don't respond, I see a crack appear in his mask as he puts down his cup, leaning toward me. "You know you can trust me, right? I rescued you from execution!"

"I know—" I try to explain, my feelings tangled in my chest as I attempt to sort through my insecurities, but he cuts me off before I have the chance.

"Remember who their father is, that he enslaved you and ordered your death." His voice is cold and cruel now, much like how I had imagined him to be, every inch the high magician. As if I need reminding, I know that every breath I take is on borrowed time. I shouldn't be alive, it's only by the grace of the Great Mother that I am still here. My whole life changed in the space of minutes, and I'm still half convinced that I'm in a dream and I'll wake any moment with those hated chains around my ankles.

Pushing away from the table, I leave my barely touched porridge and walk towards the door, hearing him sigh and begin to follow me.

"Clarissa, where are you going?"

Frustration pulses through me like I've never felt before, and with an anger I didn't know I possessed, I turn again to face him.

"Whatever the priests have planned for me will be far more pleasant than this conversation." My words lash out like a whip, and they almost seem to hurt him physically as he winces, falling back down into his seat, rubbing his hand over his face, messing up his hair in the process.

"I'm sorry," he mutters behind his hand, before dropping it and looking at me with his own frustration clear in his blue eyes. "I just feel so useless. I want to help, but I *can't*. I'm tied in ways I can't even begin to explain."

Watching him, I can almost feel his self-loathing as he leans back in his chair, scowling at the pile of papers at his side. Do I trust him? Yes, despite what I said to him, I do trust him. It's a fragile, newly formed trust, and I still half expect someone to jump around the corner and tell me this is some sort of elaborate joke. I wait by the door for a moment longer, but with a quiet sigh I return to the table, taking my seat opposite him and picking up my glass.

"Okay," I say softly, not bothering to expand or explain, and from the look of quiet relief he gives me, I know he feels the same.

"Okay," he replies, going back to his breakfast.

THE WALK TO meet Priest Rodrick is tense and silent, the only noise is the clicking of our shoes on the stone floor, almost in time to the beat of my thundering heart. Once we reach the chapel, Grayson pulls the priest to the side and has a tense, heated conversation before he storms out with barely a goodbye. Whatever the priest said to Grayson really wound him up, and from the smug grin plastered on his face, he knows it.

For once, the priest is silent as he leads me deeper into the castle, but from the sick, satisfied glances he keeps shooting me, I can tell he is enjoying my discomfort. Discomfort which turns to fear with each step taking us closer to the elf. Part of my brain is screaming at me to turn and run. After all, I'm not wearing chains anymore, I could take my chances with the guards. Dressed like this, they would pause before reaching for their crossbows, but...no, I've seen the guards train, they are ruthless—shoot first, ask questions later. I wouldn't stand a chance.

"Go." Rodrick's voice snaps me out of my thoughts and I realise we've reached the hidden staircase. Swallowing the bile that's threatening to make an appearance, I take a deep breath and step into the hidden alcove, and slowly start to descend the stairs. When I reach the bottom, the same guards lead me into the locked underground room, and the roaring sound of the forge and a hammer hitting metal greets me, a wave of heat making sweat bead on my skin.

I debate not going into the room, knowing I'm going to end up getting hurt either way, but the thought that they could take me away from Grayson if I don't comply has me stepping over the threshold. There are some things worse than death, and I know Grayson is saving me from many of those, not to mention I'm beginning to like the mage.

As soon as I enter the room, the pounding of the hammer stops, and although part of me is screaming not to do it, I raise my eyes to see the elf is glaring back at me. It's a long distance, so I shouldn't be able to see his expression, but I can *feel* his disgust. Scurrying into the cubby, I collect my supplies and take a moment to breathe and calm my racing heart.

Returning to the same place in the room from the other day, I ignore the dagger-like stare of the elf and frown down at the floor. There is a patch where the marble of the floor is starting to peer through, but there's still muck coating it and the surrounding area, so I set to my task. Last time I mopped the floor first and ended up turning the dirt to mud, which made my task that much harder, so I decide to sweep the floor first, removing as much of the surface dirt as possible. However, this means I have to leave my little corner of relative safety.

You've survived in situations far worse than this. He's a prisoner, just like you. Get on with it, my inner voice chimes, and I realise that it's right—I *have* survived worse than this. The elf might hate me, but he hates the guards more.

Gripping onto my broom as if it's a weapon, I begin to sweep, refusing to let him terrorise me. I'm acutely aware of his presence and ignore that tugging *pull* I feel every time I'm near him. A couple of times I think I see him raise his hand to his chest, rubbing at a spot just under his collarbone, but every time I lift my head to look, he's studiously ignoring me.

After the first hour, I realise I'm waiting for something to happen—what, I'm not sure—but when it doesn't come I find myself falling into a trance. The work is menial, I don't really need to focus, and as I switch from sweeping to mopping the rest of the dirt ground into the floor, I switch off. Although as a slave you're always alert, waiting for the next task or punishment, you begin to tune out of the tasks, your mind taking you somewhere more pleasant. You have to, otherwise the reality of your life would drive you mad. So although I'm aware of the elf, that pull in my chest telling me where he is even when I'm not looking, my mind starts to drift.

I lug my second bucket of clean water over to the spot I've been cleaning when I start humming under my breath. It's quiet, and I'm far enough from the elf that he shouldn't be able to hear, especially over all the noise he's making as he pounds the metal against the anvil. I don't know where I learned the song, perhaps from one of the other slaves, or from some long-lost part of my past, but it comforts me. If there are any words to it, I don't know them, but the tune is lilting and always struck me as magical. When I hum it, I feel strong, protected, like I've got someone watching over me, and even if that's all stuff I've made up in my head, it helps me through my days.

I'm so caught up in my task and the song that I don't

realise the ring of metal on metal has stopped. The elf seems to have a routine, putting the metal into the forge and then working it on the anvil only to repeat the whole process until it suits his standards, so it's not unusual that the hammering halts. However, I should have noticed when he was quieter than usual.

"What are you singing?" I almost drop the mop when he speaks, my head jolting up so quickly that my neck screams in pain as I jerk a muscle. He's watching me, his slanted, feline eyes tracking my every movement. I think about not responding, I don't owe him anything, after all, but seeing his frustrated expression makes me pause. He doesn't want to talk to me, that much is obvious, but he can't hide his curiosity, and it's clear to see that's annoying him.

"I don't know," I reply honestly.

I could elaborate, tell him that the song comes to me in my dreams, always when I'm at my lowest, like the Mother knows I need to hear it. But I don't, I simply stare at him. I wish I wasn't, but I can't seem to pull my eyes from him. He's shirtless, wearing only a leather sash that crosses over his chest with various tools hanging off it, his dark leggings hugging his legs. Tattoo's cover his chest and back, some are words, all in a twisting font that seems to wrap around his body. I don't recognise the letters as our own, so even if I could read, I still wouldn't be able to understand what they say. On his back, he has a large tattoo of a huge, twisting tree. I want to see it up close, see the detail and run my fingers along the—

What are you thinking? He's an elf, the enemy! my inner voice chides, and I rip my eyes away, lifting my mop once more as I drop my head, using my hair to hide the furious blush covering my cheeks.

"It's one of the songs from the mountain tribes. I

recognise it." My mop stills, his words reverberating through me. The mountain tribes, formidable people who are used to living in harsh conditions. Their warriors are renowned for their ferocity in battle, and as a people they're very protective of their women. How would I have learned a song from them? The Kingdom of Arhaven doesn't have the best relationship with them, although I don't know why. I once saw their party of dignitaries they sent to the peace talks several years ago. I had been scrubbing the ground in the front courtyard when they arrived, covered in furs and emitting a vibe that felt anything but peace-like.

Why is the elf telling me this? He doesn't have to give me this information, I haven't asked for it, so why would he do this? Frowning to myself, I continue with my task, my thoughts twisting with the new information I have, and the confusing elf who gave it to me. Silence stretches between us, and the shuffling of chains and banging of metal begins again, so I know the elf has returned to his work. I'm not sure how long we continue like this for, but I have refilled my bucket of water several times before he speaks again.

"Your injuries—they're healed?" Blinking at his sudden words, I realise I had zoned out, my thoughts completely caught up on the mountain people. I don't know why, but I've always been fascinated by them, and now I find that I've been hearing their song in my darkest hours, it's making me think.

I don't reply, but I can feel his gaze burning into me, so I stop mopping and when I glance up, I see he's watching me once again. His expression is confusing. Whilst his words were carefully neutral, like he was just asking about the weather, he looks angry, no, furious, enough so that I flinch away when his eyes flick up to meet mine. What have I done to invoke that kind of hatred? Is it because I'm human? Is it as simple as that?

Don't play coy. You hate him because of his race as well, you shouldn't be so surprised. Sure, we're mortal enemies, but it's not hate I feel towards him, I don't know what I feel. Scared, anxious, curious... My feelings are just so tangled that it's difficult for me to separate any of them. Does that make me a traitor to my own people?

I certainly don't like him and don't want to be around him, but that's because of how he acts, not because of his race. Why should I blindly hate someone who hasn't done anything to me just because we are told to?

I don't know what he sees as I go through this thought process, as something in his face changes, almost a flash of surprise before he's scowling again and turns away to work on his task.

"Yes." My voice is quiet, barely loud enough to be heard over the roaring of the fire in the forge, but his head whips up as he catches my words. "High Mage Grayson healed me."

He contemplates what I said, shifting his weight as if he can't stand still. "A mage healed you? A high mage at that." His words are more to himself than a real question for me. He seems to mull over my words before something in him snaps and he grabs the unfinished sword from his workstation. In a movement too quickly for my human eyes to track, he appears in front of me, sword pointed at my chest. "Who are you?" he demands, suspicion lining his face, his voice sharp. Instinctively, I jump back a step, but I don't run away, some deep part of me knowing he won't hurt me. I don't know where this feeling came from, he's not exactly exuding calm.

"I'm no one." I'm proud of myself that my voice

doesn't shake as I face down the elf. I push the truth of what I'm saying into the words, I *am* no one. Giving me a fake name and dressing me in pretty clothing doesn't take away that fact, no matter what Grayson keeps telling me.

"A high mage wouldn't heal a nobody, you must be important," he comments, but even he sounds unsure, my calm appearance throwing him off. Most people wouldn't be composed when facing the threat of death, but then I'm not most people. As a slave, I spent every day wondering if this would be the day I died, so I'm embracing these brief periods of freedom, even if it's temporary. Taking a deep breath, I step forward so the tip of the blade is just touching the delicate skin beneath my collarbone.

"I've faced pain and death every day of my existence, you don't scare me." Again, my voice is steady, even though my traitorous body begins to tremble under his stare. Hearing the truth of my words, he drops his arm down to his side, the unfinished sword still clutched tightly in his grip.

"Are you being punished?" His slightly accented words are laced with confusion, as if I'm a puzzle he can't work out.

Pushing up the cuff of my dress I show him the marks on my arm, the slave number and black X's that mar my skin. "I'm just as much a prisoner as you are." Judging from the shocked expression on his face, I've surprised him. Feeling self-conscious under his intense stare, I pull my arm back to fix the cuff of my sleeve, but his hand darts out and grabs my wrist. A gasp escapes my lips, his hold firm but not painful as he turns my wrist over, his thumb rubbing over the raised brands, then the Goddess mark above it. That sensation of power rolls through me again, the strange pull I feel toward the elf igniting in my chest. Our eyes meet and fire, determination, and an emotion I can't name greet me in his gaze.

"A slave." His words are so quiet I almost don't catch them. The elf shakes his head slightly, opening his mouth to say something else when the sound of booted feet marching towards us has us both backing away. As soon as he lets go, the pull lessens, but the feeling of power, of strength, stays with me for a moment, lingering, like it's giving me the chance to remember what this feels like.

The elf returns to his work just as the soldiers enter the underground room. Looking down at the patch of floor I've scrubbed, my gut clenches as I see how little of it I've actually managed to clean—less than a quarter of the room.

"You call this clean?" The voice makes terror flood through my system as the guard repeats the same words from the last time I was here. He circles me and I finally get a good look at him. He's wearing the green uniform of the royal guards, but his jacket is lined with gold, showing his seniority. Scanning the room, his eyes narrow on the elf before coming back to me, suspicion making his otherwise handsome face look cruel. "You're alive and—" His eyes run over my body, lingering on my breasts, making me blush, but I refuse to hide my face. "Alive and unharmed."

Spinning on his heel, he stalks towards the elf, his every step promising violence until he stops just in front of the work bench. He's either brave or stupid getting that close to his prisoner and goading him, or he trusts in the aim of the guards who are now standing in the doorway, their crossbows aimed at the elf.

"What's the problem, filth? We give you a new plaything and you leave it alone. You killed all your other minders, what's different?" he spits, provoking the elf who looks frozen. Not frozen in fear, but frozen with a quiet rage, his eyes promising retribution, but the senior guard doesn't realise or doesn't care. "Is it because she's a girl? Pretty thing. Shame really." Clicking his fingers, the two guards from before come forward and grab my arms, dragging me back, putting space between the elf and me.

My heart hammers in my chest, my breaths ragged and uneven. I know what's going to happen, but that doesn't stop the fear from threatening to swallow me whole. Something in my chest shifts, an undeniable pull, and my eyes flick up to the elf who is watching me carefully. He doesn't say a thing, he doesn't even move, but I feel like he's trying to tell me something, to be strong, like I had been with the sword pressed against my chest. I knew he wasn't going to hurt me and that assurance made me brave. But no matter how much I wish it was otherwise, I'm not strong. Shaking my head, I tear my gaze from the elf and look around for any signs of mercy, but am met only with unforgiving expressions. That warm, tingling sensation I'm beginning to associate with my Goddess mark fills me, and a sense of calm washes through me

"Stay strong, daughter."

Gasping, I look around to see if anyone else heard the lilting, comforting voice of the Great Mother, but quickly realise she has only spoken to me. Whatever her plan or reasoning, she needs me to experience this, it's all for some greater purpose. At least, that's what I tell myself. I have to believe that my suffering is for a reason.

Taking a deep breath and drawing courage from the fact the Mother is with me, I meet the eyes of the elf just as the first booted foot kicks into my leg, causing me to fall to the ground. The cry that escapes me is filled with shock, pain, and anger, so much anger. As I lie on the dirty marble floor, their sharp kicks and jabs shattering my body, that anger builds and twists. They may break my body, but they won't break my mind.

Chapter 15

The next couple of days fall into a routine. Grayson and I eat breakfast together, and then he takes me to the priest, who in turn takes me down into the bowels of the castle. I scrub away in that underground room until the guards come back and beat me in front of the elf before making me climb the stairs where Rodrick meets me and takes me back to Grayson. The magician is always quiet as we walk back to his rooms and he heals me, my strange gift of amplifying his magic making the process so much quicker. My presence as Lady Clarissa hasn't been needed since the other week, and although I hate my daily task, I don't have to pretend to be anyone else.

Grayson, Wilson, and I are sitting around the table in his dining room as I eat the stew Jayne prepared for me. She's been slowly adding richer food to my diet, and I've started to notice the difference in my body. I feel stronger, like I have more energy, although that could be the daily healing from Grayson. My figure is starting to slowly fill out, my bones not sticking painfully through my skin any longer. It will be a while before I don't look gaunt and half starved, but I feel better than I have in years.

Wilson has joined us for the evening, as he often does, chatting away happily about some gossip he heard about one of the ladies who is visiting court. He seems to have made it his mission to make me laugh, and each evening he has another wild tale to tell me. I have no idea how much of what he's telling me is true, but I look forward to seeing him and hearing whatever ludicrous story he has for me that day.

Today, he's telling me about one of the ladies that plied a palace magician with alcohol and then convinced him to use his magic on her to make her more beautiful. Leaning back in the chair, I watch as the young magician weaves his story, his hand gestures getting bigger the more enthusiastic he gets.

"—and then, her hair fell out! Right there in the middle of dinner!"

"You're exaggerating," Grayson critiques, but he's smiling as he leans back in his chair nursing his glass of wine, the most relaxed I've seen him in days.

"Ha! She's now fashioned the remainder of it into some ridiculous comb over. Next time you see her, have a look and then tell me who's exaggerating."

I can't hold back my laugh at Wilson's feigned hurt expression at the thought we might not believe his crazy story, but I have to admit this one has more of a ring of truth than most of his nightly updates.

"Well, there you go, don't drink and use magic folks." Grayson sips from his glass of wine again and then chuckles at the irony of his statement. I had tried the bitter liquid, but recoiled at the burning sensation, and I still don't understand the draw.

"So, magicians shouldn't drink?" I haven't been around many magicians other than Grayson and Wilson, so I'm still learning what's acceptable and have come to realise they are bound by a far stricter set of rules than the rest of us.

"It's discouraged. One glass with dinner is accepted, but drunk magicians make mistakes."

Frowning at Grayson's comment, I fight a shudder that runs through me. I've witnessed first-hand what alcohol can turn a person into, and the thought of what a magician, an individual with that much power, could do is a scary thought. They seem to have a strict set of rules that I can't understand. Why is this allowed when simple things like getting married isn't permitted without the approval of the higher magicians? "Why not ban it then?"

"Sometimes magicians need to forget some of the things we see..."

The haunted expression on Grayson's face makes me regret asking the question. He doesn't talk about it much, but I know he's been stationed at the front line of the war with the elves for a long time. He feels guilty that he left his legion behind to come save me and that he's stayed here since. It can be seen in the tightness of his shoulders and the tension around his eyes. Not that he would tell me, but I've seen him standing at the windows with a glassy look, and I know he's not really seeing the view.

"That reminds me of the time when Balin visited the castle!"

Wilson weaves another impossible story that has me laughing and the high mage smiling as he sips his wine. Grayson likes having the young mage around, and I'm not really sure how they know each other, but they have more of a sibling type relationship rather than a mage and his superior. I have to admit that I look forward to Wilson coming over in the evenings, especially since he acts as a buffer between myself and Grayson, always filling any empty silence with chatter. I'm very fond of him and his cheery disposition.

Does that make him my friend? I've never had friends before, so this is something I'm not used to. I enjoy seeing him, he makes me smile, I trust him not to hurt me, and I would be upset if anything happened to him.

Smiling at the thought, I lean back in my chair as I watch the mage. My friend.

Movement to my left has me glancing over as Grayson shifts in his chair. Does that make the high mage my friend too? He's done nothing but help me, he heals me daily, and makes sure I'm fed and comfortable. He scares me sometimes, but I do trust him not to harm me. Under the table so no one can see, I tick off the same criteria I used with Wilson on my fingers.

I enjoy seeing him, yes. He makes me smile—it's not as easy as with Wilson, but he does—and I like being around him, he makes me feel safe. Would I feel upset if he was harmed?

An anger so deep and fierce rises within me that the glass in my hand shatters at the thought. I don't even notice as the shards cut into my hand, the room going silent they turn to stare at me and the broken glass. They seem to realise something is going on with me, that this wasn't just a clumsy accident.

"Clarissa, are you okay?"

Taking a deep breath, I meet Wilson's concerned eyes and see him recoil slightly at the anger there. I immediately feel guilty, but it's not enough to stop the swirling rage that's building inside me.

"Clarissa." Like a cornered mountain lion, I follow the voice and spin my head to look at Grayson, narrowing my eyes at the command in his tone, the top of my lip curling back in a snarl. "Stop." The command rolls through me. "Everyone is safe. I'm not sure what's upsetting you and I can't help unless you talk to me."

I continue to stare at him, the swirling anger twisting with something else as I try to comprehend his words. "Has she gone into *euisa*?" Wilson whispers, but I don't take my eyes off the high mage.

"No, she doesn't have magic, she couldn't have," he tells the younger mage, but there is a note of uncertainty in his voice. He keeps his eyes locked on me as he speaks. "But we've triggered something, look at her wrist."

Following their gazes, I see my wrist is glowing despite the cuff that's covering my mark, the purple glow shining through the fabric. A fierce need to protect rolls through me and I push out of my chair and stalk towards Grayson, our gazes locked together. That is until Wilson coughs awkwardly and pushes up from his chair.

"I should go—"

"No," I snarl, cutting him off. Prowling around to him, I grab him by the collar of his uniform and drag him with me as I go back to Grayson. Then, in a move that's completely out of character for me, and one I'm sure I will look back on with horror, I climb into Grayson's lap, pulling Wilson so he's draped over me. It's awkward, and the high mage grunts a few times as I shuffle into a more comfortable position. However, with the two of them wrapped around me, I feel safe, the fierce need to protect placated.

"Okay... guess I'm staying then," Wilson mumbles, his words echoing through me as his jaw presses against my head. He says it like it's a chore, but as his arms close around me, I can't help but let out a contented sigh.

We stay this way for a while, the passing of time

strange, but the longer I stay in Grayson's lap, the more I relax, and the anger starts to disappear, only to be replaced with mortification as I return to myself.

"What just happened?" Voice tight, I try to keep as still as I can, ignoring the heat of Grayson's taut chest and how good the warmth of his body feels against mine. The comfort I'm getting from Wilson draping himself over me is different, but no less calming.

"I'm not sure," Grayson replies honestly, his arms tightening around me as he starts rubbing small circles on my back. "You reacted a little like you'd gone into *euisa*. The protectiveness is similar, the need to be close to the person who set it off." Frowning, I try to lift my head to look at him, but this turns out to be impossible with Wilson draped over me. Grayson has continually told me that I'm *not* a magician, that I have no magic, so I couldn't have gone into *euisa*. It makes no sense. "What happened?" he asks gently, and I know what he's asking —what set it off?

"I was thinking about friendship." My throat tightens and I clear my throat before I continue, "About how I've never had friends before…and about what I would do if either of you got hurt."

Both men still, and I worry I've said something wrong, that I've offended them. But then Wilson peels himself away from me and turns, placing a hand on my chin. He lifts it so he can look at me, Grayson's arms loosening around me so I can move if I want to.

"You consider us your friends?"

"Um, yes? If that's okay, I know I'm not—"

"Shut it," Wilson says with a grin, so I know he's not serious. "I'd be honoured to be your friend. I know that's not easy for you. Right, Grayson?"

The high mage stiffens beneath me at the question

and insecurity starts to creep in. "Yes, of course. Friends." Although he said it, I get the impression he wants to say something else, something more, but as I twist in his lap and look up at him, his expression softens. Suddenly realising I'm sitting in a grown man's lap, I start blushing furiously. Grayson's never made any moves on me, or demanded anything sexual from me, but sitting here, realising how close I am to him, I hope he doesn't think I'm trying to put my advances on him.

"I suppose I should get off your lap now." With an awkward laugh, I climb off of him and pull at my dress, making sure it's straight, unable to meet his eyes. "I'm going to head to bed now. Thank you for dinner." Bowing my head, I hurry from the room intending to hide for the rest of the night and mull over every agonisingly embarrassing moment.

"Clarissa, wait." Freezing as Grayson calls my name, I glance over my shoulder at him. My heart flutters in my chest, and I'm not sure what I expect him to say, but it's certainly not what he says next. "You won't be working with the priest tomorrow."

"Oh." I try to hide my disappointment, but I'm not convinced I pull it off from the sympathetic look Wilson's giving me. "Night." Hurrying away, I leave the room and head to my door, but I don't miss Wilson's snort.

"Smooth."

※

I SLEEP SURPRISINGLY WELL despite my twisting and churning thoughts about how I acted at dinner. But after a hot shower, I curled up in the large bed, surrounding myself with cushions, and fell straight to sleep.

A knock at the door announces Jayne's arrival as I sit

at the desk in front of the mirror, looking through the selection of lotions and makeup.

"You're Lady Clarissa today," Jayne announces as she bustles into the room, pulling open the wardrobe door and searching through the clothes with vigour. I have no idea where all these clothes came from, all of which are in the colours of the magicians. An uncomfortable thought comes to me as I watch Jayne through the mirror.

"Jayne, where are these clothes from? They're not Grayson's sister's, are they?"

"No, they didn't belong to Opal," she replies with a sad sigh, pulling out a dress and hanging it on the door. The garment looks lovely, but my thoughts are caught on something she said. Opal. Grayson sees me as a sister. Something twists inside me, something that feels like disappointment, but I push it aside. "Grayson made a couple with his magic, but the rest were made by the royal tailors." I'm not quite sure how I feel about this, and I have no idea how the tailors were able to make anything for me without measuring me. Perhaps Grayson told them. Shaking my head to rid myself of those thoughts, I stand and walk over to the maid where she's brushing down the skirt of the dress she selected.

"They're all blue."

"Yes, I'm sure it's a way to protect you, by claiming you as one of theirs."

The ladies I've seen walking around the castle have been dressed in many different colours, but so far all of my dresses, including the one I wear when I work with the priests, have been blue. Casting my eyes over the dress, I see it's much grander than the one I had worn to the library the other day. The top is fitted, deep royal blue in colour, and has sleeves that end at my wrists. The dress is fairly plain in design, but the golden stitches and edging on the bodice make it stand out much more. This is a statement in a dress if I've ever seen one.

With Jayne's help, I slip into the garb, and with the bodice laced up tight it accents what little bust I have, making me look more womanly now that I've started to fill out. The skirts are pleated, so they fall in a way that shows off my hips, with delicate golden patterns stitched into them. From a distance it just looks like the skirt is sparkling, but if you look closely, the patterns are actually the Great Mother's symbol delicately stitched over and over again.

There's a knock at my door, and after a moment Grayson walks in, his gaze immediately taking me in. His eyes skim over the fine dress before rising up to my face. I feel the tingle of magic, resisting the urge to reach up and touch my hair as his magic changes my locks from black to blonde.

"You look lovely."

Shaking my head, I try to ignore the tight feeling in my chest at his compliment, catching sight of one of the now curling blonde strands. "What's going on?"

I obviously didn't give the response he was looking for, as he reaches up and runs a hand through his hair as he sighs. "Prince Rhydian has returned from the warfront, there will be a meal and ball in his honour tonight." I understand why I'm wearing a nicer dress, but if the meal isn't until later in the day, why am I dressed up now?

"Your time is your own this morning. I've got a meeting I have to attend, and I'll come find you later to escort you to the meal." He turns to leave but pauses in the doorway, his back tense as he looks over his shoulder at me. "Be careful today."

As he leaves, I get the feeling there is something more going on than he was saying, and I realise that today is going to be difficult. With that thought plaguing me, I finish dressing and eat breakfast alone.

I try to decide what to do with my free time, knowing at the very least I'm going to leave these rooms and get some fresh air. As I exit Grayson's quarters and walk through the corridors, I can't shake the feeling that's hovering over me. Something is going to happen today, something important.

Perhaps I'll see if I can find Wilson, I muse to myself. The young mage has a way of always being able to lighten my mood. Now having a plan, I feel more confident as I enter the main corridor of the castle. It's much busier here. The wing where the magician's room is located is always quiet, but I suppose that's because most magician's don't spend much time here, being required either at the academy or on the frontline.

As I look around the hallway, I see many groups of young ladies, all of whom are watching the lords as they strut through the castle. I fight the urge to roll my eyes at the obvious ogling of both the males and females, and simply ignore it and walk past them. I still feel uncomfortable under their gazes, so used to being unnoticed before, but I can't let them see that it gets to me. Whispers follow me but, thankfully, no one tries to talk to me. My thoughts are too twisted to attempt to navigate a conversation with the vipers disguised as ladies.

I continue to search the castle for Wilson, sticking only to the areas I know and have already been shown. I don't want to get into trouble for wandering into some forbidden area out of ignorance. Although this part of the castle is carpeted and there are tapestries on the walls, I can't help but feel uneasy, like I'm being watched and they know I shouldn't be here. That I don't belong.

"Lady Clarissa, right?" A voice cuts through my musings, making me jump slightly, and put more distance between myself and the person who's appeared at my side. Looking at the woman who surprised me, I can't help but wonder what's happened to me, how she managed to sneak up on me. I've always been very good at knowing my surroundings, but this last week it's like I've lost that ability.

"Yes, I am," I reply, looking over the lady again and realising I recognise her. She was the one next to me in the choosing ceremony who stood up to the snobbish lady. She's wearing the same colours from the ceremony, but her dress is much less formal, her bright, curling auburn hair falling free around her face. "You're Lady Aileen?"

"You remembered my name." It's a statement rather than a question, but I don't miss the slight note of surprise in her accented voice, like she hadn't expected me to remember her.

"You remembered mine," I counter, the corner of my mouth lifting in amusement.

"Aye, but I wasn't the one who received a Goddess mark and then disappeared."

"Grayson has been keeping me busy—" I start to explain before realising how what I just said would sound. Blushing furiously, I try to clarify, mortification filling me. "Not in that way. I've been working with him, helping him," I babble, my words coming out in a rush which I'm sure makes me look all the more guilty.

"Aye, I believe you." An amused smile spreads across her freckled face. "You're fun to wind up. Will you be attending lunch today?" I'm still trying to decide if she truly believes me or if she's joking—the laughter in her eyes telling me the answer—when I realise she's asked me a question.

"I hadn't realised it wasn't mandatory."

"Oh, it is. But you're Goddess blessed *and* a friend of a high magician, so the same rules don't apply to you." Shifting uncomfortably under her gaze, I simply shrug at her flippant comments. "I'll see you there," she chirps abruptly before spinning on her heel and walking back the way I've just come from. Remembering my own mission, I call out to her again.

"Oh, Lady Aileen, have you seen Mage Wilson?"

At my question, she quickly turns back to me, her eyes wide as a ferocious blush covers her cheeks. Shaking her head violently, she practically runs away from me and I have to fight back a laugh. Seems Wilson has an admirer.

Chapter 16

After aimlessly wandering around the castle and not finding the young magician, I finally get tired of all the stares and whispers following me, so I head to the one place I've always found peaceful. The farther I walk away from the main part of the castle, the quieter it gets, and as I reach the Queen's Courtyard and push through the doors, I smile when I see it's completely empty.

Although the country is in the grips of winter, with the pale sun breaking through the clouds and a gentle breeze caressing my skin, it's pleasantly warm and I don't need to worry about a cloak. The four fountains are working, the gentle sound of flowing water and the chirping of birds are the only sounds I can hear. Around each fountain is a circular border of exotic plants and flowers, with a stone bench built into each. As I stroll through the courtyard, I marvel at how peaceful it is even though it's surrounded by the castle on all sides. I've never seen anyone in here, only ever the occasional person hurrying through to get to the chapel on the other side.

I reach out and brush my fingers against the plants, a gentle smile on my face as I amble around each fountain, admiring them. The plants are that of some of the southern cities in Arhaven, the land is very different there. Where we have long winters and mountains, the other side of our kingdom—where we originated from—is full of deserts, rainforests, and pounding heat. By all means, these plants shouldn't survive here, but I can feel the faint, sticky feeling of magic coating them, and it makes me wonder who would waste magic keeping these plants alive when no one ever visits them.

Following the path of the fountain, I continue around until I reach one of the stone benches, taking a seat parallel to the other fountain. It's going to be a busy day and I can already feel the tension building in my neck. These days, where I'm required to be Lady Clarissa, I find them harder than when I'm working down in the underground room. Even though I'm humiliated and beaten, I don't feel like I have to pretend. Maybe some part of me still thinks I deserve it? Yet, if I follow the teachings of the priests, I have been deemed worthy of her blessing, and one step further than that, I've been given her mark. Instinctively, I reach across and touch the symbol, actually the words, in the language of the Goddess.

My beloved. A tingle runs through me, along with a sense of love, and I know that she's with me. Then why is it so hard for me to be Lady Clarissa? This is my life now.

My thoughts turn to the elf. Will he wonder where I am? I've been working in the underground chamber for the last five days. Will he think it's strange that I'm not there today? He mostly ignores me, but when the guards come to get me, he always stops his labour and watches them beat me. At first, I thought it was because he enjoyed it, enjoyed seeing a human being struck, but I've come to realise that the anger I see in his eyes is not aimed at me. When he observes and our eyes meet, and I get the feeling he is urging me to be strong. Sometimes, when I feel like I'm going to pass out from the pain, I think I can hear him. That strange pull, the tug that I always feel when he's around, it's like it connects us, and my delirious brain thinks that he's talking to me through it. Telling me I can get past it and not to let them win. I know it's all a delusion, that I'm not actually hearing him, that some part of my brain is creating what I need in that moment, but it's comforting nonetheless.

"Lady Clarissa?" The voice catches me so unaware that a shocked gasp escapes me as I twist on the bench to see who snuck up on me. Eyes widening, I quickly jump to my feet as I see Prince Jacob and, sketching an awkward, shaking curtsy, I try to calm my pounding heart. I never, *never* would have let someone get so close to me without my knowing before. What about me being "Lady Clarissa" turns the instinct off? Do I truly feel so safe that I drop all of my reflexes?

"Please, don't worry about that." His voice is closer now and his hand appears in my field of vision. Placing my hand in his, I straighten up and take in his slightly chagrined expression. "I'm sorry if I startled you."

"Don't apologise, Your Highness. My thoughts were miles away."

"You looked like you had a lot on your mind. Is there anything I can do to help?" He sounds sincere, and there's a slight crinkle between his brows as he gestures for me to sit back down. Perching on the bench, I shuffle over to make room for him next to me.

"That's very kind, Your Highness—"

"Stop with the 'Your Highness.' I thought I told you to call me Jacob." At first I think he's angry, but his smile tells me otherwise as he angles himself closer to me.

Raising my eyebrows at him, I look around to check that no one can overhear us. He must know that if I was caught calling him by his first name that I would be whipped, or worse. "I didn't want anyone to overhear me calling you that and think I was overly familiar," I reply in the politest way I can phrase it, as that's the other risk. People might think that the prince and I are… being intimate, and then Grayson would find out. I don't know why that is so important to me, it's not like I don't like the prince. He's handsome and kind, and there isn't anything going on between the high mage and me, but I can't help but think back to last night when I sat in his lap.

"You don't need to worry. No one really comes here," Jacob informs me, interrupting my musings, although I blush slightly at being caught out. "Do you know why?"

Shaking my head, a grin spreads across his face. "They say it's haunted." I bark out a chuckle before covering my hand with my mouth. Ladies don't laugh like that, but then Jacob starts laughing too, his infectious amusement encouraging my humour. Once we've settled down again, he picks up his story.

"This courtyard was created by my father for my mother. I'm not sure what was here before, there are no records in the library—I checked." Of course he did. That is exactly what I would expect of the scholar who was born as a prince. Smiling at his comment, I nod for him to continue his story.

"My mother was married before she married my father. She was the daughter of an important lord, and very young at the time—just turned eighteen. She was married off to one of the men from the mountain tribes." I can't hide my surprise at this piece of information. I had heard the queen had lost a lover and this was her place of mourning, but I didn't know the other details.

Nodding, the prince continues, "Her and her new husband lived in Morrowmer, but he had to travel back to his people a lot. It's said that they loved each other very much, despite her young age, and that the match was made for them. She and my father met at some of the court gatherings. I know that he had designs on her, but since she was married, she was untouchable. He was older than her and had just inherited the throne when his father, my grandfather, abdicated." I hum in acknowledgement, leaning back against the bench as I listen.

"One day, when her husband was on his way back from visiting his tribe, he was attacked by the elves and killed." My heart aches for the queen. I knew this story wasn't going to end well, but I can't imagine how much pain she must have been in, losing a husband so young. "My mother was not only a widow at eighteen after losing the love of her life, but her father had also just died—she was distraught. She knew she would have to marry again if she was to survive. My father was there when she needed him, and eventually they were married and the rest is history." He smiles, gesturing to the space we're sitting in. "This courtyard was built for her as a place of reflection, for her to visit when she needed to escape, a place of mourning."

We are silent for a couple of minutes as I mull over everything he just told me, but it's not a strained quiet, it's comfortable, companionable. "That's a sad story," I finally reply, before raising my eyebrows with a small, teasing smile. "It doesn't explain the rumour of it being haunted though."

"Ah, the rumour is that his ghost lingers here, trying

to find his way back to his lost love." Shuddering at the thought of being stuck here after death, I can't help but shake my head.

"That's funny, I've never found this place anything but calming." Looking around the space, I let a small, peaceful smile tug at my lips as I listen to the soft trickling of the running water, enjoying the silent presence of the prince next to me.

"Are you attending today's meal?"

The question comes out of nowhere and I frown as I sit forward to look at him. "Why do people keep asking me that? I thought it was mandatory?"

"It is." He shrugs, not answering my query before tilting his head to one side as he contemplates something. "You've become a bit of a mystery, Lady Clarissa."

"I see, you get to call me by my title, but I can't call you by yours."

"Oh hush, I'm teasing," he says with a grin, and I can't help but return it. "You see, you appeared out of nowhere on the day of the choosing ceremony on the arm of one of the most eligible men in the kingdom, and a high mage at that. You are then blessed in a way no one has ever witnessed before, only to disappear. You don't attend court, or any of the other social things noble ladies seem to enjoy. You're a mystery, one that I, and many other noblemen, would like to get to know better."

My heart jumps into overdrive, pounding in my chest as I jump to my feet. I can't afford for people to think I'm different, I'm supposed to be blending in. But if the prince has heard I'm not acting how the other ladies do, then I'm not doing a very good job of it. Jacob's eyes widen at my panic and he stands, reaching out as if to stop me from leaving, but I back away. "I better go, Grayson will be looking for me."

"Are the two of you together?" His voice sounds calm, like he's asking about the weather, but his fists are clenched until I shake my head.

"No."

"Then I'm going to keep pursuing you until you tell me to leave you alone."

I should tell him now, tell him to leave me be, that I don't want his advances, but for some reason that I can't explain, I hold my tongue. Instead, I nod and turn away, retracing my steps and heading back into the castle.

Hearing a hurried set of footsteps behind me, I glance over my shoulder to see Jacob striding towards me, his charming smile in place as he offers me his arm.

"Let me escort you, we are going to the same place, after all." My heart flutters in my chest as he links my arm with his, that ever-present blush reappearing on my cheeks with the contact.

"I'm supposed to meet—"

As if just thinking about the mage had summoned him, Grayson strides around the corner, stopping in his tracks as he sees me with the prince, his eyes going straight to our linked arms. All of a sudden, my skin feels like it's alive, every nerve ending alight as a wave of dizziness overtakes me. Closing my eyes, I take a moment to centre myself before opening them again, only to see myself linking arms with the prince.

What in the underworld is going on? Perhaps I'm coming down with a fever and it's making me delirious. Raising my hand to my head, I try to feel my skin to test if I have a temperature, except my hand doesn't move.

Why is she with him? She's blushing, I bet he's working his charm on her. She wouldn't be so close to him if she knew the truth. The thoughts keep coming, except they aren't *my* thoughts. Distinctly masculine, they feel familiar. *She looks so beautiful in the dress. Who are you kidding, she always looks beautiful, even in those rags the first day you found her.*

Grayson. These are Grayson's thoughts. I'm in his head. In a panic, I fling myself against his mind, hurling myself back into my own body. What just happened?

Looking between the two men, I'm relieved to see that neither of them look suspicious, especially not Grayson who is just scowling at the prince.

"Clarissa," he greets me, his voice cold but polite. "Prince Jacob." Acknowledging me before the prince would be a whipable offence if it was anyone else other than Grayson, but being a high mage has its advantages. Shuffling my feet awkwardly, I glance between them.

"High Magician," Jacob replies, with barely concealed dislike, before turning to me with a bright smile that promises all sorts of trouble. "It's been a pleasure, Lady Clarissa, I look forward to seeing you at the ball tonight. Perhaps you'll save me a dance?"

He doesn't give me time to respond before taking my hand in his and raising it to his lips, pressing a gentle kiss against my skin before scowling at Grayson and striding away. Watching his back as he leaves, I contemplate asking him to take me with him rather than having to deal with a now grumpy Grayson.

"What did he want?"

Flinching at the malice in his voice, I step back, putting some space between us, not that he notices, his narrowed eyes are still locked on the retreating prince. I debate not telling him, but I know that will only make him think we were discussing him.

"He was telling me a story about the Queen's Courtyard." This pulls his attention back to me, but his frown is still in full force. Before he can launch a barrage of questions regarding what we discussed, I decide to give him some of his own medicine. He seems to respond better to direct questions, so that's what I'll do. "What is your problem with him?"

Surprisingly, his defensive posture droops and he lets out a sigh, rubbing a hand across his tanned face. Closing the distance between us, he places a hand on my arm and starts to lead me through the corridor back towards the main part of the castle.

"The magicians and the royals have a bit of a tenuous relationship."

Confusion rolls through me. How is it a tenuous relationship when they work together against the elves? "But you fight for our safety. The magicians protect us, protect the kingdom."

"I'm glad you see it that way."

Frowning, I know there's more to this story than what he's telling me, but we're entering the more heavily frequented parts of the castle now. Ladies gathered in giggling groups seem to be around every corner, the short journey to the dining hall taking much longer than it should as we have to keep stopping to greet them. I can tell he's just as frustrated by the slow going as I am from his tight smile and polite tone his voice takes on as he greets them with his aloof, high magician mask. I'd be lying if I said I didn't feel slightly smug that he lets that mask down around me, not that I'd ever let him know that.

Eventually, we reach the hall and I can hear the buzzing of many voices echoing from the large arched roof. Anxiety lines my stomach as we pause at the huge wooden doors. Glancing up at Grayson, I give him a questioning look, which he returns with a smile.

"I'm just giving you a chance to prepare yourself. Whenever we are around large groups of people you tend to get this startled rabbit expression and you glance around as if looking for somewhere to hide."

"Oh…" Frowning, I pull my gaze from his, looking down at the stone floor. This is not good. I'm supposed to be a lady. If people notice me acting that way, they are going to start trying to search for answers. My eyes lock onto my free arm which is crossing my body to rest on Grayson's forearm where it's linked with mine. The cuffs of the dress hide my slave marks, but I can almost feel them burning on my skin, making themselves known, a constant reminder.

"Don't worry, it's subtle. I only notice because I watch you—"

"You watch me?" My head snaps around to Grayson once more, and his eyes widen slightly as he realises what he's said.

"Well…Yes. I mean, you know—because the Great Mother tasked me with your protection."

A smile curls my upper lip as I watch him bumble through his words, so unlike the strong, sure high magician he usually is. Ignoring the small pang in my chest at the implication that the only reason he's with me now is because he was told to be, I simply force a chuckle.

"Don't worry, Grayson. I'm under no illusions that you harbour any desire for me."

"Why would you say that?" His voice is carefully neutral, a simple, light question, but I can feel his eyes on me waiting for my response.

"You're a high magician," I explain, surprised that he really needs me to spell it out for him. Looking around, I'm suddenly aware that there are other people milling about the doors and that anyone could hear us. Nodding towards an alcove, I lead him away from the entrance, lowering my voice once we reach it. "You would never want an ex-slave as a romantic partner."

"You have such a low opinion of yourself."

"No, I have a realistic opinion of myself. I was a slave, I must have done something, some crime—"

"You. Were. Eight," he spits, anger flashing in his eyes as he takes a step closer. My back is pressed up against the stone of the arched alcove, so I have nowhere to go as I watch him rage. "How could an eight-year-old do something so terrible that you were stripped of everything, even your *name*?" His words stir something inside me, something I keep locked away, that familiar anger awaking and stoking the dangerous thoughts that infiltrate my mind. Growling with frustration, he reaches out and places a hand on my shoulder, and I gasp at the sudden contact. "Clarissa, don't you see how people look at you? You're beautiful. You may have come from a different background than the rest of us, but you *are* a lady now." I snort, shaking my head. I have nothing and it wouldn't take much digging from one of the other nobles to figure that out. Sensing my despair, Grayson sighs and his hand leaves my shoulder to cup my chin, lifting my gaze to meet his. "If you were to go to Lake Haven you would find an estate with your name on it, including staff who are running it while you're here at the castle." His voice is quiet, and he looks like he's afraid of my response.

"You bought me an estate?" I ask, staring dumbly at him, not quite registering what he said. An estate, all in my name. A place to call my own. "You bought me a home?" I've never had a place to call home, so the fact he would do this for me... My breath catches in my throat as I fight back the sobs that threaten to rack my body. Eyes welling, I see him watching me with part happiness, part concern. With a huge, shuddering breath, I throw myself forward and wrap my arms around him. He lets out a slight "oomph" then he stills for a moment before returning my embrace, his chin coming down to rest on my head.

I'm not sure how long we stay like that for, long enough that I can hear people whispering as they pass us and enter the hall. However, I simply don't care. Right now, heart aching in my chest as I'm enveloped in the arms of my saviour, I feel at peace. He would stay like this for as long as I need him, I know he would, it's the type of person he is, but the longer we stay out here, the more rumours and whispers will follow us.

"So, you fancy me then?" My voice is muffled as I talk into his chest, enjoying the deep laughter he emits as he takes a step back with a broad smile, which is just for me.

"Clarissa! Looking good, my lady." Wilson's enthusiastic voice fills the hall as he squeezes into the small gap between myself and Grayson, so he's almost pressed up against me. "Oh, hello, High Magician Grayson, I didn't see you there," he says as he looks over his shoulder, spotting the magician just behind him. "I was too busy looking at this beautiful woman. Stop hogging her, it's my turn."

I can't fight the giggle his comments bring as he wraps his arms around me. I thought being touched by so many people would upset me, after all, I've avoided physical contact for so long. But I instigated the hug with Grayson, and even though Wilson's spontaneous hug startles me, it doesn't make me feel uncomfortable. In fact, after a brief pause, I return his embrace. Over his shoulder, I can see Grayson watching us with an unreadable expression on his face.

Once Wilson pulls away there's an awkward pause and he glances suspiciously between the two of us.

"Did I interrupt something?"

"No," both Grayson and I blurt, making Wilson grin as he nods and raises one eyebrow.

"Oh yeah, sure. I believe you." He snorts, a sly grin letting me know that he *doesn't* believe us. Walking out of the alcove, he glances over his shoulder to see if we're following him. "Come on, or we'll miss the toast."

"Are you ready?" Grayson's deep voice pulls my attention back to him, and as I look up at him, his smile gentle and eyes knowing, I feel my own smile form. I know he's asking me about the banquet, but I can't help but feel he means more than that—if I'm ready to truly become Lady Clarissa of Lake Haven. Taking his offered hand, I straighten my back and nod, my smile still firmly in place.

"Yes, I am."

Chapter 17

I've just settled myself at the table when a loud trumpet fanfare starts, and everyone in attendance pushes to their feet in unison. Following their lead, I stand, glancing at Grayson for a hint of what's happening when the royal family enters the hall. Prince Rhydian is walking alongside his father, the queen and the other two princes following behind. Seemingly as one, the room bows and I hurry into a curtsy, holding it until I hear the scrapes of chairs. Peeking up, I see the royals taking their seats at the table at the head of the room.

The rest of the hall has been set up with long tables along each wall, forming a square of free space in the centre of the room. Grayson and I are sitting at the table to the left of the royals, closest to the royal table. He informed me beforehand that there's a table plan and everyone is sitting by hierarchy, so as a high mage, Grayson is only just below the royals. Sitting with us are several of the king's advisors and other nobles, and I notice that Wilson has been placed further down the table. I wanted to ask why he's so much further down, but a slight shake of Grayson's head has me pausing, stilling my tongue.

The king remains standing as the rest of the royals take their seats, his gaze scanning the people gathered before him. He looks cruel. He once could have been handsome, but years of scowling have lined his face, his golden hair more white now than blond. But it's his eyes that make me nervous, a cruelty shines through that makes me want to avoid him at all costs. Eyes like that promise violence and remind me of the advisor I met in the library with Jacob.

"People of Arhaven, you are here to celebrate the return of my son, my heir, Prince Rhydian. He has been working with the soldiers on the front lines, fighting for our freedom against the elves." The king pauses, allowing the room to fill with hissing as the lords protest and bang their fists against the table when our enemy is mentioned. "So eat, drink, and be merry."

I flinch as loud cheers fill the room, tankards and glasses being banged on the table. A hand slips into mine —Grayson. Keeping my attention on the king, I absently squeeze Grayson's hand, silently thanking him. The simple act helps ground me, reminds me that although I'm surrounded by people who would kill me in a moment if they knew who I was, I have a friend here. I am not alone.

Clearing his throat, the king waits for everyone to quiet down again, his face falling into a scowl. "In other business, we have some guests." Sounding less than enthusiastic, the king waves his hand and the large wooden doors are hauled open again. Although I don't know much about etiquette and how these things are run, I'm sure that introducing guests this way, as an afterthought, is an insult, and seeing the frown Grayson is throwing at the king, I think I'm right.

Murmurs fill the hall as the seated lords and ladies

whisper, watching as the new arrivals file into the centre of the room. There's a lot of them, I lose count after fifteen of them stride in. Mostly men, but even the females are large in stature, their hair dark like mine with feathers threaded through their braids. The men range from having long braided hair to none at all. Tattoos cover their skin, and they wear clothes fashioned from animal pelts. The male leading the group is wearing a headdress complete with a set of deer antlers. They fascinate me and I can't seem to drag my eyes away. One of the males in the middle of the group scans our table, his eyes appraising me for a second before moving to the others around me then flicking back and locking onto me. My breath catches at his intense gaze, his eyes narrowing before he looks away. Taking a deep breath, I lean back in my chair once his attention is no longer on me, the feeling of light-headedness making me dizzy.

What in the underworld was that? I can feel Grayson's eyes switching between me and the mountain man. Glancing over at the royal table to gauge their reactions to the newcomers, I see frowns of concern, even a flash of hatred in Rhydian's eyes. When I reach Jacob, I flush when I realise he's watching me. I'm starting to feel hot under all these gazes, so used to blending in that having this much attention, especially *male* attention, is making me uncomfortable.

Or is it? Don't lie, you enjoy having the mage and the prince watching you, my inner voice chimes in, and I have to admit it's right. There is something exciting about having them stare at me this way, looking out for me, but I'm sure that's all it is. Nothing would ever be able to come from a relationship with either, they simply want to protect me, possibly even be my friend, which is enough for me.

"A diplomatic party from the mountain tribes. They will be staying with us for a few weeks," the king continues once everyone has hushed, less than enthusiastic as he dismisses them with a flick of his hand, gesturing towards the row of free seats on the table opposite mine. The leader of the group scowls, confirming my suspicions that the king is not following diplomatic protocol with the visitors. Holding his position, the leader of the mountain folk glares at the king for a second with such hatred and disdain, that the atmosphere in the room suddenly changes. The guards subtly reach for their weapons, tension filling the hall as they wait for the order to attack, but thankfully it never comes.

Spinning on his heel, the leader of the mountain tribe strides towards the table, taking the seat at the top, the rest of his kinsmen following suit. The man who caught my attention is sitting second from the top, his eyes scanning the space again as if he's looking for someone, stopping as they land on me. He freezes, his body seeming to grow as he stares at me, his already impressive physique becoming *more*. I want to look away, his gaze too intense, but I can't. A sense of familiarity hits me so strongly that it's like a physical blow to the gut.

"Everything okay?" Grayson whispers, lowering his mouth to my ear. He's so close that his breath brushes against my skin, making me shiver at the sudden intimacy of the action. The man opposite scowls, his hand holding his knife in a white-knuckle grip. Around us, servers are bringing in large platters of food, the general noise rising as conversations start up.

"Who are they?" I nod towards the newcomers, and Grayson follows my gaze then leans back in his chair, taking a sip from his goblet. Following his lead, I reach for mine, bringing it to my lips and pulling a face as the bitter taste of wine coats my tongue. Quickly putting the goblet down, I push it away, feeling Grayson's amusement as he watches me.

"They're from the mountain tribes," he begins, before taking another sip of his wine. "They live in separate tribes all across the mountains, but they have representatives from each tribe, and an elected leader who helps unite them." I guess that explains the different clothing, tattoos, and hair styles.

"Why are they here? They look…angry."

"They always look that way. They're a serious lot. Life is hard for them in the mountains, and we haven't had the best relationship with them over the years. This is a big step and a show of peace having them come here," Grayson admits.

Looking around the room, I see many people are watching the tribesmen with suspicion, and Prince Rhydian is practically glaring at them. To their credit, the mountain people mostly ignore everyone else, talking boisterously amongst themselves as they tuck into the food served in large plates on the tables.

Placing some fish and potatoes onto my dish, I flash Grayson a grateful smile as I start to pick at my food. My appetite is increasing, but I still have to be careful. As I slowly eat, I tune out the sound of Grayson as he makes polite conversation with the men next to us, my attention on the mountain people and the man whose gaze never leaves me for long.

AFTER THE MEAL we retire to our rooms, Grayson leading me away, and I can feel eyes on me as we leave.

Not only of the mountain man, whose name I still don't know, but I can also feel Jacob's heavy gaze, which didn't leave me throughout the meal. I was relieved when Grayson suggested we leave.

I spend the rest of the afternoon with Jayne, chuckling at the stories she tells me of the servants' antics when the nobles aren't looking as she helps me dress for the ball. The gown she helps me into is stunning, a tight bodice with light, flowing organza sleeves which gather together in a thick cuff at my wrists. The skirt is multi-layered, the bottom tier hitting the floor with the top layers falling from my waist and gathering up behind me, making my hips look wider, giving me the womanly shape I'm lacking. The most beautiful thing about it is the colour. Still blue, but the deepest blue of the night sky, and scattered on the dress are tiny sequins that are unnoticeable until I move, the light catching on them and looking like glittering stars. My hair is styled up into a bun with some blonde curls framing my face. Settled on top is a diadem with a single, deep blue gem resting on my forehead.

"I can't wear this." Reaching up, I place my hand on the diadem to take it off, but Jayne slaps my hand away.

"Yes you can. Master Grayson picked it himself."

I try not to preen at the idea that Grayson selected this for me. I don't know why it makes me feel warm that he personally chose my clothes, that he imagined me in them. My cheeks grow hot and I know Jayne notices as she smiles smugly, playing with some stray strands of my hair.

"It looks like a crown, won't the royals be upset with that?" From what I know of them, they are cruel and fast to punish for any misdemeanours. The last thing I want to do is draw even more attention to myself. There is already enough whispering and attention on me without needing a glittering dress and crown to stir things up.

"They would expect you to dress up for a ball like this, anything less and they would take it as an offence against the prince. They'll assume you don't think he's worth dressing up for."

Rolling my eyes, I stare at myself in the mirror as I ponder Jayne's words. Either way, there will be a lot of attention and gazes on me. At least I'll have Grayson there to fend off anyone who tries to talk to me.

As if on cue, there's a knock on the door. Jayne goes to open it and I turn from the mirror, smiling as I wait for the high mage to enter the room. For the first time I feel good. I know I look nice and I want to see his reaction when he sees me. I try not to delve too deeply into *why* I'm so eager for him to see me in this dress.

The door swings open and Wilson strides into the room with his usual gusto, and I have to work really hard not to show my disappointment when Grayson doesn't follow him through.

"Mother above, Clarissa," he whispers as he reaches my side, circling me with wide eyes. He's uncharacteristically quiet, and it makes me nervous. Shuffling from foot to foot, I glance over my shoulder where I see he's still walking around me, a gobsmacked look on his face.

"Do I look okay?" I hate how vain I sound, but I trust Wilson's opinion and I don't know how to interpret his silence. He finally comes back around to face me, his eyes wide with wonder and a strange feeling falls over me. It's the same tingling feeling from the choosing ceremony, and my eyes lock onto the young magician as his magic flares for a second. It's over before I know it, and confusion settles over me, but before I can say anything, Wilson takes my hand.

"You look like a queen." Kneeling before me, he presses his forehead against my hand and stills, as if waiting for me to say something. Panicking, I raise my eyes and look at Jayne beseechingly, but she just shrugs, looking as confused as I feel.

"Um, Wilson. What's going on?"

My voice seems to shake him out of his stupor as he stands back up, his eyes boring into mine, and I can see the moment his eyes clear. I've seen Grayson do this a couple of times, and it's always when he receives a vision, so I'm assuming that's what's happening now. With a wide grin and slightly awe-filled expression, he takes hold of my other hand and takes a step back, admiring me.

"Sorry, the Mother sent me a vision," he says, confirming my suspicions before pulling me into a hug. With an "oomph," I'm roughly pulled into his embrace which I return with a chuckle, but after a second I push back from his touch. He's not getting away that easily.

"Are you going to explain what just happened? You kneeled before me." Pushing the fear away at the thought, I try to sound authoritative, but I know I failed because he just grins and shakes his head.

"I can't tell you, the Mother was explicit in that." Scowling, I try to walk away, fed up with never knowing what's happening. Quicker than I would have thought possible, he grabs my wrist and pulls me to a halt.

"Know that you are exactly where you need to be." His voice isn't his own, his eyes glazed over again, and I swear I hear the Mother talk *through* Wilson. Heart pounding in my chest, I nod dumbly, not finding any words. If the Mother says this is all I need to know, then I have to trust in her that she knows what's best.

Eyes clearing once more, Wilson blinks and looks

down at where his hand is clutching at my wrist. With a noise of surprise, he quickly let's go, shaking his head as he mutters something quietly under his breath.

"Are you okay?" I inquire timidly, needing to know that Wilson is once again in charge of himself. Trusting in the Great Mother and seeing her take control of someone I love are two completely different things. I won't lie in saying that she doesn't scare me, especially when I see exactly how powerful she is.

"Yes, the Mother *chose* me. To send a vision to *me*." The awe in his voice breaks my heart a little. Grayson told me that Wilson has had a difficult life, and when he was chosen to be a magician that life didn't get any better. He had a tough time at the academy and eventually came to work in the capital as one of the castle magicians. He's never complained about his position or his lot in life, even though I've seen the looks that the others in the castle give him.

"Anyway, we should go. Grayson's in a meeting, but he'll meet us there."

It's only then that I realise he's dressed in his smart uniform and I have a sense of déjà vu from the last ball I attended. Linking my arm with his, we walk through to the dining room, and with a quick good night to Jayne, we leave Grayson's quarters.

The journey to the ballroom is quiet, we don't speak much, content with each other's company, but as we enter the main corridors the noise of people talking hits us. The hall is full of beautifully dressed people, much like the last time Wilson and I took this walk, and the voices dull to a hush as we walk through, many sets of eyes watching us, whispers following us.

"They're just jealous that we look so damn good," Wilson whispers to me, which puts a smile on my face.

It's a small one, but a smile all the same. Reaching the entrance of the hall, we pause as we're announced before walking into the grand room and heading straight for the buffet table.

"I hate these things," he whispers to me as he nods at a portly gentleman, the only other person by the food. Snagging a glass from the tray of a passing server, Wilson drinks half of the pale, sparkling liquid in one go.

"We don't have to stay long, right? We just have to show our faces?" I question hopefully, as I glance around the room, spotting Aileen and the gentleman who I assume is her father from the resemblance between them. Wilson's chuckle pulls my attention back to him, and I raise one eyebrow at his expression.

"I can leave as soon as Grayson arrives. It's you I feel sorry for."

"What do you mean?" A sinking feeling fills my stomach.

"You're the shiny new plaything. I've been hearing rumours about you." His smile widens as he sees my expression, laughing at my discomfort at the prospect of people talking about me. "I think Grayson is going to have to share you with others more. The fact you disappear for days without an appearance is starting to become noticed."

I still. This is more serious than a couple of rumours. If people are noticing that I'm not about, they might start to ask questions and go hunting for answers, which we can't afford for them to discover. Wilson is glancing around us, his attention caught on someone else on the other side of the room rather than my internal panic. Grabbing his hand, he looks back at me, frowning at my severe expression and realising something's upset me.

"Does Grayson know?"

"Yes, but—"

A loud banging causes the room to fall silent, the music stopping as everyone turns to the archway. The hall is full of well-dressed people now, and I'm sure that there can't be many more arriving.

"Announcing, the King and Queen of Arhaven."

Dropping into a curtsy, I feel Wilson bowing next to me, silently pleased that I didn't need to be prompted this time. Perhaps I *can* do this after all. Rising, I see the king and queen walking towards their thrones, holding hands as the crowd parts for them. "Their Royal Highnesses, Prince Rhydian, Prince Michael, and Prince Jacob."

"The king didn't attend the last ball," I whisper to Wilson, as we watch the finely dressed royals take their thrones, the princes following closely behind.

"No, neither him nor the queen usually attend these things. It's only because Rhydian is back that he's here. He'll stay for an hour before finding a young lady and then invite her back to his quarters. Oh…" He stops as he sees my wide eyes, realising he's said too much. Lifting his glass to his lips, he throws back the rest of his drink before cursing under his breath. "I didn't say that."

"The king is sleeping with one of the ladies?"

He snorts, and I'm pretty sure I hear him mutter, "One of," before raising his gaze to mine. "I said too much. I had a drink before I came to pick you up and it's loosened my tongue," he says with a sigh. "Please don't say anything."

"Of course I won't."

The atmosphere in the room changes, and as I glance around I see everyone is facing the arched doorway once again. Standing there, wearing their leathers and furs, are the men from the mountain tribes.

The steward by the door appears anxious as he looks over them, and after a brief conversation with the men, he finally clears his throat.

"The men and women from the mountain tribes," he announces loudly, but he needn't shout however, as the room is so quiet you could hear a pin drop. Everyone watches the tribesman, but I turn my attention to the royals. The king and Rhydian are watching with barely concealed disgust. Michael just looks bored, his roaming gaze on the ladies mingling nearest his throne. Jacob is watching the advancing folk with interest, nodding his head to the leader as they come to stand in front of the thrones, dipping their heads once in acknowledgement before turning away and breaking off into groups.

The person whose reaction is the most interesting is the queen's, and I remember the story Jacob told me in the courtyard—the queen had once been married to one of the mountain people. She's leaning forward in her throne, her eyes wide as she skims her gaze over them. She tries to hide it, but I see the mix of excitement and pain that having these people here is causing her, and I'm not the only one. The king places a hand on her arm and whispers something to her that has her back stiffening and her face tightening. Nodding once, she pulls her arm from his grip and stands up before storming from the room.

If anyone thought her behaviour odd, no one comments on it, and as the musicians start playing again, couples gravitate to the centre of the hall and begin dancing.

"Mage Wilson, I see they let you out to terrorise us all again." Anger fills me from the insult aimed at my friend, but Wilson just grins as we turn to face the familiar woman.

"Ah, Lady Aileen, I had hoped to get through most of the ball before you sought me out, you hateful wench."

I stand awkwardly between the two as they glare at each other. Wilson's grinning like the cat who's got the cream, so I don't think he's offended by her comment, and just as I'm about to step in they begin laughing. Throwing his arm around her, he pulls her into his embrace before turning that grin on me, but I don't miss the adoring look she shoots Wilson.

"Clarissa, have you had the honour to be introduced to this pitiful excuse of a lady?"

I look between the two of them again, fairly sure they are joking based on the grins on both their faces, but I have no idea how to answer. I'm also pretty sure that Wilson is completely oblivious to the fact that Aileen is in love with him.

"Oh, have pity on the girl, Wilson. She looks like she's about to implode." Aileen grins, strands of her wild, curly red hair falling out of her updo. "We have met before, at the ceremony."

"Oh yes, I always forget you're still a baby," he says as he frowns down at her with mock disapproval.

"So you two know each other?" This much is obvious, but I don't know how to politely ask about their history, especially as they are throwing insults left, right, and centre. Thankfully, Wilson takes pity on me.

"We grew up together. Aileen's father came here for diplomatic work and brought this brat with him. I saw her threatening to beat up one of the spoiled children from the houses if they didn't share their toy, and I knew we were going to be friends."

"He adopted me, and seeing as we were both outsiders, we decided to stick together," she explains, turning to the buffet table behind us and filling up a plate with sweets and pastries. They start playfully bickering once again and I study them. They're easy around each other, and Wilson is relaxed and happy in a way I only see when we're alone and away from the prying eyes of the nobles.

I like her, I realise, a faint smile gracing my lips as I watch them. She's always seemed different to the other ladies, having views on the lower classes that others don't share, not to mention she's friends with Wilson.

I'm glad he's got someone here other than me, in case... I pause at the thought. In case of what? That I wouldn't be here. If I was killed by the beatings from the guards, or it's discovered who I am, or a whole host of other possibilities...I just have to hope that if anything does happen to me, he's not involved in any way. The thought of him getting hurt because of me makes me shudder.

"Lady?" a gruff, deep voice interjects behind me. I turn quickly, my skirts spinning around my legs, and find someone standing very close to me. Pressing my hand to my chest as if to still my pounding heart, I eye the man who spoke. It's the tribesman, the one who was watching me during the meal earlier. That tingling sensation returns as soon as our eyes meet.

Not this again, I think to myself as I rub my arms, as if the action will take away the feeling. His eyes lock onto my movements, as if he knows exactly why I'm doing it.

"I didn't mean to startle you," he states, and some might take that for an apology, but from the lilt in his voice I know he finds the fact he took me by surprise amusing.

He's tall, like the rest of his tribesmen, and his loose linen shirt and the wolf pelt thrown over his shoulder does nothing to hide his muscled physique. His sharp jaw and piercing, dark eyes bore into me, as if he can discover all my secrets with just one look. Dark hair reaches his shoulders, but the right side of his head is shaved and a tattoo marks the skin there, a swirling design the arches around his ear and down his neck. I can see a hint of a tattooed chest from the opening at the top of his shirt. He wouldn't be considered classically handsome, but his looks are striking, and I can't deny that there's a…pull. Not like the one with the elf, but like being around him makes me feel powerful.

Realising how close we are standing to each other, and that I'm staring at him, I take a step back and knock into the table, the plates rattling against one another. Hearing the commotion, Wilson turns around and, realising I hadn't followed him and Aileen down the table, hurries to my side, his face uncharacteristically serious.

"Is everything okay here?" His voice is polite as he places a hand on my arm. The tribesman follows the movement, narrowing his eyes at the action. I get the feeling Wilson isn't actually asking *me*, but I open my mouth to answer anyway.

"Will you dance with me?" The tribesman grinds out, his whole posture stiff and promising violence, but Wilson doesn't back down. He takes a step closer to me, his gaze still locked on the other imposing man.

"Clarissa," Wilson murmurs, his hand tightening on my arm, and his voice filled with caution and a warning. If I decide to go with the tribesman then he can't protect me. I don't know what type of agreement Arhaven has with the mountain tribe, but it seems fragile. Turning to the mage, I place my free hand on top of the one he has on my arm, squeezing it gently.

"It's okay, Wilson, I won't be far."

He turns to me, his eyes portraying the words he

can't voice. *Don't go, it's not safe. I can't protect you. Please.* Taking a deep breath, I squeeze his hand again and step toward the tribesman, placing my hand in his outstretched one. Ignoring his smug smile, I glance over my shoulder as we walk away, giving Wilson an apologetic look.

I know I'm safe. I have no evidence to prove this, but something about him tells me that he won't let anything happen to me. As we step onto the dance floor, he pulls me to a stop.

"Clarissa. Interesting name." His deep voice makes me shiver. I stiffen slightly at the way he says my forename, like he doesn't believe me. Clarissa might be a new name for me, but it *is* my name now. At least, that's what I keep telling myself. He places his hand on my hip and stares down at me as if he's trying to figure me out. Looking around, I notice people are watching us as we stand in the centre of the room, not dancing, not moving, just…standing. I raise an eyebrow and gesture to the others around us, but he grins at me. It's not the friendly, jolly type of grin, but one that reminds me of a wolf when it captures its prey. "This was the only way I could get you alone. I *don't* dance, at least not with your kind."

Blinking, it takes me a moment to process what he just said, then anger and outrage builds as I take a step back from him, not wanting his hands on me.

"My kind?" I spit, shaking my head in disgust at his attitude. If he really knew who—*what* I was—he probably wouldn't even be talking to me. "If we are so abhorrent to you, then why did you seek me out?" My eyes are burning as I stare him down, fists clenched at my sides.

His expression changes, as if he's seeing me for the first time, and something akin to shock forms on his face.

It's like he's reassessing me, seeing the fire and anger that burns within me. A knowing smile spreads across his lips and he takes a step closer, putting us within touching distance again. "There's something different about you, *Clarissa*." My heart speeds up, pounding in my chest. "I know you won't tell me, but I *will* figure it out."

Staring up at him, I refuse to let him see my fear. Not fear of him, but fear that he knows more than he should. Knowledge is dangerous. Instead, I make my face a mask of boredom.

"You know my name, are you going to tell me yours?"

He laughs, as if he can see straight through me. "Torsten, but my clan calls me Tor."

I'm just about to reply when I see movement over his shoulder. Leaning slightly to the side, I spot the youngest prince, with an expression of concern on his face, at the same time I feel a familiar presence at my back. Glancing over my shoulder, I see Grayson and fight the urge to groan.

"Clarissa, are you okay?"

"On first name terms with the prince, I see."

"What's going on here?"

They all speak at once, their voices merging so I can't tell who says what as they glare at each other with me in the middle. With all of them this close, my skin feels like it's on fire, my breath coming in pants and my body tingling. My vision closes in and I know if I don't get away, I'm going to pass out. There are too many sensations.

"I need air," I gasp out, as I push past Tor and Grayson, hurrying to the door. They call after me, my name cutting through the music, and I know everyone is watching me, but I need space. I'm worried someone will follow me, but I see Wilson nod at me before hurrying over to the squabbling trio of guys behind me.

I don't know what compels me to run to the Queen's Courtyard, but as soon as I step into the space, the cool night air brushes against my too hot skin, and I feel like I can breathe again. Uncaring that the stone is freezing and will seep through my dress, or that I might catch a chill out here, I take a seat on one of the benches. I'm lucky the cold doesn't seem to affect me as much as my fellow Arhaviens.

Leaning back, I look up at the stars above, enjoying the quiet peace, the only sound the gentle trickle of the fountains. When I was a child, I used to believe the stars were far away spirits that looked over us. I used to pray to them, ask for them to rescue me, to save me from my life as a slave. That soon got beaten out of me.

"You made quite a scene when you went running out of the ballroom."

With a gasp, I jump up from the bench, seeing Crown Prince Rhydian leaning against one of the other fountains. Cheeks flushing, I quickly drop into a curtsy. Why do people keep surprising me today? He must have been moving quietly, as I hadn't heard anyone enter the courtyard.

"Your Highness, I apologise, I just needed some space."

He watches me, his body completely still, the only noise between us is the water in the fountains. I don't know much about this prince, other than he's been fighting on the front lines, but I'm getting an uneasy feeling around him, like I shouldn't be out here alone with him.

"I can see why they're all fighting over you, you are quite alluring." He takes a step toward me, and I have to fight again the shudder his words induce. I become more tense with each step he takes, his movements quiet and fluid. Shaking my head, I look around to see if there is anyone else around us, someone who could help should I need it, or act as a distraction.

"I don't want anyone fighting over me."

Snorting, he shakes his head as he continues to prowl toward me, one slow step at a time. The closer he gets, the stronger my gut instinct is screaming, *get away!*

"Isn't that all you ladies want? Princes and magicians fighting for your hand."

"I'm sorry to disappoint you, Your Highness, but I'm not like most ladies." My voice hardens, my anger starting to flare up again. I'm tired of being treated like an object, something to order around, to fight over. His eyes light up as he steps in close, his hand snaking out and landing on my hip. My unease doubles and something grows within me, something unfamiliar and unknown. I want to push him away, to shout at him to never touch me again, but this is the crown prince. Goddess blessed or not, I would be executed faster than I could blink if I laid a hand on him.

"I'm beginning to see that." Like a viper, his other hand shoots out and grabs my left arm, turning it so he can see the mark on my wrist, his thumb brushing at the fabric concealing it. If he keeps doing that, he will see my other marks hidden below the cuff. Fear courses through me and I know I need him to let go before it's too late. Even through the light fabric, every time he brushes over my Goddess mark, nausea runs through me.

"Prince Rhydian, what are you—"

"Lady Clarissa, there you are. I've been looking all over for you." The queen's voice fills the courtyard, and

I've never been more glad to see anyone in my life. I swear Rhydian's eyes flash with something inhuman for a second before he pastes a smile on his face and takes a step away from me. As soon as we lose contact, a wave of relief floods through me, but I try not to let it show as I slowly back away from the prince as he focuses on the queen.

"Mother. What are you doing here?"

"I came for Lady Clarissa, we have some things to discuss."

There's a pause as the prince stares down his mother. It's obvious he doesn't believe her, and from her flushed face I would guess she came here for an entirely different reason. However, she holds her own, smiling pleasantly at her son, who simply narrows his eyes before nodding.

"Mother. Lady Clarissa," he says as a way of addressing his goodbyes, before stalking out of the courtyard with that unnatural grace of his.

The courtyard falls silent as the queen runs her eyes over me before sighing and walking up to one of the fountains, running her fingers through the water. She looks like she carries the weight of the world on her shoulders, and although I don't know her, I wish I could offer some way to help, to lighten that burden. I probably shouldn't, after all, her husband was the one to sentence me to a life of slavery as a child. But something about her is familiar, perhaps it's the shared feeling of loss that makes me feel close to her.

"You wanted to see me, Your Majesty?"

"I know you're smart, there's no need to pretend. You needed rescuing from my son, so I provided you with an excuse. I love my son, but he's too much like his father."

How am I supposed to reply to that? If I agree, then

I am insulting not only her son, but the crown prince, their heir to the throne. Instead, I walk up to the fountain she's leaning against and stand beside her, facing the water as I speak.

"Thank you." My whisper is so quiet I'm not sure she would hear it, but her soft smile and the incline of her head tells me otherwise. We stand in companionable silence, the queen and the ex-slave.

"Do you know why this courtyard is here?"

"I was told that it was a gift from your husband. There were some other stories too, but…"

"You are too kind, you can speak freely with me," she assures, before starting her story. "I was previously married, but he died. And my current husband, the king, had always wanted me. I was in this very spot when he told me that my husband had been killed. The ladies of the houses whispered that this was a romantic gesture, that the king built me a private place to grieve a lost love. But it wasn't. He is a jealous man, my husband. He built this place to remind me of the day when my whole world changed."

"Why do you keep coming here then?"

"I come here to remember, to remember exactly the type of person my husband is."

I want to ask what type of person that is, but I run out of courage, instead staring at the water. The sound of footsteps echo around us and the queen lets out a small sigh as she pushes away from the fountain.

"Good night, Clarissa, it was nice to meet you formally."

"Thank you, Your Highness."

Finally alone, I collapse onto one of the stone benches and stare up at the stars, my thoughts confused and tangled. It's been such a long day and I'm craving my ridiculously puffy bed, but I can't face the prospect of running into anyone else in the corridors. So, I pull my feet up onto the bench and wrap my arms around my knees, my skirts long enough that they cover my feet. Instead of praying to the stars that don't listen, I pray to the Great Mother for guidance and courage, because I get the feeling I'm going to be needing a lot of it soon.

Chapter 18

"You didn't come yesterday." The elf's lilting voice reaches me where I'm scrubbing the floor. There's a particularly stubborn patch of dirt on this section of the flooring, so I'm down on my knees again, scrubbing brush gripped tightly in my hands. It's tiring work, but something I'm used to, so I barely have to pause to look up at him.

"I had...other obligations to fill." He wouldn't understand if I told him part of the time I'm masquerading as nobility, it wouldn't make sense. Hell, half the time it doesn't even make sense to me.

I'm not sure how long I stayed in that courtyard last night, but eventually Grayson found me curled up on the stone bench. I was freezing and knew I needed to get up and get warm, but I was just so drained that I couldn't face it. The mage had sat down next to me and was quiet for a while before he sighed and lifted me onto his lap. He rubbed at my exposed skin, his hands moving in comforting circles as he rested his cheek against the top of my head. Minutes or hours later, I wasn't sure, he stood up, taking me with him in his arms as he took us back to his rooms. I heard him talking to someone in soft tones, but I was just so *tired*. I woke up this morning and shared breakfast with a solemn Grayson who informed me I was working for the priests again today.

"You seem different today. Sad." The elf's voice pulls me out of my musings, and this time, I *do* stop what I'm doing, dropping the brush to the ground as I meet his gaze, frustration rising in me at his pushing.

Someone's chatty today, I grumble internally as I watch him, his eyes tracking me wearily, as if scanning me for something.

"Why do you care?"

My question seems to take him by surprise. In fact, I surprise myself, but it's something I need to know.

"I get bored. At least things are different when you're here." Truth. I can hear it in his voice, but not the whole truth, he's holding something back.

Returning to his work, he starts pounding the sword on the anvil, his actions seeming harder, rougher than usual. Frowning, I watch his back as he works, his tension obvious as he takes out his frustrations on the metal. Shaking my head, I grab my scrubbing brush once more as he growls and spits something in a different tongue. The anger in his voice has me jumping to my feet, spinning back around to face him. He hurls his hammer to the floor and I flinch at the loud noise, watching him warily as he whirls around with an unnatural grace.

"Enough," he growls, his face twisted into a glare as he strides towards me, and for the first time in this last week, I fear for my life. My hands start to shake, but I hold my ground, clenching them into fists at my sides, refusing to back away. I don't know what I've done to upset him, but I won't die a cowering nobody.

"I had accepted my fate—that I would die in the hands of my enemy, as a traitor to my people." His voice is quiet as he hisses at me, stalking ever closer. "I had accepted it, until *you* came along."

He's within touching distance when he finally comes to a stop, his feline features twisted with rage as he scans my face.

"Why can't I get you out of my head? What magic have you woven over me?" Frustration is evident in his tone and I know how hard he's trying to fight this, this *need* to be close to me. I know this because I'm fighting exactly the same thing. I want to touch him, to be close, to inhale his woodsy scent and roll around in it until it clings to me like a second skin.

"I'm sorry." Voice breathy, I take a half step forward before I can stop myself. Being this close to him is making it difficult for me to control that need. It's not a sexual need, but more like he is the other part of my soul I hadn't realised I was missing. "Do you feel it? The pull?"

"You feel it too?" His words are quick and sharp, like he doesn't believe me, or doesn't *want* to believe me. Cursing in his strange, lilting language, he turns away from me, pacing a few steps before spinning back around to face me. "No, that's not possible. You're human."

I raise my eyebrows at that comment. I know he's at war with my people, but the disgust that coats his words hurts. It shouldn't—he's my mortal enemy, right? But it does hurt, his words wound me. Shaking my head, I push away those thoughts and try to focus on what he's saying.

"I don't understand."

Making a cutting gesture, he points at me, his anger rising once again. "Who are you? Why are you here?"

He already knows I'm a slave, he's seen my marks. Do I tell him? He hasn't deserved to hear my story, he's only treated me like crap. Grayson can dress me in pretty clothes and give me a name, but I will always be a slave for as long as the priests still have the amount of control they do now. Staring at the elf, I realise we both have that in common. Slave. Shaking my head, I decided to tell him, even if it doesn't change anything, or makes him hate me more.

"My name is Clarissa, but until a week ago, I had no name."

His body stills, his frown deepening as he tries to understand what I'm saying. "What do you mean?"

"You know that I am—was—a slave." His eyes run over my body again and I know what he's thinking—how painfully thin I am and how the guards treat me each evening, like I'm nothing. Reaching over, I push up the cuff of my dress which hides my marks, his eyes darkening with anger when he sees my brands again. He steps forward, reaching out and gently, oh so gently, runs a finger over my Goddess mark. I have to bite back a moan at the sensations his touch sends through me, igniting a part of me that I thought had died years ago. His eyes shoot up to mine as he scents my arousal and he quickly stops touching me, taking a small step back.

Pushing away the disappointment his actions fill me with, I awkwardly raise a hand to my hair and tuck it back behind my ear. I shouldn't be embarrassed, desire isn't something to be ashamed of, but the fact that it's for an *elf*, a prisoner of war...I move my fingers to the mark he had just been touching, but I only get the pleasant tingling feeling I usually do when I touch it, unlike when Grayson or the elf do.

"One of the high magicians was sent a vision by the Great Mother, our Goddess, and he saved me from being executed. This—" I gesture around us and at the dirty floor. "This is the only way the priests would allow it."

"Even though your Goddess decreed she wanted you safe through the vision?"

The look he sends me is incredulous, and I just nod my head in agreement. It's true, while the Mother sent Grayson to save me, the priests should take that as an affirmation that the Goddess wants me around. However, she never specified that I shouldn't be a slave anymore.

The elf snorts and starts to pace again, watching me as he does, his eyes never leaving me for long. "What did you do to be made a slave?"

Raising my eyebrows at his blunt question, I try to decide if he deserves an answer or not. I want him to trust me, I don't know why, he's supposed to be my enemy after all, but I just don't get that feeling about him. Sure, I don't particularly like him right now, and he scares me, but we have something in common. We know what it's like to have nothing, to *be* nothing.

"I don't know, I was eight at the time," I answer with a shrug, my fingers tracing the marks on my arm. "I don't remember my life before that."

"Your people made a *child* a slave?" That familiar anger rises in his features again, showing his disgust at the thought of child slaves, and I have to agree with him. It's disgusting, but what could someone like me do about it? The elf pauses as he sees something in my face, that strange pull between us almost vibrating with the rage we both feel.

"What did you do to deserve execution?" he demands, and I get the feeling he's trying to justify why I'm here. I don't know why he feels this is important, but it's practically thrumming off him.

"I reached the cut off age."

There's a pause after I speak, our gazes locked on

each other before he breaks away with a laugh. It's not a happy laugh, it's the stunned, incredulous laugh of someone who can't believe what they just heard.

"And your people call my race uncivilised?"

Your people. I don't know why those words anger me so much, perhaps it's the implication that I'm associated with a society who put children into slavery. His arms start to shake slightly, rage and frustration taking over his body.

"Why are you here?"

It's a question I've wanted to ask since I first saw him. How did an elf end up a prisoner here, and why isn't it common knowledge? Surely it would raise morale if the people knew, it would seem like a victory. The elves are stronger, faster, and are better at healing than us, so although we have the numbers, they are far superior in battle. Not to mention their weapons, which are branded with magic and cause devastation when used.

He looks surprised, but I get the impression it's because I had the nerve to ask rather than the question itself.

"I got caught. It was a trap, and they bound me with these." He raises his wrists which are encased in thick, metal cuffs that have symbols engraved into them. I noticed them before and had wondered about their purpose as they didn't seem to shackle him at all, unlike the chains around his ankles. The cuffs glow slightly and I notice his arms are shaking more now, his face showing discomfort as he slowly staggers backward, like he's being dragged away from me. "Even now, the magic in them is punishing me for being too far away from the forge." His explanation makes me realise that I was mistaken earlier. He wasn't shaking because of his anger, but because he was fighting against the magic in the cuffs. "It forces me to make weapons against my own kind." Disgust. That's what I'm seeing now as he faces the forge once more, his whole body trembling as he picks up the hammer from the floor. "I would rather take my own life than make anything that would harm my people, but these stop me."

Shaking my head, I take a small step closer. I can't imagine how he feels, being forced to make something that will harm your own people. It's no surprise the king ordered this, it makes sense from a battle perspective, but I'm horrified.

Are you feeling sorry for an elf? He is the enemy! my inner voice reminds me, and I nod to myself. I need to be harder, stronger. I must remember I can't trust this man.

"So you're trapped here with magic?" I try to keep my voice neutral as I speak, like I'm asking about the weather, but my heart twists painfully at the thought.

He doesn't reply, simply returning to make his weapons. It's fairly obvious he can't leave here, and those softly glowing cuffs are giving off the aura of magic. I didn't notice it before, the strange *pull* between us making it difficult to focus on anything else.

"Why didn't you kill me that first day? I saw the hate in your eyes."

"I thought about it," he admits, glancing over his shoulder, his piercing eyes boring into me. "But you looked so small, so pathetic. That's when I realised that's exactly what *they* wanted."

He's right, that's exactly what the priests hoped, that he would kill me. That would give them the perfect alibi and Grayson couldn't do anything about it. I ignore the slight blow to my pride that he only decided not to kill me because he thought it would anger the guards. I'm starting to see him in a different light, and I don't think he's all that different from me. Walking right up to his work bench, I watch him labour, the strong muscles in his shoulders and arms as he hammers the hot metal on the anvil.

"We're the same, you and I." I'm not sure where my boldness came from, but I say it with a surety that has him looking up. "Both slaves and traitors to our own people." For a second, I think I've offended him, his body stiffening when I called him a traitor, but then he snorts and shakes his head, going straight back to his work.

Turning away, I head back over to where I left my scrubbing brush as I kneel down and start to scour again. Sneaking glances at the elf, I berate myself. *What am I doing?* Even if he's not *my* enemy, he probably hates me just as much as he hates the rest of us.

The elf probably won't even remember your name, he doesn't care about you, he pitied you. That's why you're still alive. That thought makes me pause, and sitting back on my heels, I look over at him again.

"What's your name? I can't keep calling you 'the elf' in my head." An awkward chuckle leaves my lips at my awful attempt at a joke, but I'm rewarded when he pauses his hammering and flashes me a smile. It's not the pure happiness type of smile like Wilson's, or the comfortable smiles from Grayson. This smile is only really a half smile, the right side of his mouth twitching up, and one eyebrow rises, making me want to clench my thighs together.

"You think about me often then?" he replies, and I suddenly panic.

Is he flirting with me? I'm way out of my depth here, this was not what I was intending, but I can't help the little part of me that's thrilled by this attention. Opening my mouth to reply, but coming up with nothing to say, I end up opening and closing my mouth like a fish out of water. I'm sure I look ridiculous and I'm about to run away to the storage cubby to hide my burning face when he barks out a short laugh and takes pity on me.

"It's Vaeril."

The name rings through me, like I've known it all along. "Vaeril," I whisper under my breath, testing it out. I'm still looking up at him when heavy footsteps approach us, a shadow falling over me. With a gasp, I spin to see one of the guards has left his position by the doorway and is now looming over me.

"Back to work, filth!" he spits, ramming his message home as he smacks the butt of his crossbow into my face. Pain flares across my cheek as the force of the hit causes me to fall to the dirty floor. The room goes silent as Vaeril stops working, and even the roaring fire in the forge seems to grow quiet. My breaths come in quick, gasping pants, but I stay pressed against the floor so I don't anger the guard any further.

The guard grunts behind me, and after a few seconds I hear him walk away, but I stay on the floor. I know that tonight's beating will be worse than usual, that guard will see to it. Fear is a powerful motivator, and as I stand quickly to pick up my scrubbing brush, I ignore the feeling of wetness rolling down my face and get back to work.

"Are you okay?" The words are quiet, and I can tell from the slight bite in them that he doesn't want to ask, but he can't stop himself. Keeping my gaze down and locked on the floor, I simply nod my head. After a few more silent, agonising seconds, the sound of hammering starts up again and I release the breath I hadn't realised I'd been holding.

. . .

WE STAY mute for the rest of the day and I start to get a sinking feeling of dread with every minute that passes by. Eventually, the pounding of several sets of booted feet reaches my ears and my heart speeds up as fear floods my system. The lead guard enters the room and looks around the space, his gaze immediately focusing on me as if he can sense my fear. A smug smile crosses his face before he turns and says something to the other guards. Two of them immediately walk over to me, roughly grabbing the tops of my arms and dragging me into the centre of the room, positioning me so I'm facing Vaeril. He starts to put down his hammer, frowning as he watches, but I shake my head slightly. If he stops and gives them a reaction, then they get what they want. His frown deepens, but he picks the hammer back up and starts working again, however I can tell he's not paying attention to his task.

A large guard steps in front of me and punches me in the gut, my breath leaving my body with an "oomph." My knees buckle, and the only things keeping me upright are the two guards who tighten their grip as I dangle from their hold. He hits me again and again, changing his punches to my face and then back to my gut. I try not to cry out, my breath coming is gasps as silent tears roll down my face.

"I hear you were feeling chatty today." The punches suddenly stop as the guard speaks, stepping around so he's in my line of sight. As I look up, I see Vaeril watching us, watching me, with an anger so hot I'm surprised it doesn't burn me as his eyes scan my bruised and bleeding body.

A slap hits my face, my vision darkening for a second as I see stars.

"Pay attention!" the guard growls, grabbing my chin roughly, causing me to groan as pain racks my body. "Perhaps I should cut that tongue of yours out. Or cut up that pretty face to warn others to keep away from you?"

A hammer drops to the ground and the guards around me shift uncomfortably as the sound of chains clinking together echoes around the room. Slowly, oh so slowly, I lift my head and see Vaeril inches away from us, his face twisted into a snarl, his teeth bared. The guards raise their crossbows, all pointed at his chest, and I know if they fire right now the elf will die. A part of me screams and thrashes, bellowing to be let out as my Goddess mark starts to glow. The guards holding me begin to mutter, shifting uneasily again, probably wishing they had their crossbows in hand.

"No," Vaeril snarls, his voice lower than I've ever heard it before, his accent strong as he takes another step. The chains that keep him here scream as he strains against them, the metal links starting to gape against his supernatural strength. The guards around me shuffle, looking to the head guard for instructions, and I know with certainty they will shoot him if he takes another step.

"Vaeril." My voice is croaky, and every second I keep my head raised causes a wave of pain to shoot through my body, but fear and adrenaline makes me stronger. I don't want to look too closely at the reason behind that fear, why warning the elf is more important than saving myself some pain. His eyes dart to mine as I shake my head, the pull, that link between us going tight.

Just as I think it's all over, a wave of magic engulfs

me, and I recognise the feel of the magic immediately before he even speaks. Grayson.

"Stop." That one word, woven with magic, makes everyone freeze as he strides over to me. He's behind me, so I can't see him, but I can *feel* him. His magic is coated with anger as he gets closer and closer until it's embracing me like a safety blanket. "Let go of her." His voice is eerily calm, but infused with his powerful magic.

The guards immediately follow the order, stepping to the side as I drop to the ground. Except I don't fall far, a cushion of magic catching me before gently lowering me down. Grayson steps around the guards, his face a careful mask as he sees the state of my face, but I can feel the fury rolling off him. I need to calm him down, otherwise he's going to kill everyone in this room, I can tell from the look in his eyes, or perhaps it's this strange bond we have between us? I know I shouldn't care if the guards live or die, but I can't have their deaths on my conscience. Surprisingly, I'm more concerned about the elf, Vaeril, but I refuse to face the reasons behind that, pushing those feelings down.

"Grayson," I call, having to spit out a mouthful of blood before rattling, racking coughs overcome me, my ribs painfully shifting in my chest. He watches me and I shake my head, hoping he understands what I'm trying to say.

Don't kill them. Don't let them turn you into that person, you are better than this. I repeat the words in my head over and over like a mantra, hoping it will come across in my silent communication. His expression is blank, and I worry he's going to go into *euisa*, the strange battle calm I triggered previously, but he just seems to be wearing a different mask today—the mask of a vengeful high mage.

Turning away from me, he faces the head guard who suddenly clutches and claws at his neck, his face turning a shade of purple as he gasps for breath. The other guards shift, as if they want to do something, but the magic is still wrapped around them, filling the room so much it feels like I'm trying to move through treacle.

"Grayson," I call again, pushing up slightly into an upright position, but I can't hide the wince as my abused body protests against the movement. I think he's going to ignore me, to carry on and kill the guard, but I feel a flex in his magic and the guard drops to his knees, spluttering and coughing as he takes big, shuddering breaths.

"Return to your jobs. This isn't the end of this," Grayson commands, his magic wrapping around the guards who turn and leave, throwing scared, confused looks over their shoulders. The lead guard hurries to his feet and practically runs from the room, his face still red as he departs, fear easy to see in his eyes.

Grayson turns to the elf, his magic returning to him in a flash, and I can almost see it rippling and churning around him, reacting to his hatred and anger.

"If you've even laid a hand on her—"

Vaeril bares his teeth, falling into a defensive stance. Standing like that, with his hair falling forward, revealing his delicately pointed ears and the forge glowing behind him, he looks completely fae. For some reason that doesn't scare me. It would have two weeks ago, but instead all I fear is that they'll get hurt.

"I didn't touch the girl, *Mage*. Her own people did this to her," Vaeril spits, and I can hear the groaning of the chains around his ankles again. I'm not the only one, as Grayson's eyes narrow and he takes up a defensive stance.

"Grayson, please." My pain laced voice seems to

break through to him, his magic relaxing and flowing back into his body. "I just want to go."

Turning, he kneels in front of me, making sure to keep Vaeril within his sight as he gently slides an arm under my knees, and with a hand around my shoulders, he lifts and cradles me against his chest. Without another word to the elf, we turn and he walks from the room. Raising my head, I peek over his shoulder and see Vaeril is still watching us, his posture rigid, a heavy crease between his brows.

"Thank you," I mouth, hoping he can see with his enhanced fae vision. When he stumbles back with a shocked expression, I'm assuming he saw. Is he that surprised I would thank him? We may be mortal enemies, but he risked death when he stood up for me. He may hate me and my kind, but he did the right thing, and I won't forget that.

Resting against Grayson, we exit the room in silence, and I start to worry. He's mad, more so than I've ever seen him, and I don't know what he might do later once he's assured I'm safe. He hurries up the stairs and I wince as I'm jostled against his body, but I try to hide it by burying my face into his chest.

"Sorry," he murmurs, slowing his climb. I can tell he wants to say something, so I don't reply, simply letting him work through whatever is upsetting him. "You lied to me."

Raising my face, I frown up at him. "I've never lied to you."

"You didn't tell me you were working with an *elf*. Omission of something that important is just as bad as lying."

I don't bother to explain I was trying to protect him

by not telling him, or the fact I'd been threatened if I said anything. He's upset and that's because of me.

"I'm sorry," I say, which is true. I am sorry I hurt him. However, I'm not sorry I kept this from him, I still believe I did the right thing. He blows out a long, frustrated breath and I feel him relax slightly, although I can tell there's something else still bothering him.

"Grayson, I'm okay." My statement would have made more of an impact if I hadn't gasped with pain as his arms shift to open the door at the top of the stairs. Frowning, he shakes his head, a dark mood settling over him as he hurries back to his quarters.

"I'll do everything I can to get you out of this."

Chapter 19

Grayson lived up to his word and spent the next couple of days working to try and get me released from the arrangement with the priests. This meant I didn't get to see much of him, which upset me more than I had anticipated. Sure, Wilson spent a lot of time with me to keep me company, and he even took Aileen and I for a walk around the palace grounds. It was great to get out of the castle and have some fresh air, I especially loved seeing the two of them bicker and joke around. I like Aileen. Her fiery temper and sense of humour have me chuckling when I'm feeling anxious.

Whatever Grayson has been doing to stop me from having to work for the priests hasn't worked, *but* it has helped. When I returned the next day, the guards didn't touch me, simply kept a wary eye on both the elf and me. Vaeril barely spoke to me other than a curt question asking if the mage had healed me, but I could feel his eyes watching me as I cleaned. I didn't work as long, Grayson collected me after only a handful of hours and dropped me off in his rooms before he disappeared once again.

I don't know how long this will last as I've seen Priest Rodrick glaring at me from the staircase, and I know he's plotting ways to make me suffer. However, I make the most of this brief moment of respite.

"YOU WON'T BE WORKING for the priests today," Grayson informs me as we eat breakfast, and I don't miss the disgusted way he says "priest." The fact that he hasn't been able to break the arrangement with them is a major source of frustration to him, and I can see it's beginning to take its toll. His face is lined with tension, and he looks exhausted all the time. His hair is a mess this morning from where he's been running his hands through it.

"Oh?" Raising my gaze from my porridge, I watch him from across the table, getting caught up in his expression. He's looking down at a report, his brow creasing with a frown, and I find I want to run my fingers through his hair, feel the silky strands as I brush it back into position. Scowling at the rogue thought, I shake my head slightly and sit up, trying to pay attention to what he's telling me.

"Prince Jacob has requested your company," he announces wryly, but there's a hint of bitterness in his voice. I assumed I would be Lady Clarissa today as I woke with the familiar feeling of magic clinging to me, and when I looked in the mirror, blonde hair greeted me before Jayne had dressed me in one of my finer gowns. Finally looking up at me, he meets my eyes before flicking them away. He's been doing that a lot recently, as if it hurts to look at me, and although I try to hide it, it distresses me when it happens.

"If it was anyone else, I would refuse, but he's the prince."

I wonder what the prince has planned. I'm looking

forward to a day away from the priests, but Grayson's words bring my thoughts to a screeching halt. He would *refuse*? There may have been a time when I would have allowed others to make decisions for me, but those days are over. Putting my spoon down, I sit back in my chair and stay silent until Grayson realises something's going on and looks over at me again.

"Can I not make my own decisions?"

He at least has the decency to wince and look apologetic when he realises his mistake, but I'm not going to let him off that easily. A thought comes to me suddenly as he starts trying to explain himself.

"Of course, but I'm just—"

"Has anyone else 'requested my company' and you've declined on my behalf?" I should feel bad for interrupting him, for not letting him finish his explanation, but my temper gets the better of me. However, his silence and guilty expression soon takes away that feeling. "Grayson! If you want me to truly accept this life you've created for me, you have to let me actually *live* it!"

"I was jealous, okay?" he retorts suddenly, throwing his hands up in the air in exasperation, although I get the feeling his frustration is aimed at himself rather than me. If I wasn't already leaning back against the high-backed chair, I would be from his comment. Shock, disbelief, and a little bit of pleasant surprise runs through me as I try to come up with a response.

"What?" Not the most intelligent of responses, but my confusion is evident.

"I was jealous that he gets to spend time with you. One word from him, and you're excused from working with the priests, yet I can't convince them to let you go."

A small part of me is disappointed he's not jealous about the prince's personal feelings for me. He's only jealous that the prince has more power than him, that Jacob can get me out of my situation with the priests and he can't. Like I'm an obligation he can't fulfil.

Don't be daft. Why would he want to get into a romantic relationship with you? He's been your friend throughout, of course he's upset he can't help you, my inner voice chides and I realise it's right. I shouldn't be surprised, he's tried to help me from the start. That's the only reason he's jealous, because he's my friend and wants to protect me. I continue to try and convince myself of that as I eat my porridge, the awkward silence between us stretching.

A knock at the door saves me and I hear Jayne talking to our visitor before entering the dining room, a slight smile on her face as she looks at me.

"The prince is here to see you, Lady Clarissa," she tells me. I know she's using my title only because of his presence, but I have to smile slightly and shake my head at her antics.

"Thank you, Jayne." Pushing away from the table, I leave my half-eaten breakfast and look over at the magician who's watching me with a concerned frown. I'm still frustrated with him, but I can see why he did it. "I'll see you later."

He stands and strides to my side, grabbing my hand and stopping my exit. Turning, I look down and watch him brush his thumb over my Goddess mark, seemingly without even realising it. That tingling feeling fills my body as I feel his stare on me.

"Just be careful, I don't trust him. Please."

Glancing up, I see his worry and something within me clenches, wanting to make him feel better. Even if I could say no to the prince, I *want* to spend the day with him. I like Jacob, and although Grayson says I can't trust him, I get the opposite impression.

"I'll be careful, I promise." I give him a smile as I say this, the one I reserve for him. It's not guarded or forced like they are most of the time, and sure, it's not an unrestrained grin full of happiness, but it's one of trust. Grayson stares at me for a long time before returning my smile with one of his own and gesturing for me to go.

"Don't keep the prince waiting."

Rolling my eyes, I walk from the room, feeling his eyes on me as I go. The prince is waiting by the front door, looking handsome in his royal green jacket, a small circlet of gold resting on his blond hair. He smiles as he sees me, lighting up the whole room before dropping into a small bow. I quickly hurry into a curtsy and he chuckles, offering me his hand.

"Good morning, Lady Clarissa. You look beautiful today."

"Thank you."

The atmosphere in the room suddenly changes and Jacob stiffens, his grip on my hand tightening. Following his tense gaze, I see Grayson has trailed after me and is staring at the prince.

"You'll take care of her?"

I'm not sure what I expected him to say, but this wasn't it. Glancing between them, the prince nods, his expression serious.

"With my life."

Grayson seems to relax slightly, and after a quick glance at me he walks back into his chambers. Letting out the breath I hadn't realised I was holding, I glance up at the prince who is still staring where the magician had just been, a frown marring his features.

"Your Highness?"

My soft question pulls him out of his thoughts as he

drops his attention to me, smiling again as he guides me from the rooms and into the corridor.

"What have I told you about calling me 'Your Highness?'" he teases lightly with a smile, so I know he's not cross.

Entering the main corridor, we turn and immediately bump into someone. Letting out a surprised "oomph," I glance up and realise it's Tor. I haven't seen him since the ball other than fleeting glances, but now, up close, I remember just how big he is. Not only in height, but in build too. He towers over the prince and I. That strange feeling in my chest starts again and I get the sensation of familiarity. His eyes are locked onto me, his gaze so piercing I feel him stripping pieces of me away. When he looks at me like that I feel raw, exposed.

"Speaker Torsten, what are you doing in this part of the castle?"

When I jump slightly as he speaks, Jacob pulls me closer, as if to protect me from the mountain of a man before us. What I can't tell him is that it's not me who needs protecting. I don't know how I know this, but I do know he would never hurt me. The prince on the other hand…

"Just exploring, Your Highness," Tor replies facetiously, finally pulling his eyes from me as he sizes up the prince. Jacob is by no means small, but compared to Tor he looks like a boy. After a few silent, tense moments, the mountain man snorts and nods once to me. "Clarissa," he says in farewell, before stalking away.

Jacob lets out a deep breath before chuckling slightly, leading me away.

"Sorry about that. We have a bit of a tense relationship with the people from the mountains."

Explaining the obvious, I think to myself, but simply nod.

This is my opportunity to learn more about these people. The king had been fairly unimpressed by them at the ball welcoming the crown prince home.

"Why are they here?"

"We are trying to form a treaty," the prince explains, and I raise my eyebrows. They hadn't seemed particularly friendly just then, and they want to form a treaty? "I know, things aren't great at the moment. We used to work together years ago, but everything fell apart about two decades ago, and this is the first time they have responded in any positive way. We could really use their help in this war. I've been talking with them. They are strong and fierce, having them at our side would help us win this."

He's passionate, and I realise it's probably only because of his pushing and determination that this meeting is even happening. As the third and youngest son, he will most likely never take the throne, and in his father's eyes his only use would be to marry him off to an influential family. From our conversations recently, I've learned he's really devoted to his people and forming alliances to help us, and he was the one to liaise with the mountain people.

Feeling my attention on him, he glances at me, a slight blush coating his cheeks as he looks away again quickly. "Anyway, I won't bore you with any more politics."

We continue to amble through the castle, with Jacob making small talk as we go, pointing out different things and telling me the history of them, or whispering stories of courtiers we pass. I can't help but think back to Tor and his interaction with the prince, how hostile he had been, but I push those thoughts away, focusing on the prince. Reaching the front of the castle, he takes me towards the huge, towering double doors and I realise he's taking me outside. Raising my eyebrows, I slow my steps slightly until he turns to me with a questioning look.

"Where are you taking me?"

He smiles then, gesturing for me to follow him through the doors. Taking a few timid steps, I walk through the large arched egress, stepping outside the castle for the first time as a free woman. I blink against the bright winter sunshine, and it takes me a few moments to register what I'm seeing—a large carriage, painted with the royal crest, and two gorgeous black horses attached at the front. Gasping, I walk straight past the prince and hurry down the steps to the horses, a genuine, happy smile stretching my face as I reach their sides.

I've always had an affinity with animals, they seem to like me, and as I coo both horses turn their heads to look at me, whickering in response. Smile still in place, I walk up to their heads, holding my hand out flat for them to sniff, and then raising it to stroke down their long faces. The horse on the right has a white star in the middle of his forehead and the longer hair around his hooves is also white, whereas the one on the left is fully black.

"Hello, you gorgeous creatures," I say quietly, continuing to stroke them, laughing at the one on the right who's pushing his head into my hand, getting jealous of my attention to his companion.

"So this is all I needed to do to see you smile."

Glancing up from my horse friends, I beam at the prince, shrugging my shoulders slightly. It's cold out here, seeing as it's still the middle of winter with snow lining the ground, our breath forming into clouds of mist. Thankfully, one of the stewards hurries forward with two thick, fur lined cloaks, a blue one for me and a green and gold one for Jacob.

"I've smiled at you before," I reply, as I pull the cloak around me, nuzzling my nose against the warm fabric, and then I immediately turn back to the horses.

"Not like this." The prince's voice makes me hesitate for a second before I continue stroking the stunning animals, whispering sweet words to them. "When you smiled before it was like…like you've had so much heartbreak that even smiling is painful. Whereas now, it's like the sun breaking through on a cloudy day."

My heart hammers in my chest. If the prince noticed, will other people? Is it just because he's been paying attention, or have I just not played my part well enough?

"We should go." The prince saves me from having to answer, and while I'm grateful for the excuse, and to get out of this cold, I will miss my newfound friends.

"Bye, gorgeous boys," I whisper, pressing a kiss to their noses before following the prince into the carriage.

Settling into the plushly furnished carriage, I arrange my skirts and smile at the prince who takes a seat opposite me.

"Are you going to tell me where you're taking me now?"

Laughing, he leans forward and takes one of my cold hands in his, rubbing it between his own before blowing on them to warm them up. It's a strangely intimate act and I find it's not the only part of me that starts to heat. Glancing up from my hands, he smiles slightly when he sees my now red cheeks. If anyone asks, I'll blame it on the cold winter wind, but the look he gives me tells me he knows exactly what effect his actions are having on me.

Letting go of my hands, he sits back and gives me his bright smile.

"I'm taking you on a tour of my favourite places in Arhaven."

THE NEXT TWO hours are magical. I've never seen any of the city beyond the castle, so I don't have to hide my amazement as the carriage takes us through cobbled streets, the snow making everything look picturesque. There is a large pond in the centre of the city, and the city hall is built at one end with a large park behind it. I always expected the city to feel cold and barren, like the people, but I'm starting to learn that as a slave, I only saw the worst of society.

Jacob was polite, funny, and considerate the whole trip. At one point we stopped at a bakery where he bought us both sweet cakes. I'd never had anything like it, and as soon as I popped a small piece in my mouth, I couldn't stop my groan of pleasure and quickly inhaled the rest of it while Jacob laughed. He immediately gave me his untouched piece, stating he didn't really want it anyway, which earned him a small smile from me.

I'm actually disappointed when the sun starts to set and Jacob announces that we needed to return to the castle. On the carriage journey back, I can see the dark stone fortress coming into view. It's huge, a monstrosity of twisting towers with gargoyles peeking over their plinths down onto the people below. The closer we get, the darker my mood becomes, until the oppressive feeling fully settles over me again. I hadn't realised how much I hated it here until I was taken away and shown how different my life could have been.

. . .

ONCE WE ARRIVE BACK at the castle, Jacob jumps out of the carriage and offers me his hand to help me down. Giving him an absentminded smile, I accept his assistance, walking arm in arm back into the castle. It must only be about five o'clock but the corridors are uncharacteristically quiet. This is usually prime time for the court ladies to be gossiping in the halls before attending dinner. When he squeezes my arm slightly, I glance across at the prince, unable to stop my smile when I see the way he's looking at me. Like I'm his favourite person in the world.

"Will you be joining us in the banquet hall?"

Most ladies from the houses would kill for an invitation to dine at the royal table, but I simply shake my head.

"Thank you, but no. Grayson and I eat in his rooms."

It's true, but I also need to put some space between the two of us, take a breather. My feelings are all mixed up and tangled. Not to mention I don't want to be anywhere near his family, particularly the king or Rhydian. Jacob is quiet for a while, obviously thinking over his response, and when he does speak it's with a carefully blank expression.

"You and Grayson are…close. Is there anything going on between the two of you?"

My face immediately flushes red and I choke on my quick inhale at the unexpected question. We are just friends.

Then why are you blushing so much? Why is your stomach churning and your breath catching at the prospect of being more than friends? Ignoring my inner monologue, I take a step away from the prince, needing some distance so I can come up with a response. I can't think when he's touching me.

"I—Well. No. No, he's just a friend. He's helped me out of a very difficult situation, and he's very protective of me."

Another heavy pause fills the space and I feel his eyes on me, watching my every move. Taking a step forward, he closes the gap between us and takes my hand in his. Raising my head slowly, I see his soft smile.

"That gives me some hope then."

"What do you mean?" I'm confused, one moment he's asking me about Grayson and now he's talking about hope. His smile widens at my bewilderment as he raises his free hand up and pushes one of my unruly curls behind my ear. His touch makes my skin tingle, not in an unpleasant way, but in a way that makes me want more. Shifting his weight, he brings his face closer to mine and I realise he's going to kiss me.

"I—"

"Prince Jacob!" Jerking away, the prince spins around to face the person who called his name. I can't decide if I'm disappointed that he didn't kiss me or not, my mind spinning through different scenarios.

What about Grayson? What about your connection with Vaeril and Tor? Taking a deep breath, I push away those thoughts, guilt making me feel unwell. I'm not sure what I'm feeling guilty for, I didn't do anything, nothing happened. Heavy booted footsteps reach us, and I glance over at the uniformed guard who has obviously just run here, his breath coming in large, gasping pants.

"Yes?"

"Your Highness…you are needed…immediately. Your brother—"

Jacob's expression darkens at the mention of his brother and he nods at the guard. "I'll be right there."

The man nods and spins on the spot, running back the way he came. Frowning, I watch the whole episode with confusion, not quite understanding what's going on. Which brother needs Jacob, and why does he look so angry? He turns to me now, his expression changing to concern. Glancing around, he takes my hand and guides me over to one of the little alcoves before pulling me close to him, so close that I have to put my hand on his chest to stop myself from falling.

"Clarissa, something is happening, it's been building for a little while now." His eyes dart around the empty corridor as if someone is going to jump out at any moment, his voice low as he explains.

"What do you mean?" I repeat my question from earlier, although it has a whole different meaning now. The fun, flirty atmosphere from our afternoon together is gone, tension and a calculating expression appearing on his face that I've never seen on him before.

He opens his mouth to say something but closes it again, cursing. "I can't say much." He swears again, and a small burst of magic seems to emit from him. I want to ask what he's doing, he doesn't have magic—or so I thought. But I can't ask him because *normal* people can't feel magic. That's when it hits me, he *can't* tell me. He's being silenced by magic. Fear starts to creep through me. What is serious enough that a magical gag is placed over one of the princes?

"Things are about to happen, awful things. I hadn't realised it was going to be so soon, I had hoped..." The look he gives me is that of a young man full of faith, but that quickly shutters and he takes a small step away from me, putting distance between us. "Stay with

Grayson, he should be able to protect you through this."

"What—"

A pained expression crosses his face before he shakes his head and starts to walk away. "I have to go, I'm sorry."

Moving away from the alcove, I watch as the prince storms away. Anyone who doesn't know him would think he was calm, but I can tell from the way he's walking, back stiff and a stride I don't usually see from him, that he's worried. The fact that he hasn't escorted me back to my rooms is a big indicator that something is wrong, and that concerns me. Something bad is about to happen, I can feel it. My mark is almost humming.

I need to return to my rooms, another wave of tingling power from my mark assuring me that I'm right. Grabbing the front of my skirts, I start the journey back to Grayson's rooms, the corridors still eerily quiet as the winter sun sinks behind the horizon, leaving only the light from the lanterns illuminating my way. As I move, my mind wanders, all the horrible possibilities of what could happen swirling in my head. Are the elves going to attack?

A noise snaps me back to the present, my head immediately lifting and looking for the source of the sound. Frowning, I realise I'm by the Queen's Courtyard. This is not on my route back to Grayson's quarters, but somehow I've instinctively come here and the sense of assurance rolls over me again. For whatever reason, I'm supposed to be here.

I walk out from the corridor into the courtyard walkway, wrapping my arms around myself against the sudden change in temperature. It's dark out here, only the lights from inside the castle reflecting against the water from the now still fountains. A murmuring has me pausing and I realise it's someone talking. I start to walk away, I shouldn't be listening to other people's conversations when they obviously came here for privacy, but something stops me. A feeling, deep in my gut, and I know it's the Mother trying to tell me something, something I *need* to know.

"You risk too much." The rough, accented voice is familiar. Tor. What is he doing out here?

"I can't keep pretending, dear friend." The queen's whispered words reach me and my eyes widen as I raise my hand to my mouth to keep in any sound. Whatever the queen and Tor are discussing, they do not want to be overheard, otherwise they wouldn't be out here.

A sense of urgency runs through me, but it's not my own. The Mother is trying to tell me something. A tug in my chest makes me take a step toward the still open door to the castle corridor and I see a group of four guards marching our way. Panic floods my veins, something bad is about to happen.

"We can't risk—" I cut off whatever Tor was going to say by hurrying over to the fountain they are hiding behind.

"Guards are coming!"

The queen's eyes widen and I see the panic flash through her gaze before she nods and gives a pointed look at Tor. "Thank you, child." Turning, she hurries to a dark corner of the courtyard and seems to disappear. There must be some sort of secret entrance there and I vow that when I have time, I'll explore it further.

The sound of booted feet now fills the courtyard and I see the guards spreading out before thoroughly searching the area. I feel Tor's eyes boring into me, as if he can peel away my skin and see my thoughts and feelings.

"Freeze!" one of the guards shouts as he comes across us, with more guards swarming around us, hands on their weapons as if they mean to use them at any moment. "Captain, one of *them* is out here."

One of them? What is happening? My thoughts spin, I don't think they mean me, so they must be talking about Tor. Turning my confused expression to him, I see him frowning as he realises the seriousness of the situation. His hands drop to his sides, hovering near the decorated axe that hangs in a sheath at his waist.

"What is the meaning of this? I'm here on a diplomatic mission." His voice is authoritative, but given the tension of the moment, his tone is much calmer than I had expected. He eyes the guards as he moves forward and casually slides in front of me. The Captain of the Guard, in his smart green and gold uniform, steps forward, frowning as he scans the area around us, as if he was expecting to see someone else here. His attention returns to Tor, his scowl deepening as he glances over his shoulder and sees me.

"What are you doing out here? And why is Lady Clarissa with you?"

I'm surprised the Captain of the Guard knows who I am, but I guess he's seen me with the prince, so he's made it his business to know my name. I've always liked the current Captain of the Guard, he's never been overly cruel to any of the slaves unlike his predecessor. Once or twice when I was starving and I didn't think I'd make it through the night, I would find scraps of bread left next to where I was laying, and when I had the energy to lift my head I could just see his back as he walked away. So it's strange to see him now, and I have to hope he doesn't recognise me from before.

"The prince and I just returned from the city. He had to leave on important business, so I just came to clear my head before I returned to my rooms," I explain in a pretty voice, like I'm a young lady who's been thoroughly wooed by the prince. His gaze turns to me, his bright eyes examining me. His face is much more lined than the last time I saw him.

The guards continue to search the courtyard around us while the captain continues to flick his eyes between Tor and I.

"I was looking at the stars. I miss sleeping underneath them and I saw it would be a clear night, so I came out to view them," Tor reasons, and I can't fight the surprised noise that escapes me. He glances once over his shoulder before turning back to the captain. I know he was meeting the queen, but something about what he said rings true.

"Clear!" one of the unseen guards shouts, and there's a long pause before the captain nods.

"Go back to your rooms. When you get there, lock the door and don't come out until morning." He looks at me as he says this, so I know he's warning me, and it makes my stomach sink. If the Captain of the Guard is speaking something like this, then it's serious and not a caution I'm going to ignore. As I nod, he turns away and the guards begin to file out.

Tor and I stay silent as they go, and for even longer after that, until we are both sure we're completely alone. He turns to me, studying me, and even in the moonlight I can see his troubled expression.

"How much did you hear?"

"I only caught the end of your conversation," I reply

honestly, and he nods as he spins to go, but he stops as something occurs to him.

"You saved us. Why?"

"It was the right thing to do." There's more to it than that, and he knows it, but now's not the time for that conversation.

"Do what the captain said, don't stray. The stars are telling me something bad is coming." And with that cryptic answer, he leaves faster than a man his size should be able to.

※

I DON'T DALLY, heading straight to Grayson's lodgings, Tor's words ringing in my ears. I don't understand anything he said. What do the stars have to do with anything? But his warning is eerily similar to that of the captain's and Jacob's.

GRAYSON ISN'T BACK when I reach his rooms and I end up having a quiet supper with Jayne. I keep glancing towards the door, waiting for him to appear at any moment, but he doesn't. Eventually, with lots of reassurance from Jayne, I get ready for bed, but the concern in her eyes as she tries to convince me he's okay bothers me. What is this "something" that everyone keeps saying is coming? Nightmares plague me. I dream of grabbing hands and eyes in the dark, waking up numerous times to pace the length of my room so I can try and settle myself. I eventually fall back into a fitful sleep in the early hours of the morning as the sun begins to rise.

Grayson doesn't return that night.

Chapter 20

A banging noise wakes me from my sleep. Sitting up, I look around my room groggily, trying to work out what's going on. The sun is shining through the curtains, but Jayne hasn't yet come into my rooms, so I know it must still be fairly early. A shout echoes in the hallway that has me jumping from the bed and running to the door. Just as I'm about to reach out to open it, it flies open and a large, snarling guard stands in the doorway.

Heart in my throat, I stumble back, dread filling me as he takes a step forward. Except he never does, his body seemingly frozen as he growls, struggling against the invisible barrier, and the sense of magic reaching me reminds me of something Grayson told me—no one can enter my rooms unless I say they can. Feeling more secure, I try to push away my fear as I straighten to my full height and stare down the guard.

"Why are you here?"

"Come out here, filth," he spits, his anger at not being able to reach me clear. "You're to attend a...ceremony." The way he says it makes me shudder, his sick grin telling me enough. Whatever the prince and the others have been warning me against is happening.

Glancing around him, I try to see into the corridor. Why isn't Grayson stopping them?

"Where's Grayson? I won't go anywhere without him," I state with more bite and confidence than I actually have. I want to curl up in a ball and hide, but I can't do that anymore. I *won't*.

"He's indisposed." My gut sinks again, what does indisposed mean? I know he didn't return last night, but why isn't he here now? Is he hurt, injured? Oblivious to my silent panic, the guard loses his patience. "Come with me, by order of the king."

My gaze snaps up to his. Order of the king. If I refuse, then I'm breaking the law, but I know something awful is going to happen, the Mother has assured me of it. I shouldn't go with him, and for the moment, I have a way to stop him from taking me.

"No."

His face contorts and he swears at me before backing away. I think I've gotten away with it when he strides back to the open door with a bedraggled Jayne. A fear like none other takes over me, an icy feeling of dread trickling down my spine. I'm not sure when Jayne became a person I care about, a person I would sacrifice myself for, but I do and she is.

"Come out or I'll kill the maid," he growls, and as if to prove his point he lifts one of his meaty hands up to her throat. To her credit, Jayne struggles against him, kicking, biting, and refusing to go down without a fight. All the while I have to just watch. He finally manages to grip her throat and I take a juddering step forward, my hand out in a stop gesture.

"Don't, Clarissa, you're safe in ther—"

Jayne's shout is quickly cut off when the guard's hand tightens around her neck. She starts to go red as her air supply is cut off, her arms flailing as she attempts to claw at his hands. I can't let her die. Stepping right up to the threshold of the door, I try not to let my panic show.

"Okay, I'll come with you, but you have to let her go." The guard turns to face me, gripping Jayne for another agonising couple of seconds with a look of satisfaction in his eyes. He's won. He releases her and she falls to the ground, coughing and gasping for air, clutching at her abused throat.

"Go inside my room and wait until Grayson comes back, you'll be safe in there." I hurry out of the room and grasp her, pushing her into my bedroom. A hand clutches my arm, but I don't bother turning to look at the guard as he starts to pull me down the corridor. "Remember no one can enter unless I say so, and only you and Grayson have that permission," I shout to her. She's now safely ensconced in my room, panting as she leans against the doorframe with a look of devastation on her face as I'm led away.

"Hurry up, filth," the guard growls, half dragging me as I try to catch my footing.

I want to ask where he's taking me, but I know I won't get an answer, and as he leads me through the rooms, I see there are two more guards waiting by the exterior door, their swords hanging at their waists, hands ready to grab them if needed. Staying silent, they fall into position behind us as the guard tugs me through the main doors and out into the corridor. I'm in my nightgown, the scars on my ankles on show for all to see, not to mention my slave marks, and my hair is in its natural state.

Everything is about to change.

Strangely enough, although I'm pretty sure I'm going

to lose my life, I'm not sad. In these last few weeks, I have been able to experience what it's like to actually *live* for the first time. I will be upset to leave behind my friends—Wilson, Jayne, even Aileen—and I'll miss what could have been with Prince Jacob. I wish I had gotten time to get to know Tor and his people better. Then there's Vaeril and the strange connection between us. He might be my enemy, except there's something about him... And no one should be a slave, forced to work against their own people. But I'll miss Grayson the most, my saviour.

As I'm marched through the castle, I realise where we are going as we reach the large central courtyard that leads to the church. I can hear lots of high-pitched, confused, and scared voices, and as we enter the courtyard, I see that no one has been spared, everyone has been gathered here. The cold wind bites at my skin, the freezing, snow covered ground penetrating my bare feet.

Guards stand at all the doorways, stopping anyone from leaving

"Don't you know who I am?" an elderly man, obviously some sort of lord as his pyjamas are made from the finest quality silk, protests as he tries to push past the guards. One of them steps forward and backhands him across his face, the crowd around him gasping in horror before falling into an uneasy silence.

"I don't care who you are. King's orders," the guard spits, before returning to his spot.

As the guard continues to drag me, I can see the justice pillars gleaming like a beacon. My fear ramps up. I really don't want to be strapped to those pillars, I don't want to die. However, as we reach the front of the crowd, we stop, the other guard stepping up to my other side and grabbing my free arm so I can't move.

What's happening? If they were going to kill me, I'd be strapped to one of those pillars. I look around desperately for a clue as to what's going on and spot Wilson on the far side of the crowd with a scared-looking Aileen at his side. I can see Tor and his kinsmen in a group near the front, but thankfully he hasn't seen me.

A hush falls over the crowd as the king and Prince Rhydian step up onto the plinth by the pillars. The head priest and Priest Rodrick are standing just behind them, attempting to look serene and calm but they can't keep the cruel gleam out of their eyes.

"You're probably wondering why I dragged you all out here." The King's voice echoes around the courtyard, the whistling of the wind the only other sound to be heard. "There is a poison in this castle, a dark evil that is infecting my people, and I've come to a difficult decision. I have to eradicate this evil so the rest of my people will be safe."

There are some murmurs of agreement, but I have a sinking feeling about what's going to happen. The king gestures and two guards come forward, dragging a bound woman behind them. Her hair has been shaved off, but you can tell who she is by the way she holds herself—the queen.

"This is going to be a difficult time for us all, but we must be strong." As he speaks, she is dragged to the middle pillar and strapped to it, her hands behind her back as she faces the crowd. Her face is tear stained, but she doesn't cry now, no, she stares out, her eyes landing on the leader of the mountain tribesmen. "The queen, my wife, has been conspiring against us and has been tainted."

The king's voice continues to ring out. The crowd is starting to realise what's about to happen and shuffles nervously, half-hearted protests rising. The tribesmen look furious, but they stand stock-still.

"This evil can't be tolerated," the king shouts, as he palms a knife in his hand and spins, slicing the queen's exposed throat in one quick movement.

"No!" The word is ripped from my throat before I even realise it, watching as her body slumps, blood gushing from her and covering the platform. People in the crowd are shouting, a couple turn away to vomit.

"Liv!" I'm not sure how I heard the shout over all the other noise as people panic, but the pure shock in the voice has me searching for the owner. Tor's eyes are wide as he stares at me, his gaze running over me and then back to my hair. He shouts the name again and I think he's addressing me. The guards holding me tighten their grips and start to drag me away as if by some unspoken signal. The expression on Tor's face darkens as he starts to push his way to me, that strange feeling in my chest going taut. A fight breaks out in the crowd and he gets dragged back, his gaze staying on me as I'm roughly pulled toward the chapel.

"The evil has infected some of our slaves, so we need to wipe the slate clean to make sure it doesn't spread any further," the king continues. Half of the citizens are frozen in fear and the other half are fighting the tribesmen.

My eyes are ripped from Tor as I see a line of slaves being led up onto the stage and then strapped to the three pillars. A guard stands by each one, and as one, they swipe their swords across the slaves' necks. A raw cry is ripped from me as their still bleeding bodies are unshackled and thrown off the side of the platform, and the next three are marched up onto the platform for the same treatment.

Disgust, anger, hate, and rage run through my veins like a fire, and as I turn my gaze to the king, I see he's watching me and has the decency to look disturbed before he looks away.

"Father! What are you doing?" Jacob's voice reaches me, and I see him run into the courtyard, looking up at his father in horror. "Where is Clarissa?" he asks, looking around the crowd, but he doesn't even look at me as I'm dragged away, not recognising me with black hair. I see the moment Jacob spots the body of his mother, and the rage that overcomes him as he rushes at his father. Two guards jump in front of him and tackle him to the ground.

Fighting against the guards' hold, I try to break free. I don't know what I'll do if I manage to get loose, but that part of me that has been hidden for the last twelve years is trying to take control. But I'm not strong enough to escape, and as we reach the chapel and yet more slaves are killed, I meet Tor's eyes once more.

"Liv!" he shouts again, but I lose sight of him as I'm hauled back into the darkness of the sanctuary.

The doors shut behind us and I get a second in the dark to pretend this is all just a terrible nightmare. Just a dream that my brain has come up with based on all my insecurities.

I can't do this. This isn't happening. All those slaves—the queen—just slaughtered like they were nothing. My thoughts whirl and spin in a tangled web and I have to fight back a sob. People had been attacking the tribesmen. Tor called me Liv. Why? He'd looked like he'd seen a ghost. I hope Jacob will be okay, he might be related to the king, but he's been nothing but kind to me. A deep disappointment falls over me. I don't know why I expected Grayson to turn up and save us all, but it didn't happen. Where is he? Why didn't he come?

I know where the guards are taking me, and as Rodrick appears, his smile wide, I know I haven't escaped their purge of "evil." The only evil person I can see right now, though, is the priest, the person who is supposed to guide us and teach us the love of the Great Mother.

"The time has finally come, 625, for you and that *elf*," he crows gleefully, his eyes running over me as we reach the hidden stairway. Turning, I spit at him, unable to hold back my disgust. I should have expected his sharp backhand, the pain and force behind it making me stumble, and since the guards had let go of me so I could walk down the stairs in front of them, I fell. Down I go, the sharp corners of the stone steps breaking and bruising my body. I don't know how many steps I fall down, but the priest's cruel laughter echoes off the walls and seems to follow me.

When I eventually come to a stop, I stay in place, panting and trying to focus through the pain, adrenaline running through my system.

"Get up," the priest demands as he reaches me. Biting back the agony, I pull myself up and walk down the rest of the twisting stairs. My thoughts are quiet as I use all of my energy to focus on walking and not falling down. When we reach the bottom of the staircase, the priest gestures toward the door, which the guards start to open. "Make yourself useful until we come to finish you."

"Why don't you just do it now?" It would be a mercy for him to kill me straight away, to stop this pain, both physically and mentally.

"I have orders." I can tell from his frown and clipped tone that that's exactly what he wants to do.

I stumble forward into the underground room, wanting to put as much space between the priest and myself. The door closes behind me and I take a few unsteady steps so I'm farther into the chamber. The constant sound of hammering stops for a second and I sway on my feet as I meet Vaeril's piercing eyes. The sob I've been holding back finally breaks free and I fall to my knees, pain racking my body. Curling in on myself, I try to focus on breathing, pushing away the images of all those slaves who were just blindly killed, their blood covering the ground as it poured off the platform.

"Clarissa."

I jerk back in surprise at how close the voice is to me, and as I look up, eyes wide with fear, I see it's Vaeril, his gaze scanning my body. Holding up his hands in a gesture of peace, he kneels down, the chain on his ankle keeping him from coming all the way to me.

"I need to see your wounds," he tells me, but I don't move, the horror of what I've just seen playing over and over in my head. "What happened?" His voice is soft, realising that my physical wounds aren't the only thing upsetting me.

"They killed the queen and they are killing the slaves, every single one," I gasp out, his cursing filling the space between us. The screeching sound of metal has me looking over at him again, and I watch as he reaches down and breaks the chain around his ankles with a flex of his arm. Walking slowly, cautiously, towards me, he crouches down again, taking a seat next to me.

Reaching out unhurriedly, he gently runs his hand over my arm, carefully prodding the skin and checking for breaks and cuts. I numbly let him, watching as he flicks me concerned looks. I probably shouldn't feel so comfortable sitting this close to him, but right now, I need him, need his support.

Lifting my head, I lean back slightly and he pauses, meeting my eyes.

"We're next. They're going to kill us," I say softly, and he simply nods.

"I know."

He continues to examine my bruised body, his limbs starting to shake as he keeps himself away from his work, the magical cuffs punishing him for deviating from his task.

Is this how it's going to end? In a forgotten underground room with my enemy at my side?

"What's that?" Vaeril questions wearily, backing away slightly from my glowing mark. A warm, gentle tingling feeling encompasses me, like a warm embrace, and I recognise the Mother's presence. Closing my eyes, I fall into that hug, feeling her love surround me.

"You need to be strong, my beloved. I didn't bless you without reason. Remember, I am with you, always." Her voice reaches me, not something I can hear, but I can *feel* it deep within. I feel her pulling away and I blindly reach out, grasping for her, not ready for her to leave me just yet despite what she just said.

"I don't understand. Why me? What am I supposed to do?" My insecurities rise to the surface and I feel the weight of responsibility fall on me.

"You know, my beloved. You are stronger than you think."

She leaves me with a final wave of power that floods through my body, so intense it's almost painful. Her presence fades and I open my eyes with a gasp, looking down at my now healed body.

"What just happened?" Vaeril inquires, frowning as

he looks over my body. "You have magic?" He shakes his head as if he's not actually talking to me, but himself. "No, I felt another presence, like someone else was here."

"It was the Great Mother. My Goddess," I explain as he continues to frown, but I ignore him and think back on what she said.

I know what I need to do.

Taking a deep breath, I push to my feet, blessedly pain free. Looking around the chamber, I search—for what, I'm not quite sure. A hand circles my wrist and I spin to see Vaeril has followed me, his limbs shaking more violently now.

"What are you doing?" Confusion, frustration, and anger line his words, but I ignore him. The Great Mother wouldn't have come to me if it wasn't possible, right?

"We need to escape."

He laughs, waiting as if I'm going to deliver a punch line to my joke, but his face drops when he realises I'm being serious. Anger takes over and he grabs my other wrist and shakes me slightly.

"How are we going to do that? I have these, remember?" Roughly releasing my wrists, he shoves the stone cuffs into my face. I know the disgust in his voice is not aimed at me but at the cuffs, yet the words still sting.

Instinctively, I reach up to grab his wrist to stop him from hitting me, and a shock wave runs through me the moment my fingers graze the stone. My mark starts to glow again, flaring so brightly I have to close my eyes. I want to let go, but I can't, a wave of power rolling through my body.

"What are you doing?" Vaeril asks in awe as he watches. Opening my eyes, I see his cuff glowing, more so than the usual gentle light they usually give off. A draining feeling comes over me, and as I watch the light in his cuff simply disappears.

Falling back, I stumble to keep my footing before sinking down onto the ground, my body weak and shaky all of a sudden. My brain takes a moment to catch up and I stare dumbly at the now magic-less cuff.

"How did you do that?" Vaeril questions, suddenly in my face as his expression turns to distrust. "You have magic?"

"No! Why does everyone keep asking me that? I can sense and amplify magic, it was a gift from the Mother," I explain, exhausted. The cuff is still attached to his wrist, but the symbol is gone, leaving behind a simple stone band.

"Can you do it again?" he demands, holding out his other arm, the urgency in his voice scaring me. Holding my hands up in front of me, as if I can fend him off, I shake my head weakly.

"I don't even know what I did the first time!" I protest, and he seems to pause, his eyes taking in my exhausted expression and my slumped position on the ground.

"You don't just sense and amplify, you can break spells too," he explains, but I don't understand what he's saying. Break a spell? Like, unwrite it? "I can feel it, the pull to work has lessened, and I can already feel some of my strength and power coming back."

We both look down at his now plain stone cuff. The implication of what he's saying suddenly hits me. I can free him. He could help me escape—*I could be free.* But can I release my enemy? Is he really still my enemy, though, after everything that's happened today? I can't think, my thoughts are too tangled.

"I—"

He cuts me off, placing both hands on my shoulders, and he leans in to press a kiss against my forehead, whispering something against my skin. That strange pull between us flares to life and I know I can't just let him die, even if freeing him would condemn me in the eyes of my people. I'm not even sure if I have the strength to break the spell on the second cuff right now.

I wish I could ask Grayson about this.

Grayson. Can I really leave without saying anything to him? Can I run away without saying anything to any of them?

They would understand. If it's your life on the line, then they will understand that you did what you had to. I repeat those words over and over in my head. Who am I kidding, I can't leave until I know my friends are okay. It was a massacre in that courtyard, what kind of person would I be if I didn't check? That tingle I'm starting to associate with the Great Mother runs through me, and I know that whatever I'm doing, it's what she wants me to do.

Staring at the elf, I go through my plan in my head. He's still kneeling in front of me, his hands on my shoulders, waiting for my answer.

"Okay, I'll help you."

"You can get us out of here." His voice is full of awe, a smile gracing his face, and I realise how beautiful he is when he smiles. "*Alina,*" he whispers, the word sounding beautiful with his lilting accent, and I feel something settle over me. "In my culture, that means 'my salvation.' The name is fitting, for that's exactly what you will be."

I feel overwhelmed. I've gone from having no name to having more than I can count. The pressure of what he's implying threatens to break me, but I can't let it.

Taking a deep breath, I lean back a little, needing some space.

"I will help you, but we can't leave. Not yet." His face darkens and his hands drop from me as I continue, "There's something I need to deal with first, and I'm going to need your help." I hope he can feel how earnest I am, feel the truth in my words. "Do you trust me?"

There's a long pause and I can't tell what he's thinking, his expression a blank mask. Trust is not something either of us do easily, so I know what I'm asking of him. When he leans forward again, it's with an expression of steely determination.

"What do you need me to do?"

The End

This is only just the beginning.
In the games of war and deceit, will Clarissa and Vaeril survive, or will they get caught up in the Fires of Treason?

Fires of Treason, coming soon.

About the Author

Erin lives in the UK with her husband and sassy rabbit, Jethro. She works part time as a healthcare worker and the rest of the time writes the stories that fill her brain. She started writing in 2018 when she published her first book, Hunted by Shadows. Soon after she met K.A Knight and began writing together.

Also by Erin O'Kane

The Shadowborn Series:

Hunted by Shadows

Lost in Shadow

Embraced by Shadows

The War and Deceit Series:

Fires of Hatred

Erin O'Kane and K.A Knight

Her Freaks Series:

Circus Save Me

Taming the Ringmaster

The Wild Boys:

The Wild Interview

Coming soon: The Wild Tour

Erin O'Kane and Loxley Savage

Twisted Tides

Printed in Poland
by Amazon Fulfillment
Poland Sp. z o.o., Wrocław